KU-503-598

ADVENTURE WITH A SECRET PRINCE

ANDREA BOLTER

THE WEDDING FAVOUR

ALLY BLAKE

MILLS & BOON

All rights reserved including the right of reproduction
in whole or in part in any form. This edition is published
by arrangement with Harlequin Enterprises ULC.

This is a work of fiction. Names, characters, places, locations
and incidents are purely fictional and bear no relationship to
any real life individuals, living or dead, or to any actual places,
business establishments, locations, events or incidents.
Any resemblance is entirely coincidental.

This book is sold subject to the condition that it shall not,
by way of trade or otherwise, be lent, resold, hired out
or otherwise circulated without the prior consent of the publisher
in any form of binding or cover other than that in which it is published
and without a similar condition including this condition
being imposed on the subsequent purchaser.

® and TM are trademarks owned and used by the trademark owner
and/or its licensee. Trademarks marked with ® are registered with the
United Kingdom Patent Office and/or the Office for Harmonisation
in the Internal Market and in other countries.

First Published in Great Britain 2022
by Mills & Boon, an imprint of HarperCollins*Publishers* Ltd,
1 London Bridge Street, London, SE1 9GF

www.harpercollins.co.uk

HarperCollins*Publishers*
1st Floor, Watermarque Building,
Ringsend Road, Dublin 4, Ireland

Adventure with a Secret Prince © 2022 Andrea Bolter

The Wedding Favour © 2022 Ally Blake

ISBN: 978-0-263-30220-2

06/22

MIX
Paper from
responsible sources
FSC® C007454

This book is produced from independently certified FSC™ paper
to ensure responsible forest management.
For more information visit www.harpercollins.co.uk/green.

Printed and Bound in Spain using 100% Renewable Electricity
at CPI Black Print, Barcelona

ADVENTURE WITH A SECRET PRINCE

ANDREA BOLTER

MILLS & BOON

For Ronna

CHAPTER ONE

"COME, SON, THE CAR is waiting to take us to the airport."

Ras had stopped walking after he and his father exited the Secretariat, the skyscraper building at the United Nations headquarters in New York. People were hurrying to and fro, and the numerous member flags flown in the plaza were billowing in the early autumn sunshine. Ras stared up at those flags for a moment. They waved in the freedom he was about to claim, still tethered to poles but allowed to flutter as the breeze took them.

The moment had arrived.

"Father, I'm not going home with you."

"Whatever are you talking about, Ras? You're to be married in less than two months."

"I shall be. But first, I'm going to spend some time on my own." The words fell out even easier than he'd expected them to. His conviction had been growing for weeks; years, really, in a certain way. Everything had been building to this point. And his plan had been in place well before they'd taken this trip to New York to attend a UN summit on global culture.

"Do not start with that nonsense again." Ras had brought this up previously with his father, who always dismissed him out of hand. Patiently waiting for the right time, Ras knew it was now or never. His father went on,

"We don't want to miss our runway time." The private plane would have been given only a small window of minutes to take to the skies. His father was in a hurry. Ras, however, was not.

For once in his life, he was going to breathe at his own pace, and he took in a slow, clean inhale for emphasis. Yet this was not the spot to see his father off. So he gave a yank on the small wheeled case that his father would have assumed contained paperwork but, in fact, was filled with clothing and toiletries. He'd purchase more along the way.

Since they were to leave New York today, Ras's valet had packed his wardrobe into traveling cases and saw that they were loaded into cars going to the airport, as usual. Ras did nothing to stop the process and made a point of keeping the small case with him. Now tugging it behind him, he resumed striding with his father away from the UN Plaza toward their waiting limo. "Father, I want you to understand," he explained as they moved forward decisively, sharing the same pace, "I will return home well in time for my impending nuptials. I love you, and I will always love and honor the memory of my late mother. However, in order to be whole, I must experience choice. I need to wander a bit, to roam without formalities and handlers and bodyguards. You know that mother wanted that for me. She always told me as much."

His mother had indeed urged him many times that in order to fulfill his obligations, he needed to be content. She'd had a wanderlust that she'd passed on to her only child prior to her untimely death when Ras was fifteen. And fifteen years later, he was finally going to actualize that desire. For her and for himself.

"I've told you, son, that is too dangerous," his father insisted. "And, I might add, absurdly timed." Yes, Ras hadn't forgotten his arranged marriage to a woman he didn't love.

They reached the limo where the driver was awaiting their arrival, holding the door open. "I'll be safe. I promise you."

"Ras, get in the car. Stop behaving like a child." His father slid into the limo seat. "You are bound by responsibilities."

"And I shall honor them. I'll be home in a few weeks. I'll stay in touch." He'd already purchased several untraceable cell phones for the purpose. He didn't want to cause his father worry. Yet this was something he had to go through with. "See you soon." He bowed with his shoulders before turning away from the limo.

"Go after him," he heard his father implore a bodyguard who was standing at attention nearby.

Expecting that as well, His Royal Highness Rasmayada, crown prince of Ko Pha Lano, a sovereign island nation in the Gulf of Thailand, maneuvered himself into the throngs of people surrounding the UN. Seeming to escape the bodyguard. In his fine wool but undistinguishable gray suit, Ras easily blended into the crowd. Leaving his father, His Majesty King Maho, to travel home without him.

Ras's heart pounded with exhilaration as he hurried this way and that through the streets away from the UN. He'd only been to New York and Washington, DC, on official occasions, conferences with dignitaries and meetings with politicians. Always chauffeured in cars with tinted windows, whisking him to private entrances. His plan today was easy to follow in the grid of Manhattan streets. The UN was at the East River and he was headed west to get to his destination at the Hudson River, the two bodies of water flanking the great metropolis.

Realistically, he knew that he likely hadn't fully escaped his father's surveillance. The king might employ top-notch security to locate Ras, possibly even cutting his scheme short. All the more reason he'd be sure to enjoy every moment of this time-out from the regimen of his life. In his thirty years he'd been respectful and proper, habits he had no intention of changing. Even down to marrying Her Royal Highness Princess Vajhana from the neighboring island of Ko Yaolum, a unification that was designed to combine the resources of the two nations to bring more much-needed employment and prosperity to their citizens. Vajhana was not a bride Ras would have picked for himself. While attractive and educated, she was also frivolous and petty. He'd already resigned himself to hoping for no more than an amenable partnership with her, one that would produce an heir to his eventual throne. He was not expecting passion and burning love although, secretly, he wished for what his parents had. Until the loss of his wife had turned his father into a brittle shell.

Once he'd cleared away from the UN area Ras hailed a taxi, having only seen the practice done in movies. The driver wore a turban, and the inside of the car had an artificial pine smell. As they chugged through stop-and-go traffic, horns honked and drivers yelled out their windows to curse at each other. Ras appreciated every second of being in the center of the real New York and would return to explore lesser-known parts of the city at the end of his journey. At that point, hopefully no one would be looking for him.

He hardly knew where to focus his eyes as they passed through the Times Square area. Not quite as large and pulsing as Tokyo's Shibuya Crossing, nonetheless, the bright lights of the jumbotron advertisements, the Broadway theaters, oversize stores and street vendors were teeming with activity. Continuing west, the driver brought him to his destination at the port terminal. He paid the fare and got out of the cab. Toting his wheeled case, he took in the sheer size of the cruise ship he was about to board, the vessel itself aptly named *Liberation*. It had the capacity to hold three thousand passengers, not large by cruise standards but compared to the private yachts on which Ras traveled, it was enormous.

At home in the palace when he began finalizing his design for this trip, a travel website had featured information about this newly completed ship. The maiden voyage of uber-luxury Carat Cruises' newest addition to its fleet would begin in New York, heading toward its destination of Miami, a short distance meant to showcase the lavish amenities onboard. The passage was perfect for getting Ras away from New York unnoticed. No one would suspect a crown prince to be traveling on a public cruise. Then, instead of returning to New York, he had a yacht waiting for him in Miami. When he disembarked there presumably for a day of sightseeing, he simply wouldn't return to the cruise ship.

The brisk air of the waterfront filled his lungs as he strode up the gangway to board, bluffing to the porters that his luggage had arrived separately and checking in merely his small case. He didn't proceed directly to his stateroom suite. Instead, he remained on deck to watch when the ship left the shore.

"Ladies and gentlemen, this is Captain Batista," a voice boomed through the loudspeakers stationed at various points on the deck where many of the passengers had gathered after embarking. "On behalf of the crew and everyone at Carat Cruises, welcome to *Liberation*!"

"That's something," Gracie Russo said to herself as much as to anyone as the ship left the dock. It was sometimes hard to believe that Manhattan was actually an island. With its millions of residents and twenty-four-hours-a-day verve, it had always felt to her like a small country, one that she'd traveled to many times by bus and train. But from the vantage point of a cruise ship on the Hudson, the great skyscrapers and architectural marvels were indeed surrounded by bodies of water.

"It is, at that." Obviously, Gracie's comment was loud enough to be heard. As *Liberation* turned to chart its way toward the heart of the Atlantic Ocean, Gracie side-eyed the baritone that had spoken to her. The voice belonged to a tall and attractive man gazing at the island as they left it. "The Manhattan buildings always look to me like important and purposeful men."

His expensive suit struck her as a rather formal choice for the cruise's departure. Perhaps he was an important and purposeful man himself. He certainly looked excellent in his outfit's tailored fit. Gracie wore a flowered dress and carried a cardigan in case the sea breeze brought a chill. The leaves would be changing color to welcome autumn literally any day now.

"Is this your first time seeing the city from the water?" she asked, angling to face him.

"Yes, exactly. I've only flown in, so the perspective is quite different."

Gracie was interested in the points of view of some typical cruise passengers. Although this man seemed anything but typical with an accent that suggested elite schooling and that gray suit, white shirt and charcoal tie. His skin was tan and his eyes dark; prominent cheekbones and a razor-sharp jaw added up to a stunningly fine face. She couldn't help but wonder if he was on the ship alone as there was no companion in sight. What would a man like him be doing alone on a ship? Compelled to continue the chitchat she asked, "Do you cruise often?"

She'd been learning all about cruise culture, about people who preferred that mode of travel with its all-inclusive accommodations, dining options, port excursions and carefully customized itineraries. In fact, Gracie had been learning about all types of tourism and leisure. Because she was finally going to fulfill her dream of becoming a luxury travel consultant. Truth be told, just as *Liberation* had embarked so had she. This was her maiden voyage as an industry professional. She was nervous and excited all at once.

The handsome passenger rotated his long neck slowly, very slowly, from left to right, scanning the entire vista both on the cruise ship's deck and even past it to the small boats that also rode the river. It somehow didn't seem like he was looking for anyone in particular among the many passengers who had gathered on deck to watch the departure from port. Yet his heavy eyebrows furrowed, as if he was suspicious, maybe even in danger. She couldn't imagine what someone would be worried about when they'd just set sail on a pleasure cruise, something she'd never done. Of course, his reasons were none of her affair. Satisfied, at least momentarily with his investigation, he returned his gaze to Gracie. The depth of his gaze ran right through her, forcing its way into every vein. There was something very compelling about this man. She was glad he was nothing to her but a stranger on a deck, as the last thing she needed was any entanglements when she had finally set herself free in every way. He rounded back to her original question. "Public cruises, no. I do travel quite a bit by yacht, though."

Of course, he did. He was almost out of place on this ship, despite the fact that it was touted as being ultra-luxurious in every detail and was the newest vessel in Carat's fleet, the most exclusive cruise line in the world. This man was somehow beyond even that.

"Where are you from?" Gracie inquired, rationalizing that the question was still within the realm of superficial banter fellow passengers would have.

He scoped out another panorama before saying succinctly, "Asia." She'd have guessed as much from his features, but the full stop on the end of his answer let her know that she was not going to get a longitude and latitude any more specific than that.

A moment later, snapping back from that bird's-eye survey he'd taken, he asked, "Yourself?"

She gestured with her head to the other side of the Hudson River, to the land it bordered on the opposite side from Manhattan. "New Jersey. Born and raised." If a person could call the sorry excuse for parenting she'd received *raised.* Not to mention what had gone on between *born* and the ripe old age of twenty-six. He'd have been able to guess from her bargain cotton dress that she didn't live on Park Avenue.

"Ah, so you must know the US Eastern Seaboard like the back of your hand?"

She'd lived in three places, all in New Jersey. Born in a seedy outskirt of the capital city, Trenton. Then she'd moved to the shore at Point Pleasant, whose name was a matter of opinion, with her biggest mistake, named Davis. And for the last two years she'd been in the north of the state, in Newark. Not exactly the pounding pulse of urbanity but close to New York. As to the rest of the East Coast, she knew of all the places she intended to visit so that she could advise clients. She hoped to make *nowhere* her new home, done being left behind, done being at the mercy of others, done holding anything dear because it would surely be taken from her. She had it all mapped out. She'd be the perpetual wanderer, financing her own ride with the money she made planning other people's.

"My whole life fits into four boxes," she'd said to Jen yesterday as she'd lifted them into her friend's already cramped Staten Island apartment, which, like New Jersey, was not the most coveted address in the New York area.

"Down to the essentials," Jen had commended her.

"Thank you for agreeing to keep my stuff and letting me have my mail sent here, too."

"Live your dream."

Gracie swiped the hair that had fallen into her eyes when she was carrying the boxes. "Let's hope so."

"Think of all the exotic and interesting people you'll meet," Jen had said. "Maybe even *men* people."

"Oh, you know there'll be no more of that for me. I'm a solo voyager."

Funny that Jen had been right about the interesting men, having just met one. Although he was none of her concern. "This cruise is more an introduction to the ship than a tour of the eastern US," she mentioned in case he didn't already know. "It only ports in Miami."

"Yes, I know. I'm only planning ahead to—" he abruptly reworked his own thought "—see the sights someday."

Potential client? Would it be too bold of her to give him a business card? Business card. Gracie Russo was a businesswoman. She'd studied as many popular locations as thoroughly as she could, taken courses in tourism and become certified, and learned all of the latest software programs. She'd been hired on a freelance basis by a cooperative of travel agents. The only money she'd make would be on commission, so she was going to have to work hard and make a name for herself.

She'd versed herself in all things Carat Cruises, which had held a reputation for decades as being the absolute finest. What she hadn't yet amassed were the funds to personally visit all of the travel destinations she would be selling to clients. But she had to start somewhere. Which was why when she'd read on an industry website that a limited number of travel professionals were being invited to take *Liberation*'s maiden voyage so that, no doubt, they could recommend it, Gracie jumped at the chance. Her former job as a cashier at a bus station in Newark qualifying her as a travel professional might have been a stretch. Although it was technically travel-related, wasn't it? And she was now a member of the agency co-op even though she hadn't had any bookings yet.

When she'd strode up the gangway to board a little while ago, an electric charge fired through her as she followed the check-in signs for Tourism Professionals. Her bags portered to her stateroom, she was warmly welcomed at the reception table that held no more than a list of names. She wasn't questioned about her credentials despite her trepidation that she might have been. An extensive color brochure of the ship's amenities and the numerous activities planned would await her in the stateroom, although she'd already studied it in great detail online.

It was her moment. When the cruise returned to New York after its four-day voyage, her online travel agency would be open for business. Next, she'd planned a rental car trip through New England to see the fall colors and investigate the bed-and-breakfast inns whose owners had offered travel agents complimentary accommodations to come tour their properties. With enough money diligently saved to keep her for a few months before a first commission was earned, she was filled with gusto at the future she'd been waiting for, for far too long. Okay, she was in equal measure terrified.

What if none of it worked out? she suddenly thought in a moment of panic. She'd given up her job and her apartment. It was no-holds-barred *go for it* time. Well, she mused, if it all fell apart, it wouldn't be the first time a promise didn't come true. What did she have to lose at this point?

"*Liberation* guests." The captain's voice came through the loudspeakers once again. "We'll begin our welcome festivities shortly, but let me first turn your attention to that grand monument known the world over."

The closer they approached, the larger the three-hundred-foot Statue of Liberty appeared. Although Gracie had spent her life nearby, she would never tire of seeing Lady Liberty's oxidized copper-green glory.

"Indeed, a symbol the whole world understands," said the elegant stranger still standing next to her, who was himself studying the details of the magnificent representation of a Roman goddess. For no comprehensible reason, she wished his eyes were intently on her instead of on Liberty.

Gracie glanced around at the passengers on the deck. With Carat's clientele, her shipmates were likely to be among the most privileged people on the planet. Those who demanded, and received, the best of everything. Yet she couldn't help but see a bit of wonder in all of their eyes as they took in the majesty of the statue. "Did you know that her crown has seven spikes in acknowledgment of the seven continents and the seven oceans of the world?" Gracie hoped to visit them all someday.

"Ladies and gentlemen, I am Aston, your cruise director," a strapping man with red hair and an Australian accent announced through a handheld microphone as he bounced onto the deck. "As we say goodbye to New York for a few short days, Carat Cruises has a surprise." He was accompanied by other members of the crew who dispersed to shake hands and give individual greetings to dozens of passengers. They all had big smiles and donned crisp blue shirts embroidered with the Carat diamond logo, both the male and female members wearing them tucked into fitted slacks. Smartly casual but polished. In the small bag he'd brought, Ras had a couple of leisure outfits other than the overdressed suit he was wearing, which he worried made him look conspicuous. He'd been in full royal regalia for the meetings at the UN and in suits for dinners.

Aston continued, "We hope to have your every wish fulfilled onboard *Liberation* with her state-of-the-art facilities. To kick things off, we're celebrating the rich culture of our port city, Miami, with a very special guest. You know her as one of Cuba's best-known singers. She's toured the planet with her renowned band, selling out arenas in over forty countries. Topping both the pop and Latin music charts for over a decade. Let's give a big Carat Cruises welcome to eleven-time Grammy winner, Benita Diaz!"

Ras heard audible gasps from a few people. Benita Diaz was a global superstar. No one would have expected her to be entertaining on this short cruise. A massive smile crossed the pretty face of the woman in the flowered dress he'd been talking to, whose name he still didn't know. "Ah, a brilliant publicity move," she extolled. A bubbly energy sparked off her. He had no idea why, but he took one step closer to her. Then thought better of it and retreated. She observed his faux pas but continued. "Everyone will be posting and talking about this!" He didn't know why Carat Cruises' public relations would be of interest to her. But she radiated a contagious enthusiasm His Royal Highness, sometimes thinking of his title as being something outside of himself, wasn't used to being around. He lived behind a window of propriety and control.

Her comment that people would be posting about this unexpected celebrity appearance caused Ras to scan the deck once again. Cell phones and cameras were trained on the entertainment storming the deck. There was always the possibility of Ras being recognized by the general public. He tried to reassure himself the crown prince of a very small nation halfway around the world was not likely to be noticed aboard this tourist cruise. Yet somehow, with paparazzi seeming to sprout up from under the surface of the earth, his photo did occasionally land on websites and magazines that catered to those obsessed with young royals. His flashy bride-to-be was frequently photographed at the world's biggest parties, a slave to fashion and the famous. He had always been cognizant of poise and dignity so there had never been anything tawdry the media could uncover about him. Nonetheless, every couple of years he'd been chosen as one of the world's most attractive princes or another similarly embarrassing moniker.

In any case, as a line of men in white bearing horn instruments and handheld drums began to play, Ras was sure there were no eyes on him. Cuban tempos and percussion spread across the deck, garnering everyone's attention. *"Bienvenidos!"* a female voice boomed through a microphone over the music. Dancers with long legs and colorful feathery costumes sashayed into position and began their choreography to the lively music. Then their line parted in half to welcome Benita Diaz in a sparkling red dress with massive ruffles. She bounded out almost as if from a cannon blast. "Welcome. To. *Liberation!*"

The passengers applauded and hooted. Ras glanced at the woman still beside him who began bobbing her head in time with the music. The afternoon sun glinted off her golden hair, which fell in loose waves to her shoulders. She was certainly attractive, Ras admitted in his mind. Which gave him a wicked rush he wanted more of. No wonder his subconscious made him take that step forward toward her. Thank goodness the rational part of his brain had immediately retracted the error. This personal voyage wasn't a premarital stag party. It was his own company he wished to keep.

As Benita tore into one of her most popular songs, it seemed everyone on deck cut loose and either shimmied their shoulders or wiggled their hips to the rhythm. Except him, of course. The media might choose to portray him as one of the world's most eligible royals, but while he had certainly enjoyed the company of women, he was not a playboy. His parents had taught him decorum and respect for the honor of leading a nation. His Royal Highness Rasmayada of Ko Pha Lano most certainly did not *shake his booty*. In public, anyway. That didn't stop him from enjoying the sight of the silky shoulders next to him as they shimmied.

"I love this song!" the owner of the shoulders exclaimed.

"What's your name?"

"Gracie Russo. Yours?"

"Ras." He wouldn't say more. As a matter of fact, he should have given her a phony name. Well, probably no harm so far, he told himself. A reminder that while this Gracie was friendly, he was traveling incognito and couldn't forget it.

"Nice to meet you." She flashed a smile at him that made a squiggle flitter up his spine. His shoulders arched sharply.

After Benita, her dancers and her band played several of their hits in a set that lasted about half an hour, they left the deck to thunderous applause.

Cruise Director Aston took to the mic again. "We're glad you enjoyed our *special* guest. Now we'd like to turn your attention to our coffee reception where you can sample a cup of good old New York regular and a rich Café Cubano. The brews are ready and waiting!"

Gracie turned around as did Ras to see the buffet tables set with cups, and decorated with cuttings from coffee trees, including the cherries that contained the beans. There were trays full of cookies and chocolates for the taking. Guests began making their way toward the offerings. She placed her hand on his upper arm by way of gesture. "Let's go get some."

He was unused to being touched and instinctively pulled back. After all, a prince had handlers surrounding him at all times in public, as much as a barricade as anything else. Although there was no way Gracie's soft pull could have meant him any harm, and he missed the feel of her as soon as he'd ended it. She gave him a quizzical look. Perhaps his retreat was startling to her. Especially after he'd taken a step closer to her earlier. He tried to cover his slip with, "Yes, we must try the coffees."

"Sounds great."

Even though they were among the elite on this exclusive cruise, Ras was surprised at the mad rush toward the buffet. He was sure the crew knew exactly how much refreshment to prepare and wasn't in danger of running out. Cruise culture, he noted to himself. He wasn't accustomed to being in a crowd other than when he passed through them in an official capacity, with both liveried and undercover protection. He was glad that in a couple of days, he'd be picking up his private yacht in Miami. Looking over at Gracie, though, he had this completely unprovoked notion that he'd be sad alone. Which, since he'd exchanged nothing more than a few words with her and spoken to no one else in the last hour, was simply ridiculous. Although when her caramel eyes met his for an unspoken moment of connection, something in his spirit soared. "About that coffee…" He snapped out of it to square himself and get back to business.

"This is very cute," Gracie said, surveying the buffet table once they reached it. "See these blue-and-white coffee cups with the Greek key design on them? Those cups used to be the kind every place in New York that sold coffee had before the brand-name coffee shops took over. Made of paper, of course. These are porcelain."

"What's a regular coffee?" Ras asked, having never heard the term.

"Milk and sugar already mixed in."

"Ah, yes, New York. No fussing around."

"Let's get serious about these sweets." She took one of the small plates provided and handed one to Ras. Only a cool whisper of air separated her fingers from his as he took it. He smiled as she helped herself to one of each and every of the offerings, double-checking that she hadn't missed any. There were shortbreads half dipped in chocolate. Cherry chocolate chip cookies. Chocolate cookies bursting with nuts. Biscotti. Macarons. Cuban sugar cookies. Then assorted filled chocolates as well as squares. It was a chocolate festival. "Ooh, did I get that dark chocolate oval?" She pointed.

"Yes, Gracie, I think you've thoroughly loaded your plate," he said with an exuberant laugh so unlike him. At first, he only took one each of three selections. But then, carried away by her devotion, he piled his plate just the same as hers, feeling like a greedy child at a candy shop, an experience he'd never actually had.

You only live once.

"We need our Café Cubanos."

"What type of preparation is that?"

"It's basically an espresso with sugar." Served in small cups that were brown on the outside and white inside, the frothy brew smelled utterly intoxicating. He took a tray from a stack provided. Placing the four coffees and the two overflowing plates on it, he felt like a teenager holding books for a cute girl. It elicited a sort of pride that he didn't get often, as mundane things such as this were done for him. The tray also confirmed that they headed together toward an empty table to sit at.

He stopped, tray in hand.

"Is something wrong?" she asked.

What on earth was he doing? He had no idea who this woman was. A prince didn't suddenly keep company with someone he'd met on a cruise an hour ago. Most definitely not an engaged prince. He and Vajhana had been matched by their fathers and had agreed from their very first meeting that they would put no monogamy claims on each other. Yet that didn't mean he'd abandon his usual discretion when having his occasional liaisons with women. Which did not include the open deck of a public cruise.

Ras hadn't planned to actually talk to anyone on the ship. The cruise was just a mode of transportation to reach the yacht. In fact, he'd considered having all of his meals brought to his stateroom. It was unorthodox enough that he didn't get on that plane back to the island with his father. That he'd carefully planned this sojourn to explore on his own, to experience just a taste of life outside the palace walls. To escape being a prince for brief interludes as his mother had wanted him to, and told him so when he was a teenager before she died. To learn to be simply a man with his time his own, to know what that was like. He surely couldn't have imagined sharing a snack on a public deck with a beautiful young woman. Yet, blame it on the music, blame it on the coffee or blame it on Gracie's infectious smile. It turned out Ras's freedom quest had already begun.

CHAPTER TWO

"OH, MY GOSH, have you tried the piece with nuts on top?" Gracie gestured to Ras's plate while he took a sip of his New York regular, light and sweet and smooth. She was referring to one of the chocolates in the black, pleated paper cups they'd put on their plates to sample. "It's heavenly."

Ras examined his plate. He located the confection she was referring to and studied it in his fingers. The top was studded with finely chopped almonds and sprinkled with slivers of sparkle. "The gold leaf is a nice touch."

"If you hold it a certain way, the sun glints off it. Perfect for outdoors."

"A little work of art, in and of itself." Ras couldn't say he'd ever given that much thought to an individual piece of candy. Although he did turn it right to left, forward and back, just to see the reflections. Had he been eating chocolates at an official function, neither His Royal Highness nor whomever he was in company with would have thought to admire the creativity involved. *Thank you, Mother*, he thought, silently lifting his eyes to the skies. This was a perfect example of what she wanted for him. For him to know small pleasures. To serve himself a plateful of desserts without caring whether that was proper royal conduct. To daydream, to imagine *what-*

if with regard to anything that came to mind. She'd believed it would make him a better leader, more complete and able to see the world from perspectives other than his own.

It was the kind of thing she and his father did, every so often. Yes, they were role models to an entire nation and never took an action that would be disrespectful of their positions. At the same time, Queen Sirind had made sure her family knew what grass felt like under their feet and what it was to care for their beloved Shih Tzu. It had been years since Ras thought of Lucky, so named because Sirind had told the dog daily what a fortunate destiny he had. He'd died when Ras was thirteen, two years before his mother. In retrospect, the family should have immediately replaced Lucky with another dog. That could have helped both him and his father with their grief when Sirind died. It might have helped the king continue to have red blood running through his veins as opposed to the cold frame of a man he'd become.

In his mother's memory, he'd make sure his own children ran around the palace grounds and ate unreasonable amounts of sweets once in a while. And know of the real world. Biting into the chocolate he'd been watching catch the light, the milk chocolate robe gave way to a center of more almonds mixed with a buttery brittle that had both crackly and chewy bits.

"What do you think?" Gracie watched as he savored his bite.

"Yes, it is truly divine." He popped the rest of it in his mouth while she finished hers as well. Following that, he lifted his cup of Café Cubano. "What shall we toast to?"

"To…adventure."

"To adventure." They tapped their cups to each other's

and sipped. "This coffee is perfect. Sweet enough to keep the bitterness from becoming too harsh."

"Is that a metaphor for life?"

He laughed at Gracie's observation. "I suppose you could say that."

"Have you tried the lemon macaron? I think that's my favorite so far."

Without hesitation, he put his onto her plate. "Please, have mine then."

She gave him a wistful look as if he'd just gifted her with fine jewels or something valuable. "That's so… thoughtful of you."

"It's just a sweet. There are probably more at the buffet table. Would you like me to get you some?" He was eager at the prospect, getting something for her that she wanted. Perhaps he'd watched too many movies and had a distorted view of how commoners flirted with each other. *Flirted?* Was he flirting with her? His Royal Highness didn't flirt.

Though the way she stared at him after his offer made him wonder if she'd been treated unkindly in the past, so dramatic was her gratitude for a macaron. Which made him curious about her. "No, thank you." Her voice went hardly above a whisper.

Was she on the cruise by herself? If she'd been with someone, wouldn't she be sharing heaven-sent chocolates with him? Or her? Or them? Would it be snooping to ask? It didn't matter, he figured. On a ship holding three thousand passengers, he'd likely never even see her past this interlude. "Are you traveling alone?"

"Yes," she said and then took a bite of the lemon confection. He waited for her to say more. She looked up to the sky with a hesitance he didn't understand. "For business. I'm a travel consultant. Carat Cruises invited

a number of people in the industry for the voyage to introduce *Liberation*. No doubt in hopes we would recommend it to clients."

"A travel consultant. That must be interesting work."

"It will…it is."

"Perhaps you can offer me some recommendations.
What would you suggest I see on the East Coast beyond
the typical spots?"

"The East Coast covers a lot of ground. Savannah,
Georgia, and Charleston, South Carolina are special
places. Do you golf?"

"I do."

"Water sports?"

"Sure."

"Regional food?"

"Absolutely."

"You'll find it all, up and down the East Coast. You
also might want to visit the Hamptons on Long Island,
New York."

"Thank you for the tips." He flashed on an idea that
was so impossible he forced his mind to dismiss it right
away. "You said you were from New Jersey. What do you
like in your home state?"

Was he imagining it or did her eyes mist up as she answered? "Getting out." Her gaze left his and went past the
confines of the boat, out to the ocean and sky. Clearly,
he'd touched a nerve. She flattened her palm to her stomach. After a few beats she seemed to remember that she
was sitting with him. "There's nothing to see there."

She brought her attention back to her plate for another bite and onto another topic. "What do you do for
work, Ras?"

It was a question he'd never been asked in his life.
The words sounded so unusual. He decided not to an-

swer the question at all. But then the silence became too awkward so he snapped, "I'm in a family business. We go back generations."

She lowered her head to her plate, lingering as she made her next selection, avoiding eye contact. Perhaps he came across as sharp, but his anonymity was crucial to this journey he had embarked on, so he wouldn't stand for being interviewed.

He tried to reengage, "What does *your* family do?"

Gracie barked out a laugh that was bitter and dark. "No one particular thing."

"How does that work?"

"It doesn't."

"What are they doing now?"

"I have no idea. I haven't talked to them in a while."

"You don't talk to your parents?"

"I don't know where they are."

"I'm sorry to pry. But that sounds like a difficult situation."

"It was. It's perfectly simple now."

While he and the king differed in their points of view about many things and had lost the closeness they'd had when Queen Sirind was alive, Ras couldn't imagine not talking to him even if they weren't in the same *business*. Gracie had obviously been through some trauma in her life. Ras's position meant he didn't really get to *know* people. He was mostly kept at a distance. At charity events, he might hear someone's troubles but the connection was never more than a few minutes long. He wondered what Gracie's heartaches and triumphs were.

Finally, when each and every sweet had been at least sampled if not devoured, he did a quick check to make sure no one appeared to be watching him. He'd never hear the details of Gracie's life. They were just two cordial strangers who'd crossed each other's paths for a brief repast. They'd never see each other again. As a matter of fact, he'd been out on deck and exposed long enough. It was time to say goodbye to her and retreat to his stateroom suite. His brows bunched at the idea even as he knew it was the right thing to do. He could continue to enjoy the sun, water and views from his private balcony.

"Well," he said as he pushed his chair back and stood, "this has been absolutely delightful, but I'd best be going. It was a pleasure to meet you, Gracie."

She seemed surprised at his abruptness and gazed up at him while still seated. Wow, were her eyes luminous? "Oh. Um… You, too."

He lowered his right hand to shake hers, another very unprince-like move as in his nation royals did not physically touch commoners, and he'd backed away when she'd tapped his arm earlier. He considered retreating again although that would be awkward since he instigated the contact. Plus, he had to admit to himself, he wanted to know what her hand felt like. The gesture afforded him the sensation of silk in human form as he was sure he'd never held anything as soft as her palm. Making a direct connection with those eyes, he knew the handshaking was really just an excuse not to let go of her fingers. He kept the moment one tick longer than he should have, maybe two, actually maybe three, knowing it was a once in a lifetime experience. Finally, his hand separated itself from hers, not without struggle, and he bowed his neck to her. "Thank you again for an enchanting kickoff to our passage. Enjoy the cruise."

"You too, Ras." As he walked away, the sound of her saying his nickname played over and over on a continuous loop in his brain. Ras. Not Prince Rasmayada. Not

Your Royal Highness. Ras. *You too, Ras... Ras... Ras.* The tones in her voice were like music.

He reached his stateroom suite on the most exclusive deck of the ship, which he'd booked with the assumption it would be less trafficked. He swiped his key card, entered and removed his shoes, leaving them by the door. His small travel bag was almost silly in the spaciousness, but he lifted it onto the luggage bench. The enormous living room was centered by an L-shaped sectional sofa that faced the ocean on one side and a mounted television on the other. In front of it was a coffee table that had a nice stack of art books. A black table and chairs were set up for in-suite fine dining. A modern chandelier drew the eye up to the high ceilings. The far wall had a sliding glass door leading to a balcony with another table and chairs, plus chaise lounges. After surveying the equally well-appointed bedroom and master bath, he circled back to the living room and finally took off his suit jacket and tie. He undid the top button of his shirt and then sat down facing the water. Having left the balcony door open, he could hear the ocean waves and feel the sea air circulate in the room.

As he watched the waves of the Atlantic, he thought of oceans on the other side of the world. He realized, as if for the first time, how little time he spent alone. His day was often filled with meetings, many at his father's side. Evenings were generally spent at official or charitable functions, lately in the company of Princess Vajhana once their engagement had been brokered. He was genuinely humbled by the responsibilities his position brought, which would grow even more important when the crown sat upon his head. Leading his people was a great distinction. At the same time, the confines could be stifling. He needed this break away from Ko

Pha Lano. Before he married and the particulars of being a husband, and hopefully a father, would define the next chapter of his life.

Out of his pocket, he retrieved one of the untraceable cell phones he'd purchased. Dialing a phone number known only to him and a very select few others, he heard the king's recorded greeting.

"It's Ras. As I told you in New York, I will come back in three weeks. I'm going to live out mother's wish for me. That, before I marry, I wander a bit. That I walk and think like a man not a royal." For example, boarding a public cruise ship and enjoying delicious treats eaten in the open air with a woman who had beautiful golden waves of hair. "To know what that is. Like you and she used to. I'm calling because I want to let you to know that I'm fine. I'll call again soon." With that, he tapped off the phone and tossed it beside him on the sofa.

Explore himself he did, as for the next couple of hours he stared out at the ocean, ideas coming to him one after the other. The status of the island. How when Sirind died it was not just a prince who'd lost his mother and a king who'd lost his wife. It was the whole nation who'd lost their queen. A loss that to this day it had never recovered from. The people of Ko Pha Lano needed their inspiration back. Spoiled and glamorous Princess Vajhana was not going to give that to them. Ras would need to do it himself. Even though he and his father didn't agree on the island's future. Perhaps his ultimate mission would be to change the king's mind.

His mother had been so right. He needed to see distant shores and have unfamiliar thoughts. Ideas were bouncing around his brain so fast he couldn't even catch them. That was okay. It was wonderful, in fact. But after he'd done enough brainstorming for the day, he couldn't bear to sit in his suite alone the rest of the day and evening. He decided to change the plan and take a walk around the ship.

"Oh, what are the odds?" Gracie choked out when she saw Ras heading toward her on the starboard side of the promenade deck.

Ras bowed his head. "Very unusual," he answered with a quick dart of his eyes right to left.

"Are you waiting for someone?" Had he ever said whether or not he was traveling alone?

"No, why? It's nice to see you again." He'd peered around several times during Benita Diaz's mini concert and again during the sweets buffet. She half expected to find out he was actually onboard with a wife or significant other and was trying to be sure he wasn't caught getting a little too friendly with another passenger.

Although his big dark brown eyes held a gaze of trustworthiness. When he'd looked at her during their coffee chat, he fully looked. Giving her the impression she had all his interest. It was a nice feeling and something she was wholly unused to. In any case, the deep eyes were quite entrancing as she now encountered them for an unexpected second time.

"Where are you headed?" Solo travelers were rare, and it would be useful for her to know how this obviously well-to-do gentleman was going to spend his time onboard. Was he en route to the spa? The casino?

"I was going to peruse the boutiques." A shopper? She wouldn't have pegged him for one. She'd figured him as the type to have an assistant or perhaps even a personal tailor. She noticed that he still wore the same gray suit pants he'd been in when they'd first met. Although he'd taken off his tie and changed from a white shirt to a pale yellow one that was very becoming on him. Why wouldn't it be? He was six feet plus of lean muscle and the suit had fit to perfection, if not made specifically for him. Perhaps it was his posture, the way he carried himself, shoulders back, chiseled jaw just so, that made her certain he was successful and moneyed. "Where are you off to?"

"Just browsing around." After they'd finished their chocolates and coffee, he'd abruptly excused himself from the table. Gracie made her way to her stateroom and found the porter had left her luggage there as arranged. While it wasn't one of the ship's deluxe rooms, it was elegantly detailed. On the pillow of the king-size bed was a long-stem red rose with a ribbon tied around it that read *Welcome*. The bed linens were in the signature blue shades of Carat Cruises. On the nightstand were bottles of water.

Beyond the sleeping quarters was a dressing area. A large full-length mirror stood near the ample closet. While this introductory cruise was only for a few days, *Liberation* was intended for longer voyages. Passengers who chose fine dining and entertainment might have packed quite a bit of luggage filled with evening clothes. Gracie put the two nicer dresses she'd brought on hangers. A vanity table with a mirror and a chair was a handy place to get ready for wherever she was going on ship.

She took a minute to imagine having packed a trunk full of evening wear. Garments of fine fabric and fashionable style, clothes like nothing she'd ever worn. Next she envisioned opening up a large case filled with makeup and hair accessories. Dozens of shades of eye shadow and lipsticks to choose from, and her having the knowledge to apply it all so that it enhanced her features without overdoing it and looking cheap. Finally, she'd go to the stateroom's safe to pull out whatever jewels she'd brought along to complete her ensembles.

She laughed at her own reflection in the vanity mirror. It was nothing short of a miracle that she'd even gotten this far, finagling a complementary stateroom on an elite cruise ship. She hoped none of the staff would ever find out that working at a bus station didn't exactly qualify her as part of the tourism industry.

The travel professionals onboard were going to be given a full tour of the ascending levels of accommodations tomorrow. Gracie wanted to build a client base of luxury travelers because, of course, that would mean higher commissions. Plus she assumed there would be more opportunities like this one, for her to have the *whisk you away* experiences she'd been reading and watching videos about for her entire life. With parents who'd left her alone most of her life and then a boyfriend who might as well have, now she wanted to be the one leaving for here or there, not someone being left.

After freshening up, she'd stepped out to see all *Liberation* had to offer.

"Can I tag along with you?" she asked Ras, not wanting this coincidence to end. "I'd like to see the shops."

"Come with me?" He tilted his head as he considered her request, giving Gracie further reason to question whether he was trying to keep a secret. It was a simple yes or no question.

"Of course," he finally conceded and gestured with his hand for her to follow him. What sort of destiny had them crossing paths again on this enormous ship?

The first store they came upon sold items for use onboard. Bathing suits and cover-ups, pool shoes, T-shirts. "Do you want to go inside?" she asked.

"Yes, I don't have swimming attire."

"You didn't pack for water activities?"

"It's difficult to explain. Embarking on this cruise was…a sort of last-minute decision." He was a terrible liar. His eyebrows raised until they were flat lines, and those shapely full lips of his parted in a way that made him look thirsty. Earlier, he'd bristled when she'd asked about his *family business*. Oh, well, she figured, everyone had a story. What she did know about him was that when she'd taken his arm to lead him to the coffee buffet, he'd pulled away, uncomfortable at being touched. Although, later, he'd given her a prolonged handshake. And he'd carried their tray to a table so she had to follow. When she said the lemon confection was her favorite, he insisted she take his. She wasn't used to gentlemanly gestures and kindness like that. No one had ever noticed if something was her favorite. So her inner sense told her he was a good man even if he was obviously holding a mystery.

"The ocean is too cold to swim. Will you be going to the beach in Miami?"

"Beach, pool, I don't know. As I told you, I'll be traveling for a few weeks. Might as well be prepared for anything, right?"

If you can afford to, she thought to herself.

"Absolutely, you can never have too many options," she blurted and then felt silly at her phoniness. Truth was, she'd had the same bathing suit since she was eighteen.

While he perused the rack of men's swimwear, she surveyed the knickknacks and typical souvenirs, noting that they were more tastefully designed than usual. When she came across an infant onesie with a graphic design reading *Baby's First Cruise*, she winced. Instinctively, even after all this time, her hand reached to massage her belly. Would she do that forever? Now the motion had become a symbol of everything she'd lost. Hopefully, better times were ahead.

"Are you all right?" She hadn't noticed Ras come up beside her. "Are you seasick?"

Ah, he was reacting to her hand on her stomach. "Thank you, that's nice of you to ask." Davis would have never observed if she appeared unwell. He wasn't that kind of guy. "No, not seasick at all, just a silly habit."

After he paid for his selections he said, "I'm done here. I'm told there's a men's clothing shop a few doors down." As they made their way toward the exit, Ras turned in a certain way so as to block something behind him that, evidently, he didn't want her to see. Which, of course, only made her all the more curious. As they left, she did a quick swerve to see a book and magazine stand. Hmm. Was he famous, not wanting her to see him on a book or magazine cover? Was he an actor, a politician, was his *family business* a prominent one? If he was a famous face, wouldn't she, and other people, recognize him?

Nonetheless, it was fun to see the shopping gallery, and he led her past a luggage purveyor and a jewelry store to the men's shop. When they entered its quiet hush, the walls paneled with red wood, Gracie could tell the prices were going to add at least a zero to the end of any number she was used to. "I need casual clothes," Ras explained to the salesman who wore a jacket and tie.

"I can help you with that, sir." He nodded to Gracie. "Madam."

"Hi."

"Can you tell me a bit about your preferences, sir?" The question seemed to perturb Ras so the salesman went on. "For example, do you prefer a button-down shirt or would you like a polo style?"

Ras looked at him as if that was the most difficult decision he'd ever been asked to make. He thought about it for as long as he could before sort of giving up with a simple, "Yes."

Trying to make it easier, the salesman inquired, "For example, do you like chambray or would you prefer denim?"

"Do you have a personal stylist?"

"Of course, sir. Give me a moment to see if Charles is available." The salesman rushed back behind the sales floor to some private area.

"At home, I have a valet who manages my wardrobe," Ras told Gracie.

"Of course." She nodded as she tried to unpack that statement. He has a personal *valet*. Who *manages* his wardrobe. If it needed confirming, obviously Ras was indeed wealthy. Not just well off. She'd guess dripping. And, as she'd learned at the first shop, possibly famous. This cruise was certainly getting off to an interesting start.

"Charles can assist you, if you'd like to follow me," the salesman said to him.

He seemed to consider the situation for a moment before asking, "Gracie, will you join me? That is if you don't have somewhere else to be."

"Sure." This could be instructive, to be allowed into the inner sanctum where the proverbial *haves* versus the *have nots* shopped. The salesman swiped a key card and ushered them into a salon. The room was painted ocean blue. Two rounded silver sofas formed a semicircle in front of a trio of tall mirrors that completed the circle, with a dais in the center.

A small-statured older man who wore fine suit pants, a shirt and tie with a measuring tape slung around his neck and a pin cushion on his wrist introduced himself as Charles. An attendant brought in a tray holding two glasses of champagne in tall flutes, offering one each to Ras and Gracie. They both accepted. "Madam, perhaps you'd like to sit down." Charles pointed to the sofas. Gracie sat on one of them, exquisitely comfortable. To Ras he said, "My associate tells me you'd like some assistance with casual items. May I take you to the dressing room and show you some selections?"

Ras sent a shrug and a smile to Gracie as he followed Charles, leaving her alone. Scanning the room, she saw a rack of clothes off to the side. Black tuxedos. One was a young child's size. Four more had emerald-colored cummerbunds and bow ties on each hanger at the ready. The last one on the rack was different. The cummerbund had black embroidery and a black border on the emerald fabric as did the tie, making it subtly but distinctly different from the others. Grace knew in an instant that she was looking at the menswear for a wedding. Getting married on a cruise was a popular choice. She'd imagine a ship like *Liberation* would have every possible detail needed for a world-class wedding.

She chewed her lip. Life could have gone in several different directions for her. She could have had parents who cared about her, given her the security to go after her dreams at an early age. She could have married a good man and had children. Or she could have married Davis. After he'd showed his true colors, she was glad she hadn't. He did her a favor by delivering the hurt before it was too late. Never even knowing what had happened afterward.

As a result of her past choices and those made for her, she knew who she was. She'd never form a *forever after* with anyone. Never take those vows. Not at a neighborhood church in New Jersey and not on an opulent cruise.

She was sailing alone, on this passage and beyond. That was that.

Ras and Charles exited the dressing room. Well-fitting jeans showcased Ras's long legs and a pale pink button-down shirt worn untucked was just right for relaxed elegance. While he'd looked businessman-handsome in his suit, this outfit was more easy confidence, and extremely hot, actually. "You look…that looks…great," she said, stammering.

Charles brought him to the mirrors for tailoring adjustments. Once that was done he asked, "Madam, may we show you another ensemble?"

Gracie took a sip of her champagne. She wasn't expecting her freebie ticket on this cruise to already be so much fun.

With the clothes to be delivered to his suite, Ras stood outside the men's shop with Gracie. "Thank you. It was wonderful to have a woman's eye, not to mention a helpful second opinion. As I told you, my clothes are generally selected for me." It was an unexpected pleasure to have an attentive companion along with him. If he'd been in the same situation with his fiancée and they were shopping for him and not her, she'd have bided her time on her phone and never looked up.

"My pleasure, Ras. I've never seen a private salon like that so it was fascinating. I like what you picked." Her approval made him happy in an unexplainable way.

"Well, I've kept you long enough." Once again he was to bid her farewell and, given the three thousand other passengers onboard, was unlikely to see her yet again. He fought his vocal cords from asking to. Spending time with people was not part of his trip's itinerary. He merely wanted to try being without his rigid schedule and expectations. He hadn't contemplated this voyage having anything to do with a woman. Although, he was drawn to Gracie. She had spirit and verve so unlike his interactions at the palace. It had been fun enjoying the concert and gorging on those delicious sweets, with her enthusiasm heightening the experience. That strange thought took hold again, but he knew he had to reject it. Instead, a few simple words choked out of his throat. "Goodbye, then. It's been a pleasure."

"Have a great rest of your trip." She gave him a genuine smile that shot like a beam right into his heart, sending a warm sensation to his chest that he wasn't sure how he'd get by without when it wore off. As she turned and headed away from the shopping area, he commanded himself not to watch her walk. That was, he meant to. Instead, his eyes took a slow slide from the honeyed strands of her hair, the cut of her dress and down to the shapely legs that carried her away from him.

After she was out of view, he strolled through another of the shopping lanes, one an enormous Carat Cruises office busy with people gathering information and perhaps booking for future sailings. Ras saw the glossy advertisements on the walls and knew he'd never cruise to Nova Scotia or down to the Caribbean on a vessel like this. His decree was set, and he was very fortunate indeed to be born into the humbling responsibility of the welfare of his subjects. It also afforded him almost every luxury possible. Except that of living as a common man. While he knew it was self-centered and something he'd need to work through by the time the crown sat on his head, Ras had been plagued by loneliness after his mother died. Partially it was because his father had also died, figuratively, along with her. There was no joy in the palace without her in it. He had no genuine intimacy with anyone. Certainly not with his intended, who he barely knew but didn't like. Vajhana was a quintessential party princess, a breed he'd never had interest in. Plus they'd been clear with each other about what they did, and didn't expect from their preordained marriage. Real intimacy was unlikely.

Ras did rendezvous with women occasionally. High-ranking career women who knew that a weekend with him at a private resort or on an adventure sport trip meant nothing more than a getaway. Even those excursions had grown tiresome. His mother was the only one he'd laughed with. Appreciated little things with. In her company he could be silly, say anything and truly be himself.

As Ras passed a toy store, he smiled wistfully when two parents presented a young boy, presumably their son, with a large replica of *Liberation*. It had human figurines that moved and doors that opened. A splendid souvenir. Would Ras playing with his own child someday fill up the hole that was left when his mother died?

And was it a crime, or even a surprise, that he already missed Gracie's company? He wondered where she was going. Perhaps to lay by the pool. Maybe she was taking a painting class or having a massage. Ras absolutely did not envision Gracie in a spa robe untying the belt and letting the thick terry cloth sides fall open to reveal her no doubt creamy skin underneath. He snickered at himself, at the mere thought of that.

When he passed the entrance to the casino, he noticed two Asian men wearing black suits. Was he imagining it, or were they staring at him? He knew from the minute he didn't get into the car with his father at the UN there would be a good chance that His Majesty would have his son followed. Deeming his son's grand scheme too risky to be left alone. For all he knew, half a dozen members of a security detail could have trailed him across Manhattan's Midtown and gotten onboard with him. His eyes darted to a woman in line at the casino cashier who smiled at him. So did another sitting at one of the slot machines. He suddenly felt claustrophobic.

"Would you like to do some gaming, sir?" a crew member asked. He glanced at the Carat Cruises insignia on the chest of her blue blazer. She startled him out of his web of suspicion.

"No. No, thank you."

"Let us know if you change your mind. One of our casino concierges would be glad to explain any of our games if you're unfamiliar with them. We feature baccarat, roulette, blackjack, craps and poker." Ras had visited the most posh and high-stakes casinos in the world and was adept at all of the games.

But this cruise was just a means of transportation to the yacht in Miami. He wasn't planning to participate in any of the *Liberation*'s activities where he'd be highly visible. After the ship departed, he'd got carried away with Gracie and with delectable chocolate. He'd be wise to bide his time from here on hidden in his stateroom suite until they got to port. He hoped if he was, in fact, being shadowed he'd be able to evade the detail at that point. The smart move for the moment was to return to his suite and order dinner in.

When he got back, the new clothes were nicely hung in one of the closets, the selected shoes and leather jacket at the ready. Feeling that he must, he texted Vajhana that he'd been called away on a charitable mission and would see her soon. There was no response. Pouring himself a glass of water, he ruminated on what it might be like for two people to return each other's texts the moment they arrived, as if receiving word from the other was the highest priority. He didn't have that kind of relationship with Vajhana and never would. Hopefully, they could become co-parents who formed a pact to do right by their children and their subjects. That was all that was required. Nothing more. They'd even agreed that fidelity would not be part of their agreement.

So why was Ras so listless as he stared out at the vast ocean on which he sailed? Was it more than wanderlust that compelled him to undertake this quest? He thought of that boy in the toy shop, excited about the plastic ship model that was about the size of his torso. Ras vaguely remembered being that age, happily playing with toys on the palace lawn as if it were a typical backyard. Where his two parents would often sit down on the grass and join in. In love with each other and with their son. All the smiling left when Sirind died. It was as if she took the sunshine with her. Was he here to find it once again?

After watching the waves for a long, long time, it dawned on Ras why he'd thought so much about his mother since he'd boarded the ship. She'd wanted this for him, all but instructed him to make sure to retain something of his true self before the palace demanded all his allegiance and all of his time. Yet there was another reason he was wistful and nostalgic. It was meeting Gracie. She was vibrant and riveting. She made thick red blood run through his veins in a way it never had before.

Although he'd scanned the ship's QR code to order dinner, he just as quickly put his phone down. Hiding alone in his suite would be unbearable. He'd take a chance that he'd just been overly cautious when he'd thought those people at the casino knew who he was. What he'd do was drop into one of the informal and crowded restaurants on the ship, no need for dinner attire. Maybe he'd read a book or even play a relaxing video game. Just a regular guy having a bite to eat.

CHAPTER THREE

IN A COUPLE of the ship's casual restaurants, passengers were welcome to seat themselves. All Gracie cared about was getting a window table as, to her, that was the point of being on a ship. To never forget being on the water. To take in the sheer splendor of eating while traversing oceans and seas, to watch the life of the water, to see vistas of sunrise, sunset and the cycle of the moon. It was a bit late for dinner. The afternoon dessert and coffee spread had been quite filling. So by the time she was hungry again, the moon shone high in the sky with a bright hue illuminating the ebb and flow of the waves. It was a lovely sight.

Scanning the dining room, she realized that she wasn't the only one who wanted a table with a view. All of them were full. She noted a few tables throughout the dining room where only one person sat and wondered if they were traveling alone like she was. A sneaky smile crossed her lips when she thought of her chance encounters with Ras, both as an intriguing companion with whom to stuff her face with sweets, and then later to find herself in a private salon watching him model clothes and ask her opinion of them. What a strange circumstance that was, exciting with a forbidden feel that still had her buzzing. It wasn't every day she was in the company of people who could afford clothes like those let alone be allowed into the world of shopping for them. Piece by piece the stylist built outfits for him, each intended for certain occasions. For example, if Ras was to eat in this casual dining room right now perhaps he'd be in that medium brown blazer that so complemented his big brown...

She spotted the blazer first. When he turned his head she could see that it was indeed Ras, doing his usual scan of the room. The odds were so slim that she'd run into him another time, yet there he was! Her heart fluttered a couple of extra beats when he noticed her and a radiant smile swept across his handsome face. No one had ever looked that happy to see her. Was it meant to be that she'd come down to eat right at that moment? "We meet again," she sighed to herself.

He, of course, had one of those coveted window tables kissed by the moon's light. There was no reason not to share it. Not to mention that the prospect made her skin tingle. She maneuvered her way across the dining room in order to reach him. "We are on the same wavelength. Or is it that we ate so much chocolate earlier that we needed the same amount of recovery time?" she teased.

"I'm hungry now," he proclaimed. "What about you?"

"Yes!"

"You look lovely, by the way."

"Thank you." She mashed her lips at the compliment. Knowing she wasn't dressed for one of the formal dining experiences, she was still well put together in a fitted black skirt and a red blouse with a scooped collar that came to a bow on one side. If she had to interact with anyone professionally, she wouldn't be an embarrassment. Her pearl earrings, which she'd bought herself for her twenty-sixth birthday and were the only *real* jewelry she owned, would be her adornment for everything she wore on this cruise. There was no jewel case in her room's safe. But with her black kitten heels she felt chic. Chatting with a sophisticated man on a classy cruise was a far cry from foraging for food when she was a teenager and her parents, who had left her alone, failed to send her money for groceries. After one of his pauses in which he seemed to be weighing options he said, "Join me."

An open bottle of red wine sat on the table next to one half-filled glass. "Would you like a glass of Pinot Noir? Or something else to drink?" Ras asked as he waved a server over.

"Wine would be nice."

"Another glass, please," Ras requested. A corner of his mouth tipped, making Gracie feel like they were in on a secret. "It seems I have a guest." The server pulled a menu card from his apron and placed it on the table-cloth in front of Gracie.

"Did you already order?"

"Not yet."

"What looks good?" Besides him.

"I was thinking of starting with the Vidalia onion tart. Then the herb-crusted salmon with black rice."

"I was toying with the onion tart but the sweet pea soup with quail egg sounds amazing. I'll have the salmon, too." Ras relayed the order when the server came.

"Tomorrow, the travel industry group is going to be given a full tour, including all the dining options."

"What led you to become a travel agent?"

"I've been studying destinations around the world since I was a child." Maybe someone would suppose that she'd done a lot of traveling, and that's what prompted her to pursue it as a career. That wasn't her case, but better late than never. The appetizers were served. Her pea soup was a brighter green than she'd expected, not the sludge that typically came from a can, and it was sweet and fresh with that rich quail egg as an unusual garnish. "This is delicious. Would you like to taste it?" Funny that she felt absolutely comfortable offering him her food. They'd already shared a lot together, what with the chocolate and his personal fashion show. And without censoring herself, she'd told him a little about her parents. It must have been the anonymity of their acquaintanceship that gave her license. After they parted, he'd go off to his well-to-do life and his *family business*. And she'd go forward with hers, uncomfortable history like a piece of luggage she'd always tote around.

Watching him tip a spoon into her soup did seem intimate. And she couldn't help but study him as he brought it to his mouth, those full lips parting. How did he manage to make a spoonful of soup look so sexy?

"Ever since I was a young girl, I used to look at books and watch videos and TV shows that took place in the four corners of the earth," she babbled, unable to stop. "I couldn't get enough of dreaming about faraway locales. And I knew that I would see every spot someday. Beautiful lands with beaches or big fast cities, as long as they were very far from New Jersey." It was those goals of seeing the world, of being out from under the dysfunction of her household that kept her strong. When she was cold. When she was hungry. When she was scared. And her plans helped her carry on after Davis had mangled her life.

He tilted his head to study her, maybe to judge her. There was nothing she could do about that. She was who she was. But he simply raised his wineglass in a toast. "To adventure."

"To adventure." Apparently, that was their motto. They clinked and took a sip. "Do you travel a lot?"

"Yes. Although as I had mentioned, I've spent very little time on the Eastern Seaboard save for New York and Washington, DC. My mother loved to travel."

"She doesn't anymore?"

"She died. When I was fifteen."

"Oh, Ras, I'm sorry to hear that. Was she sick?"

She could hear a little catch in his throat before he answered. "Yes. She had ovarian cancer. Then two recurrences. The third bout was more than her body could bear."

"How awful."

They looked each other in the eyes in unspoken communication, a step toward knowing one another better that they both seemed to value.

"Do you have siblings?" she asked.

"No."

"Growing up, I spent most of my time alone with my travel fantasies."

"You spent a lot of time alone because you have no siblings, either?"

"That and my parents were away a lot." She'd already told him that they didn't have established careers.

"Who cared for you when they were gone?"

"No one."

"What do you mean?"

"They left me alone for weeks on end while they worked temporary jobs in other cities or states. Until I was eighteen when they left altogether." There she went again, telling him more than she'd ever told anybody. "Then I had to let the bank foreclose on the house because I couldn't pay the mortgage and they stopped sending money." Now she'd said even that out loud. It was part of the story, anyway. Actually, it was a great purge to say it to a total stranger who'd be out of her life shortly.

"Gracie, my goodness. How old were you when they started leaving you alone?"

"About twelve."

"Twelve! Did they have personal issues? Alcoholism or substance abuse?"

"No. They were just drifters who had no business having a child. So sometimes they pretended they didn't." She touched her stomach and then removed her hand quickly. *Must stop that habit.* That was a different matter entirely. *Old news.*

"How did you manage at that age? What did you do?"

"I went to school. Back then they'd send money every so often for groceries or bills. I earned extra money shoveling snow from people's driveways."

"Yet after such a troubling childhood, you have such a pleasant disposition. Not everyone would."

She smiled, having never thought of it that way. Forward thinking was indeed her strong suit. Maybe, in her mind only, to show her parents and the Davis types of the world that she was worth caring about. Of course, it didn't matter because she'd never let herself rely on anyone ever again. "That's nice of you to say. A few other things dragged me down but now I feel like I'm on my way." She didn't need to tell him *everything.*

"I'm moved by your self-reliance."

"Oh, yes. I only count on myself. I'll be flying solo for the rest of my life."

"Here's to you, Gracie," he said as he lifted his wineglass for another toast. She clinked it with his and took a sip that tasted like validation. No one had ever analyzed her in such terms. What would it be like to be with a man who respected her, who she trusted? She'd never know. It was essential to always remember the words she'd just uttered. That she'd never get close to anyone again. Never let anyone take pieces of her heart away. She didn't have anything left to spare.

Why did she feel so comfortable talking to Ras? After Davis she was steering clear of men and, most certainly, of men from a totally different station in life, which would always be an issue. Yet Ras didn't act superior to her, even with his obvious status. She felt heard around him. It was a feeling she'd never had before. He made her think of desires she didn't allow herself. Or maybe it was that she'd never met anyone who stirred up yearning in her like he did. She could imagine moving past talking with their words. That they could communicate in a different, nonverbal language. Learn more about each other through their bodies, through bringing each other appreciation and pleasure. She bit her lip. None of that was going to happen. Even if he wanted to do that, Gracie wouldn't take the risk of starting to care about him. And she didn't know a thing about chance encounters.

They went quiet for a minute. Both of them gazing out to the distance of the dining room. Gracie noticed families. Beautiful young children were on their best behavior as parents cut up food on their plates. Older kids whispered among themselves. Other tables were filled with fours and sixes, perhaps friends who regularly cruised together. Many more tables were occupied by couples. Casual dressers in outdoorsy clothes, perhaps just grabbing a bite after an afternoon of sport. Older couples for whom just enjoying the vistas from the ship made for a lovely vacation.

Then there were the lovers, the honeymooners, the anniversary celebrants. Gracie especially liked to watch the couples who were madly in love. The way the world around them disappeared and all that existed was each other. That would never be her. But it touched her heart nonetheless.

"You wouldn't by chance want to...?" Ras leaned closer and then stopped himself. "No, of course not."

After dinner, Ras walked Gracie to her stateroom. What serendipity it had been that she'd chosen the same restaurant as he had. Truth be told, he'd felt awkward sitting alone. A group of young women had failed at subtlety as they'd obviously gestured toward him, giggling and trying to catch his eye. One even passed by his table presumably on her way to the ladies' room, sauntering slowly in hopes of engaging his interest. Then there was his own caution that he was being followed, although there was no evidence of that. Anybody could recognize him as royalty and snap photos on their phone. On top of it was always the possibility that real paparazzi were around, ready to pounce on a juicy story about the prince on a cruise ship. Ras had hoped to leave his cares behind for his weeks on this journey. Which he seemed to be able to do when Gracie was by his side. So, he was glad she was back. Of course, it helped that he hadn't told her who he was.

"What are you doing tomorrow?" he asked as they strolled, making conversation as well as asking just out of curiosity.

"In the afternoon there is that industry group tour. We'll see the kitchens, the spa, the pool areas, different stateroom configurations. Then we have a tasting menu dinner in one of the private dining rooms."

"That sounds wonderful."

"What will *you* do?"

"I haven't decided yet."

He'd triple-checked that his private yacht was ready for him to leave *Liberation* the day after to board his true vessel for his trip. Due to the private nature of his venture, he'd booked the details of the yacht himself rather than have his personal secretary do so. Given the advantage that money was no object, in fact his mother had set aside a fund in hopes that Ras would make this journey, he'd requested the best of everything. An enormous yacht would await him, far larger than what he needed but one in which he could be comfortable to breathe deeply, sleep soundly and amuse himself however he wanted to. Something he hadn't done since his mother died.

"So what will you do in Miami the day after tomorrow?" he asked, knowing this might really be the last he'd see of her. Speaking of enjoying himself, admiring the caramel glisten in Gracie's eyes and the undulating waves of her hair were quite pleasant pursuits.

"I'll do a bus tour of the city and view the famous South Beach hotels. Then a seafood dinner. Then a visit to one of the Cuban nightclubs for dancing. What about you?"

Hmm, he didn't want to explain that he'd be doing none of that because he would leave *Liberation* and head straight to his yacht. But now that he thought about it, why not see the sights of Miami, having never been there before? He could change his plans, couldn't he? Wasn't spontaneity supposed to be part of this escape? What if he tagged along with Gracie, who seemed to know what was worth seeing, and then left after that? How would he explain it to her, though, when he didn't get back on the cruise at the end of the evening?

"Is that a preorganized itinerary that the cruise line offers? On a bus?"

"Yes. It sounds like cruise excursions are unfamiliar to you?"

He couldn't tell her that was because royalty wouldn't

travel on a bus with the general public. Which didn't sound like a good idea. Close-up with a group of other passengers for a long period of time? Too much opportunity for someone to recognize him.

"I'm curious. What other excursions are offered?"

"On a typical cruise there would be dozens. But given this is such a short one, there were only a few. There were water sports. And one to explore the neighborhoods and Miami's ethnic food markets. I chose the bus because in one day it gives an overview of the city."

As they continued toward her stateroom, he thought to himself. What if he hired a car with a personal tour guide who could show him and Gracie all of those sights privately? He'd still have to figure out how to end the night and get Gracie back on the boat without him. Ah! If he wasn't heading straight to the yacht, he wouldn't have his luggage with him. They'd return at the end of the night to their respective staterooms. Then he'd get his bags and leave the ship a second time, Gracie tucked away in her bed by then.

The idea of spending the day with her in Miami filled him with elation. Yet maybe it was both unwise and unfair to steal her away, without telling her who he really was. Although it would be just half a day. It wasn't as if he was going to break her heart. Nor she break his. Hmm, strangely he wasn't so sure about that. He needed to think this out. When they reached the door to her stateroom, he held his tongue from saying anything further. Or tried to.

What slipped right out was, "Thank you for a lovely dinner. Will you have breakfast with me in the morning?" This was supposed to be his personal endeavor yet all he wanted to do was experience everything with Gracie. Harmless diversion, he figured. Besides, they'd for sure be apart the rest of the day after breakfast because she had her tour and tasting dinner. That would create some forced time away and he could settle down. It was just so nice to have her company. To hear the eagerness in her voice as she talked about her career ambitions after the unfathomable obstacles that she'd had to overcome. She was feminine and warm-blooded, which charged into his own masculinity.

"I have to warn you," Gracie said with a smile, "I've already read about the pancake sampler in the morning and I'm definitely going. They're offering ten kinds of pancakes with twenty different toppings. I intend to eat myself senseless."

Ras chuckled and then Gracie did too, and he was sure he could actually see the sizzle that flew through the air between them. "What time shall I come for you?"

"Ten."

"Until then." He caught himself leaning toward her, halfway to giving her a kiss on the cheek. Thankfully, he righted himself and instead bowed his shoulders to her. She swiped her key card and slipped into her room. When he heard the click locking her in, he figured he'd better go back to his stateroom as the Carat crew probably wouldn't look too favorably on him standing in front of Gracie's room all night. Tempting as it was.

Once in his own suite, he toed off his shoes and took off the new jacket that had felt quite comfortable for dinner indoors with its lightweight fabric. What an interesting dinner it had been. Gracie's knowledge of the East Coast was a stroke of luck. While he'd planned to roam at will, she'd given him some marvelous suggestions. It almost felt like they were mapping the trip together, which was, of course, ridiculous. He was engaged to be married and Princess Vajhana had already picked out a destination for their honeymoon, a particular Greek island. As he recalled her exact words were, "Everyone there is a *somebody*." In time he'd resume some circumspect meetups with women, but he'd play the husband game at first for the sake of appearances.

He sat down on the sofa and, uncharacteristically, put his feet up on the coffee table. Which brought a smile to his face as it was something any man might do but His Royal Highness Prince Rasmayada wouldn't. In the complete privacy of his stateroom, not a valet or assistant in sight, there was no harm in it.

He reflected over and over again on Gracie's shocking confessions about her childhood. What kind of people would leave a child of twelve years old to fend for herself for long periods of time? Not only was it immoral, it must have been illegal. And while she said it took her a number of years, and apparently some other hardships, to move into the career she wanted, she was doing it. Her grit and bravery were even more beautiful than her face. If that was possible. He hoped for the best for her from here on in. She deserved it. There was something so authentic about her, he'd found himself talking about his mother, something he hadn't done in a long time.

In contrast, he had a call to make.

"Where *are* you?" Vajhana's voice sounded irritated. Ras could hear the voices of other people in the background. In fact, it sounded like a party.

"I'm still in the States. Where are *you*?"

"Paris. I absolutely had to shop for clothes, and you know there's not a thing to be had on our islands."

"Princess," a deep voice called out to her, which Ras heard. "Look what I have for you." Vajhana laughed in that over-the-top dramatic way she had.

"Who's that?" Ras asked.

"No one you know."

"When are you going home? I'll be there in a couple of weeks."

"I will, too. I've got photographers coming from Singapore and Milan to do features on us, we still haven't finalized the seating arrangements and surely you don't expect me to go to that boring fundraiser for the Marine Biology Foundation alone."

No, certainly Vajhana wouldn't want to attend a function simply because her name might help that charity attract important donors. Sometimes Ras thought Vajhana had no idea what it meant to be a princess. That it wasn't about jewels and shoes and not having to wait in line to get into a club. Furthermore, someday she would also be queen to his king just as her older brother would sit on her island's throne someday. What Ras wanted in her was a wife and partner, someone who would set an example in kindness and rationale, someone who wouldn't take anything for granted. Of course, what he longed for was a woman like the greatest queen the island had ever known. His mother.

In Vajhana, he'd have to accept a different kind of queen. Their fathers had made the decision to unite for the betterment of their subjects. Although Ras still questioned whether caring for the land was just as much an obligation as caring for its people. He didn't like the proposals for the massive manufacturing plants they were developing with the Thai conglomerate PTG corporation.

"Oh, Princess," that male voice Ras heard through the phone cajoled. Could it be what it sounded like it was? That Vajhana wasn't even exercising the most basic courtesy of discretion in her liaisons? Ras ended the call. Annoyance began to dot his forehead. He texted a mutual friend who he knew could find out the truth about what was really going on.

"Your pancake escort has arrived, madam," Ras said with an outstretched hand when Gracie opened her stateroom door. She wore another one of her adorable flower-patterned dresses, this one white with big yellow roses. It flared out at the knees, and along with the ballet-type shoes, she looked like a New Yorker in the 1950s, hurrying through the busy streets. No wonder she was able to help him pick out clothes yesterday; she had her own personal style. With her friendly face, he supposed she'd look good in anything. After his distasteful conversation with Vajhana last night, he was in the mood for Gracie's freshness. He wasn't even sure how he'd make it through the day without her. Which was probably a sign that he needed to, to let his growing heat for her cool off. She was not a woman to have a dalliance with. He sensed that with her, it wouldn't be so easy to have a passing fancy.

"Good because I'm famished," she said, greeting him with zeal. "It took all I had to resist the snacks in the room's basket. I did have a cup of tea already."

"Pancake emergency, then. Let's go." He wanted to match her vivacity. All of His Royal Highness's moves were usually scheduled and measured, which was how it should be. Yet he felt like taking her by the hand so they could run through the ship in pursuit of their treats. Thankfully, decorum told him to simply gesture toward the corridor. He followed right behind her as they made their way to a sunny breakfast room constructed mostly of glass. It was packed with passengers, reminding Ras, in case he'd forgotten who he was, that royalty was never to be in large crowds without accompaniment. He knew the reasons were for his safety. But surely a quick breakfast didn't present grave danger. His alarm reinforced the idea he was about to spring on Gracie.

"I'll have a ricotta lemon pancake, a pumpkin pecan, a banana coconut and a mixed berry." Gracie quickly rattled off the menu items with conviction when the server took her order.

Ras could only throw up his palms in surrender and say, "Same." Which gave all three of them a giggle.

"Does anyone *not* eat too much on a cruise?"

"Not knowing firsthand," he offered, "it's definitely a pleasure to try new foods. That Café Cubano yesterday afternoon was quite memorable. I typically take coffee with only milk. The Cubano was rich and sweet, but the bitterness kept it from being sugary. What shall we eat in Miami?"

"We?" She tilted her head at him in question. Last night, he'd felt it was too much to bring up his idea, so he'd only asked her to breakfast.

"I'd like to make a suggestion." He'd been weighing his larger idea ever since it occurred to him. This new brainstorm would be a way to try out a short version, and if it didn't feel right, he wouldn't take it any further.

"What's that?" She licked a drop of pancake syrup from a corner of her mouth. He hoped she'd do it again.

"Rather than following the exact itinerary of that bus tour tomorrow, possibly having to stay too long or leave too soon at any of the destinations, I've reserved a private car to drive me around Miami. Would you join me?" He realized that was an odd proposal coming from someone she'd just met yesterday. He wished he could assure her that his intentions were respectable. Because he'd only be with her for a short time before he boarded his yacht never to see her again, he thought it best to persist in not revealing his identity. "As a travel agent, I'm sure you know the sights. In fact, can I hire you as my tour guide? I'll pay you for the day."

"Pay me?" she sputtered while taking a sip of orange juice.

"Why not? I'm not a murderer or a kidnapper, I promise you. I'm simply asking you to perform a service just as I'll be paying for a driver." He gave her a figure that was double what he was quoted to hire the driver. The fact that her eyes went quite round told him that the number had gotten her attention. "Plus, don't you think it would be more fun to tool around on our own?" Not to mention keep him out of crowds.

While he couldn't read her mind, Ras sensed she was considering the proposition, with skepticism. He understood the reluctance to trust strangers; after all, he was held apart from them. Verbal assurance that he wasn't a murderer or a kidnapper was the best he could do. She'd have to take a leap of faith.

"We'd spend the day and evening doing whatever we want in Miami?"

"Exactly."

She forked into her pancakes for a few more bites, contemplating his idea. "Okay. I'll do it on one condition. That I choose all our destinations. I want to be able to make recommendations to future clients as to the best of Miami. We can't see everything in a day, but we'll do our best."

"Deal. I'll put myself in your hands." A rush of oxygen whooshed through him at his own words.

Might she have felt it too, as evidenced by the peachy blush that came to her cheeks? There was nothing wrong with a little bit of harmless flirting was there? Other than the fact that he was soon to be married, the thought of which brought a snarl to his lips. How could he marry a woman he didn't love and who clearly didn't love him? He knew he needed to fulfill his duties to his homeland, but it was such a price to pay. His mother never would have approved of that, regardless of the impending partnership in industry. Ras knew she would say that nothing was more important than love. And she would have gotten the king to agree. They'd had a love story for the ages, after all. A gleam in the eye every time they saw each other. Secret signals and code words they had while in public and genuine smiles behind closed doors. Was Ras selfish for wanting that for himself? King Maho was very certain in his matchmaking of his son during his discussions with Princess Vajhana's father. In fact, he'd called for a meeting and made the motion himself. As Ras turned thirty, his father had made a unilateral decision about his son's matrimonial status.

Something ached in Ras's chest as he watched Gracie sip her coffee. It was a sad finality that he'd never be in love. Why did he have such a haunting, aching feeling that love was around him, like an aura that he could reach out for but never grab hold of?

Not able to take his eyes off Gracie's lovely face, a stunning insight blazed like a wildfire through him. While his father had signed deeds and contracts that the union between Ras and Vajhana was to benefit their nations' livelihoods, that wasn't the only reason for the arranged marriage. The king knew that Ras didn't love the princess. That was precisely why he thought Ras should marry her. He'd concocted this whole strategy to shield Ras from future pain. What if Ras was in love with the woman he married and she was taken from him? As the king's wife was. He didn't want his son to suffer that awful anguish and loss, the kind the king had never recovered from. He knew Ras would *never, ever* love Vajhana. In marrying him off to a woman he felt nothing for, the king was protecting his son, eliminating risk. Ras shook his head in the realization that his father was still a romantic after all.

CHAPTER FOUR

THE NEXT DAY as they walked down the gangway to disembark in Miami, Gracie tried not to let her excitement be too externally obvious. As a travel professional, she should be a bit more blasé. The truth was she'd never been to Miami and was thrilled to be there. She'd done her due diligence and taken virtual tours of all the hotels and major attractions, talked to other travel agents to get recommendations, and followed websites and social media accounts that had their pulse on what was new and cutting edge, where the latest sounds and tastes were. Nonetheless, she was looking forward to seeing everything in person. It was a bonus that *Liberation* was docking in this famous Florida city and that she'd have a chance to get to know it personally.

"There's our car." Ras pointed to the black sedan after he'd been texted the license plate identification. No driver holding up a tacky sign that read Ras. It occurred to Gracie that she still didn't know the last name of the man she was about to get into a car with. She didn't have a good track record on judging people. She fell for Davis, and he turned out to be rich in dollars but poor in character. He left her at a critical time, not wanting to take responsibility for what he helped create. Never knowing what transpired in his wake. Leaving Gracie with a double loss she'd never forget. She brushed her hand across her tummy.

She may not forgive or forget, but she was going to move forward. And apparently, in style today. Whoever Ras was, he was clearly used to the top-of-the-line in everything. She should have known he wasn't going to hire a compact car in a garish color. She wanted to sell luxury travel. Here it was.

"Great."

"Yes, please, come." He placed his hand on her elbow to help her onto the solid ground of Miami. Had he gotten over his original discomfort in touching her? Was it the breeze or his flat palm that swept over her, dredging up something that she'd stuffed deep down, a part of her that she'd been ignoring?

When they reached the car, the driver, in full uniform and cap, opened the door for them to enter. Ras gestured for Gracie to get in first. Her hand slid across the butter-soft and plush black leather of the seat. The driver closed the door once Ras got in next to her. A strong virility emanated from his body.

There was no reason for them to be sitting right up against each other, the seat was long and wide enough to hold three people, yet there they were, neither of them making a move away. Ras reached into the beverage tray and pulled a frosty bottle of sparkling water from a bucket of ice. He cracked the cap and poured the fizz into two heavy crystal glasses.

"Let the driver know our first stop," Ras told her as he handed her a glass.

"South Beach. Please take us through Ocean Drive and Collins Avenue." She took a sip of the bubbly water.

In reference to the drink he said, "I assumed we'd have

a cocktail later but that it was too early in the day now. Tell me about yesterday."

As they passed through the city streets, she gave him a description of the ship tour, saying that she was particularly impressed seeing the engine room and the inner workings of the vessel. She described a few of her favorite bites from the tasting menu dinner. What she left out was how much she'd missed him, how many times she'd thought of him. And that when she got back to her stateroom, how long the evening felt not having seen him. "How did you spend the day?"

"You might find this surprising, but I did something I haven't done in years. Ever maybe."

"What's that?"

"I laid in bed and watched movies."

She really wanted to ask him the big questions about himself. Where he was from, as the first time she'd asked he'd merely answered, *Asia*. She wondered what the family business he spoke of was that prevented him from spending a day in bed if he wanted to.

But she didn't need to know any of that and he wasn't offering to tell her, so what difference did it really make? She'd never see him again after the cruise. Although her skin felt tight at that notion. In a weird way she'd already become attached to him. She knew it was silly to get carried away with fairy tales, though. In reality, even if she clicked with Ras, she'd never get close to him because he'd desert her in the end. Her belief was supported with evidence.

The driver knew where to go. "Look at this architecture!" she exclaimed as they peeped out the window at the tall hotels. "These pastel-colored buildings make up the Art Deco Historic District."

"Fantastic," Ras agreed.

"Can you let us out here so we can take a walk?" she asked the driver, who pulled over.

Along the street, she pointed to this restaurant and that, at outdoor tables filled with people dressed in light-weight clothing. Palm trees were everywhere and the glistening beach, with seemingly thousands of people in the sand, was never out of sight.

"Was this whole area built at the same time?" he inquired.

"It was an evolution during the 1930s and '40s. Miami has always been a popular city to live or vacation in. For decades now, retirees from New York and surrounding areas move down here for the weather."

"I can see why. Shall we sit down at one of these establishments?"

"No, we're just here to walk. We'll eat in the Little Havana neighborhood."

"Okay. Whatever you say." He gave her a military salute, which made her chuckle.

After a lovely stroll, they got back in the car. "Calle Ocho," she told the driver. After the pastels of South Beach, Little Havana was an entirely different part of the city. Brightly colored paint adorned the buildings, murals and sculptures in the heart of the area. Gracie had the driver drop them off again, so that they could wander through the neighborhood on foot.

Even in the sunlight of day, Cuban music could be heard coming from businesses and street corners. "This is so vibrant and alive. I love the verve," Ras said after his customary inventory of everyone on the streets. He always seemed to worry that he was being observed. After he'd tried to shield her from looking at the magazines in the ship's gift shop, she'd gathered that he was in some way famous, maybe within whatever industry he was in.

And he didn't want her to know, wanted their connection to remain anonymous. That was fine with her, although she couldn't resist being curious.

They walked through several of the streets, admiring the artwork in the many galleries. "Ras, here's the important question."

"Oh…okay," he said, expressing trepidation.

"What do you feel like eating?"

He grinned with relief. "What's traditional?"

"Perhaps *ropa vieja*." She didn't speak Spanish except when it came to food, and then she could make her way pretty well. "Believe it or not, that translates to *old clothes*."

"Doesn't sound very appetizing."

"It really doesn't. But it's delicious. Shredded meat in a sauce of onions and peppers."

"Yes. I want to try everything," he said, making eye contact that was so strangely penetrating it rattled through her.

Gracie felt happy, the happiest she had in as far back as she could remember. This was *her thing*. This was what she wanted. She was visiting a new place, throwing all of her senses into it. And, much to her surprise, it was all the better with this interesting man by her side.

Ras pushed the plate away from him when it was empty. "Well, I should be hungry again in three or four days."

Gracie smiled after swallowing a bite. The savory *ropa vieja* was balanced with its side dish of *arroz y frijoles negro*, rice and black beans. "Yes, it's very filling."

"Scrumptious, though." He wasn't in the habit of using words like *scrumptious*. He didn't usually get emotional about food or scenery. Yet this trip was different. On this trip he did.

"You are finished?" the waitress asked.

"Did I leave a drop?" he joked.

"I will tell the dishwasher he does not have to spend too much time on this plate."

"Is this a family business?" he asked her as Gracie observed the conversation.

"Yes, my mother is at the front today," she said while pointing to the woman who'd seated them. "My aunt and brothers run the kitchen. And my son helps wait on the tables at night." She cleared the plates and left their table. Chatting with people, without that built-in distance because they were commoners and he was a prince, was exactly what his mother had wanted him to experience. He even enjoyed the unfamiliarity of doing so.

"You mentioned that you were involved in a family business as well," Gracie commented.

"Yes, in fact we have an upcoming merger with another family." He was being purposely cryptic but he almost grimaced thinking about Vajhana, off in Paris doing heaven knew what. Checking his phone now and then, he awaited a report from his old friend Niran who would scope out what was really going on.

Ras and Vajhana both knew their marriage involved the economic future of two nations and had nothing to do with two hearts. Nonetheless, Ras expected at least decorum from her. If she was going to have extramarital liaisons, he'd hoped she'd pay great attention to keeping them away from their fathers, the staff at the palaces and the public. As he would. Laughter and shrieking on the other end of the phone hadn't garnered confidence in Ras that his fiancée was behaving herself circumspectly.

"You say that as if you don't approve of the partnership," Gracie noted. Ah, so he wasn't even hiding his displeasure well.

"My father and the other interested party," he explained, meaning Vajhana's father, King Yodfa of Ko Yaolum, "are planning to work with a manufacturing conglomerate on some islands they hold guardianship of. I'm against the idea because that type of industry will cause depletion to the area's natural resources." Of course he was referring to Ko Pha Lano as well, his home and the place where the island's long-term well-being would fall on his shoulders in later years. It would be then any damage due to the decisions made now would be felt. How would he explain it to his subjects, when the waters were contaminated and the land became unfarmable?

"Do you have an alternative plan?"

"I think cultivating environmentally friendly tourism would be better stewardship." Which could provide employment to the people of both islands and sustainability to the land and its resources. Both kings had rejected Ras's suggestion. "But that's not the direction my father and the other decision maker want to go in." It was hard to say which was more frustrating, the hardheaded, old-fashioned thinking of the two kings with regard to development or to arranged marriages.

"It sounds like you care quite a bit about the outcome."

"Hmm." Of course he did; he was the crown prince. His computer was filled with files of research about ecotourism and schematics, many specifically with regard to marine conservation.

"Coffee or dessert?" the waitress interrupted.

"No, thank you. Gracie?" She indicated no, and the waitress left the check on their table. Changing to a less heated topic, he asked, "Where are we going next?"

"Do you want to do something unusual?" she asked with a little snark as if it was a dare. She was very sexy. Very. Plain and simple. He wondered if she realized how alluring she was. And why some man hadn't already swept her off her feet and made her his.

"Unusual." He licked his lips. "You have me intrigued."

"Would you like to see the Florida Everglades?"

"Why not? Are they nearby?"

"They are. And we'll see them on an airboat. There are several tour companies. I can look them up and buy us tickets."

"You mean there are group airboats?"

"Yes."

"Let's book a private airboat. Just the two of us and the driver." He handed her his phone. "Make the arrangements and then I'll pay."

"Regardless of cost, I assume?" A minute later they were booked, and she handed him the phone back to authorize payment.

"We'll be more comfortable, if it's only you and I." He sat on those words for a minute. Feeling them inside.

"Everglades National Park, here we come."

As they were leaving the restaurant, the waitress yelled out, *"Gracias."*

"Adios," Gracie said back.

The driver brought them to the national park, and they walked a trail that led to a pond where there were many species of birds. Gracie gasped. "Oh, goodness, look at the blue coloring on that one."

"Is it a heron?"

"There's an app that can identify the bird if we load in a photo." She pulled out her phone and lifted her graceful arm to get a good shot. With a few taps she quickly got the result. "Yep, a great blue heron. Common to wetlands areas."

They studied a flock of spoonbills.

"There's an egret," Ras said, pointing in a different direction.

"Wow, I don't think I've ever seen one of those before."

Ras loved this. One minute they were in the hipster South Beach, the next in the culturally rich Little Havana. And now in serene nature, reminding him that he didn't want to see the natural beauty of Ko Pha Lano disintegrate from decades of exposure to toxic industry.

"Gracie, you're doing a great job as a tour guide. I wish I could hire you to be my personal travel agent." There he went again, saying something that could be interpreted as flirty!

"Hold your praise until you see if you like the airboat."

When it was time for their ride, they arrived at the plank wood dock to be welcomed by a white-haired man with a matching beard who introduced himself as Captain Clyde. He handed each of them a pair of headphones. "Welcome aboard. You'll be wanting these as the boat is loud, and they also let you talk to each other and hear me babble." They both grinned as they took their seats. "Have you ever been on an airboat?"

Both Ras and Gracie shook their heads no.

"Basically, it's a flat-bottomed boat that uses an aircraft-type propeller." Captain Clyde pointed behind him at the giant propeller wheel in its cage. "You'll want to refrain from letting your arms or legs get near the propeller if you'd like to take them home with you."

As they started away from the shore the sound was, indeed, deafening, and they immediately put their headphones on.

"The Everglades National Park is home to dozens upon dozens of species of wildlife." The captain's voice came in through the headset as they skimmed across the water.

"That includes over two hundred thousand alligators. We might get lucky and see a crocodile or two as well, this being one of the only places in the world where the two coexist."

They traveled through mangrove tunnels, the parts of the water where the coastal trees didn't grow. Birds flew up above, and the wind blew in their faces. Ras felt far away from everything, in a magical world that didn't belong to humans. So when his phone buzzed and he glanced down to see it was Niran, he stuffed the device back into his pocket. The news about Vajhana's escapades could wait.

The captain directed them to notice a family of raccoons, climbing through and among dry twigs above the water. The black masks around their eyes made them distinct from every other animal Ras could think of. He knew that even though they looked cuddly, they weren't. Nonetheless, they were magnificent to watch.

Gracie studied the baby kits, three of them, as they frolicked around their mother. Her smile was so celestial there were almost tears in her eyes. Ras reached over and put his hand atop hers, immediately reacting to how tender her skin was. Funny, but touching her had become the most natural thing in the world to him. She turned to give him a half smile, which covered him like a ray of sun peeking through the thick sawgrass of the marshes.

Captain Clyde's voice continued in their ears as he gestured to a huge, scaly sunbather. "We've spotted ourselves a crocodile. Do you folks know how to tell the difference between a crocodile and an alligator?" They both shook their heads. "You can tell by their snouts. The croc's is long and pointy whereas the gator's is shorter and rounded."

The crocodile, asleep with his mouth wide open,

looked ominous, but the captain told them that was normal. Then, from under water beside the boat, an alligator popped its head above the surface, startling them. Another sprang up on the other side of the boat. Gracie's eyes opened wide.

"Now, you folks don't want to be getting too close to the gators. Although they don't eat humans," Captain Clyde explained reassuringly. "Not so far, anyway."

Without question, theirs was the only chauffeured car driving out of Everglades National Park. That was sightseeing, Ras style. The driver pulled onto the highway returning to Miami. They'd had a wonderful time on the airboat marveling at all the wildlife they saw. Now they were headed for an evening at Club de Magia, which translated to Magic Club, one of the city's biggest Cuban nightspots. After that, they'd reboard *Liberation* and sleep while it looped northward, making its way back to New York.

"Captain Clyde was quite a character," Ras chuckled. "Especially when he told you that the alligators…"

"That's gators, to the locals," Gracie corrected him.

"When he told you that particular big daddy we saw had a penchant for blond hair."

She scrunched up her mouth. "Yeah, he had me for a minute there."

"I couldn't blame the gator if it was true, though." With a tilt of the head, she studied him. "Why are you looking at me like that?"

"I'm not used to receiving compliments," she said. Everywhere they'd been, money and luxury were no object. He still hadn't said specifically what he did for a living but had spoken of stewardship of land. Not that it mattered any to her, yet she was still bemused that the man who'd hired a private tour guide and driver was also so nice to the waitress serving him *ropa vieja* at an informal lunch.

"You should be, Gracie. Is it too personal of me to ask if you've been in a relationship?"

"I never will be again."

"Oh, that's right, the wanderer with her online travel agency."

"Right."

"After you've fulfilled your dream, could you see yourself settling down? Having children?"

She looked past him out the window as the car sped through the miles. When she concentrated hard enough, she'd learned how to swallow back the tears. All of them. *Do not put your hand on your stomach.* "I wouldn't know anything about having children. I told you, my parents didn't exactly set any kind of example." The truth was, she adored children. Certainly she'd spent time contemplating whether having her own, loving and caring for them, would be the best revenge for everything she'd missed out on. That's why she'd been so happy at first when it looked like all the pieces were going to fit with Davis. What a disaster that was. And now, even though she'd never get into a relationship again, there was always the possibility of having children alone. She did think about that. A lot.

"I think you'd be a terrific mother."

"I was in a long-term relationship once. His name was Davis."

"What happened?"

"He left me."

"Why?"

"After the way my parents were always off doing whatever they wanted, I was desperate for someone who would stick around. I met Davis and moved from Trenton to a beach house in Point Pleasant his grandmother left him when she died."

"That sounds like a promising start."

"You would assume so. But he was out all the time, not bringing me along. He was very controlling, wanted me to live with him and be faithful even though he was never around."

"That's odd."

"Not really. He was from a wealthy family and I was born on the wrong side of the tracks. I was good enough to be kept at home but not to be seen out with."

"Oh. I see."

She wished Ras would have sounded more indignant but with his mergers and islands, he probably only dated the *right kind* of girls, too.

"I was so relieved to have a steady job and a place to live, not having to panic if a check from my parents didn't arrive like I used to, that I went along with it. And then…" She stopped herself. She hated this part of the story and so she didn't have to tell it. She barely knew Ras. He didn't need all the details. He was clearly keeping some secrets of his own.

Do not put your hand on your stomach.

"Anyway, it just didn't work out."

By the time they got back to the city, it was nighttime and the clubs were beginning to fill up. Gracie had chosen Club de Magia because it was one of the most renowned, and they featured live music all night. They walked into the sounds of a horn section and Latin percussion. The club was massive. The inner circle held the stage and an enormous dance floor. The next level was filled with tall cocktail tables and barstools. And the top level was for tables and booths. "Shall I get us a booth?" Ras asked. She nodded and he approached the hostess, a stunning woman in a tight orange dress and bright lipstick.

They were shown to a half-circle-shaped booth in the center of the top tier. Ras had probably arranged it because it was so big and tall that it was quite private. The seat was upholstered in a deep purple velvet. Before they were asked, a server came over with two drinks on a tray. "*Buenos noches.* Can I offer you a mojito?"

"Ooh, yes, those look fabulous," Gracie answered quickly. The waiter placed down two coasters with the club's logo of a top hat and rabbit, homage to the traditional magician's trick. He placed the drinks on top, frosty highball glasses with big sprigs of mint.

She lifted hers to toast with Ras. "To adventure. From Art Deco to *ropa vieja* to gators to salsa," he said with a clink of his. "You've shown me a day I'll never forget."

"To adventure. The night is still young." They sipped.

"Oh, my gosh, that is the best thing I've ever tasted."

"Simple perfection. Rum, sugar, sparkling water, lime and mint."

"It's been many hours since we've eaten. What shall we have?"

"Do you feel like a sandwich? I want you to taste the classic Cubano."

"Whatever it is, I'm in," he said with a laugh. "I'm so glad I decided to hire you, Gracie. You're not like most of the women I know." His smile quickly faded like it had just dawned on him that he'd forgotten something.

"Is something wrong?"

He took a long pause to consider the question. "Absolutely not."

The waiter approached and Ras gestured to her to order. "Two Cubanos."

The band launched into a fiery rhythm that prompted many people to make their way from the tables to the dance floor. "What do you think? Shall we?" he suggested.

"I'm game if you are."

Ras stood up and reached his hand down to take hers. Gracie didn't know what it was, but between the music, the gentle clasp of her hand and his sincere smile, she felt like she was leading someone else's life. Thoughts she hadn't had in years kept popping up. What it might be like to truly *be* with someone. To share life. Weather the ups and downs. Create a union together that was bigger than the sum of its parts. That meant something. That meant everything.

No, Gracie reminded herself. It was fine to play pretend for a couple of hours in a city where they were nameless tourists. In reality, she'd never put her heart on the line again. She'd charted her course, and she was going to stick to it.

Even if Ras's eyes made her speculate beyond anything she'd ever dared before.

Once they got to the dance floor, the beats drummed into her body and she started to sway. Ras faced her as they found the tempo. "Do you know how to salsa?" she asked him, making an assumption that he might be more the waltz type. Yet he surprised her by taking the lead with the basic left, right, together, right, left, together steps. Within a few bars, they got into a groove. She placed her hand on one of his muscular shoulders. The flat of his large palm against her back made her eyelashes flutter.

Gracie felt the sexiest she ever had. Was it her imagination or was it in the way Ras looked at her? Goodness, even though she'd only known him for a hot minute, it was going to be hard to say goodbye when this wild ride ended. Would that be tonight when they returned to the ship? Or would they spend the rest of the time until they returned to New York together? Her convictions about staying away from men were fraying at the seams when she was with him.

After a few songs, the band segued to a slower rhythm. The couples on the dance floor brought each other to a close embrace. Gracie took an immediate step backward, figuring Ras wasn't going to want to dance as lovers do, and wasn't going to pull her close. She thought she'd save them from awkwardness.

However, she apparently had it wrong because as she started to move away, he wrapped his long arm around her waist, encircling her in a way that made her core melt. His other hand took hers and brought it to his collarbone. She was almost woozy as they began to sway, quickly finding their flow. His body melded into hers until she could feel every bone underneath his skin. And no matter how wide she swung, that firm anchor of his arm brought her back over and over. To him. *To him*.

After the trance they reached, he eventually snapped back to survey the crowd in the dim lighting of the club, perhaps reaching his limit of the sensual dancing, ending the moment and providing both of them with relief. "We'd better return to the table before our Cubanos get cold," he suggested. Leading her by the hand, they slid back into the booth and had a sip of their refreshing mojitos. The sandwiches did arrive shortly after. Ras took a bite and then rolled his eyes in a comic way that made her laugh. "Why do you keep feeding me one delectable thing after the other? What alchemy is in this deliciousness?"

"It's ham, roast pork, cheese, pickles, mustard and bread placed into a sandwich press so that the center gets gooey and the bread becomes crusty. Another very simple combination that yields a yummy result."

They chatted about travel. On the West Coast of the US, he loved Seattle and San Francisco. He started to say something else, then scrapped the idea. A minute later it returned.

"Let me share something with you," he began. "I'm not returning to New York on *Liberation*."

That was strange.

"Oh, is everything okay?"

"Yes. This has always been my plan. I've got a private yacht waiting at the Miami harbor. As I told you, I'm going to tour the East Coast."

"By yacht?"

"Yes. That way I can go wherever I want and decide how long I want to stay. Just as we've done today rather than in a group."

"Why did you board *Liberation* in the first place?"

"I'm recognizable, so I wanted to throw any possible followers off my track. I figured no one would expect me to be on a short public cruise."

"You're not sleeping on *Liberation* tonight?" In spite of herself, she felt a little disappointed. She, too, had a spectacular day today. In fact, the most fun she'd had in ages.

"Gracie, I have a proposition for you. Just as we've done today, I'd like to offer you a job as my tour guide. For the time that I'll be here. I'll be much less noticeable if I'm traveling with a woman, as if we were just an ordinary couple. Plus I'd love for you to show me all of the great spots."

"A personal tour guide?"

"Yes. You name your price."

"I'd stay with you on your private yacht?" While Ras

had been nothing but a perfect gentleman, Gracie found his offer more than a little unusual. "And this would be just as your guide and traveling companion?" She didn't want to insinuate that he'd be less than honorable, but this was not a typical offer.

"Of course. You'll have your own suite onboard. The yacht I've chartered is lavish. Top-of-the-line, with a pool, a cinema, a spa, deluxe bathrooms, three dining rooms."

Her first impulse was to say no. She'd only just met him, and he obviously had some skeletons in the closet. No one in their right mind would take off on a yacht with a stranger. Even one whose touch made her breath sputter. To whom she'd opened up about some of her own past, details that she'd never told anyone. A man who made her feel desirable and indispensable. Even still, this couldn't be a wise idea.

"Ras, I don't even know your full name, where you're from, what you actually do for a living. I'm sure you can understand that it seems less than prudent for me to go sailing away on your yacht."

He smiled wistfully, as if he'd just contemplated the proposition from *her* perspective. "Of course. I'm sorry that I'm not able to share the details of my identity. I can assure you, though, that the yacht crew will be on board with us at all times. And I give you my word that your safety, comfort and protection will be at the forefront of our journey."

It was a hunch that could prove disastrous, yet her gut told her his words were true, that he'd make sure no harm fell on her.

"I'd have total control over our destinations and sights?"

"Why yes, that would be the point. Wouldn't that benefit your travel career?"

Yes, it would. She'd never be able to afford to travel in the style Ras did. Top shelf, money no object. It was a chance to see things she'd never seen through a once-in-a-lifetime lens. Afterward, she'd be able to speak with firsthand knowledge about deluxe experiences on the East Coast.

What difference did it make that Ras was a mystery? This was just a business opportunity.

"So, what, we'd go back to the ship to get our bags and then disembark again?"

CHAPTER FIVE

RAS HAD WAITED long enough. He'd been having such a beautiful evening with Gracie, he didn't want to let real life interrupt. Especially when they'd danced with their bodies so close and in sync to the Latin beats, both of them losing themselves in the loud music and in each other's rhythms. The club was dark enough that his concern about being spotted was abated. How they'd organically moved through the salsa, and the rhumba and, especially the ballads. Like they'd been dancing together for ages, anticipating each other, welcoming each other. And the smell of her perfume had sent a surge through him. He could still inhale a whiff of it next to him in the car as it took them back to the cruise ship to pack up.

But now it was time to truly face the music. He needed to read the text his friend Niran had left him about Vajhana, what she was doing in Paris and with whom. He held his phone toward him, already suspecting, no, knowing, in his heart what Niran's messages were going to be.

He wasn't wrong.

Didn't realize this was news, sorry to be the bearer. Vajhana is in flagrant cahoots with a British earl named Cyril. Sources saw them checking into various Parisian hotels. Her Royal Highness was photographed sitting on the earl's lap while they smooched at a club. They're inseparable, traipsing in and out of shops on the Champs-élysées. Again, assumed you knew. He's not the first.

Ras's jaw clenched, and he could almost hear the ticking where the bones met his ears. His breath became very fast and his hands turned to tight fists. In fact, all of the muscles in his body tightened as he leaned deliberately back against the seat. The sheer shamelessness of her behavior made him see red, even if it wasn't a surprise.

"Is something wrong?" Gracie sensed the changes in his body language.

"An unfortunate report on the business proposal I was telling you about."

"I'm sorry to hear that." The kindness in her voice reached his subconscious. With deep breaths, his oxygen intake gradually slowed. His mouth relaxed, releasing the gritting of his teeth. After the sting of the confirmation subsided, he realized that he felt nothing. It was humiliating that she was behaving so indiscreetly, but it was just information. They were going to need to come to better terms than these if they were going to have an enduring partnership.

When they boarded *Liberation*, he and Gracie parted to pack up their belongings, agreeing to meet back at the same spot in twenty minutes. The tiniest curve of his lip told him just how glad he was that she had agreed to travel with him. She was a delightful companion. He genuinely enjoyed every moment he'd spent with her. Her gusto for all the sights and sounds and tastes they'd experienced was contagious. With her, he felt that freedom that he'd set out to find. And honest conversation flowed between them. Well, honesty on her part. On his personal identity, not so much. She didn't know that he was a prince, let alone an engaged one. Nonetheless, this chance partnership was exactly what he needed. Now more than ever.

There was nothing wrong in spending time with a woman he met on this trip. But he did make a mental promise to himself that even though he was physically attracted to her, he would not let anything happen between them. Gracie was off-limits. She didn't deserve to be treated as a secretive, short-term fling. Which she wasn't at all. He knew she'd been hurt by parents who didn't meet her needs and by a boyfriend who'd treated her badly. He wasn't going to add to her list. He did have a moment's lament after hearing about Vajhana's carelessness, a wish that he was set to marry a woman he loved and who loved him, like his mother would have wanted. A woman like…

It took a mere few minutes to pack up the small case he'd brought along from New York and the new bag he'd bought on ship for his purchases from the menswear shop. His Royal Highness was still quite unused to carrying his own luggage. A simple act he quite liked. Once he joined Gracie at the meeting spot, with a tug he took her bag, too.

"Ready?" he asked.

"Ready."

As they left *Liberation*, he informed the attendant that they wouldn't be returning to the ship. Soon he, the bags and Gracie were back onto Florida ground. A limo was waiting. This time, it was to take them to the harbor. They were headed even further away from reality.

When the yacht's captain reached for Gracie's hand to help her step aboard *Destiny*, she couldn't believe her eyes. While she'd studied private yachts online and had even gone to look at them at local harbors, nothing had prepared her for the grandeur and size of the vessel Ras had reserved.

"My gosh, this is spectacular!" she exclaimed, taking in its sparkling clean hull and polished brass railings.

"Welcome to your home away from home. I hope you'll be comfortable."

"Good evening. I am Captain Ernesto. May I introduce you to the crew?" The captain was a trim man with short gray hair and a short beard, who wore a traditional uniform. "This is David and this is Neo," he said, pointing to the two men, both in crisp khaki shorts and white polo shirts.

"Hello."

"It's our pleasure to serve you in every possible way so do let us know how we can best accomplish that."

"Thank you."

"If you'd like, I can show you around the ship and then perhaps you'd like to settle in for the night. We'll set off in the morning. Can we bring you a late supper or some snacks?"

Ras looked at her to decide. Even though they'd had those delightful Cubano sandwiches, after all their dancing, she wouldn't mind a little bite before bed. "Gracie?"

"Some snacks and a cup of herbal tea would be nice, thank you."

"If you'll follow me, then," the captain said, "let me show you the cabins."

They went up the stairs to the top deck. When they stepped inside, it was beyond Gracie's imagination. The entire deck, from bow to stern, was devoted to one master bedroom suite. The perimeter was lined with 360 degrees of shaded glass panels so that guests could see out in any direction but no one could see in. The whole deck was one room! Gracie didn't even know such a thing existed.

Within the area, a salon had contemporary sofas and chaise lounges, all done in earthy colors. Side tables were placed here and there with a huge display of pink flowers on the coffee table. Nearby was a bar area, its own private pub with shelves of liquor, beers, wine and soft drinks of every conceivable variety. A half dozen bar tools were arranged on a stand at the ready.

Sliding glass doors opened out to a wooden balcony. At that late hour, both the water and the moon glistened. They stepped out while the captain adjusted the night lighting so they could see. A row of lounge chairs with stuffed cushions surrounded a lap pool. There was a section for entertaining as well, a big wraparound sofa with white and red cushions that created a separate space. Yet a different part of the balcony had a dining table set with chairs for eight. In another nook was a king-size bed strewn with dozens of decorative pillows, a canopy, and curtains for privacy. An outdoor bed. For lazy naps breathing in the sea air. And… Her mind thought all sorts of things that it shouldn't.

Captain Emilio briefly showed them some of the convenience systems. Various areas of the outdoor deck had remote-controlled awnings to allow as little or as much direct sun as they wanted. "Of course, please ring for a crew member to assist you with anything."

It was probably past midnight after their long day of sightseeing, Miami's neighborhoods and the Everglades tour, finishing up with the dancing. A shiver ran through her as she replayed key moments of their time on the dance floor. Ras had such a sexy way of moving his body. He was swept into the music and the mood, and brought her right along with him. Slim hips that easily swiveled and his strong posture gave his dance moves such a confident air. He was all man without wearing his masculinity in a controlling way. Ras's power was absolute but quiet. It didn't need to shout.

He was as luminous as the moon itself and seemed pleased with this paradise of a yacht he'd chartered. His hair blew in the night, his eyes sparkled and his fine cheek and jaw bones deflected light and shadow. Clearly he'd been upset about something earlier. He'd glossed over it, saying something about a business problem. He was incomprehensible indeed, as she still didn't know what his daily life was like. And probably never would. It really wasn't important, though. She'd found herself on this unexpected journey, but he'd been very clear that he was only in the US for a couple of weeks and had many things to attend to at his unspecified home in Asia.

"Perhaps you'd like to tour the rest of the ship tomorrow?" the captain asked.

"Yes, that's a good idea," Ras agreed.

Back inside the massive master suite, Gracie's attention turned to the bed. The gigantic bed with pillows propped up against a quilted headboard, the piece arranged to look straight forward through the glass panels. There were curtains operated by a remote control to give that particular section of the room even greater privacy and climate control. A bed on the balcony. A bed in the suite. A hot enigma of a man. Gracie's pulse sped up at the thoughts she was having. About how maybe her vow to never be with a man again was too harsh. Maybe there was a man out there for her. Not Ras, but perhaps someone else? Somehow, being with him gave her twinges of loneliness. It reminded her that she had no one to count on. Everyone had abandoned her. Her parents, who came and went without warning. Davis, who wasn't going to make a lifetime commitment to someone he felt so superior to. And then even the product of their union had left her alone, in the most tragic way. Why wasn't she entitled to someone she could trust?

She reminded herself not to let her pleasant exterior fade. Ras was being so generous, the least she could do was be good company. Their midnight snack and warm chamomile tea in heavy stone mugs was a comfort. When they were finished and the wee hours of the night were approaching, Ras rang for David to take Gracie to her stateroom one deck below, where the guest cabins were.

"Good night, then," she said, with a bit of sadness at being separated from him.

"I had one of the most marvelous days of my life."

She gulped. She could say the same, but the fact that he articulated it shot into her heart like a moonbeam.

"Thank you for this opportunity. I look forward to showing you Savannah tomorrow," she replied.

"Yes."

The finest stateroom on the lower deck had been prepared for her. It was as extravagant as the master suite although, obviously, nowhere near its size. A private balcony, a sitting area, two televisions, a bathroom stocked with amenities. After washing up, she crawled into the comfortable bed. She decided to text Jen and let her know that she was on a yacht named *Destiny* embarking from Miami. Just so that someone in the world would know where she was.

Jen wrote back.

What's his name?

   Gracie laughed out loud.

I told you. No attachments.

We'll see.

   Jen added an emoji of a face with hearts for eyes, which made Grace giggle again.

   Surveying the room from the perspective of the sumptuous bed, she planned to slowly make a mental memory of all of the carefully chosen details of the decor. Instead, she fell asleep replaying the image of dancing with Ras, the way he never once took his eyes off her.

   She slept long and soundly. When she woke up, she stepped out on the balcony to see that they had traveled during the early hours and were ported in Savannah, Georgia. She showered and readied herself for the day. A knock on her door was the polite Neo, there to tell her she was expected up in Ras's suite for breakfast.

"This is certainly charming," Ras noted as he and Gracie strolled through Forsyth Park.

   "It's one of Savannah's most well-known landmarks."

   They approached the central fountain with its tall and wide spray. It was no wonder there were a lot of people taking photos to remember it by. Ras bristled at the number of people and took Gracie's elbow to steer her away, taking notice of her always smooth skin. They could do without a photo or a selfie. Ras was certain he'd remember everything about this trip for the rest of his life. "Tell me about these trees."

   "They're oak, dripping with Spanish moss. Savannah is famous for them. They like parks here. There are twenty-two city squares."

"Can we see them all?" Ras was feeling lighthearted this morning. Yesterday's unpleasant news about his fiancée's exploits reminded him that he had so much to attend to when he returned home, including, apparently, helping his future wife to become a proper monarch.

He so appreciated that, unexpectedly, he was accompanied by such a charming companion. Last night after Gracie went to her cabin, he had spent some time in his absurdly large master suite alone idly thinking about her. She had such joie de vivre in her, and it was something he'd been missing in his life for so long now, he'd almost forgotten it existed. He'd never been so drawn to a woman. She absolutely intoxicated him.

As to visiting the city parks, Gracie said, "We have a tee time not long after lunch so we'll choose our sights wisely and see some of them, how about that?"

"Deal."

Last night, Gracie had told Captain Ernesto that their next port out of Miami would be Savannah. So this morning at breakfast, after Ras had expressed an interest in golfing, she'd checked online to find the best course in town and he'd booked it for them. When they were ready to leave, he'd smiled at the look on her face when the captain and crew operated the controls to open the storage compartment on the yacht that housed a Porsche 911 silver sports car. "Are you kidding me!" she'd exclaimed incredulously, in a way that made him laugh. "There's a car too?"

"Ah, the travel professional hasn't seen every level of luxury yet?" he'd teased.

"I have to confess I haven't."

"We'll see what we can do about that," he'd replied

in a raspy, sexy voice that he'd never heard coming out of his mouth. How could he help but flirt with her? She was irresistible.

"Savannah has the largest National Historic District in the United States," Gracie said as they continued their walking tour, the car parked in a garage at the moment.

She directed them to a couple of those city squares. They sat down on a bench. The dripping Spanish moss provided not only shade but a sort of hush. He stretched one of his arms across the top of the bench. He sensed her shoulders along his biceps and hand. A battle erupted within him. He wanted to lay that hand on her to bring them closer on the bench. He knew that he shouldn't, yet her body made a shift closer toward him. He sensed it was involuntary and not something she had planned. But she moved her back against his side and, when she did, rockets shot through every blood vessel in his body. Confusing him. If she continued behavior like that, he wasn't sure how long he'd be able to hold out before returning it.

"This is all you promised it would be," he declared a bit later as he scanned the golf course from the elevation of the clubhouse. The whole of the historic downtown was visible from the expansive view. And the course itself, by a world-famous designer, was endless yards of expertly maintained grass and foliage, with canals, ponds and a central lake, pristine in the afternoon sunshine.

"Founded in 1930, it's always been considered one of the best courses in America."

While Ras requested they walk from hole to hole, Gracie had booked a premier package and they were assigned a caddy who followed them in a cart holding the clubs they'd rented. The fresh air and grass reminded him of the palace grounds, of blissful years running around with Lucky on those manicured lawns, his mother giving him license to play and get dirty.

"Do you golf much?" he asked.

"Not until recently. I took lessons because I figured it was something future clients might be interested in."

He so admired that despite the rough times she'd endured, she was moving forward with her life. Chasing her dream. What a unique woman she was. "You?"

"Oh, yes, lessons as a child. My mother liked a lot of sports. Said it was good for the brains as well as the brawn." She chuckled at the cute expression. "In fact, some of my favorite memories are of golfing with her. Just the two of us. Sometimes we'd only take two clubs and just whack the ball toward each other like it had become a game of ice hockey. Just to be silly and to laugh. My mother was good at laughing."

He went silent for a moment as his words pulled his gravity downward. If only he could look forward to a future as happy as his past had been. He knew that wasn't likely, that he and Vajhana might ultimately be able to find a working alliance, save for marriage vows, but they'd never have the sheer family joy that filled the palace when Queen Sirind ran barefoot through the halls.

The caddy presented them with tall plastic glasses. Inside was sweet and icy tea, most welcome after they'd traversed the green. He watched Gracie sip, feeling more connected to her than he had to anyone in his life. She got him thinking about every subject under the sun. Somehow, in the middle of the golf course, he was having memories that hadn't occurred to him in years. She was a splash of color bursting into his black-and-white heart. They stood close as they drank, appreciating their surroundings. Pulled by a supernatural force, he bent his face closer to her, just as he had on the park bench when she'd inched her body just a perceptible bit toward his. Her full lips glistened from the sweet drink. He wanted to taste those lips. Maybe just once. Or maybe until eternity. Then he leaned in a little farther still, until their mouths were only inches away from each other. He could all but feel her breath.

He startled himself, came to his senses and backed off.

Did he notice a little sign of disappointment on her pretty face?

CHAPTER SIX

HAD RAS BEEN about to *kiss* her? Gracie couldn't stop replaying the moment on the ninth hole when they'd stopped for a glass of iced tea. As they stood together and surveyed the golf course, it seemed like he had been moving toward her. If she was being honest, she'd have to admit to herself that she absolutely, desperately, emphatically wanted him to kiss her. Even though she knew it wouldn't have meant anything other than succumbing to a momentary urge.

Just as when they'd sat on that bench and he seemed to be putting his arm around her. Her body, without being asked to, had brought itself closer against his, all of her molecules questioning *what-if*? It was all just dalliance, but she couldn't stop herself. Obviously, she and Ras could never be together. He deserved a real, live, enduring love, and that was something she could never give him. Her scars would never heal. She still didn't have a picture of his life, but when he spoke of his mother she could tell that only someone capable of great love could be capable of the great hurt he'd suffered by her loss.

After they'd finished the eighteenth hole, they returned to the pro shop to check the clubs back in and settle the account. Gracie idled around in the shop, browsing the sunglasses and hats. Along one wall of the shop were shelves with a nice selection of international news-papers and magaz—

What? She couldn't believe her eyes. They must have been deceiving her. She glanced back to Ras who she could see in profile as he spoke with the club manager. And then her eyes shot back to the publications. To Ras, then to the third shelf of the display. To Ras, then to the magazine called *World's Young Royals*. To Ras, then to the photo that took up half of the cover, a man in full royal regalia identified as His Royal Highness Crown Prince Rasmayada of Ko Pha Lano. The second half of the cover showed a photo of a woman with long dark hair in a revealing designer dress that left nothing to the imagination. She drank from an open bottle of champagne in one hand and her other arm was thrown around a blond-haired man who had a royal sash over his jacket, named as a British earl, Lord Cyril. The caption read: Prince Ras and Princess Vajhana: On or Off?

Gracie couldn't make sense of the information overload. She'd known he was a person of notoriety, he'd all but told her so. But a royal? After he settled up at the counter, he found her and froze in front of the magazine cover as well. She could hear him swallow before he whispered, "Let's get out of here."

The valet had brought the Porsche to the exit, so they quickly got in. Ras pulled out onto the gravel road as they headed back to the main street. Gracie was seeing stars; she simply couldn't bring her thoughts together. "You're a prince?"

"Yes."

"A prince. Like with a crown and a throne?"

He smiled. "Theoretically, that won't be until my father dies and I become king, but yes."

"A prince of an island in the Gulf of Thailand who boarded a public cruise in New York?"

"I wanted to travel without being noticed. As you can see from the magazine cover, and you'll find on numerous websites, people's fascination with royalty can be oppressive."

"So, when you spoke before of your family business…"

"Yes, I meant that my father is sort of the CEO and I'm next in command."

"And about that *merger* you got some bad news about?"

"Yes, well, as you saw on the magazine cover, I'm to be married."

As they traveled back to the harbor, among her many emotions was hurt that he hadn't told her who he was sooner. And especially about the woman he was to *merge* with. Not that it should be any concern of hers. Except, somehow it was. She'd pressed her body into his, he'd almost kissed her, or so she'd sensed. And everything that had come before. The smiles that told her he'd been pleased when they kept running into each other on the cruise, the sharing of chocolates, the dancing that was unmistakably sensual.

He'd mentioned being recognizable and was always looking around as if he suspected he was being followed. She supposed he didn't want to be photographed alone in the US if he was engaged to be *merged*. Although from the looks of the princess, she didn't seem to share the same worry. Still, it all stung. That he didn't trust her enough to tell her who he really was, didn't think she was worthy of the information. It made perfect sense from his point of view. Irrationally, it hit her like a rejection.

"As you could see from the cover photos, my arranged marriage to be is a bit of a sham."

"Arranged marriage, crowns, do you have a scepter, too?" She sounded a bit snitty so restrained herself. There was no logical reason to take offense. She hadn't told him everything about herself, either. "How do you feel about a wife being chosen for you?"

"I have an obligation to my people and she to hers. Our marriage will be part of our jobs and never anything more."

There was something wistful in the words he said, singed around the edges with sadness. Maybe even longing. Something she well understood. For all her proclamations about a life untethered, she knew that was going to be a lonesome path. Especially since she still longed for something that was taken from her forever. Her palm went to her belly.

"The business *merger* you talked about."

"Yes, a collaborative effort of both of our fathers to a large agenda of bringing manufacturing to the islands."

"Whereas you think developing eco-friendly tourism is a better idea."

"Yes. Marine conservation, for starters."

"There's a big interest in voluntourism."

"I know. I have to convince my father not to go forward with their plans."

"What does your fiancée think?"

"What did it look like on the magazine cover? She has no interest. But she's going to at least need to keep her unprincess-like behavior out of the media or we'll both end up humiliated. Our engagement was only announced to the press months ago."

"I don't know anything about your royal rules but, of course, you don't want photos like that one splashed across the news." Ras shook his head in distress, like he was at a loss. So was she, for a different reason. Somehow, learning he was a renowned captain of industry or some other reason for his fame would be far easier to fathom than him being a prince. But, okay, she was on a voyage with His Royal Highness. This was a once-in-a-lifetime experience in so many ways.

"I'm so sorry. I was just trying to have a little getaway on my own before I got married, as my mother wanted me to. I've been trying to keep all of this under wraps. At first I thought my father was having me followed to either force me home or track my every move. But by this point, I doubt that. Then there's the possibility of being recognized by the general public who'd love to snap a compromising shot and sell it to the press. On top of that are the ruthless bona fide paparazzi relentlessly trying to get any juice they can. The photo of me on that magazine cover is one of my official portraits, but Vajhana on the lap of an earl is a fresh catch."

They parked the car at the harbor. When they reached the yacht, Ras handed the fob to Neo who would return the car to the boat. Gracie felt like she was being pulled with the tide, from the golf shop to the car to the harbor and now onto the yacht.

"Did you have a good day of sightseeing?" Captain Ernesto asked as he welcomed them back onto the ship.

"Fine," Ras said brusquely.

"Do you still desire dinner onboard?"

"Yes." They'd talked about it earlier because Gracie thought it would be nice if they took a night sail to look at Hilton Head and Myrtle Beach islands. And they'd decided to make it a dinner cruise. In the morning they'd head northward to their next destination.

"Shall I have two masseuses come aboard in an hour for massages in the spa?"

"Yes."

"May I show you the activities deck where the spa is located? Since you arrived late last night, you didn't have a chance to see it."

"Fine." She knew Ras well enough by now to perceive from his tight voice and straightened eyebrows that he was still rattled about the magazine cover. A massage should help. Although she could hardly blame him for being upset. It was sad that the only way he could find some peace and reconciliation about marrying a woman he didn't love was to steal away on a secret trip away from her.

As Captain Ernesto led them to the activities deck, Gracie continued to be impressed by the details of the yacht. It was, indeed, meant for royalty. "The cinema," the captain said as he ushered them into a theater. Gracie quickly counted twelve plush red-velvet-covered reclining chairs. Between each was a small wood table for refreshments. Behind those recliners were a couple of rows of traditional movie theater seats, which Gracie figured came into use if there were additional guests. A glass snack bar lined one of the walls. It held a popcorn machine and a soda dispenser, and underneath the glass were shelves full of popular movie theater candy. The screen itself was theater-size, framed by a red velvet curtain that matched the chairs.

There was a fitness studio, a clean room with exercise equipment positioned to face seaward and several screens directed at different angles for video entertainment while working out. Weights, yoga mats and Pilates apparatus were at the ready. "When you'd like to participate in water sports, I'll be delighted to show you our equipment."

"Thank you."

Next, he showed them a party room, a large space with a hardwood dance floor and cocktail tables set up along the windows. Gracie could imagine whoever was chartering the boat hosting events onboard. The captain opened a pair of wooden double doors. "And here is our chapel." A white room, with wallpaper that depicted delicate cherry blossoms, held six white upholstered pews. Two simple chandeliers gave the room a special feel without being over the top. The floors were lushly carpeted, and at the front of the room stood a white pulpit. Behind it were windows to provide beautiful views.

Ras took a deep inhale. Gracie imagined he was considering his own upcoming nuptials. She was sure his royal wedding would be a massive affair with hundreds or maybe even thousands in attendance. What a unique agony was his fate. She wondered, for only a quick minute, what it would be like to be his bride. This man who made her feel so good about herself. A man she could talk and listen to for hours on end. With whom she could share everything she felt, without fear of uninterest and belittlement. Not to mention after the brushes of physical contact they'd had, she imagined what his big hands would feel like on her, how his full lips would be pressed against hers.

She forced all of those thoughts away with what felt like a literal push. She could have just as easily ended up standing at the altar with Davis. After being so ignored and irrelevant to her parents, she'd been desperate for Davis's attention. In the beginning, she would have married him in a minute. He'd looked like stability, someone with whom to build a life, to raise a family. She'd been such a poor judge of character, so hungry for care that it took her a while to notice that he didn't regard her well. How he'd talked down to her, always reminding her of her miserable childhood, telling her she was fortunate he took pity on her. Until he didn't even do that and, after receiving the news of what would be their next step, he'd walked out on her. Thank heavens she never got as far as wearing his ring.

Ras turned his back and headed out of the chapel. That wouldn't be a part of the ship either one of them would need to return to. "We'll see the rest another time, Ernesto. Kindly take us to the spa."

The spa was as carefully designed as the rest of the yacht. Done in a tropical motif, both tall and low-lying green plants were everywhere, creating a dense lushness. A waterfall feature provided nature's music, not a gush, just a gentle rain of drops that instantly lowered his blood pressure whether he'd willed it to or not. Within that space, Gracie looked so pretty, like a mythical creature in her natural habitat. It had annoyed him that on seeing the chapel, his mind had immediately gone to Vajhana and the disappointment that he'd probably be dealt over and over again in his coming life with her. The kind of love his parents had was not to be his. Making the chapel feel like a charade with its promise of true marriage. But somehow when his thoughts returned to Gracie, it was as if a ray of light penetrated through the dark, filling him with hope.

Her radiance was becoming a safe aura for him to bask in. She'd been open with him, prompting him to want to give her that kind of candor in return. Yet what had he chosen in return? Deception and secrecy. He should have told her who he was sooner, should have gauged that she'd hold his confidence. For her to find out by accident was insulting. He wished he hadn't let it play out that way. Although her finally knowing was like a long sigh of relief. He took her hand, whether he should have or not, to walk around the spa and see its unique features. Resting areas featured furniture in a leafy print fabric. He commented, "It definitely feels like stepping into a different world." In more ways than one.

They turned to an inner alcove. "I like how they made the salon chairs that would be used for hair styling or facial treatments look integrated, like you'd find them in nature." The tools and products were probably behind the closed wood cabinets.

Beyond a wall of bamboo were two massage tables, surrounded by flowering plants emitting their sweet fragrance. A disturbing thought crashed through what would otherwise be a blissful tableau. Were he and Gracie about to get side-by-side massages on those tables? Massages. Where people were generally naked. Captain Ernesto asked, "Are you ready for Ovia and Coro to begin?"

Now or never, Ras thought with a smile to himself. "Certainly."

"While they set up, if you'd like to use the changing rooms—" he gestured to a wooden door "—you'll find robes and slippers as well as showers and towels. After the massages, I highly recommend the rain forest shower with its ten water jets, built for two."

Ras's gut, or maybe it was lower, twitched at the idea of sharing a shower for two with Gracie. She lowered her eyes as well, obviously uncomfortable at the suggestion. First the park bench, then the almost-kiss at the golf course? What was he thinking? Although, he considered, as a wicked thrill washed through him, why not? The *why not* was that it wouldn't be fair to Gracie. Perhaps it was part of his journey, of this whole escape, to fully fathom and accept what he and Vajhana were, and weren't, going to have. To find his place in it. Maybe, but not with Gracie. They'd already reached such a forbidden closeness that he knew it was going to be wrenching to say goodbye when this was all over. It would be a terrible mistake to make that any worse for both of them.

There was no scenario that could keep them together. Even if he wasn't engaged and she wasn't closed off to a romantic relationship, he was no different from that snob Davis who thought Gracie was too far beneath him. Ras's mother was a commoner, but from a wealthy and thoroughbred family. Crown Prince Ras had to marry for his country; he couldn't just marry *anyone*. That was a fight he would never win.

He and Gracie entered the spa's dressing areas, and he was glad to see there were *his* and *her* sections with the aforementioned grand shower between them. He took off his clothes, imagining Gracie doing the same on the other side. Was she in front of the mirror at the vanity table, as conscious of her nakedness as he was his? The erection that reflected back at him was powerful. Not needing the validation his title bestowed on him. A man and a woman, stripped to their essence. What soul-searching might they share and wounds might they salve if they allowed themselves to? He'd never know.

"Ready?" she called across the shower. They met in the middle, both in thick, white terry-cloth robes.

The masseuses were waiting for them in the massage area, two uniformed women with their hair pulled tightly back. "If you'd like to lie down on the tables, madam and sir," one said with a gesture. They both assisted Ras and Gracie onto the tables, shrouding them with sheets as they took their robes off, affording much modesty. Although as he fit his face into the headrest he was keenly aware of Gracie beside him.

"This feels amazing," he heard Gracie coo as her treatment commenced. Her voice coated him in equal measure to the scented massage oil being applied to his shoulders. You *feel amazing*, was what he wanted to say in return but, of course, didn't. As the massage went on, he was washed over and over again with Gracie's declarations of pleasure. His only regret was that he wasn't eliciting them from her himself.

After an expert combination of Eastern and Western bodywork techniques, the masseuse helped him back into his robe. It took all of his concentration not to turn to watch Gracie doing the same.

They moved to a terrace to relax in reclining chairs. She eased into one and pushed it all the way back until it was in a V shape. "I love these zero gravity chairs. They take all the pressure off your back."

"Yes, we have some on various balconies at the palace." He sat down and pushed the seat back to its full recline.

She giggled. "That probably feels very natural coming out of your mouth. But you can imagine how unusual that sounds to me." She used an exaggerated fancy voice, "Oh, yes, I held a charity ball at the palace last night."

"Is that how I sound?" he teased.

"No, but you get my point."

"Indeed," he laughed.

"There you go again. No one says *indeed* in real life."

"You better watch yourself, smart mouth." Indeed, *indeed*, did she have a smart mouth. Not to mention sexy, the way her two lips parted slightly in repose. He'd come so close to kissing said smart mouth before and was ready to pounce upon her zero-gravity chair right now.

Of course, those were only fleeting thoughts he would never act upon. But Gracie's uninhibited way about her made him want to act the same. "Once again, I'm sorry I withheld my identity from you. Every time we ran into each other on the cruise I assumed it was the last, and then it just snowballed."

"I guess there's nothing we can do about that now, Your Royal Highness." Her good humor was appreciated.

Once they returned to the dressing area, the rain forest shower for two still stood tauntingly at the ready. He summoned his self-control as the dilemma had an obvious solution. He couldn't be expected to get into that shower with her and not sponge her shapely body, an activity that he thought might take him hours. A force had genuinely begun inside him as he found more thoughts than not had become about her. But he wouldn't treat her as she had become unfortunately used to, cast aside when no longer needed. He had to keep things to the acquaintanceship they'd settled on, a friendly tourist and tour guide who happened to open up their souls to each other, a rare occurrence in the world.

"Please, you take this rain forest shower and observe all of its features. I can tell you, extravagant personal care facilities like this are definitely something the high-end traveler wants."

"What will *you* do?"

"There are other showers in the men's changing room. I'll meet you back in the relaxation area. Take your time and enjoy yourself." Two things he'd like to be doing. With her.

He proceeded to shower and dress. When she exited the changing room door to reunite with him, she was a vision. Her wet hair was tousled and her skin positively glowed, as if it had been kissed by the sun. "How was the shower?"

"Exquisite. You absolutely have to try it while we're aboard."

He was unable to shut down ideas of making it an activity for two. "I'll take it on your recommendation."

She poured them two glasses of the coconut water that had been provided and he grabbed a bowl with dried fruits and nuts. They sat down in front of the waterfall on another one of those sofas that were large enough to be beds, probably seated more intimately than they should have been, yet they were there before he'd had a chance to decide against it.

"This is really divine, Ras." He swallowed. Looking into those light brown eyes, he fell into a trance. He was quite sure he could stare at her for an indefinite period of time. Maybe forever. "Can I have some of those snacks?"

He picked the plumpest almond out of the bowl. Pinching it between two fingers, he used it to slowly outline her lips, which parted in acceptance of the sensation. After he made a circle all the way around her mouth he placed his fingers ever so slightly against her lips and watched her tongue dart to grab the nut. A slight smile moved across her face as she chewed. "That tasted especially good."

"Do you want another?" a voice so low it was almost a roar came out of him.

"Yes, please."

This time he selected a Brazil nut, smooth on its surface. It's bigger size glided along the fullness of her lips. She bit it in two as he fed it to her, his body vibrating as if it were a guitar with strings that had been plucked. "More?"

"Delicious." He directly fed a couple of dried cranberries onto her tongue.

And then rational thought couldn't hold him back any longer and he leaned over to replace his lips for the snacks. Her mouth was plush and tender. The tip of his tongue explored in the same circle the nuts had before. Then the fullness of his lips pressed into hers. Those guitar strings thrummed inside him. Which urged him forward to seal their mouths together as the kisses became longer. Their lips opened and her sweet taste was as divine as he'd envisioned it would be. He brought a hand up to caress her cheek, coaxing her even closer to him. He dotted her entire face with kisses, his lips hardly knowing where to go first.

His mouth found the furrow of her neck, provoking a tiny moan from her. Tracing down to the hollow of her throat, he breathed into the smell of her skin. Back up to her mouth, which he had to take again and again, starving for more and more still. His fingers laced through the velvet strands that were her hair.

"Gracie," he murmured softly but, really, it was a flag speared into the dirt. A claim. A home.

That was probably a mistake, Gracie thought in her cabin as she dressed for dinner. Succumbing to Ras's considerable appeal and feeling bonded to him after all they'd shared over the last couple of days, she had no strength to deny the kisses that he'd instigated, yet both wanted. Genuine, robust and urgent. His kisses came from the heavens, they belonged to the universe, pure demonstrations of human emotion that could not be bound by logic. They were so monumental, they had to be honored. She felt them down into her core, like no kisses she had ever received or given before, and the fact was she wanted more.

"You look stunning," he said as she came up the last

stairs leading from her cabin to his. While she didn't have a lot of clothes with her, originally thinking she was only on a cruise for a few nights from New York to Miami and back, she was glad she hadn't yet worn the dress she had on now. It was black with a halter tie at the neck, the front plunging low. It was long, past her ankles, and fit slimly all the way down. She thought of it as her glamour dress, and she felt sexy in it. A long gold chain and a pair of hoop earrings added to the look that she finished with black platform sandals and a shimmery gold wrap in case it got cold in the night air.

"May I serve you a first course?" David appeared wielding a tray. A formal table had been set for them with a fine brocade tablecloth and napkins in cobalt blue. Polished silverware was arranged for several courses. A bottle of champagne chilled in a metal ice bucket on a stand. An arrangement of purple and blue flowers made for a vivid centerpiece.

"Shall we?" Ras gestured to Gracie, and they approached the table. He pulled out a chair for her, and she sat as he pushed it in. He then took the chair opposite. They were extraordinarily comfortable for dining chairs with cushioned armrests. Gracie took note of how painstakingly they must have been chosen.

David moved in to lift the champagne out of the bucket and wait for Ras's nod of approval at the label. He popped the cork with the most minimal sound, the measure of an experienced server. Pouring the bubbly into two flutes, he immediately retreated from the table to allow the two of them a private toast.

"To adventure."

"Adventure." They clinked their crystal and sipped.

Once they'd had a few minutes, David returned with two plates. "Heirloom tomatoes from the farmers' market in Savannah." Gracie liked the detail of the specific place where the tomatoes were purchased. While she and Ras were sightseeing and golfing, the crew was attending to their voyage, including buying things like tomatoes and fresh flowers.

The artfully arranged plate contained yellow, orange and brown-hued tomatoes. "The drizzle of balsamic reduction really brings out their sweetness," Ras commented.

They chatted a bit about the agriculture on Ko Pha Lano. "Have you heard about the mineral accretion technologies?" she asked. "There are coral reef restoration programs that use low-voltage electrical currents to aid the health and growth of coral reefs and other marine life."

"Yes. Other islands in the gulf are doing that. And we need more farming. The massive amount of importation we do for food and other goods drives prices up, contributing to the stagnant economy."

"Hence the manufacturing industries the two kings want to bring in as a solution."

"Honestly, I don't think my father truly understands how the island never fully recovered from my mother's death."

"How so?" she asked as she speared her fork into a tomato.

"The mood, the disposition of the entire nation. Which is now transferring down to the children of the subjects who were of my mother's era."

"She sounds like both an accomplished queen and an amazing mother."

A smile broke on one side of his mouth. Yet there was a glint of sorrow in his eyes. "She was. Her monthly addresses from the palace balcony drew thousands."

David replaced their appetizer plates with the main course. "Grilled crab legs, corn *elote* with chili, lime and cotija cheese. And sauteed fresh spinach."

"Thank you." Ras nodded and dismissed him.

"What did she talk to your people about?"

"That was what was so wonderful. She spoke about both civic and ordinary things. A success I might have had at school. A challenge to one of our districts, such as roadwork that was creating a traffic problem. A benefit concert she was organizing. She had such innate humanity. I think it was because she was a commoner. She understood the lives of people outside the palace."

"You said that's why she wanted you to take this trip."

"Yes, and she set aside a fund for me to do so, that I shouldn't spend the nation's money on my own pursuits."

"She was thoughtful."

"Yes, and my father's approach to ruling is nothing like hers. He dutifully keeps the needs of his subjects foremost in his mind, but he's icy and distant. Especially after my mother died. He hardened."

"What a terrible tragedy you both endured."

"As have you, from what you told me. Parents who basically abandoned you, and a fool of a man who didn't treat you as the precious jewel you are."

Gracie all but swooned. Those words were like balms to parched skin. Ras had a way of making her feel so valued. Fate had dealt her a cruel irony in meeting a man like him, a man she couldn't have.

"I haven't yet told you about my loss far greater than that."

He tilted his head, intrigued. "Go on."

There was no reason not to confide in him. "I became pregnant with Davis's child." Her hand reflexively went to her belly, as it had thousands of times before. "He told me I wasn't the kind of woman he and his family would want to continue the family name. That the best thing would be for me to get rid of it."

"*Get rid of it?* What does that even mean?"

"I suppose that I should either have an abortion or that I should give the baby up for adoption so there would be no connection to his or her true parentage."

Ras gritted his teeth. "What a disgusting human."

"I didn't want to do either of those. When that became obvious, Davis left and told me never to get in touch with him ever again. And that if I ever told the child who his or her father was, he'd crush me under his heel. Those were his exact words."

Ras reached across the table to cover her hand with his, so big and strong. He caressed her with the pad of his thumb, back and forth in a tender and soothing motion. "I can't even imagine the abandonment you must have felt."

"That wasn't all of it."

"You had to endure more?"

"Weeks after Davis left, I had a miscarriage. That was the pinnacle. There's no loss, no desertion, that could be worse than that."

CHAPTER SEVEN

A WAVE OF sorrow crashed over Ras at Gracie's admission. She was right, there was nothing more tragic than a parent losing their child. Even the child they'd never met, one who was growing inside his or her mother. "Gracie, I'm so sorry."

As they'd finished their entrée, Ras stood up and moved to her side of the table. Her face had taken on a pallor so unlike her usual glow. He was glad that she didn't try to hide it from him.

"Let's walk around the deck," she requested.

They strolled the perimeter. She held his hand, and he had no intention of letting it go unless she wanted him to. It seemed she had more to say to him, and he wanted to give her the opportunity to do so. "You said Davis had already left you when you miscarried. What was his reaction?" he asked gently.

"He didn't know, Ras. It happened a few weeks after he'd thrown me out of his house in Point Pleasant. After he'd confirmed how small and insignificant I was to him, I got the bus station job in Newark. He never found out I lost the child he wanted me to *get rid of.* It ended up as what he wanted, not having a child with me, but he never found out why."

"Why didn't you tell him?"

"What difference did it make? I couldn't stay with him after all of that."

Ras shook his head in disbelief. "You're surely better off without him."

"I am."

"And you didn't tell your parents, either?"

"No. I couldn't have even if I wanted to."

"Why not?"

"I had no idea where they were. I still don't."

Her words caused another stab to Ras's heart. He squeezed her hand as they stopped along the portside railing, with very few lights illuminating the area. They peered out at the ocean in its darkness. The sound of the water crashed like a symphony.

"Gracie, you've been through so much. How are you so resilient?"

"I don't know that I am. If I've learned anything, it's that I can only count on myself. That I'll never fall in love with anyone ever again. I'll never rely on someone else." Something about that tugged at Ras. In the strangest way, he wanted her to rely on him. He knew he'd never betray her. He could give her the solid ground that she deserved to stand on. To walk through life never trusting anyone was a horrible fate. It was one he faced, too. His matrimony to Vajhana was not to be built on trust or honor. It was concocted for purpose.

"What happened after you moved to Newark?"

"I got a tiny apartment. After work and on the weekends, I started taking classes in the travel sector. And slowly but consistently, I learned and formulated my outline for the rest of my life." Her certainty about an existence without love tapped against Ras's chest. Because he'd decided on the same thing. He'd marry the princess, he'd produce an heir, he'd serve his people. Yet in the process he would become like his father, not the joyous mother who had exuberance for life and living. There was no point in lamenting; that was the path in front of him. Just as Gracie had decided on hers.

She turned her head to make eye contact with him. Her hair whipped around her face in a wild storm. Her lips were ripe and plump. He swooped down and brought his hands underneath her hair, to the back of her neck. And then all of a sudden his lips pressed into hers and he was kissing her again. "Gracie, Gracie. You make me wish for things that are impossible."

When she lifted her arms up and around his shoulders, yearning coursed through him. His hands slid down her sides and to her waist, where he pulled her tightly against him, wanting to shore up any gaps between their two bodies. With her back against the ship's railing, he moved into her, a crush of their bodies with every kiss, using the groove he created with her in the Cuban nightclub of Miami. But now they provided the melody themselves in a dance only for them. And the ocean. And the moonlight. And the heavens.

His lips brushed against one cheek and then the other, her skin like milled talcum. She made many utterances of pleasure that were like kisses to him. His hands slid from her waist, along her hips. Blood rushed to his center as he pressed into her, stiffening him to steel. Tomorrow no longer mattered. Of course, he could have no future with this enchanting and emotional woman. Both had decisions they'd made and both had barriers. Although, if she was willing, they could have this moment, easily the most exciting of his life.

Suddenly, he was picking her up and into his arms, carrying her along the deck, the smashing sound of each wave urging him on. The wind billowed his white shirt into a sail as her warm lips furrowed into his neck. With a kick, he opened the aft entrance to his suite. Striding across the room to his opulent master bed, he whispered to her, "Can we be together tonight? I want you so much."

"I do, too, Ras," came the answer he needed to hear.

He looked at her lying curved in the center of his bed, a magnificent sight. "The only thing that could look better than you do right now would be if you were naked."

Although the panes of glass surrounding his suite were completely privacy darkened and no one could see in, he grabbed the remote control to shut the curtains that surrounded the room, making their lair all the more only theirs, even hiding from the Atlantic. When he assured himself that operation was complete, he retrieved the condoms he'd wistfully noticed in the toiletry basket beside the sink. Then when he turned his attention back to Gracie, his breath caught in surprise. She'd done exactly what he'd stated as his wish. Her clothes were in a pile on the floor. She'd quickly removed them and lay there naked with a sly smile, one arm propping her up, her head leaning back a bit, all of it forming the most seductive S-shape ever in the world. His eyes glazed.

"Is this what you had in mind?" she purred.

"Oh, yes, I was right. This is even better than that sexy black dress you had on."

He snaked onto the bed to join her. One hand slid ever so slowly across her hair, down her face along her jawline, into the crook of her throat. With no reason to stop there, his thumb traced her shoulder along her arm down to her fingertips, which led him across her hips and to her thigh. He felt behind her knee and then down the rest of her leg to her foot. Every part of the exploration was magnificent, if one-sided as he made a mental note to remember the other side of her body next time his hands made their travels. And there would be many next times; in fact he couldn't keep his touch off her skin. His hand cupped her breast, so pliant and creamy that his second hand had to have the other one. He held them, reveling at their perfect fit in his palms. Until the tips of his fingers became itchy to caress and pull on her nipples, making them hard with just a few satisfying strokes. As he did, her head fell back and a slow, delicious moan vibrated from her throat.

His mouth found hers and their tongues wrote more music together, one he knew he'd replay in his memories for the rest of his life. He couldn't get enough of this woman. She was in his blood. In every inhale and every exhale. He'd never imagined the affinity he felt with her, the tie. And to bring that joining to the physical as they did now, in perfect sync, was a gift from the hereafter.

His hands explored every vertebra of her spine. Hers searched to untuck his shirt from his pants, sliding her hands underneath to make contact. The hairs on each inch of his body stood on end at her electrifying touch, skin to skin. She unbuttoned his shirt, slowly, tantalizingly, to place her palms flat against his chest. Next, her hands roamed over him, learning him. Any way she touched him was ecstasy. He wanted to give himself to her completely. He gasped when she reached into his pants and wrapped her delicate fingers around his hardness. Quickly unzipping his fly he worked his pants down, all the while her supple hand swelling him more than he'd ever thought possible, coursing him with not want but need. Finally naked as she was, their arms and legs tangled into one creature, desperately taking and giving with their hands and mouths until no part of either was neglected.

When he couldn't take it any longer, he rolled her onto

her back, sheathed the condom onto himself and got on top of her. His knees urged hers open as he angled himself to enter her. Only one inch at first as he wanted to read her body and her face. Her smile encouraged him and he slipped farther into her.

"That feels so good, Ras." When he entered her all the way, she cried out in arousal as he centered himself and fastened to her. Despite her sounds of pleasure, she couldn't possibly know the rhapsody and rapture she was causing his body and soul.

They rocked, at first gently and then not so gently. Slow and deliberate, and alternately fast and frenzied. They rode each other like the high tides of the ocean surrounding them, the ebb and flow, over and over and over again. Until it crested them over and they crashed, grasping each other like life preservers.

The next morning, Gracie took Ras to the breakfast restaurant that she'd selected for them in the Charleston City Market. Within the two-hundred-year-old brick buildings, over three hundred shops and restaurants attracted visitors from all over the world. She'd read about this particular restaurant and had decided that would be their first stop of the day. Captain Ernesto had known that he was to set off from Savannah early in the morning for their brief stop at the historic city of Charleston in nearby South Carolina.

She'd spoken to Captain Ernesto last night. Before dinner. Before heirloom tomato salads. Before she'd told Ras her most painful truth. Before the walk on the moonlit deck. And before they'd retired to private quarters to discuss things further. Er, that was to say communicated in a non-verbal way. One that had left her feeling boneless and dazed this morning. Even as they strolled arm in arm through the colorful streets of Charleston.

"Good morning. Breakfast for two?" the hostess asked as they came into the cheery restaurant.

Gracie responded, "Yes, and if you have a table by the window, that would be great."

"Follow me." She sat them at a lovely table in its own little alcove that overlooked the comings and goings of the famous old marketplace. "Is this your first visit to Charleston?"

"Yes."

"I'll send your waitress right over," the hostess said with a big-toothed smile, making Gracie glad that she'd chosen this restaurant known for its southern charm. The open room with its white tablecloths and wooden ceiling fans was a lovely destination from where to start the day. And before the waitress could arrive, the hostess returned with a pot of hot coffee that she poured into the red porcelain mugs on the table. She laid down a basket. "These are our mini biscuits. Looks like today we have pimento cheese, blackberry and buttermilk." Ras and Gracie looked at each other with a smile, silently agreeing that hot biscuits served with soft butter was a quite appealing way to start their morning. Of course, their morning had already begun back in his bedroom suite. In fact, appetites had been satiated starting at dawn, but that was a different hunger entirely. Ras winked at her as if he was remembering their earlier activities as well.

When the waitress arrived to greet them, Gracie took charge. "We'll both have shrimp and grits."

"Good choice. Anything else I can get you?"

"Not at the moment, thanks." Once she walked away Gracie said enthusiastically to Ras, "That's a historic dish down in the Lowcountry, as they call it."

"You surely do your homework," he said as his mouth caressed the rim of his mug to take a sip. Lucky mug, she thought to herself. She could watch his lips all day long, so full and expressive. Those lips had wanted to know everything about her last night and again this morning. They knew how to coax a reaction out of just about every spot on her body. The crook of her elbow. On a shoulder blade. Her hip bone. Ras was an intense lover, completely focusing on either the giving or receiving he was involved in. It had been a night and morning of lovemaking like she'd never known existed.

Although, she was well aware of what it didn't mean, too. When the food arrived, she took one bite of the juicy seafood forked up with the buttery grains of the grits. And then put her fork down to state plainly, just to get it out of the way. "Ras, I know what happened between us last night and this morning didn't mean anything."

"You're wrong. It meant a lot."

"Thank you. What I'm trying to say is that I understand that we'll say goodbye forever at the end of this trip. You'll tread your path and I'll go mine."

His face turned somber. "Don't ever think that it will have been easy for me."

A corner of her mouth ticked up. "No. We stumbled upon something really special in each other, didn't we? Maybe that's why we can't have it forever. It's like a meteor that shines so bright it has to explode."

"So, we'll have this time together. Let's make the most of it."

"And then it won't be as hard to part as it could be because we'll know that's how it was supposed to end up. We'll be ready for it."

"I have to marry by contract, and you'll never marry at all."

"You see, it's all decided already." Neither of them believed a word they were saying, but it was probably useful to state.

He bent across the table to bring his mouth to hers. His kisses swirled her insides, hypnotizing her, like she could get lost in them and lose all track of time and space. "It's a shame though," he whispered in between, "because I think I might like to kiss you for the rest of my life." They narrowed their eyes at each other, as if someone had issued a dare. Until he broke the eye lock and proclaimed, "Now about these biscuits."

After breakfast, they strolled through the market, taking special note of the artisans who sat weaving sweetgrass baskets from the local marshland. "It's a tradition of African Americans who live in the Lowcountry and speak the Creole language of Gullah."

"Shall we buy some?"

"As souvenirs?"

Ras realized what he'd just suggested. It wasn't as if he could return to Ko Pha Lano with armfuls of gifts for his father and fiancée. "Let me buy some for you, then."

"No, but thank you. Remember, I'm a nomad now. I have nothing to put in baskets."

"Look," he said, pointing to some very tiny ones. "Surely you'll have a use for a small one like that. You can use it to hold my kisses."

Her lungs swelled at the specialness of that thought. And in sadness because that was all she'd have of him, an empty basket filled with clandestine kisses. "Okay. We'll get one for you, too."

"And why don't we buy some larger ones for the yacht crew."

After the purchases Gracie suggested, "Let's go look at Rainbow Row."

"Wonderful. What's that?"

Once they turned onto the street she intended, Ras had his answer. The Georgian-style houses were painted in pastel colors one after the other. "The most well-known street in Charleston."

"I can see why."

Later, they walked back to the yacht where the basket gifts were appreciated. As they entered Ras's suite, which had been cleaned and the bed made up with fresh linen, Gracie said, "Our next port is Washington, DC."

Ras's brows furrowed. "I shouldn't spend much time in the capital. I've been there too many times for official functions." Was he still concerned that the paparazzi would catch him? Worried that someone would see him on his bachelor freedom quest and post it on a gossip site or in a magazine? She admired that he didn't want to bring any shame to his family. They had a reputation of propriety dating back generations.

"Okay, we'll just go to touristy places, and you can wear your most casual clothes that you bought on *Liberation*."

"Yes… I'm sure that will be…okay."

"We're at sea tomorrow," Gracie reminded Ras even though he hadn't forgotten.

"Yes—" he scratched his chin "—however will we pass the time?" He winked at her and was gratified by the smile he got in return.

"Well, for this evening, how about we watch a movie?"

After they changed into comfortable clothes, they made their way to the cinema they'd only taken a quick look at. David prepared a popcorn buffet with buttered, cheese and caramel flavors. He also made them mini hot-dogs, soft pretzels and put an array of sodas on ice. Ras and Gracie plopped onto the center seats that were the best in the auditorium. "Now, what to watch?"

"Action movie?" Gracie suggested.

"Or comedy?"

"No weepy dramas. I want total escape."

David made a few suggestions, and they picked a superhero movie that neither had seen. He set the projection up for them and then left them to it. The sound and picture quality were outstanding, not that Ras would have expected anything less.

The movie played on, explosions and superhuman feats performed on the screen. Yet his mind was a million miles away. He was daydreaming, on the palace balcony where his family had always addressed the citizens. He saw himself wearing the crown, standing next to his bride. He was formally introducing her to the island's people, her face shielded by the brim of a large black hat.

The population of Ko Pha Lano was clapping and cheering loudly, yelling out welcomes and hurrahs. His subjects looked optimistic, like they had when Queen Sirind used to address the crowd. In turn, Ras was overcome with joy and with hope that his reign would be a good one for the citizens he had the great privilege to serve. In the vision, he put his arm around his bride's shoulders. He was in love, the enrapturing, all-consuming force he'd imagined it to be. He remembered seeing it in his parents and knowing what it was. So grateful to have it for himself, he nodded to his father who sat off to the side, smiling at the young couple. Ras turned his beloved so that she could better see the people and they her, because her face was obscured by that hat.

When he did, the blond waves of her hair caught the light and her beautiful face emerged like a mirage. Only, it was not Vajhana beside him, ready to lead as queen.

No, it was Gracie. It was Gracie the people were admiring and approving. The ovation was for her. Ras had to close his eyes for a minute to take in the sublime perfection of his hallucination. It was the best he'd ever had.

Then his mind ricocheted, wishing to but suddenly unable to re-create the pure bliss of his waking dream. Contentment in the present moment was all he had. Following that theory, he decided on their next activity. When the film ended, he summoned Gracie. "Come with me."

"Where are we going?"

"It's a surprise." He led her down the corridor, everything dark on board save for some safety lighting. Silence allowed only the sound of the ocean, fierce in its turbulence. He led them to the spa, where they'd shared their first kisses. What they hadn't shared was that magnificent rain forest shower. An omission that had tantalized him ever since and was about to be remedied.

The one night-light provided a silver glow. He swept his arms around Gracie's waist and under the loose blouse she was wearing. Lifting it right over her head in one fluid motion, he tossed it to a nearby chair. "I've been wanting you naked for hours," he rasped and with that, eased her pants down and helped her step out of them until he got his wish. The shadows played against her skin, creating light patches and dark stretches, all a gorgeous work of art that aroused him to the point that he had to rid himself of his own clothes as well.

Taking her into the shower, he positioned her under one of the heads so that he could get all of her hair wet, working with purpose as he ran his hands through the locks, taking one break for a long, hot, needy kiss. He ran his palms everywhere, from her breasts to the small of her back to between her legs and groaned when he felt her press her sex into his cupped hand. He held it steady and let her set the tempo that was right, stroking her until she came apart, making him the luckiest man on earth. He wrapped his arms around her and held her close until she settled down, although he was far from done.

With water jets spraying them from every angle, he backed her against one of the shower walls and pressed himself tight to her. "I want you so much, Gracie."

"Mmm…" Her seductive meow egged him further, until he maneuvered them so that he could lift one of her legs, giving him leverage to enter her with a pendulous swoop. Her cry of excitement echoed. He took her slow but solidly, his body deciding for them as his passion was urgent. Again they joined in the new dance they'd created together. Ras wanted it to go on forever although, eventually, their bodies reached a height, a summit, a peak where they slipped into free-fall together, holding each other for stability.

Once they found their footing again, they kissed gently, lovingly. Ras used the strawberry- scented shampoo to wash Gracie's hair, wanting to see the suds he created and then watch them cascade down her shoulders when he used a handheld showerhead. Then, in turn, she lathered his body with a soap that had a refreshing citrus aroma. Such power did she have over his reaction that he became stiff again. He sat down on the stone bench inside the shower and pulled her onto his lap. He couldn't have this woman on his continent, in his palace bedroom, by his side on the royal balcony. But this he could have, this he could allow himself. Although an ache in the center of his being told him loud and clear that he was in danger. What he felt for her went far past carnal. And had maybe become something he wasn't going to be able to live without.

Many hours later a pink and dewy Gracie rolled over

toward him from underneath the pearly gray sheets.
"Good morning?"

"I don't think so." His fingers instinctively brushed
aside a few strands of hair that were in her face. "We've
slept well into the afternoon."

"Well, it was our sea day, anyway."

"After all, we were up so late."

"I'm glad we got a chance to visit the spa again."

"Maybe today I should give you a massage." She shot
a smile into his heart.

He called an order in to David. Meeting him at the
door, Ras carried the tray to the bedside. They ate lei-
surely, occasionally popping something into the other's
mouth. Afterward, they sat by the pool, taking a swim
here and there.

"Okay, we're going to avoid places like the White
House and the Pentagon when we get to DC."

"More than that, Gracie. I don't want to be anywhere
near Dupont Circle where a lot of the embassies are.
There are a lot of danger zones in that city."

"How about the Smithsonian museums?"

"Better not."

"What were you planning to do when you visited?"

"I hadn't decided that I was going to. Remember, I
had no itinerary until I met you. My only agenda was
to have none."

"Hmm, let's see… I'm assuming a dashing prince such
as yourself is an airplane pilot."

"At your service."

She picked up his phone. "I'm making reservations.
Take me flying."

CHAPTER EIGHT

RAS APPROVED AS they were shown to the plane Gracie had rented them outside the no-fly zones of the nation's capital. Helping her into the cockpit, he surveyed the appointments, such as the sleek leather seats and modern design. "Nice details. Good research." After she was comfortably seated, he swooped in for a kiss on her cheek.

Gracie didn't know the first thing about airplanes but when she was scrolling through the options, she went for the well-reviewed and the best money could buy. That's how Ras seemed to like it, and why would she argue?

"Ready for takeoff?" he asked as he settled himself beside her in the two-seater, single-engine plane. The crew had pulled it out of the hangar so all that was left was for Ras to fly away. He performed some safety checks and radio communications to the controller, all effortlessly as if he flew a plane every day. Fortunately, he held pilot licenses in many countries including the US. "Here we go."

He soared them into the air as if they were a great winged bird, taking them up higher and higher. "This is wonderful."

"It's a great feeling, that's for sure." Once he was at a leveling altitude, he used one hand to reach over and squeeze her knee in a gesture of togetherness before returning it to the controls. This was another marvelous escapade they were on together. She quivered thinking about all they'd been occupied with for the past few days. Missions such as finding creative activities to do in a shower. Proving that nighttime might be used for pursuits other than sleeping. And so on. Even though it made no sense, and what happened in the Atlantic Ocean was going to stay in the Atlantic Ocean, they had been writing poetry together, with their bodies and with their souls. Making an unexpected meeting in the middle that had her concocting forbidden fantasies.

Everything about Ras had jolted her into realizing that her proclamations about spending the rest of her life alone were based on misinformation. Her parents and Davis had been her education in human relations, and they weren't good teachers. In fact, the instruction she'd received from them was terrible. She'd never understood the deep well-being of feeling supported and cheered on. The empathy and compassion and sincere concern she and Ras had for each other wasn't to be found in that incomplete guidebook she'd been handed. The world with him was as new as the open skies in front of her. Or maybe it was just the fresh lens she now saw it through. She'd never be the same after him. And feared that she couldn't bear there to even be an *after him*. Yet she knew the rules so she breathed in to take it for all it was worth, gliding through the skies.

"Take the controls," Ras said after a while.

"What?"

"You do it. You fly the plane."

Shock widened her eyes. "Ras, I don't know how to operate a plane."

"I'll talk you through it. Take hold of the yoke." He pointed to the U-shaped handle that was twin to the one he was using to maneuver their flight.

"I can't. You don't want to die, do you?"

His laughter bounced around the cockpit.

"We're not going to die. I'll manage our speed. You'll be in charge of altitude. The yoke is your means of going up and down. Get it together, Gracie baby, because you're about to cross the sky."

"Wh-what?" With hands that were shaking, she put both where he showed her. Her heart pounded a million times a minute. He had to be joking, letting her pilot the plane. But she sure as heck wanted to do it, wanted to feel the power to keep this mechanical bird in the sky. Nerves were fine as long as she concentrated. He knew what he was doing.

"Pull back on the yoke to nose up, push it forward to slant down. Here we go," he said as he flipped a couple of switches. "You're in the hot seat now."

At first, all she could do was try to keep steady, too afraid to make any moves, every muscle in her body tense as stone. "Oh, great, no big deal. Are you saying I have our lives in my hands?"

"No, ultimately I do. Your job would be to keep us from crashing into other planes, tall mountains, that type of thing."

She gritted her teeth and steeled her eyes. "Ooh!" she cried out.

"Okay, now, do something. I'll keep my eyes trained for any notification. We should be fine. Take her down a little bit."

"Are you kidding?"

"How else would you get the hang of it?"

"Ah! Here we go." She pushed forward on the yoke, which moved the nose of the plane slightly downward.

"Now level it out."

"Am I doing it right?"

"Good." She then reversed the motion, pulling back on the yoke to raise the nose upward. "Atta girl."

"This is great." Gracie had to admit it was exhilarating, all that ability in her hands. Soaring through the sky. Until she accidentally pushed the yoke too far forward and the nose began heading down at an unsafe angle.

"Gracie!" she heard Ras's voice tell her, "Gracie, pull up."

All of a sudden she got confused. Her heart raced.

"Ras?"

"Pull up!"

She summoned all of her focus and yanked back on the yoke until they reached a level position.

After they were stable he asked, "What happened?"

"I don't know. I froze."

"You recovered beautifully, and that's what matters most." She blew out a breath and acknowledged his encouragement. "Keep going."

When it was time to land, Ras resumed control of the plane. What an amazing thrill that had been, the one bobble notwithstanding. She'd surely never pictured even being in a two-seater. And she loved that Ras was confident enough in her to let her give flying it a try. After they deplaned and walked toward the hangar he asked, "Would you try it again sometime? You did great."

"Good heavens, yes. It was so much fun."

"Everything with you is fun."

She reached in her purse for her sunglasses and slipped them on, feeling cool and glamorous with the handsome prince by her side.

"Welcome to The Rosecrans." A valet took the fob for the Porsche from Ras so they could enter the fine-dining restaurant Gracie had chosen in Washington, DC, after they'd agreed that a lunch in town wouldn't result in too much visibility. Although as soon as he'd stepped out of the car and observed the comings and goings on the steps and under the welcome veranda, he was uncomfortable. Seeing people in traditional dress from every corner of the world mingling with business people in suits and women in designer fashions and elaborate jewelry, he felt noticeable. Just as he'd remembered, everywhere in Washington, DC, seemed to be teeming with visitors in town for official functions, conferences, meetings, benefits and so on. There was no avoiding the international melting pot, which was wonderful on the occasions when that had been his purpose here. Now, as a stop on his *time off* from being His Royal Highness, he didn't want to belong.

He cast his eyes downward, a move Gracie noticed right away. "Is this not to your liking?"

"I'm sure it's wonderful, just the type of place a crown prince would eat."

"Oh. Shall I find us somewhere else?"

"This is how Washington is. It's probably fine. Just a shock after our morning in the skies." What an enjoyable time he'd had high above it all with Gracie. He'd loved showing her a bit about how to pilot and watch her attempt it. Even if she was afraid, as he suspected she was, she still charged forward with all of her might. She never ceased to fascinate him. In fact, he was quite sure she never would. Not that he would have that chance to experience life with her.

When they entered and approached the reception podium, Ras immediately noticed the facial features and name badge of the hostess as being Thai. While his island was a sovereign nation in the gulf, he was naturally much more well-known in Thailand than anywhere else.

She gave him a look, perhaps just acknowledging that they were both likely from the same part of the world. But what if she did recognize him as the prince? Would she mention it? To him or to anyone else? This was just what he was hoping to avoid. Being seen far from home with an unknown woman, especially given that his fiancée's entertainments were already being well documented.

Nonetheless, he allowed the hostess to seat them as Gracie had wisely reserved a secluded booth in the back of the restaurant. The hostess walked away but then quickly returned, seemingly looking at something on her phone. She walked past their booth but the whole encounter made Ras very uneasy.

After they ordered Ras said, "I know our agreement was that you would choose our entire itinerary during our time together. But I'm just not comfortable here in Washington, so let's leave after lunch. At the reception desk, I felt like I'd met everyone I laid eyes on at a state dinner or some such. A person can easily get lost in New York. Not here."

"I'd been thinking that next we'd spend some time in the Hamptons, and then finish up in New York City."

"I love that idea. Why don't we give up the yacht and rent a house there? We can cook and swim and find some other private pursuits."

"To adventure," she said, offering the toast with a wily smirk.

"Adventure." They clinked glasses and that sexy smile of hers tightened his belly in the most delightful way.

Arrangements were made. After eating, they returned to the yacht to gather their items and Neo drove them to a helipad. In the air, Gracie grabbed his hand and her palpable excitement transferred to him as they descended into Bridgehampton, Long Island, one of the cluster of beachfront towns where the rich and the famous escaped the bustle of New York and just about everywhere else in the world.

Ras had been brought out to Long Island by limo to attend parties and summits over the years but had never stayed long. The oceanfront mansion Gracie selected had access to a private bay for water activities. He'd asked her to find a very special property, and it appeared she'd heeded his request. Upon landing, they were met by the rental agent, Miranda, who walked them in through the entry foyer with wide open glass doors and marble floors. "You have eight thousand square feet of living space." Ras had no idea what they'd do with that much house although every square foot meant that much more seclusion. He was already letting out sighs of relief from leaving Washington as quickly as possible.

"What a kitchen," Gracie remarked as Miranda led them farther into the mansion. "The granite countertops blend into the white cabinetry, which gives it a kind of homey look."

"And this is just your front kitchen for poolside snacks or a breakfast on the terrace. You have a full catering kitchen in the back." As they followed Miranda for the grand tour, Gracie took in every detail. "Formal dining room comfortably seats twenty. You have a total of four fireplaces, three here on the first level and another in the master suite."

"Billiards room." Gracie leaned in to ask Ras, "Do you play?"

"Sure."

"We'll see about that. We Jersey girls know our way around a pool table." She winked at him, which might have set his heart on fire.

"Private office, top-of-the-line connectivity, of

course," Miranda said, pointing. The next area she showed them was done in woods and dark greens, with leather furniture and lots of end tables. "That's your den and full bar, and the game room beyond."

She walked them through another set of double doors to the sunroom, completely enclosed in glass and open window screens with an unobstructed view of the ocean. The furniture was wrought iron, cushions in uplifting yellow and orange tones. Ras noted that there were no other buildings anywhere around them.

Miranda suggested they explore the outdoor amenities on their own, and took them up the grand central staircase in the foyer to the second level. She pointed out a couple of the guest rooms and brought them to the master suite.

"I love all the white!" Gracie exclaimed. The wrap-around room featured a sitting area on one side and a gigantic bed with a white gauze canopy on the other. The same white gauze floated across every window, allowing breezes in and out, and a 180-degree view of the ocean and the rolling green lawn leading to the bay. A fireplace faced the bed.

"Double dressing rooms, a furnished terrace with rocking chairs, loungers and a breakfast table."

He indulged in a long gander of Gracie from the hair on her head to the sandals on her feet while she chatted with Miranda. This bedroom suite was so complete, he wondered why they'd even bother with any other part of the house.

Once they settled into the Hampton mansion, Ras was in a much better mood. It hadn't occurred to Gracie that even with a baseball hat, jeans, T-shirt and other manners of casual dress, he'd still feel exposed and not even want to visit museums and monuments. That was okay. Seeing the Hamptons on a best-of-everything basis was going to be great.

"Eight bedrooms. Is that what Miranda said?" she asked Ras as they unpacked. When the rental agent was here, she'd tried to get her mind off her goal to spend time with Ras in each and every one of them during the week they'd planned to stay.

"That's what she said," he replied, smiling. She watched him bend to reach for a case, the sinewy muscles of his back taut against his sky blue shirt. Oh, how she'd enjoyed reaching around him to hold those muscles when he was on top of her. "What are we going to do about food?"

"Miranda said the kitchen was well stocked, and she emailed me a list of local restaurants."

"Let's avoid restaurants as much as we can, if that's okay. I just want to relax in this house while we're here."

"Do you want to go downstairs and visit the kitchen with me?"

"Absolutely."

They descended a second staircase that led to the back rooms of the house. "Oh, my goodness." Miranda wasn't kidding when she said the small front kitchen off the entrance was just for light fare. The main kitchen was not to be believed. A catering space ample for large parties, there was an island in the center at least four times larger than a typical kitchen would have. At one end of it sat four barstools for a casual cup of coffee or bite, positioned to face the wall-mounted television. "What beautiful choices with this custom cabinetry, countertops, floors, lighting. It's traditional but understated."

"It is finished in nice colors," he commented, regarding the tan paint with green glass accents.

Above the center of the island, a rack displayed at least two dozen pots and pans, and the perfect tools for whatever the task.

Gracie opened drawers and cabinet doors here and there, finding an amazing assortment of dishes, from those made of unbreakable materials for poolside to the finest china for the dining room. She slipped between two double doors and then called out to Ras. "You have to come see this."

She stood in a massive pantry. Shelves lined every bit of it, of varying heights dependent on what they were to hold. There were dry goods, canned foods, baking supplies.

"Do you like to cook?" Ras asked.

She liked being in the center of the pantry with him. While it was plenty big, it still gave her an intimate feeling. Like this food was theirs in their actual life today. Like this wasn't just a big fantasy that would come to a crashing end and leave her alone. Her plan had been to tour the New England B&Bs after this time with Ras. Alone, and homeless to boot, with the contents of the boxes she left at Jen's all she owned. Not even a shelf to store a can of tuna fish. That was what she had wanted. Most unexpectedly, things had changed and her decisions didn't entirely match what was now in her heart.

But for the moment, there was Ras. She looked into those welcoming eyes that always seemed to be seeing her through a complimentary lens. She could rest in his eyes for their time in this house; she could trust them. Why not give herself over fully to what had transpired between them? They both knew it wasn't forever. She could take that much risk. "I'd love to cook in a kitchen like this."

"What would you make?" He ran his fingertips from behind her ear down to the base of her neck, producing a shiver through her.

"Do you cook?" she moaned, her voice altered by the sensations racing through her body.

"As a matter of fact, I do on occasion. Naturally, the palace staff cringes when I enter their territory. But my mother taught me how to make a decent Pad Kra Pao, a meat stir-fry, and Som Tum spicy and sour salad."

"You're making my mouth water." She *might* have been referring to the description of the food.

"I'll cook them for you. We'll order the ingredients and have them delivered. But I still want to know what you're making me tonight."

"Let's look at what else is here. Where are the fresh foods?" Unsurprisingly, she found a second pantry containing more bins and baskets brimming with fruits and vegetables. The walk-in refrigerator was filled with perishable meats and cheeses. "What I was thinking of but am not seeing here are lobsters. Nearby Maine is where the most famous American lobsters come from."

"Order some. Have them delivered immediately."

"I'll call the grocery store in town that Miranda recommended. I'm sure they'll take care of it."

And sure enough, within two hours the doorbell rang. By the time she and Ras got from the back of the property where they were walking in the garden to the front door, the delivery truck was pulling away. What remained was a large cooler on wheels. Ras grabbed the handle and pulled it into the kitchen. When they flipped open the top, they were both startled at what they found inside. Four lobsters. Alive!

"Hello," Ras greeted them.

They both bent over to get a better look, and when one of the lobsters seemed to snap its claws at Gracie, she jumped back. "I didn't know I needed to clarify that we wanted them...well, you know...dead."

"At least we know they're fresh." One snapped its claws again to make the point, and Ras closed the top of the cooler. "For safekeeping. How were you planning to cook them?"

"I saw a big lobster pot. I assumed we'd just steam

them and have them with drawn butter. The classic American way."

"Carry on."

Gracie quickly looked up the recommended amount of water and salt to boil. When it was time to put the lobsters in, though, she was hesitant. "The instructions say headfirst."

"Are you ready for me to open the cooler?"

She swallowed hard. "I suppose it's now or never."

He flipped back the lid again. All four of the crustaceans were moving around. "Can you do it for me?" she pleaded.

"No, no, Miss Gracie," he teased. "You said you were going to cook for me."

"They just seem so…alive."

"That's usually the order of things, alive to dead to food. The other way around is a challenge."

"Come on, you own an island. I'm sure you're used to a lot of live fish and seafood."

"Yes, but I'm a prince. I don't have to kill it." He let out a belly laugh that gave her the giggles, too. "And I don't actually own the island."

"I can barely squash mosquitos that suck my blood in the summertime."

"I thought you said you Jersey girls were tough?" She rolled her eyes.

"I'm calling that little one Lucky," Ras continued. "That was my dog's name when I was growing up. My mother used to tell him how lucky he was to be in such a privileged family. I think she was teaching me a lesson about humility."

"Lucky? This Lucky is *lucky* to be in the company of two people who could just eat something from the pantry."

"Do you want soup?"

"I'm calling that shinier one Diamond."

CHAPTER NINE

WITH THEIR NEW friends Lucky, Diamond, Amphitrite and Hampton ensconced in the refrigerator for the night, Ras and Gracie went upstairs. They'd eaten the canned chowder and fresh bread with butter as they sat on the stools at the kitchen island watching a baseball game on TV. Ras loved the simplicity. The topic of lobsters, with the help of the internet, added to the dinner entertainment.

"'Why do lobsters make lousy friends?'" she asked, reading from her phone.

"Why?"

"'Because they're shellfish.'"

His turn. "A lobster reported a crime to the police. They asked him to be more Pacific."

"Did you hear about the lobster who couldn't go to the gym because he pulled a mussel?"

"What do you call a lobster that's afraid of tight spaces?"

"I don't know," she said as he buttered two more thick slices of bread and put one on her plate and the other on his.

"*Claws*trophobic."

"What about one that's overworked?"

"Um…a…frustr*acean*."

"Ha. Very good."

They volleyed back and forth until they finished eating.

"How does a lobster answer the phone?" she asked, finishing her jokes.

"Shello?"

They put the dishes into one of the dishwashers. Miranda had let them know the housekeepers' schedules, which Ras memorized.

"Let's take some dessert and tea upstairs for later," she suggested, grabbing what she wanted and then stopping to open the refrigerator. "Good night, Lucky. Good night, Diamond. Good night, Amphitrite. Good night, Hampton. Have a chill rest."

"What are we going to do with them tomorrow?"

"Let the housekeeping staff enjoy them. I'm sure they'll be able to deal with it once they have their morning *claw*fee." With that, they shut the lights in the kitchen and went giggling upstairs.

Out the bedroom windows, the sky was a shimmering blue, the moon pearly as it cast beams onto the ocean. Even Ras, who'd been around the earth, had to take in the tranquil beauty of it all. Not to mention the beauty of the woman in the room, who he'd come to feel more natural with than without.

She lit the candles that had been thoughtfully placed throughout the suite, no doubt left by staff who acknowledged the romance of the setting. With that flickering orange of the flames surrounding them, Ras slipped off the sundress Gracie had on and all but gasped at the glow of her skin. With only undies beneath, he hastily slid them of. Quickly shedding his own clothes, he pulled her onto the bed. "You've changed my world, Gracie. I'll never be the same after this time we've spent together."

"I know," she replied gently, running her fingernails

along his arm, shocking his body to attention. "I will always remember this."

"I don't want it to ever end."

"It has to, Ras. You have your duties to fulfill."

"Yes. My obligation above all else is to produce an heir, so that when my reign is done, the monarchy will continue."

"Even if you have to marry someone you wouldn't have chosen."

"You've shown me…" Ras cut himself off. He did not want to say aloud what he suspected was in his heart. He didn't want her to hear it. He didn't want to hear it, either. Because it was of no relevance anyway. She understood the situation exactly as it was. And if he had been an unattached man, royal or not, she would never have let things go this far. His very unavailability was what made this possible. She knew how to protect herself and so only allowed this because soon he'd fly to the other side of the planet and they'd never see each other again. For her as much as for himself, he'd bite back the words that he wanted to sing.

"You might be surprised about the heir, though. You could end up with a child to adore." Her hand went to her belly, a motion he hadn't seen her make in a while. He tapped a light kiss onto her shoulder.

"My parents adored me. I could see it in their eyes. They loved each other, and I was an extension, a product of that love. That made all the difference."

She measured what he said. "I would have thought that, too. But when I was pregnant…"

A lump formed in his throat that she had to say *when I was pregnant* knowing there was no baby at the end of that reminiscence. "Continue."

"Even though Davis wasn't a good man and I never

felt secure in my future with him, having a baby grow in my belly was the most amazing thing." Her voice took on a crackly tone he hadn't heard before. "Somehow, as soon as I found out I was pregnant, I envisioned that little being inside me. He, or she, I never did find out, was real to me. My blessing and my responsibility. It was truly awesome."

"I can't imagine how painful that loss must have been. Especially without a partner."

"It was almost as if the baby was my partner. Before that horrible day in the bus station bathroom when the stabbing pain told me it was over. It was like the baby and I were invincible. Together, we could do anything. Everything that my parents were, and weren't, didn't matter. I was going to set everything straight, right all the wrongs."

"You'll have the opportunity again if you want."

"I told you, no men, no babies. It's just me against the world now."

"If I had the chance to, I'd show you that wasn't how it had to be." He wrapped his arms tightly around her, completely encircling her. The way he wanted it. They way he'd always want it. The way it would never be.

Gracie woke early and turned to admire Ras's sculpted cheekbones and jaw in repose. Not wanting to wake him, she slinked out of bed and slipped on a pink silk robe, tying it at the waist as she edged out of one of the double doors onto the deck. Her bare feet padded the wooden planks to reach the back staircase, which she trotted down while admiring the pale sunrise. Reaching the first floor, she went straight for the kitchen. There she met Ini, the kitchen manager.

"I'm Gracie. Did you get our note from last night?"

"Yes, ma'am. I come in very early. The groundskeeper

removed the lobsters from the refrigerator and brought them to my *grandmalita*'s house. We'll have a fine dinner, thank you. Do you want coffee? I'll be happy to make a tray before I leave and place it on the table outside the master bedroom."

"That would be great."

Gracie stepped back outside, the early- morning air moist and thick, feeling the coolness under her shoeless feet. She went out to the edge of the walkway that led to the bay. The dock had a small paddleboat, kayaks, even surfboards. She turned around to look at the mansion, and the open door on the upper deck helped her locate the master bedroom she'd just came out from. Where Ras was hopefully still resting in peaceful slumber.

Cinching the waist of her robe again, she absentmindedly caressed the lapel up and down, her finger mimicking one of the many kinds of touch Ras had bestowed on her. The way he had held her so tightly she thought he'd never let her go. The way she didn't want him to.

"What's going on down there?" Ras appeared on the deck. His hairless chest was bare. That she could see the tops of his pelvic bones above the deck's railing made her believe he was totally naked head to toe. He raked his long fingers through his hair.

"Just breathing in the morning. I didn't want to wake you."

"How kind of you."

His smile would give the noonday sun a run for its money.

The scene was idyllic. She could imagine it was real. That they were together, coupled, partnered, friends. All of which she'd have never dreamed of as a child. When she was brutally alone with a neglect that branded into her skin like a hot iron. Unwanted, cast aside, insignificant. When she was young, she thought she'd done something to deserve her parents' lack of interest in her. But by adolescence a steely instinct in her grew, telling her that she was a victim of circumstance. That it wasn't her fault. Although she'd always have that cross to bear.

She heard the sound of a truck backing out along the driveway that flanked the backyard. Ini was driving, with the groundskeeper in the passenger seat. They waved goodbye. Ini wasn't kidding that they really did work an early shift.

That left her alone with her own personal angel who'd been sent to her when she was making the gigantic changes in her life that had taken all of her wherewithal. The fates were so benevolent to send Ras to her. She was so, so grateful. Why were tears spilling down her face?

"There should be a tray with coffee right outside the bedroom door," she yelled up, wiping her eyes with the backs of her fingers.

"Are you coming up? Better yet, I'll bring it down. Let's sit outside."

She held her breath long enough to get the drops to stop falling from her eyes and called, "That would be lovely."

Last night was the most she'd ever confided about the miscarriage. Sure, Jen had come to visit, and brought her sandwiches and extra blankets. But there hadn't been that much to say. The doctor explained that these things occurred with a prevalence higher than people realized, but that Gracie was young and healthy and there was no reason she couldn't start trying for another baby soon. The doctor, of course, not knowing that the father of the miscarried fetus was not around and not coming back into the picture. Sure, on occasion, she'd considered using a sperm donor or other alternative arrangements people made. But the ordeal was too much of a heartbreak to return from. Losing the baby was another desertion, and she was not going to take any more chances on that. She'd been left enough for a lifetime. Her edict was signed, sealed and delivered. Then she'd met Ras.

"Why are you crying?" Ras approached with both the tray and a worried look on his face. He'd pulled on a pair of pajama bottoms.

"No reason," she told him, brushing more tears away. Neither of them bought her false bravado.

"No one cries for no reason," he said as he put the tray down at a table and chairs by the pool. He wrapped her into his arms. The way he constantly hugged her like that was almost unbearable in its promise.

"I'm just happy, Ras. You've given me this amazing opportunity. And you've been so nice to me."

"Your parents and that horrible Davis were fools," he whispered into her ear. "I wish I could spend every day of the rest of our lives showing you how you should be treated."

She laid her face against his smooth chest and tried to compose herself, knowing that what he said could not come true and wondering how she was going to live without him.

While they had breakfast, he placed an order with a grocery store for the ingredients he needed for the Pad Kra Pao and Som Tum he'd promised to make her.

"I need green papaya, fish sauce, dried shrimp, long beans, palm sugar," he said, going over his list with the grocer. It being the Hamptons, a wide variety of gourmet and international foods were available for the asking so Ras was sure he'd get all the specific items he needed. That a queen had taught her son the crown prince to cook a few family favorite dishes tickled Gracie's heart.

Not to mention the permanent taste of bitterness that her parents hadn't even provided her with food half of the time when she was growing up. "And you have the holy basil? It can't be sweet basil…oh, from a local grower? Fantastic!"

"All set?" she asked when he was finally done with the long list.

"Be prepared to be dazzled." He winked at her.

Without another word, he stood and slid off the pajama bottom he had on. And, in one fluid motion, dove naked headfirst into the deep end of the pool and swam across its considerable length before his head popped up on the other side. He shook out his hair and smoothed it back with two palms. "Join me."

It was a week of relaxation and bliss. He showed her how to use a mortar and pestle, and together they created those spicy and enticing dishes from his childhood that made her tongue tingle. From the house's extensive digital music library, she played him all of her favorite songs and they danced naked around the empty rooms of the mansion, arms outstretched like children. She beat him at billiards, and then they used the pool table for a different purpose. They also tested out all of the other beds in the house…for comfort. They went out on the water every day. One night they made a bonfire in the backyard pit and roasted marshmallows on long sticks. Feeding each other the gooey mess necessitated licking it from each other's fingers. They took long walks on the beach, so long, in fact, that sometimes they'd just collapse to rest a bit before continuing, lying on their backs in the pillowy dry sand, watching the sun come up or fade down. Ras felt safe. He left another voice mail for the king that he was fine and would see him soon.

Too quickly, the week was done. "So it's into New

York City tomorrow," he said while stroking the hills and valleys of her body as they lay on a thick rug in front of one of the downstairs fireplaces.

"Yes, sir. I've chosen a hotel penthouse with a private entrance and elevator."

"The big city and the masses."

"Would you rather not go?"

"No. I'd love to see New York. With you."

"If it's okay with you, we'll go to the Met Museum and to a Broadway show, and I've got reservations for a trendy Scandinavian restaurant." His brows crossed. "What's wrong?"

"Only that it will be my last week with you. You're the sight I most want to see. How will we say goodbye after next week?"

She gulped air. "What choice do we have?"

Bright lights, big town. The driver who had picked them up at the house in Bridgehampton now opened the door for them to exit at the side entrance to the five-star Manhattan hotel where their personal elevator awaited. Per the instructions they had received, she punched in a key code at a small gate and they gained entry. Inside the elevator there was only one button, labeled *P*, and up they shot to the sixty-fourth floor.

"This is even better than the photos on the website," Gracie stated. She was right, the penthouse was magnificent.

A master bedroom was partitioned off with half-walls that came from the center of the space like spokes in a wheel. From there, they passed through to the master bath, also partitioned off to create separate areas. Farther around the circle was a dressing area and relaxation room. Next came a full living and dining suite.

"You did good. I love it." With all the windows, it was like having a home on the observation deck of the Empire State Building. From the green of Central Park to the north and the towers of Wall Street to the south, Ras was reminded that Manhattan was the start of his journey, meeting beautiful Gracie as the cruise ship made its way around the Statue of Liberty. Cuban coffee and sexy dancing in that Miami club, what an odyssey it had truly been. Though, on leaving his father at the UN he'd had no idea that it would turn out to be a voyage of the heart as well. One that would change him forever.

But there was still a glorious five days left. He turned to his tour guide to ask, "What are we doing first?"

"Tonight, we have a box at the opera." She moved through to the dressing room and opened the closet doors wide. A tuxedo and all of its accessories hung waiting. "I hope you don't mind, but I ordered this to be delivered. I took a guess at your size."

"You are a clever one. You are really getting the hang of this." He gave a full press of his lips to hers. Although he would be delighted to apply a half million additional kisses to her from head to toe, he refrained. "What will you be wearing?" he asked, remembering that she had some pretty dresses but nothing to wear to the opera.

Opening the closet on the other side of the room, a shimmery gown encrusted with crystals, sparkling shoes and a silky wrap were ready. "I also rented this, charged to you, of course." She grinned.

Carried by the strong emotions of *La Traviata*, they enjoyed a bottle of wine in their opera box. Once the performance ended, they stepped out into the night at the Lincoln Center and walked around the fountain. Gracie was resplendent in her iridescent gown. It really could have hardly been more glamorous. Befitting a prince with the love of his life. He internally cautioned himself to get that thought out of his mind. The longer he let it live, the harder it was going to be to forget it. Not that he ever would.

Then, suddenly, it started to rain so they ducked into their waiting limo. Back at the penthouse, Ras removed his jacket and tie and sat down on one of the couches. Gracie slipped out of her dress and into a robe to join him. He wanted to check his phone for the weather forecast to see if that might necessitate any changes to their itinerary tomorrow. Happy to read that the light rain was expected to pass by morning, on a whim he decided to check a news outlet for the weather in the Gulf of Thailand, something he hadn't done in over two weeks. While there had been heavy downpours, that wasn't the news that caught his eye.

At the bottom of the screen was the click button for the *People* section and right next to it, sure as day, was a photo of His Royal Highness Crown Prince Rasmayada of Ko Pha Lano and Gracie Russo holding hands.

His gut sank. "Oh, no."

"What is it?" Gracie moved over to sit right next to him and he showed her the photo. He clicked through, dreading what he might find.

"Ras, I'm so sorry." There were two more photos of them. One with his arm around her, one a closer shot of them smiling at each other like newlyweds. "These were taken at that restaurant in Washington."

"Remember that hostess who I thought looked at me suspiciously?"

"The one who showed us to our table."

"Then she passed by us again and she was on her phone. She was taking photos. Which she must have sold."

"I'd like to report her to the restaurant management."

"Sure. Although the damage has already been done."

"Disgusting."

He tapped into one then another of the gossip sites that concentrated on young royals and the photos had made their way everywhere, just as he knew they would.

His Royal Highness is having quite a bachelor's last hurrah before marriage.

Ko Pha Lano's crown prince doesn't have eyes only for his princess.

And on it went.

Equally awful were new photos of Vajhana with her British earl. The gossip hounds didn't miss anything. Aboard a boat on the Seine with the glistening night lights of the Eiffel Tower behind them, the princess with a designer coat falling off her. "She and I deserve each other. We are royal embarrassments."

He stared out to the New York skyline, feeling Gracie's warm body beside him. Now he questioned the wisdom of this whole trip. He'd gained what his mother had wanted him to, but he'd taken it too far. She'd wanted him to explore himself. In the process, his spirit was set free. And it had found Gracie. His heart had discovered a reason to beat. It had learned the most fundamental emotion a human could have. Which would hurt much worse than never knowing love at all.

CHAPTER TEN

THE PARTY WAS OVER. It had been going to end anyway. Yet Gracie wished it was on its own terms, not having it decided for them by some restaurant hostess with no ethics. "We knew we were doomed, Ras. Fortune put us together to bolster us to walk our own paths." Her spin didn't even sound convincing to her, so she was sure it wouldn't to Ras, either. Still, she pressed on. "We still have a few more days. We can make the most of it." Yet she knew she wouldn't. Couldn't. Everything had been spoiled.

"You're right," he uttered in a low voice that was just as unconvincing. It was late but they still sat on the penthouse couch, overlooking the magnificence of New York. They were as physically close as could be; she could feel his body next to hers from shoulder to ankle. "The most of it…" he echoed, but trailed off.

For all of the constant conversation they'd had, there was suddenly nothing to say. Eventually, they got up and went to bed. Lying naked, her in his arms, they didn't engage in the celestial lovemaking that had shown them both pleasures sent from heaven. They held each other nonetheless, not wanting to let go any sooner than they had to. She woke up alone in the gray of morning. She found Ras at the dining room table, drinking coffee on hotel china that was poured from a silver pot he'd no doubt had delivered.

"I couldn't think of what to order for breakfast. Can you take care of it?"

"Of course," she replied with a squeeze to his shoulder. She poured a coffee and sat down opposite him.

"I'm sorry you and I, what we shared, has to end with a taint," he said as if he'd been pondering it. "With a bad taste in my mouth. Someday I'll wear the crown, I'll produce the heir and carry on the legacy. But my record is marred. There will always be this as a footnote, showing me to have been reckless and impulsive. And you're not a footnote, Gracie."

"It wasn't wrong for you to have followed your instincts."

"I've let my people down. I've let my father down."

"Ras, your mother wanted…"

"I don't think she would have wanted this."

"I don't think she would have wanted you to marry someone you didn't love. Not from what you've told me of her."

He almost angrily snapped a retort but pulled it back and pierced her with his gaze. And took a slow breath. "What now?" It seemed like a question loaded with layers.

There was only one she could address. "Let's go to a downtown deli for a ridiculously big breakfast and then see some Soho galleries."

The idea brought a crack to the corner of Ras's mouth. "Carry on regardless, is that right?"

"Or we could stay here and mope around the penthouse all day."

He stretched his hand across the table for hers. He

brought it to his mouth and kissed it. "Oh, my Gracie, you are one of a kind."

After their bellies were bursting from breakfast, Gracie created a route through the streets of Soho for them to walk. Despite it not being a particularly bright morning, he wore sunglasses and was dressed in faded jeans and his black leather jacket. They roamed the blocks where artists carried large canvases into their studios and boutiques sold small-label fashions. She'd researched and picked out a couple of galleries to visit. They discussed the art as they strolled. Honestly, though, the solemnity covered them like the dark clouds above. The joy was gone. Only the inevitable remained.

That night they dressed nicely for their chef's table at one of New York's most talked about restaurants that served updated versions of traditional Scandinavian food. They were brought into a private dining room. Although the smoked, dried and pickled fishes and the savory dumplings were delicious, Ras and Gracie were deflated and there were lulls in the conversation as both stared absently around the silent room that almost felt like a prison. She understood most fully that this was how Ras lived, separated from much of the world; his life could indeed be very lonely without the right person to share it with.

He finally said, "I think I should just go home tomorrow."

Her eyes opened wide, and she willed back the tears that were threatening. "I see."

"The sooner I get back to Ko Pha Lano, the sooner I can be seen fulfilling my typical schedule. The more I do that, the more my prenuptial follies will fade into the background. Hopefully Vajhana's, too. And our people can begin focusing on the upcoming wedding, which always raises morale."

"Will it raise yours?"

"I will do what is expected of me. It shouldn't be such a great sacrifice."

Giving him up would be a great sacrifice to her. He was right, though; he was born to rule over his people and that's what he'd do. Emotions had no part in the equation. Which did nothing to silence the thudding in Gracie's gut.

She scrapped their plans to go to a jazz club after dinner as neither of them was in the mood. In fact, Ras wanted to go back to the hotel and make arrangements for a private plane to fly him back to the island the next day. She began packing her things, as she'd be leaving as well if he wasn't going to be sharing the penthouse with her.

He offered to fly her anywhere she wanted, but her next destination was already set. After touching base at Jen's apartment, she'd go forward with her plans to rent a car and learn about New England B&Bs, where she'd be able to acquire complimentary nights from the owners. How gorgeous the changing leaves of autumn would have been, seen with her arm through Ras's, but that was never on the books and nothing had changed on that score. She tossed and turned in bed, not even able to relish her last night with this man who had rocked her world. Her stomach hurt. Perhaps the salted fish had been too strong.

In the morning, a car was waiting for them and they left the hotel as invisibly as they had come in. Ras had booked a plane at a private airport and asked her to see him off, after which the car would take her to Jen's. They laced fingers in the back seat, where she tried to memorize the feel of those big square hands that would never touch her again.

"What was your favorite place that we visited?" she decided to ask, even though chitchat wasn't going to ease the pain that saying goodbye was going to bring. "Did you see what you wanted to?"

"Gracie," he answered quietly, "what difference does any of that make? I met you. I got to spend this time with you that was far more important than a monument or a tourist attraction."

Once they arrived at the airport, a crew member took Ras's bags and they walked out onto the runway where his plane was waiting. The boarding staircase had been lowered and stood waiting for its one and only passenger. It was almost unbearable to look at. Each stair would take him farther and farther away from her.

They kissed passionately. Her hands slowly traversed up his back until she could wrap them around his neck. They hugged for dear life. Tears streamed down her face, uncontrollable. They held each other so tightly that the world disappeared. Until they were frozen in time, no airport, no island on the other side of the world. Only him. Only for one last moment.

Finally, it was he who broke the hold and took her by the shoulders. "This is it."

"I know."

"I'll think of you every day of my life."

"And I will you. Remember the things your mother told you. Stay human, stay grounded, stay loving."

"Goodbye, Gracie."

"Goodbye, Your Royal Highness."

With that, he pivoted and headed toward the plane. He had to. A minute longer and he never would. He was off to do what was right. She watched him ascend every step, each one stabbing her deeper as she knew it would. When he reached the top, he turned to give one last wave.

Then he ducked his head to step into the plane, the last she would ever see of the most magnificent man on earth.

Ras kept his eyes on the window as the plane ascended to the skies. He didn't move his watch point until the clouds obscured the skyscrapers of New York, turning the past weeks into a puffy hallucination. The cruise. Miami. Savannah. Charleston. DC. Bridgehampton. And then New York. Had that all actually happened or had it been one long fantasy? Had Gracie really happened?

He sucked in an inordinate amount of air as he finally faced front in his seat. Upon boarding, he'd hardly noticed the amenities on the plane. There was a bedroom and full bathroom so that he could sleep and shower. A crew dedicated to his every comfort. Which began with an attendant placing a tray on the side table next to his seat. It contained everything from a wet washcloth for his face to a plate of finger food to a cappuccino, and a card spotlighting movies and podcasts he might find diverting during the flight. All very well intentioned although he stared at it blankly with no interest. The only thing he cared about was what he had left behind.

He instructed himself to take another set of measured breaths. And, with each exhalation, to let out what was to now become his distant past. To release it into the world as simply positive energy that should find its way to someone who needed it next. Because he had no use for it anymore. He reclined his chair into a chaise and breathed himself into a nap. When he woke, he was grateful that a couple of hours had passed. Since he was headed away from the person his heart had come to define as the very definition of home, he just wanted to get back to the island as soon as possible.

In fact, he opened his tablet on which he'd downloaded

a prospectus from a manufacturing company that his father and King Yodfa were considering. He did an internet search to look into published reports on what effect similar industries had on the environment, and it was as he thought. Depletion of natural resources and polluted waters were hard to avoid without expenses so prohibitive they left no profit. Ras still didn't think this was the best direction to go in to bring more employment and prosperity to the islands.

He was going to confront his father to strongly disapprove of these proposals. While he wouldn't be king for hopefully several decades of his father's good health, he would assert his beliefs and not let them fall on deaf ears. He reviewed the proposals he himself had been compiling, large-scale marine conservation and ecotourism. A smile crossed his face. Gracie knew a lot about ecotourism and conservation. He'd forever be inspired by her ambitions, her wherewithal to overcome all she'd faced. In spirit, across the miles but soul to soul, he'd always be proud of her. And he'd want her to be proud of him.

"Oh, you're back," King Maho said with a bite of sarcasm as Ras marched through the central hall of the palace toward his quarters.

"I am, Your Majesty." He stopped in front of his father and bowed his head. Then, like it or not, he gave his father a hug. His absence had not been meant to hurt the king. He was genuinely sorry if it did. "Had you been following my whereabouts?"

The king resisted his son's embrace at first, perhaps to punish him. Ras's insistence finally resulted in a brief hug with a pat on the back from his father who answered, "One of our people saw you board the cruise ship, I received your voice mails, and left it at that."

"I appreciate you not pulling me away from my trip."
Away from Gracie.

"No matter, though, as I was kept regularly informed
along with the public that you and your fiancée have been
traipsing halfway across the world with other compan-
ions. I hope the two of you can get your prenuptial restlessness out of the way so that the wedding can proceed
as planned."

"I'm sorry to have been a worry. You remember what
my mother said…"

"Yes, son, I remember everything about your mother."
The great man paused as remembrances softened his
expression. Which he then caught and corrected. "Fine,
you've had your ramble. You're to enter into a mutually
advantageous marriage in a few weeks. There's much
work to do for our subjects, our primary purpose. I'll
expect no further…distractions."

"About our guardianship of the island, Father." He
looked the king in the eye. This wasn't easy. His father
had suffered so much. But as a result, he'd lost touch. He
was probably unable to absorb that many peoples of the
world were unwilling to see economic growth as a justi-
fication for doing harm to the earth. His father and King
Yodfa had old ideas that didn't fit with what was important to the new generation. "I read the final prospectus
for the partnership with King Yodfa. And I don't like it."

"I don't believe you are to be king any time soon, and
while I sit on the throne we shall do things my way."

"Do you hear yourself, Father? Single-minded, not at
all willing to acknowledge another's point of view?" He'd
become both hardheaded and hard-hearted. Ras understood, more than ever. The man had lost the love of his
life, the only woman who had ever meant anything to
him. After that, days and nights had just become an ex-

istence. He had no enthusiasm for new ideas or to achieve great things. The vigor had been drained from him.

With his lips pressed into a thin line, Ras silently promised Gracie that he wouldn't let that become his fate, too. He owed it to her not to shut down.

"You must be tired from your…pleasure trip, Ras. Get settled back in. I'm sure your good senses will return."

"Oh, believe me, my…" Ras stopped himself. He had taken a very long way home. His father was right about that. Ras had to think of a different way to broach conflicts with the king. "If you'll excuse me, Your Majesty. Princess Vajhana is coming. I thought she and I would have a private dinner on the terrace."

"Very good. I'm sure the two of you have a lot to talk about."

After attending to the paperwork that had been stacked on his desk while he was away, he met Vajhana on the helipad at the castle. "Ras, *daahling*."

Yes, she really did use that exaggerated tone of voice like she was a movie star from olden times. She tripped a little bit on her high-heeled shoes and grabbed his arm. He reached to steady her, having forgotten how bony she was. He'd gotten used to Gracie's ripe and pliable body.

"Let's relax with a glass of white. I brought my tablet with so many wedding decisions to make."

Ras snarled a bit at the prospect of discussing whether pale peach or pastel orange roses would make better centerpieces at the reception. Didn't anyone understand that the wedding day was just an expense of money and pomp? What counted was a life together, the day in, and day out of how people treated each other and viewed themselves. One person understood that. And it wasn't Vajhana.

After he'd helped pick out as many songs for the band

to play as he could, he adjusted his chair so that he was close and eye to eye to his intended. "Princess, I want you to listen to me. I did not appreciate one bit seeing photos of you carousing with that British earl. It was unseemly and beneath both of us."

"I could say the same about you. I was actually kind of surprised, Ras, when my cousin sent me those photos from Washington. You usually keep under the radar, don't you?"

"Yes, that was a horrible misjudgment." The photos, that was. He would never in a million years describe Gracie as a misjudgment. Quite the opposite. "I won't do it again. Can you say the same?"

This was the woman he was going to spend his forever with. They had to establish better ground rules for their relationship. "We still have our old agreement, don't we, Ras? About how we're going to survive being matched up by our fathers with no say in the matter."

"Behind closed doors. Not on the lap of an earl. Can we agree to that?"

"I'll try." This couldn't be easy for Vajhana. She hadn't asked for any of this, either. They barely knew each other past the superficial. Perhaps deep in her heart she was also lamenting that she'd never have a chance to fall in love.

"We're to have children. We must appear as a family." His jaw clenched.

Oh, Mother, he called out in his mind. *I want a marriage like yours. I want to love like you did. A love that made you and Father both better people. Better parents. Better leaders. I won't have that with Vajhana. Who am I serving in this lie? Who is this best for?*

"Jen, thanks again for letting me crash here these past couple of days," Gracie said, coming out of the bathroom while toweling her wet hair. Her friend was eating a piece of toast at the tiny two-person kitchen table wedged between the refrigerator and the sofa where Gracie had been sleeping. It was a compact apartment as far as could be from the penthouse where she'd been living that *other* life. The one that had died on a private airport runway days ago.

"You're heading out today?"

"Yup. I pick up the rental car in Midtown, and my first B&B is in Massachusetts."

"The autumn leaves are going to be gorgeous. Why do you look so gray?"

Gracie laughed. "I look gray?"

"You know, pale. Is it because of that guy?" Gracie hadn't felt it right to give out Ras's identity, so she'd only told Jen that she'd met a man on the cruise and they'd ended up doing some additional traveling together on his yacht and in the Hamptons.

"My stomach has been funny. Must be something I'm eating." After getting ready, she grabbed her two travel bags packed and ready by the door.

"Have some toast before you go."

"I want to hit the road."

"Okay, take a piece with you."

Gracie nodded and took the toast and a bottle of water. "Thanks again for continuing to keep my four boxes. They're really all I've got now." She had that roiling in her belly again that brought her hand to hold her stomach. She'd broken herself of the habit of doing that whenever memories of the past were conjured up. There was no reason to start again. She gave Jen a hug and headed out the door with the very real feeling that more changes were to come.

Driving out of the city was great. Obviously, she

couldn't snub being driven in limos and town cars, but there was something to be said for getting behind the wheel herself. She spent the drive to her first destination absolutely *not* wondering what a handsome prince nine thousand miles away was doing. *Not* remembering what his embrace felt like. *Not* recalling the luminescence in his big eyes when he looked at her. Definitely *not* replaying the rumble of his robust laughter that echoed through the wide-open rooms in a Bridgehampton mansion. In fact, she so *didn't* hear the sound of his voice saying her name that she cranked up some loud music to keep her company as she careered down the highway.

"This building is a hundred and fifty years old," the owner of the Beaves Inn located in the Berkshire Mountains told Gracie as she gave her a tour. "As you can see, we've kept the Victorian decor in all the rooms. Yours is one of our most requested rooms, ultrafeminine, with cream, peach and sea green as our inspiration colors. Guests love it."

"I can see why. The white iron bedframe. The fireplace." Would Ras have liked this? His tastes tended toward the modern. Gracie smiled at the older woman who was rightly so proud of her property.

"Will you be joining us for dinner? We serve a three-course meal with two menu options for an additional charge. If not, I can direct you to half a dozen local restaurants."

Dinner didn't sound too good. She'd forced herself to finish the toast that Jen had given her in New York. Maybe sinking into that claw-foot bathtub would soothe her tummy ache. "No, but, thank you so much."

"I'll let you get unpacked."

"Thank you."

A while later, after deciding against the bath for fear of

nausea, Gracie chose to go for a walk. The air was crisp and, indeed, the fall foliage was just as spectacular as it had been touted. The leaves in almost psychedelic hues of red, gold and orange were like observing art. In fact, that's what they were. Nature's art.

She wished that she could be sharing the moment with Ras. She wished that she could share any moment with him. As she walked the dirt path, the sun's rays casting shards of light against the flora, she felt at one with the world. Connected, part of something. Even though she was alone, she was the opposite of lonely. Because she had started living. She'd done it. She'd evolved into the next version of herself. Her truth blossomed like a seedling that finally had enough light and water to grow. It was Ras who had tended her garden. He was the nourishment she'd needed. He'd given her something she'd never had before. Love.

Love.

Not a word she'd ever thought was going to pertain to her. It was a word she didn't have faith in. Because love might lead to hope. And, in her experience, hope always led to disappointment. The child who waited by the window for the parents who didn't come home at night. Or the young woman who hid in the bathroom until she heard the man she'd come to dread walking out the front door. No, hope wasn't supposed to be included in her marching orders. She was going to exist on sheer self-sufficiency and determination.

Why did the fates have a different idea? It was the cruelest of jokes they'd played to make her fall in love with a man who could never be hers. *Fall in love*. Yup, there was no other way to describe it. She'd tumbled head over heels in love with His Royal Highness Crown Prince Rasmayada of Ko Pha Lano. Her heart clenched and then that swell in her belly did, too. She loved him. With all of her heart and soul and every cell in her being. Tears streamed out of her eyes as she trekked, fallen leaves crunching under her feet. She cried because now she had more to tote. The burdens of her past would have to make room so that she could keep the love she had for Ras close for the rest of her life. A job she'd accept willingly. Her recollections of moments with him were the best possessions she had. She'd cherish them forever.

Gracie spent the next days touring New England, taking in breathtaking displays of color. She stayed in a room that had a mahogany sleigh bed and another with a built-in window seat. She went for a bike ride and came across a covered bridge. She'd never seen one before. It was agonizing not being able to show it to Ras, but she convinced herself that she was in some way. That he was with her wherever she went.

One day toward the end of her travels around the area, she was walking around a gentle lake, the reflections of the trees and leaves mirrored on the surface of the still water. Nausea rolled through her insides, and she ran quickly to a trash receptacle to vomit. The sensations in her body that she'd been denying had been increasing. She did some mental math and couldn't ignore the solution to her equation.

The rain forest shower on the yacht. Making love under the jets of the water. They hadn't thought to bring condoms in with them.

Later, she asked the innkeeper to direct her to the nearest pharmacy. After the short drive and once back in her room with its claret-painted walls and Italian mosaic-tiled floors, she performed a very modern test. Its answer came as no surprise. It was more than merely memories of Ras she was carrying.

CHAPTER ELEVEN

RAS PACED HIS QUARTERS, looking out from the cliff where his rooms stood. He thought he might pace until his shoes were worn to shreds, letting the wind whoosh in from his windows as he trod back and forth, back and forth. His discontent left him tired in the daytime and wide-awake in the wee hours. His daily schedule was met without gusto. He was unhappy with every conversation he'd had with his father since returning to the palace. And despite his intentions when he got on that plane to come home after his voyage, he wasn't able to put it behind him. Quite the opposite. All he did was think about the trip. Not about the Spanish moss in Savannah or the lobsters in the Hamptons. *Her.* He couldn't stop thinking about *her.* The woman who had transformed the universe as he knew it. A world he couldn't seem to fit back into. Plain and simple, there was no ground without her. Without Gracie.

His lack of kilter was especially worse when he was with his fiancée, which was quite a sorry state of affairs. Vajhana could hardly seem sillier to him, a spoiled real-life princess who didn't care about anything but herself. With no interest in building a working pact with him or in the future of their nations. He found it hard to conceive of her being a good mother, either, when the time came.

It wasn't her fault. She didn't really want this marriage, either. It also wasn't her fault that she wasn't the woman he was in love with.

He stopped moving long enough to stare out past the palace grounds. Arms crossed, a stance with legs apart, tension stiffened his body. Nothing would ever be right without Gracie. Nothing ever could. He needed to reunite with her, to profess his love in case she hadn't guessed how he felt. To beg her to be his forevermore. At any cost. Yet the reality of that need produced almost insurmountable obstacles. To call off the wedding to Vajhana would be to disobey not one but two kings. Gracie was a commoner. An American. No ties to the region whatsoever. At least his mother had come from a family of standing on the island. Gracie didn't even know the whereabouts of her parents. It was almost impossible.

He retrieved the little Gullah basket they'd bought in Charleston that he now kept on his desk by day and beside his bed at night. He ran his thumb along the tight weave of the grass. Although it was a small item it was solid, sturdy, enduring. He'd told Gracie to hold his kisses in hers.

Almost impossible. *Almost*. Why, he thought as he returned to his pacing while holding the basket in his fingers, shouldn't he have the love of his life? It would transform him into a stronger man. More importantly was the opposite concern. That he didn't know what would become of him if he didn't have the woman who made him whole at his side. He'd be beaten down. Embittered. His insides would turn to ash like his father's had. Preventing him from becoming the king he should be. He had to have Gracie back. Impossible. *Almost*.

"Your Majesty." He charged into his father's rooms

after calling the king's personal secretary to make sure he was available. "I haven't told you everything about my time in the States."

He explained it all, from the Cuban coffees to the fact that the woman he was photographed with was not a vacation fling. That he was madly, desperately, eternally in love.

The king's response was anything but what Ras had hoped. A decidedly inflexible, "Absolutely not," came roaring out of King Maho's mouth. "I told you this when you first returned home from your little carefree whirlwind. You have a duty to our people. That's the only calling you'll answer to."

Ras was unable to accept the answer, so strong were his feelings for Gracie. Why was his father entitled to love yet Ras wasn't? It was because the king had forgotten. Forgotten what life had been like until he'd buried a wife long before he should have. Forgotten the bond they'd shared, the joy, the closeness. The way any problem could be solved if they put their heads together. Forgotten the little smiles and the romantic gestures that made every day special. Or maybe it was that he remembered it all too well and was determined to protect his son from the heartbreak he'd faced.

King Maho's face changed as if he indeed was overcome by the sadness for what had been lost. His eyes opened into glassy circles like those of a child. But only for the briefest of moments. He stood up tall. "You and Vajhana will marry as agreed," he continued. "And that's the last I will hear of it."

In anger and defiance, Ras stormed out of the palace and off the grounds. He had to get away from the palace for a moment. The time in the US was successful in showing him that he could be a man among men, walking freely. Especially as no one expected to see him roaming through the streets alone. Although royal surveillance had followed him, they were in plain clothes and had the decency to stay a considerable distance behind.

Ras had to find a way to get through to his father, make him see what was best for the family. Once he met Gracie he'd be sure to like her; that kindness, so like Queen Sirind's, would be palpable to his father. They could make this work. Ras *had* to. Being with Gracie was life or death for him. Without her, he'd have no heart at all.

What if she wouldn't have him back? She was deeply into her New England tour now. As a matter of fact, it was coming to an end if his mental calendar served him right. Knowing her, she'd secured her next undertaking, which was to visit and rate the luxury accommodations in Boston. By now she'd probably booked clients into the places she'd visited with him, had probably made her first commissions and was off and running in her career. He couldn't bear to tear her away from something that was so important to her.

An idea struck him like a thunderbolt. It was a solution to a multitude of problems all at once. It was easily the best idea he'd ever had. Although there were many steps to take before it could be put into place.

Thoughts racing through his mind, he noticed two people walking their small dogs on leashes along the street, one going north and one south. When the dogs met they began circling and smelling each other, bouncing around each other at the thrill of a new acquaintance. One was a Yorkshire terrier and the other a Shih Tzu. Which of course reminded him of his childhood Shih Tzu, Lucky. How much fun Ras would have with his parents and Lucky, how happy his fa…

The second great idea of the day brought a mischievous smile to the prince's face. He pulled his phone from his pocket.

Later that day, he asked his father to meet him on the west lawn. That was an area on the grounds that had always been just for the family's use. The press was kept away, and no addresses or large functions took place there. As his father approached, Ras let go of what he hoped was going to be a messenger of détente. Who went running straight toward the king.

"What on earth is this?" King Maho shouted as he closed the gap between himself and Ras. The king bent down to pet the Shih Tzu who was jumping around him. The first dog in the palace since Lucky died.

"Remember Lucky, Father?"

"Of course I do."

"How he used to run around this lawn fetching sticks until he was panting with exhaustion."

"Yet always wanting to do it again," the king chuckled. Ras couldn't think of the last time he'd heard his father laugh. The king froze in place, looked into Ras's eyes and then shifted his gaze to the middle distance of the lawn, as if memories were flooding back to him.

"Remember those happy times, Father?" Ras pushed the point. "With mother so fun loving and caring? Her inner spirit touched everyone on our island."

"She loved everyone in the world, son," the king murmured in a soft voice.

"But no one more than you and I."

"Those were some…exceptional times."

"Gracie is like that, Father. She's the warmest person I've ever met besides mother. She's impossible not to love."

The dog was hopping onto the king's leg, which prompted him to reach down and pick him up. As he began to pet him, the dog nuzzled his face against the king's chest. Without giving it a second thought, King Maho's fingers scratched under the dog's chin, a sensation that got a heavenly reaction.

"I think Mom's death took the best of you from us, Dad." He used the informal endearments he hadn't used in years. "I think the island could be a place of good cheer again. We can all mourn the loss of Queen Sirind for the rest of our lives yet still move forward with progress and pride. She'd want us to."

While in thought, the king didn't object when the dog squirmed up to kiss his face. Then, when he noticed, he shooed him off and the stern expression that had become his typical mask returned. And then he thought about something else. That made his eyes soften at the corners. A long, almost unbearable, pause followed.

He finally declared, "All right, son. Marry your Gracie. You deserve the happiness you are asking for."

Spontaneously, Ras hugged his father, the dog in the center of the embrace. The two men chuckled. Then Ras got back to business. "And I have some new proposals for you about the island. I assume when I break the engagement to Vajhana, King Yodfa will no longer be our partner."

"You'd better be darn sure of yourself then, Ras. You've got our whole nation depending on it."

"I am. I am." The dog gestured to be let down to the lawn. At which point he ran to explore every plant, every smell. The king and the prince stood side by side watching. "What shall we name him, Your Majesty?"

"We'll call him Lucky Two."

Gracie entered the Beacon Hill carriage house that had been converted into the lobby of an exclusive hotel in

Boston. She had a spring in her step and was feeling well for a couple of reasons. One, the morning sickness that had been so torturous a few days ago had subsided a bit. Two, she'd booked a dozen clients for Carat Cruises' Nova Scotia voyage on *Liberation*, and would soon be receiving her commission. And three, today was the day she was going to tell His Royal Highness Rasmayada that she was pregnant with his child. She'd waited until she was away from the rural spots she'd visited in the New England countryside, where the bucolic serenity sometimes came with spotty phone and internet service. When she did reach him, she wanted to be sure he could hear her loud and clear.

After being shown to her room, she dipped her hand into her bag to retrieve her phone. Instead, she pulled out the little Gullah basket that she and Ras had bought in Charleston. He'd told her it would hold his kisses for her. She wasn't going to let it be a receptacle for her tears. Holding it in one hand, not letting go, she found her phone with the other.

She and Ras had had several conversations about Gracie's determination to no longer be tied down to anything that could disappoint her like her parents and Davis had. That she wouldn't even make one place her home. During one of the talks, Ras got very serious and punched a number into her phone. He'd told her she could forget about having it and that she never had to call. However, if she was ever in trouble, if she ever needed him, no matter how many years had gone by, she could always dial that number. He was going to be quite surprised to look down to his phone screen and see that she was calling him after such a short time. Sadly, he'd have to endure a moment of worry that she was taking him up on his offer because something was wrong. But she'd quickly inform him that she had gotten in touch for quite another reason.

After all, he needed to know about the miracle. That his child was growing in her belly. She touched her stomach like she had a million times before, only it was different now. As soon as she'd gotten to Boston, she'd seen a doctor and everything seemed to be fine. Of course, she could suffer another devastating miscarriage, but something inside told her she wouldn't. That the foundation she and Ras had created when their bodies met for those incredible expressions of togetherness would hold her womb strong, would protect the life growing within her.

Ever the realist, she had expectations of what Ras would do once he heard the news. Nothing. After all, what could he do? He was obligated to marry Vajhana, and together they would breed a proper successor to the throne. It was the approved alignment of stars in the sky. It was what was right.

Gracie understood that. Yes, it would be a perfect universe if she and Ras could be together, could raise their miracle as a couple in love. Just like his parents did before his mother tragically died. She'd never known the love of a family and still wouldn't. That tightness of a unit that, surrounded by love, looked out for one another. And shared private joys. Once again that was not her lot. She was destined to be left behind. But in this case the consolation was a magnificent gift.

Yet she couldn't not tell him about it, couldn't hold the secret within her for the rest of her, and her baby's, life. Ras was entitled to know he'd be a father. She assumed he would not want, or be able, to have anything to do with her. That he couldn't, wouldn't, shouldn't ever even meet the baby. As years went by, she'd explain the blessing as being assisted by a sperm donor who had sold his seed for money and had no interest in knowing the results of his actions. Women did that all the time.

The irony, of course, was that Gracie never thought she'd get pregnant again. Never thought she'd want to. She'd considered it, but had never really seen herself going through with it. She was supposed to be alone in every way. Not taking any chances. Yet it turned out she could hardly have felt more opposite. She was filled with nothing but optimism and glory. She had Ras's baby inside her! Who already had a personality. She didn't know the gender, but he or she was someone Gracie already knew. Because the fetus inside her was half Ras. Every cell in her body recognized the new life as belonging to love. If she couldn't have him, at least she could have his child.

She loved Ras so much that she was more than willing, ecstatic, to bring his baby into the world. Even if no one ever knew who his or her father was. Because that little human was going to be as magnificent, as strong and noble and intelligent as Ras. It would be her honor to raise this child who would bring good wherever he or she went, bring magic to anything she or he touched. It was a brand-new day.

And she wanted Ras to know all of that. So she tapped the phone number that he had given her. If after she gave him the news he asked her to keep the number in case she or the child were ever in dire need, she would. But she'd vow never to use it.

The phone rang three times before she heard the recipient's click. "Hello."

"Ras?"

"Gracie?"

"Yes."

"I can't believe it's you. I was going to call you today."

Hmm, Gracie couldn't imagine why, although he'd taken her phone number as well. They'd left nothing unsaid. The teary farewell at the airplane hangar in New York was about as final as anything could be, with them basically wishing each other a sweet life. Spent apart.

"I have to tell you something, Ras."

"Are you okay?"

"More than okay."

"Me first, then. I love you." His voice was like gold. In the very center of her, she glistened at hearing that he loved her. The words made her eyelashes flutter. She stroked the tiny basket in her hand with the pad of her thumb.

"I love you, too."

"I have to see you."

"I… I don't think that's a good idea."

"I have to be with you."

"What are you saying, Ras?"

"Can you come to Ko Pha Lano? I'll send a plane."

"Ras, what about your fiancée? Your father?"

"I can't live a life that isn't mine."

"Your subjects need…"

"Our citizens remember my mother. They remember a time at the palace when her zest touched everyone. They will return to that with you here, Gracie."

Alone in her Boston hotel room she shook her head without anyone to see it. "It can't be, Ras."

"It can be. It will be. I don't want to clip your independence. You can be free to pursue anything you want to, my love. We, and the people, will work it out. In fact, I think you might be interested in an idea that I want to talk to you about. In person."

"I have something I need to tell you, too."

"Save it for *in person*. I can't wait to hear it." That remained to be seen. Would he regard the baby as good news? A pregnant American suddenly on the prince's arm when he was engaged to be married in mere weeks.

"But…"

"But what?"

"I…" Was she going to protest, when the man she adored had confessed his love for her?

"Get to the airport."

This wasn't possible, wasn't supposed to be. She literally pinched her arm to make sure she hadn't fallen into what just had to be a beautiful dream. After all they'd been through, all the while knowing their ultimate destinies had already decided their outcomes, it couldn't end with her getting the prince. Could it?

Ras could hardly believe it when he watched the love of his life descend on the plane that had transported her to his home. He rushed to meet her on the tarmac. The wrenching farewell that he'd thought was permanent had changed course!

"Gracie, Gracie, Gracie…" Saying her name took turns with kisses delivered all over her face. He took her by the hand and led her to the waiting car. In the back seat he turned to look into her eyes. "You're here."

"I am, Ras. As the plane was landing, I was amazed at all of the natural beauty of the island and the clear blue of the water. I can see why you feel so protective of it."

Once they arrived at the palace, he ushered her into a salon where they could talk. He saw her touch her stomach, that habit she had been working on breaking. "Are you nervous?" he asked, gesturing to her motion.

"I am. That's not all. There's a reason I've been instinctively cradling my belly lately. A reason I hope you'll be happy about."

Her words were an explosion as he interpreted their meaning. "Are you saying you're…"

"Yes, my love. I'm pregnant. I don't know what kind of chaos that might wreak, so I haven't told anyone."

"Chaos? That's the most beautiful news I have ever heard." He swallowed hard, overcome with emotion. "I'm the father of your child!" He rushed closer to touch her belly, which, now that he noticed, actually did feel a tiny bit rounded.

"It's too early to sense any motion."

He caressed her over and over nonetheless. "No. I can feel him or her. I'm sure of it." She laughed, music to his ears. "Do you realize you're carrying the future king or queen?"

"I am acutely aware of that," she said, smiling. "It's quite nerve-racking. Especially after…"

"We'll get you the finest doctors. And we won't make any announcements right away." He bounced in his boots as he hugged her, then brought her to a chair to sit down, then kissed her cheek, then went to pour her a glass of water. "I'm giddy. Thank you, Gracie. Thank you for the most amazing miracle anyone could receive."

"But what about your obligations? Princess Vajhana? The partnership of the two islands? The manufacturing development?"

"I've already broken things off with her. That's why it was such perfect timing when you called. I was just going to call you. To make arrangements. Because it's you I'm going to spend the rest of my life with."

"What did she say? What did your father say?"

He explained that Vajhana was in Dubai when he'd reached her. That she'd said she was relieved because she didn't want to get married yet. Apparently, the freedom quest Ras was on in the States with Gracie wasn't anything compared to the wild oats Vajhana still needed to sow. And Ras had explained to Gracie about convincing his father that being with the woman he loved was to everyone's benefit. "I had help from a four-legged friend."

That night, Gracie met Lucky Two and His Majesty King Maho. She became fast friends with them both, as Ras knew she would. Over dinner, he told the king that he was to be a grandfather. The grin that cracked over his face made him look fifteen years younger. "Well done, Gracie," the king said, nodding to her.

"And I wanted to talk to both of you about something else, so I'm very delighted to have you at the same table." He retrieved the laptop he'd put on a side cupboard before dinner. "Father as you know, when we were to partner with King Yodfa and the people of Ko Yaolum, I was against anything that might rob the island of its resources. I believe this is what's best for our nation," he said firmly while showing them the prospectus he had been working on, essentially for years.

"Hmm." The king let out a sound of interest that encouraged Ras.

"Then you'll consider it, Father?"

"I can see you've done a lot of research. I have a number of questions about the feasibility."

"I promise you I have all the answers. And Gracie is a licensed travel consultant with an endless supply of good ideas. I want her to be one of the creators of our program. Will you, Gracie? Will you help our island become all that it could be?"

"Of course! I'd love to!"

Ras wasn't finished. He stood from his dining chair and approached Gracie's. He got down on one knee and removed his mother's wedding ring from his jacket pocket where he had been touching it throughout dinner. Something must have told him that he would need it someday as he had never given it to Vajhana. He held it in his open palm. "Will you officially join our family and all that it entails? Will you marry me?"

"It will be my honor."

Bursting with elation, he slipped the ring onto her finger and they kissed. Then Gracie rose and went to the king's chair. He stood. She bowed her head and then hugged him. "Thank you," she said, knowing that without the king's approval none of this would be possible.

After a conversation that lasted late into the night, the four of them proceeded down the palace hallways toward their rooms. The king, the crown prince and his pregnant love continued to exchange thoughts, come to conclusions, energize with specifics. Alongside them Lucky Two romped, understanding the many meanings of his name.

* * * * *

THE WEDDING FAVOUR

ALLY BLAKE

MILLS & BOON

My books are not the books they are without
my wonderful writerly friends: those suppliers of
laughter, bastions of empathy and lighters of creative
fires. This story owes so much to Kali Anthony,
for her boundless love of romance and dazzling
"glitter bomb" lightbulb moment, and to
Amy Andrews for her spit-take-worthy
NSFW insights and invaluable word sprints.
I am so grateful for you both.

PROLOGUE

THE FIRST TIME Emerson Adler's heart broke she was ten years old.

Well, ten years and one day to be exact. Her actual birthday had been wondrous—her dad surprising her, and her mum, for that matter, with a caramel-coloured fluffball in the shape of a cocker spaniel.

The bigger surprise had come the morning after, when her dad had roused her from her sleep before the sun was even up, tweaked her on the nose, called her his favourite girl, and said, "Life ebbs and flows, kiddo. When it feels hard, remember it'll be okay. It always gets better."

Then he'd kissed her hair and walked out the front door. Never to return.

Emerson's mum had coped by turning her naturally cheerful nature up to eleven, starting a mini-orchard in their small back yard as a symbol of "growth", hugging her daughter a hundred times a day, and adoring Pumpkin, the puppy she'd had no say in taking on. Throwing in the occasional telling words of wisdom of her own, such as, "Take care when falling in love, as things that fall often end up broken." As if quips and dauntless sunshine might make her daughter bombproof to the shock she herself had endured.

Unfortunately, as it turned out, that first heartbreak

had created some kind of crack in the space-time continuum, making young Emerson a conduit for heartache.

So many heartaches that she—like a prisoner scraping tallies in the walls of her cell—had kept count. Of the big ones, especially. The ones that took something from her. That changed the course of her life. Though in lieu of fingernails on concrete she'd used a pen with a pom-pom on the end, and a dedicated notebook with a sparkly cartoon cactus on the cover.

Heartache Number One: ten years old.

Dad left. Obviously.

Heartache Number Two: eleven years old.

Mrs Abernathy, the teacher who gave her extra stars on her homework and seemed to know when her mum was not feeling quite as sunny as usual, had also upped and left! Retired, they said, but how could she be sure?

Heartache Number Three: twelve years old.

Kailey Deluca, best friend, turned up on the first day of high school with a new haircut, new earring holes, new boobs, new clothes…and new friends. Totally awful.

And so the Heartache List had gone on.

That was its name, scrawled in big black bubble writing on the front page, begun in reaction to:

Heartache Number Four: fourteen years old.

A devastating, unrequited high school crush which had soon morphed into a detailed, annotated roadmap penned in a special notebook, ruling and shaping Emerson's decisions in the hopes she might one day figure out how to make sure she never broke her heart again.

And then…

Heartache Number Eight: twenty-five years old.

Her beautiful mum passed away, after a breathlessly quick battle with cancer.

After that there would be no *Heartache Number Nine.* For surely it would be the end of her.

This story starts nearly two decades on from that seminal heartache.

The Heartache List, with its spiky cactus cover and pages filled with detailed ramblings and deeply felt promises, has long since gone.

Emerson no longer has need to keep track of heartbreaks, for hers is a meticulously curated life, vigilant in its setting of boundaries. She enjoys a small crew of trusted friends. Work at Pitch Perfect, her very own bespoke recruitment firm, is immensely satisfying. Her life is no longer fettered by the assumption that it all may be whipped out from under her at any moment.

For she knows that everything comes to an end eventually. Opportunities, employment, favourite restaurants, favourite lipsticks, relationships. The trick, she has discovered, is in the accepting and the moving on.

It is a warm spring day on the glorious Mornington Peninsula of southern Victoria, and a wedding has taken place. The bride, Camille, is Emerson's very best friend in the entire world, and the groom, Phillip, is an utterly lovely guy who would not dare break his bride's heart—

due, in no small part, to the fact he'd have Emerson to deal with.

Dusk is settling over the gorgeous reception marquee perched at the edge of a forest a short drive in from the coast. Birds flutter and chatter as they fill the sky, following the last rays of the sun. And the air tastes like the first lick of spring after a long, cool, coastal winter. It brings with it the scent of impending change.

While inside the marquee, Emerson has no clue that her comprehensively fortified heart is about to be put to the ultimate test…

CHAPTER ONE

THE TIDE OF anticipation rippling through the crowd was palpable, voices ascending, glasses clinking, dresses shimmering in the buttery light of a marquee strung with enough fairy lights to bring a plane safely home on a cloudy night.

All the single ladies—along with a handful of convivial and unattached guys—stood in a loose group at the edge of the dance floor, shifting from foot to foot, jostling for position, eyes sharp on the deviously grinning bride who stood alone beneath a spotlight waving her lavish bouquet back and forth like some kind of lure.

Emerson Adler alone remained immune to the collective fervour.

As Maid of Honour, Emerson felt duty-bound to at least *appear* as if she was taking part. Though the bride was hardly what one might call traditional. Emerson's place card read "Best Woman/Sister/Wife" and her dress—as chosen by the bride—was less pastel eighties prom, more backless glittery bronze *va-va-voom* Vegas hostess. The bride was nothing if not extra.

Speaking of the bride… Camille planted her bare feet, backside wiggling dramatically as she readied to make the toss, and the rowdy crowd held its collective breath. Then a *whoop* split the evening air as the bouquet arced high in a tumble of white roses, orchids, moonflowers, and faux pearls.

The group surged up and to the left—like a rugby scrum, only better dressed. While Emerson and her glass of warm bubbly took a deft step to the right.

The bouquet landed atop a shelf of groping hands, then bounced—once, twice—leaving those in the bullseye in an entangled heap on the parquetry floor. Finally, like a whale breaching the surface of a stormy sea, Bernadette, sweet younger cousin to the bride, leapt to her feet, brandishing the bunch as if it were Excalibur.

Congratulations ensued before the competitors moved off to reclaim their partners, their drinks, their chairs. While Emerson sighed in contentment, happy that she'd navigated that whole affair with subtle aplomb.

Or so she thought, till she caught the bride's gaze across the crowded room.

Camille, being Camille, grinned broadly as she waggled a *naughty, naughty* finger Emerson's way, clearly finding Emerson's mini-rebellion hilarious.

Emerson offered a sly shrug, lifted her bubbly in salute, downed the lot in one gulp, placed the empty glass on the tray of a wandering waiter, found a gap in the crowd, and took it.

Camille's bark of laughter was loud enough that it could be heard above the band, who'd just heralded their return to the stage with a clash of cymbals and blurt of a trumpet.

"Dance with me, Emmy!" one of Phillip's groomsmen begged as she slipped by.

Emerson took his hand, spun deftly beneath his arm, and let go, before disappearing into the throng, stopping only when she reached her desired destination—the

empty, moody, dimly lit, back corner bar, half hidden behind a screen of stripped willow.

Catching the eye of the bartender, Emerson motioned
to the fresh tray of glasses filled with golden bubbles.
Chewing on a toothpick and drying wine glasses by hand,
he lifted his chin the barest amount in confirmation. Not
a chatty one. Perfect.

While the soft strains of moody, forties jazz filled the
marquee like smoke, bringing the slow dancers to the
floor, Emerson plonked her clutch bag on the bar, leaned
her back against warm wood, and took a moment to herself for the first time in what felt like days.

Without busy work keeping her occupied, it wasn't
long before she noticed the uncomfortable feeling that
had grown in her belly, incrementally, as the day had
gone on. Not hunger. She'd had the fish, and the chocolate mousse. More as if her innards were being pickled
in something bittersweet. More as if she felt a little…
downhearted.

It made no sense, for the wedding had gone off without a hitch, the ceremony whimsical, the after-party dec-
adent and joyful.

So why these…*feelings*?

If the Heartache List had taught her anything, it was
that *feelings* were messy and perilous. Far better to keep
them squished deep down inside where they might shrivel
up and die due to acute lack of oxygen.

And yet, as she watched the crowd on the dance floor
part, right as Phillip swept Camille into his arms and
twirled her about, before hauling her close and slow dancing as if they were the only people in the room, and her
two favourite humans move on to the next stage of their
lives in real time, a stage that would no longer include

her, Emerson dropped her hand to her belly and the— dare she even think it—*ache* therein.

"Then again," she muttered, "maybe it was the fish."

Shaking off the feeling as best she could, Emerson rolled her shoulders, closed her eyes, and drank deeply, the bubbles biting winningly at the inside of her throat on the way down. She nudged a high heel off one foot, releasing a small sound of relief as she stretched her toes, twirled her ankle and—

"Emmy?"

The voice calling her name, invading her moment of sanctuary, was a masculine one, deep, rumbling, and lit with the expectation of conversation returned. "Emmy Adler? Of East Kew High? Or, more particularly, the cracked hard plastic chairs outside the guidance counsellor's office?"

Emerson took a small breath before twisting to face the interloper now leaning back against the bar beside her.

Used, as she was, in her work as a professional recruiter of human resources to determining first impressions in a blink, Emerson took mental bullet points: tall, great hair, hell of a jawline, beautiful suit, exceptional tailoring required to contain those mighty shoulders, slow smile tugging at the corners of a wide mouth, rather lovely crinkles at the edges of a pair of magnetic eyes the colour of a coming storm—

All too late a skitter of warning thundered its way down Emerson's back, knocking against the bumps in her spine like a pinball.

The jaw, the shoulders, the stormy eyes, the *cracked hard plastic chairs outside the guidance counsellor's office*—they belonged to none other than Holden Roarke.

Aka *Heartache Number Four*.

Emerson's eyes skewed to the dance floor, seeking

Camille—the very person who had bought the sparkly cactus notebook in which the Heartache List had been etched, right after the guy now standing beside her had broken Emmy's teenaged heart.

Holden's voice cut through the fog. "It is Emmy Adler, right? If not, then the words echoing disastrously inside my head must sound like the most dubious line."

Realising that, bar bolting for the exit, there was no way out of this moment but through, Emerson forced a neutral smile onto her face, then held out a hand, as if this was all cool and normal.

"Holden Roarke," she said, her voice admirably even. "Yes, it is me. Though I go by Emerson. Mostly."

"Emerson," he said, smiling into her eyes, her name sounding like an endearment in that low, slow, velvety dark voice. "Mostly."

Then he took her hand in his. Encompassing, cool, good pressure, she'd have given him a big tick next to the "handshake" box if she was taking him on as a client. Though the shimmer of warmth that shot up her arm as he held her hand was overkill.

But he was not a prospective client. He was a guy who had, at one time, made her cry into her unicorn pillow-case simply because he existed.

Emerson let go first, her hand springing back as a zing sparked from his hand to hers. A zing that seemed to spark in his eyes as well. Though that was more likely from the fairy lights. There really were a lot of them.

Wishing she'd waited a minute before mainlining a glass of champagne, Emerson pushed her near empty glass across the bar.

The bartender, finding within himself a sudden burst of helpfulness, slid a full one her way.

"How long *has* it been?" Holden crooned. Well, he

didn't croon exactly, but he had the kind of voice—all warm and deep—that, when combined with the acoustics in their little alcove, made it sound just so.

When Emerson blinked, rather more slowly than was natural, the bartender coughed, his eyebrow flickering, a knowing smile growing around his toothpick.

Emerson narrowed her eyes meaningfully at the guy, then turned her back on him to shoot Holden a quick, bland glance. "How long? Aeons, at least."

"That long?" Holden asked. "And there I was, thinking it had only been ages."

Unfortunately, Emerson's quick glance had somehow stuck, meaning she was forced to bear the full brunt of those stormy blue eyes crinkling in that very particular, effortlessly charming, entirely discombobulating way that had put her under his spell all those years ago.

Aeons. Ages. Once upon a time, when she'd been a dreamy young thing, desperate for some guy to see her oodles of wondrous potential.

Emerson grabbed herself by the metaphorical collar and yanked herself back to the present, only to nearly topple sideways, having forgotten she was wearing only one shoe.

Stomach swooping, she white-knuckled the bar behind her and glanced down at the floor to find no sign of her own missing heel, only a gleaming, Holden-Roarke-sized shoe cocked roguishly out in front.

"Having a good time?" Holden said, his shoe kicking back further, so that the toes faced the ceiling.

"Of course," she said through gritted teeth as she swept her bare toes behind her.

"Big fan of weddings?"

"A fan of *this* wedding," she managed as she sank a little lower, her toes searching a little farther.

"Mmm. I'd put good money behind the bet you have no plans to star in one of your own anytime soon."

Now manically searching for her shoe so she could extricate herself as quickly as possible, Emerson muttered, "Now, *that's* a dubious line."

After a beat, Holden burst into laughter, the sound deeply relaxed and entirely unselfconscious. "I wouldn't dare. If I *did* dare, I'd hope I had better material."

Emerson's foot stopped mid-search as she realised what she'd just intimated.

Of course, it hadn't been a line. Even at sixteen he'd smiled with ease, made eye contact and held it, listened when people spoke. At fourteen she'd mistaken it to mean something other than what it was, and had been proven mortifyingly wrong.

She would not be making that same mistake twice.

"I'd hope so too," she said, holding eye contact to show just how undaunted she was. "Or you'd be the kind of guy who'd follow up with a little, *Hey, aren't you the Maid of* Dis*honour?*"

Holden's smile was broad. And when he turned his body towards her he blocked some of the light. "Then I'd come at you with a little side-eye and a dare—fifty points for a kiss with a stranger in the cloakroom, a hundred for landing the bride's garter, twenty-five points for getting Aunty Verna sloshed."

"Poor Aunty Verna. Seems a tad low."

"Turns out it's not that hard."

His smile grew, yet again, and she felt her mouth kick into a quick smile of its own, despite itself. Damn those eyes, with their lovely crinkles. And zillion lashes. How could she have forgotten about all those lashes?

"How many points for making a bridesmaid blush?"

Emerson blinked her eyes back into focus as she felt heat creep into her cheeks. "Now, that's definitely a line."

This time when his smile flashed, she glimpsed canines. "Not at all. A purely academic exercise, as we stand here together, a part of the festivities and yet not. Outliers in arms."

Before Emerson could unpack all that, the bartender piped up with, "If blush is a euphemism for what I think it is, two hundred and fifty points, at the very least."

As one, Emerson and Holden turned to face the bar. Emerson asked, "That much?"

"I've done a lot of weddings. And a lot of bridesmaids." With that the bartender moseyed off to serve someone at the other end of the bar.

"That, ladies and gentlemen, is a line," said Holden.

"And from such an unexpected source." Out of the corner of her eye, Emerson saw Holden slowly lift a fist, knuckles out. What choice did she have but to bump it back?

A waiter came by, grabbed the tray of bubbly from behind the bar, readying to swish it out into the crowd. It took half a millisecond for Emerson to decide to nab another glass. For her shoe had obviously disappeared into some alternate dimension and she'd just fist-bumped Holden Roarke. Bubbly seemed the only sane choice.

"I've been thinking," said Holden, looking back out into the crowd. "If I was a line guy, you'd know it."

"Would I, now?"

"I wouldn't throw them out there without a care. I'd take my time. Curate them, incessantly. Until I had a small but specific set. Instant classics. World class. Legendary."

He's more playful than I remember, she thought. What she said was, "Settle down, Casanova, I get it. If you *had* taken it upon yourself to hit on me, I might never have recovered."

Her eyes were on his when he smiled—a slow, deliberate lift of the corners of his mouth. A wave of heat swept from her cheeks to her toes.

"What are you doing here, Holden?"

He blinked. "At this very moment? Having an unexpectedly delightful exchange with an old acquaintance. You?"

Emerson didn't let the sudden rough edge to his voice distract her. "I know the guest list back to front and you're not on it."

"Open yourself up to the universe and the universe provides, don't you find?"

Emerson coughed out a laugh. For no, she did not *find*.

Holden leaned in, as if about to bestow upon her a secret, and she caught his scent—freshly cut grass, bubbling brook, warm male skin.

"My earlier quip, such as it was," he said, "was in reference to the fact I've never seen anyone less interested in a bouquet toss."

Emerson followed the lift of his glass, to see the bouquet in question now waving its way through the crowd, a snake of conga dancers falling in behind.

Oh. Her spare hand moved to her neck. "Was I that obvious?"

"Not at all," he said, gathering his glass back towards the snowy white shirt straining against acres of broad chest. "You were the very picture of discretion. I just happen to have a keen eye for understated insurrection. I'm a bit of an expert, you see. Years of experience given to the cause. It's not often I spot a kindred spirit, then there you were."

There she was. Holden Roarke's kindred spirit. It was all she could do not to burst into laughter.

Holden's eyebrow lifted, slowly, in question. As if it was her turn to say something.

"Yes," she said, her voice a little breathless. "I mean no. It's not my thing. Not even in my top hundred."

"Fighting over a used bunch of flowers?" A pause to give her an extra centimetre of smile. "Or marriage?"

"Both," she shot back.

"And not a moment's hesitation," he said, his voice tinged with awe.

She shrugged, unapologetically.

Holden Roarke's stormy blue gaze followed the move, landing on her bare shoulder for a beat, before moving to the shift of a dangly diamante earring against her cheek, then sweeping back to her eyes with such a rush, Emerson felt herself sway. And it all happened in a single heartbeat.

It was all too bizarre, standing like a flamingo, under a starfield of romantic fairy lights, with *Zoot Suit Riot* blasting in the background, as she talked marriage with the man who had dashed her teenaged heart into a thousand tiny little pieces.

"Now, what do we have here?" Mr Heartache murmured, placing his drink on the bar before dropping to an easy crouch, reaching under the closest barstool and coming up with her shoe. Just like that.

His gaze dropped to her feet—well, one foot, for the other was tucked away inside the matching four-inch heel. "Yours, I presume?"

At which point Holden Roarke dropped a knee, and held out a hand.

Emerson blinked, the ridiculousness factor having

just turned up to eleven. Enough that she actually gave her arm a quick pinch.

Wobbling on her one heel, Emerson snapped her fingers at Holden. "Up. Up, up, up. I can do it myself."

"I have no doubt," he said, his gaze stuck on hers. "Yet here I am, shoe in hand, knee in the dust, willing and able to do you this small favour."

That voice of his—deep, unhurried, and laced with humour—wound around some delicate, unprotected part of herself she was too flummoxed to keep locked down.

A small favour. Over in a jiffy.

"Fine."

Taking great pains not to feel like freaking Cinderella, Emerson looked away as he slid his hand along the soft, sensitive underpart of her foot, leaving prickles and shimmers in his wake, before his long, strong fingers moved to curl around her ankle. At which point the prickles and shimmers rushed up her calf, the back of her thigh, higher, as if connected directly to nerves, muscles, tendons, the very marrow of her bones.

Five hundred points, she thought, *at the very least, for making a Maid of Honour blush. No euphemism required.*

Then it was over before it began, with Holden shucking the heel neatly into place and gently lowering her foot to the ground. Entirely G-rated. No lingering touches, or signs of fetishism. Just a guy helping a girl he'd once known, out of a jam.

Though when Holden stood, sweeping to his feet with a whoosh, dragging a hand through his hair leaving thick, dark tracks in its wake, he had noticeably more colour in his cheeks. Was it possible the prickles and shimmers weren't hers alone?

Emerson shook her head. She'd lived half her life since Holden Roarke had broken her heart. Had survived several shiny new heartbreaks since. Those collective experiences building up the phenomenal resistance she had today. Yet, standing here beside him, it was if she'd learned nothing at all.

Now that she had both shoes on, it was time to vamoose. "Look, this has been—"

Emerson cut herself off when Holden spun dramatically to face the bar, his fingers tightening on the wood, as if he was thinking about leaping over the thing.

Intrigued, despite herself, she asked, "What's happening right now?"

Holden's jaw twitched. "Did she see me?"

"Did who—?"

A high-pitched voice called from the crowd, "Holden!"

Emerson followed the sound to find Bernadette, bouquet gripped in her hand as she battled her way through the dense crowd now dancing to a wild, fast, jazz rendition of *Dancing Queen*.

"Holden! Where are you?"

"Ah. So that's how you got in. You're here with Bernadette," said Emerson, mad at herself for the sting that brought on.

He shook his head. "We met half an hour ago when she tried to slip her room key into the pocket of my suit pants."

Emerson coughed on her surprise. "Front pocket or back?"

Holden's mouth twitched before he turned her way, his voice low, and intimate, as he asked, "Why? Is one worth more points than the other?"

"Goes without saying. But, actually, don't tell me. I've known Bernie since she was eight." A thought. "Do you still have it? The key?"

"No, I don't have the *key*. I tactfully declined." He sounded abashed. Which was unexpectedly…adorable.

And finally, for the first time since he'd ambled up to her and said her name, she felt the dynamic shift. This she preferred, by far. "I'm not sure you were as clear as you imagine you were. In fact, it seems congratulations might be in order."

Frowning, Holden leaned in a little closer in order to pick up her voice, his upper arm making contact with hers.

"She won the bouquet," she said, eyes flicking between his. Meaning she caught the moment his hunted look dissipated and a glint took its place.

Their arms still touching, Emerson could feel the man's body heat. The rise and fall of his breaths. Their faces were close enough she could make out the swirls of blue and gusts of grey around his deep, dark pupils. Count those glorious lashes, including the one that had fallen to his cheek.

She would *not* lift her hand to sweep that lash away. *She would not.*

Her voice was a little husky as she said, "Don't think, just because I am not into the bouquet-toss-winner-is-next-to-marry thing, you can't be all for it. Truly. More power to you."

Slowly, as if time stretched, Holden's eyes seemed to narrow, even as the eye crinkles returned, deepening deliciously. Till his expression turned wolfish. And very, very grown-up. "Emerson."

"Mm-hmm?"

"You know that small favour I did for you, not too many moments ago?"

"Favour?"

"Helping you with your errant shoe. I'd be hugely grateful if you'd allow me to ask for one in return."

Emerson felt, with every fibre of her being, that she ought to say no. To give him a light, chummy punch on the arm, wish him luck, then go on about her Maid of Honour duties for the rest of the night.

But his words, simple and respectful, hooked her, like a claw in a buttonhole.

"What do you need?"

The man grinned—the move so bright, so joyful, she felt it in the backs of her knees. Then he turned, lifted his arm over her head, and placed it behind her along the bar, so that she found herself tucked against his big, warm, hard body, wondering how the heck she'd ended up there.

Bernadette's big doe eyes lit up as she spotted Emerson, before she slipped through a gap in the crowd and was upon them. "Emmy!"

"Emmy?" Holden murmured.

"She gets to call me whatever she wants. She's special."

"There you are!" said Bernadette.

"How you going, Bernie?" Emerson asked.

"I'm wonderful. Such a gorgeous wedding! And you look amazing. That dress! *Phwoar*." Only then did Bernie seem to spot Holden. "Oh, hi! I was looking for you! And there you are too!"

"Here I am too," he said.

Then he shifted, just a fraction. Enough that Emerson felt surrounded by the guy. On all sides. Trapped in a haze of his scent, his warmth, his shelter.

For all that he presented as relaxed, it was suddenly all too clear that it was an act. Calculated misdirection. An ocean of energy pulsed through him, deep, rich, barely contained. Ready for anything.

"Look!" said Bernadette, oblivious, holding out the bouquet and waving it under Holden's nose as if it might put him in her thrall. "I won!"

"We saw. Hell of a leap you have."

On the "we" he lifted the arm he'd positioned behind Emerson, his fingers curling around her elbow on her far side. So aware of him was she, Emerson had been waiting for it. Her body primed for his touch before he'd even moved.

Which was when she heard the alarm bells go off deep inside her, echoing, as if they'd been ringing for some time but she'd only just begun to notice.

Bernadette pointed the bouquet towards Emerson, nearly poking her in the eye with a rose. "Hey, do you know Emmy?"

Holden's hand slid up Emerson's arm to find her shoulder, then the back of her neck. There, his thumb shifted back and forth over the small covered button holding the halter neck of her dress in place as he said, "*Emmy* and I go way back."

Emerson nudged an elbow into his side, his wince evidence she'd hit the mark.

Bernadette's eyes grew wide and she said, "Now it all makes sense." After which she gave Emerson a big, slow almost-wink, then she spun on her heel, gaze dancing over the crowd as she called, "Barry! Barry!"

And then she was gone, the air around them fluttering back to normal, like leaves in the wake of a whirlwind.

"Barry?" Holden asked, removing his hand from the back of her neck, the hairs there lifting, as if reaching for his touch.

"One of Phillip's hundred-odd groomsmen," she said. Then, "A hundred and fifty points, at least." She felt

Holden's grin even though they were both still facing the crowd.

"Far more cache than a mere guest," he added, his voice a low burr.

"Oodles."

"So we actually did *her* a favour."

"Gosh, I hope so. If she remembers even half of it, she's going to be mortified."

"No need. Only way to find out if someone you like likes you back is to be a little brave."

Unable to help herself, Emerson glanced at Holden's face, expecting a glint of humour. But his expression, as he looked into her eyes, was keen. Direct. It nudged against some soft, unprotected part of her.

Then the music changed. Slowed. A sigh coming over the crowd as the opening strains of *The Way You Look Tonight* began to fill the space. A spotlight hit a disco ball, which sent shards of warm light scattering over them both.

Feeling warm and a little light in the head, for one moment, a single breath, Emerson opened herself up to it. To the full force of him. To see if, after all this time, she could.

Time seemed to stretch, the sound of the band muffled, and everything at the edges of her vision became a blur. Her breath turned a little slow and viscous, her skin tingly and tight. She may have even felt herself sway towards him, just a smidge.

Turned out, despite excellent inroads into self-actualisation since she'd moved on from the Heartache List, testing it was a form of sadomasochism.

Emerson pulled herself back from the brink, just, and asked, "How did you end up here, Holden?"

He watched her for a few long, drawn-out moments,

before a smile tugged at the corners of his eyes. "Ours is not to reason why, young Emerson. Ours is but to enjoy what is, in fact, a damn fine band, pretty good plonk, and excellent company, all on someone else's dime."

Her dad's voice suddenly floated up out of the deepest recesses of her memory. *Loosen up, little one, so you don't snap. It'll be okay.* He would say *It'll be okay* quite a bit, her dad. As if that might make up for any number of disappointments.

Funny that she'd thought of him now, while talking to someone else on her Heartache List. Funny ironic? Or funny cautionary?

Before she could decide, Holden took a distinct step away from the bar. "I've been keeping you. I'm sure, as Maid of Dishonour, you have many duties."

"Many," she agreed, breathing out hard. "Lots. A plethora."

A crease, like a super-dimple, formed at one corner of his mouth, heaven help her.

"It was really good to see you again, Emerson." He nodded, as if surprised by the truth of his own words. "Now I must be off, perhaps even to indulge in my new-found respect for a good pick-up line."

"Or perhaps not," she offered.

He touched the side of his nose in agreement, before dipping an invisible cap, and ambling back out into the fray.

Mere seconds later, Camille burst through the edge of the crowd. So much for finding a quiet corner.

Camille held up her middle finger. "I broke a nail. Help me before I snag."

"On it." Very glad to have a purpose, a distraction, Emerson found an emery board in her clutch bag, then grabbed Camille's outstretched hand and buffed away the ragged corner.

"Whoa. Slow down, honeybun! Everything okay?"

Emerson eased back before she buffed the nail clean away. "Did you know Holden Roarke was here?"

Camille's eyes popped. "What's that, now?"

Emerson waved a hand at the crowd. "Holden Roarke—aka *Heartache Number Four*—is out there. Right now." Possibly trying out dubious lines on unexpecting—and unresisting—guests.

Camille growled, "Phillip."

"Phillip?" Emerson asked.

Camille took her hand back and nibbled on the nail. "Okay, so Phillip banged into the guy a couple of weeks back at some ex-uni networking thing where Holden was the guest speaker. Turns out they went to uni together for a tiny bit before Holden dropped out. Did you know that? That he dropped out? No, unlike the rest of us you don't keep tabs on those who did you wrong. Anyway, apparently he's some app design genius—infamously retired in his early twenties when he sold his first app for zillions, so I guess it's more like he 'dropped up' than 'out'. Everyone at the networking thing was drooling over him from a distance, while Phillip being Phillip walked up and said, 'I'm getting hitched, you should come!' Thankfully—for Phillip's sake—Holden politely refused, so I figured it best to leave it at that rather than stir everything up for you unnecessarily. I had no idea he'd actually come!"

Emerson puffed out a don't-worry-about-it breath, surprised to find her lips were slightly numb. After nursing one glass of champagne all evening, she'd somehow gone through a few in a short burst.

Camille's eyes narrowed as she peered out into the

crowd. "I've done enough bride stuff today. I'm now on keep-Holden-Roarke-away-from-my-beloved-Emerson duty."

"We already spoke. And it was fine. I'm a big girl. I handled it."

Camille's eyes skewed back to Emerson's. "Of course you did. You're a brilliant, mature, magical unicorn." Then, "So, what was he like? Smarmy? Flirty? A douche? Ground down by the weight of the world? Still a total hunk, or has the middle-aged spread hit early? Often does with the big guys."

Emerson let go of a sigh before she even felt it coming.

"Really?" Camille said, drawing out the word. "That good, huh? Hey, remember that time I thought I saw Kailey Deluca at a shopping mall, two tiny, screaming children clinging to her knee-high Ugg boots?"

Kailey Deluca, aka *Heartache Number Three*, aka Emerson's best friend in primary school, who'd dumped her on day one of high school.

"If she hadn't turned weird we'd never have found one another, and would not be standing here, together, right now." Camille's hand slid through the crook of Emerson's arm and they leaned towards one another, skulls gently knocking. "Thank you for being my best woman. No one else could possibly have fitted that title. Much less that dress."

Emerson glanced down at her slinky sparkles. "It is quite a dress."

Camille grinned. "Has it worked?"

"In what way?"

"Did you not wonder why I allowed you to look hotter than me on my wedding day? I was hoping some dashing friend of Phillip's would man up and sweep you off your feet, then you'd fall in love and be as deliriously happy as I am. Then we could buy houses side by side and have babies together…" She stopped to take a breath. "Was that too much to ask?"

It seemed Emerson wasn't the only one sensing change in the air. Her heart squeezed—not an ache, but it was close.

She held Camille's face between her hands and gave the cheeks a wiggle. "The night is still young; who knows what it might yet bring? Now, is this a party or is this a party?"

"It's a party!"

With that Emerson downed the last drops of her third—or was it fourth?—bubbly, grabbed Camille by the hand, and together they boogied out onto the dance floor.

Where the rest of the night slid by in a beautiful, ache-free blur.

CHAPTER TWO

HOLDEN'S GAZE GLANCED off the minutiae of a wedding done and dusted, cake stand empty bar a few stray crumbs, tablecloths no longer centred, centrepieces pilfered by light-fingered guests.

He righted a chair that had fallen to the ground, as Barry—the groomsman young Bernadette had taken a belated shine to—came out of nowhere to slap Holden on the back for the umpteenth time of the night.

"Last man standing!" said Barry. Then, "It was really good to meet you, mate. Don't be a stranger." When Barry looked ready to move in for what looked to be a teary hug, the remaining groomsmen descended, midway through the umpteenth rendition of *Sweet Caroline* of the night, and dragged Barry out of the marquee's gently flapping exit.

And all was quiet once more.

The noise and light had done an admirable job of drowning out Holden's thoughts, but the moment they could they returned with a flourish, unhappy memories, unprocessed regrets…all of them wrapped up in this damn city.

He had meant it when he'd declined Phillip's generous invitation, for he was back in the country for a limited time and a specific purpose and had every intention of getting the hell out of Dodge the moment he was done. Then the weekend had whipped around, and with it hours of dead time looming before him.

An hour-and-a-half drive to Sorrento—late enough to miss the ceremony, early enough to fill the evening with the perpetual blur of cheerful company, innocuous conversation, blunting distraction—had seemed just the ticket.

It had delivered. Not two minutes had passed all night long without him finding himself cornered.

You're that app guy, right? Heard about you. Are you really retired?

Ostensibly.

As good as it sounds?

People were usually happy with a quick, *Yes*. They didn't want to hear that dreams of sitting on a beach for the rest of time lost their lustre faster than expected. That sitting still in any place for too long made that place feel like any other.

Or perhaps that was just him. The chase the thing that drove him, rather than the spoils.

So-and-So said you live in Sweden/San Francisco/ Singapore. Or are you home for good? Some new opportunity we could get in on?

A sage smile, some linguistic prevarication, and flipping the questions their way was the fastest route out of that rabbit hole.

At least the chatter had ably filled the time.

Till the bouquet toss. More specifically, the woman glinting darkly at the edge of the group, blithely refusing to partake.

While everyone else shifted and shuffled, she'd seemed so unruffled. Above it all. No, not *above*. Extrinsic. Enjoying their enjoyment, but not a part of it.

As if—despite that dress with its gravity-defying architecture, and magical fabric sparking light in a thousand directions, despite her loveliness even beyond the bewitching dress—she believed herself unseen.

Something had uncoiled inside him then, some flicker of recognition, as she watched the world as if from the other side of the looking glass.

He'd had no intention of approaching her, his plan being to take the path of least resistance. Then someone had called out "Dance with me, Emmy!" as she'd stalked past.

Swap the glossy waves for wild curls, and the tiny bag clutched in her hand for a unicorn backpack, and it was Emmy Adler—his one-time hallway buddy.

How could he not say *hello*? And then, after finding her unexpectedly crisp and zesty, like that first hit of lime in a glass of iced water, how could he not stay? For, surely, she would be the most perfect distraction of all.

A chatter of voices broke into Holden's reverie as the clean-up crew bustled through the marquee entrance hauling trolleys of supplies and packing crates. He lifted a hand to intimate he'd move out of their way.

A glance at his watch showed it was a minute before midnight, and he had a long drive ahead.

Picking his way around the detritus, he made it to the exit when he heard a commotion. He turned to find Emmy, an open magnum of bubbly in one hand, the heels of her shoes dangling from the other, her clutch bag under her chin as she bore down on the cleaners.

"Let me help," she insisted. "Do you have spare gloves?"

A murmur from one of the cleaners was followed by, "I know. Such a great wedding. Though bittersweet, you know?"

The cleaner nodded, while also clearly looking for a way out.

Holden worked his way around the maze of tables and chairs. Long drive or no, he wasn't going anywhere till he knew she was okay.

"My very best friend in the whole wide world," Emmy continued, her voice lifting. "My sister by choice if not by blood, just stepped onto a conveyor belt that runs perpendicular to my own."

When she pointed off into the distance her bag dropped to the ground, and she sank to pick it up. The cleaner saw his chance and bolted.

"I didn't expect this. Not today," Emmy muttered from her crouch. Then she lifted her hand—the one holding her shoes, not her bubbly—to her heart. "The ache, right here. I thought I was done with all that. That the List had made me immune."

"The list?" Holden asked.

Emmy looked up, her eyes wide, her mouth a comical "O". Her voice was a stage whisper as she said, "Holden Roarke. There you are again. And how on earth do *you* know about the List?"

Holden held out a hand. She offered up the near empty bottle for him to use as leverage to get her back to her feet.

"You're taller than you used to be," she said, punctuating her accusation with a slow blink of those big bright eyes of hers, a rare, mossy green, fringed by insanely long lashes and tinged with mistrust.

Holden bit his lip to stop himself from laughing. "Only because this time you're completely barefoot. Now, what's this about a list?"

She waved her shoes towards him, nearly blinding

him with a heel. "You can't use it against me, if that's your nefarious plan."

Holden held out both hands in surrender. "I have no plans, nefarious, dubious, or otherwise."

"Good. All that matters is that, while my heart might feel a little squidgy right now, I will survive this. The List taught me that. Where is everyone?" She looked around.

"We're it. Camille and Phillip left some time ago."

"Yes, they did." Emmy lifted her bottle in salute, only to find it was empty. She slowly placed it on a table by her side, the way she unwound her fingers from the neck almost ceremonial.

Then she took a step sideways, teetering so that Holden reached out to cup her elbow, to steady her. Soft, smudged, and slanted, she looked up at him.

"Gosh you smell good," she said, breathing deep. Then, "Camille made me wear this dress. So we could have babies together. Then *you* turn up smelling like fresh cut grass. It really isn't fair, considering my insides already feel like a soufflé on the verge of collapse."

Holden tried to keep up, he really did, but it was a lot, what with her leaning against him, smelling rather lovely herself. *Citrus,* he thought, *citrus, and some wholly female concoction she wore on her skin. Or maybe it was her skin. All on its own.*

"Apologies?" he murmured.

"For what?"

"I have no idea." Holden took the opportunity to lean back, so that he might breathe air not filled with her. "While your current lack of a filter is extremely enjoyable, I think the clean-up crew would love to see the back of us. Come on, let's get you home safe. Unless…"

Holden looked around to see if there were any other stray

guests. "Unless you came with someone?" He wasn't entirely surprised to find discomfort in that notion.

"Are you kidding? I get a thousand trillion points for *not* bringing a plus one."

"Because…"

"Bringing a *date* to a *wedding* is as indefensible as actively going for the bouquet."

"I hear that," he said. But only because it made getting the heck out of there easier. "Shall we?"

"Shall we what?" she asked, her hazy gaze dropping to his mouth before lifting to his eyes. And his discomfort became…creative and focused.

"Shall we…blow this joint?"

The haze cleared, pushed aside by indignation. The woman was a veritable pot luck of reactions and it was mighty entertaining.

"I'm not 'blowing' anything with you, Holden Roarke," she said, using liberal air quotes. "Or doing you any more 'favours' for that matter. I mean, the guy shrugs his big, manly shoulders, and flashes his fetching eye crinkles, and thinks he can get away with anything."

"Can't believe I'm about to say this… Fetching eye crinkles?"

Emmy blinked.

Holden smiled. "Take care you don't reveal your secret crush. Or your banking password—"

"Kevin Costner," she shot back.

"Crush, or password?"

She ignored him, her pupils growing dense, her expression dreamy. "*Field of Dreams. Bull Durham. Hidden Figures.* Sigh… How about you, Holden Roarke? Ever had a secret crush?"

When her eyes moved back to his they were so dark,

so deep, he felt the ground beneath his feet shift. Just a smidge.

"Crush, sure. Secret, no. Now, Emerson Adler, do you call everyone by both names, or should I feel special?"

Emmy shot him a look.

"Special," he muttered. "Well, that's nice, then. I'm still not giving you my passwords, so don't ask."

Her indignation cracked and she glimmered. There was no other word for it. Her eyes filled with light, and that dress—all those bronze sparkles wrapped about her as if she'd been sewn into the thing—reflected any and all atmospheric light that remained in the semi-darkness.

Holden breathed in. Emmy breathed out. And the night seemed to spin out around them.

Till Holden remembered himself, held out an arm, and gently shepherded her towards the exit.

Stepping over linen napkins, bruised flowers, a dropped fork, they made their way outside, where the forest was dark, the trees tall. And up above, the stars twinkled like sugar spilled across a black velvet rug.

Emmy stopped, looked up, rubbing her bare arms as a breeze swept off the nearby bay. "Don't move," she said, shifting a little closer. "You're warm. Like you have your own personal furnace."

Holden didn't move a muscle.

"I understand why people see stars as pretty," she said, "but they've always felt more poignant to me."

"And why's that?" he asked, tucking his hands into the pockets of his suit as he looked up at the night sky.

"I can never tell if they are happy or sad."

"I find the most beautiful things are often both."

After a few quiet moments he glanced down to find her eyes were on him. They were huge, sparkling in the starlight. A curl of dark hair dangled beside one eye. And when she smiled, she appeared completely lucid. "Holden Roarke, aren't you a surprise and a half?"

Right back at you.

Then she frowned, and shook, as if the cold night air had snapped her decision-making faculties back online. "I think it's time to go."

Holden couldn't agree more. "Where are you staying?"

"The Bay Inn with everyone else," she said, pulling her room key out of her bag. "Don't panic. I'm not about to stuff it into your pocket."

The edge of his mouth flickered. "I appreciate it. Come on, I'll drop you off before I head home."

"You're not at the inn?"

"Coming tonight was a…last-minute decision."

Funny. If she'd asked him why, with the forest shifting gently around them, and all that starlight pouring into her big, dark, attentive eyes, he might even have told her.

Instead, her eyes squeezed shut as she let go of the world's biggest yawn. Then she slipped on her shoes, one at a time, and went delving into her tiny bag for her phone as she said, "Thank you, I will accept a lift to my hotel. Though, since I do barely know you, I will send Camille a message to let her know you have me. That sounded wrong. That you're taking me— Nope. That's not right either."

Holden huffed out a ragged laugh.

"Just come here." Emmy grabbed him by the arm and hauled him close. Her cheek hovering near his own, she held up her phone. She frowned so hard he grinned, right as she touched the screen.

While she tapped at her phone, Holden ushered her to his rental sedan. Once he had her settled in the front seat, her eyes drifted closed. As if she was unable to hold them open a single second longer. As if—despite her protestations—she knew him enough to trust he'd do right by her. Which brought on a rush of affection he hadn't seen coming.

Keying the Bay Inn into his GPS, Holden took off down the coast road. Soon the gentle growl of the engine and the repetitive flash of the cat's eyes set the pace for his flickering thoughts.

Dazzling fairy lights above. The hum of the sound system at his back. Emmy, exquisitely still, at the edge of the bouquet toss. That moment, right when he'd started to enjoy her rebellion, for its own sake, when she'd turned, a slow, sensuous, bolshie upward tilt of her lips as she'd lifted her glass in salute to the laughing bride, before disappearing into the crowd.

That moment he'd found himself stuck. Literally unable to move. Till she'd swept by him. And someone had called her name.

Slowing as the road curved with the coastline, Holden spared a glance sideways. Head tipped towards the glass, her face in the reflection of the window was soft with sleep. The moonlight shimmered over the coppery sparkles on Emmy's dress. Her hands—nails short and painted almost black—lightly clutched her bag, as if even in sleep she was on guard.

Who was this woman? Spectral and defiant as she had been on the dance floor? Wary and witty as she'd been in the bar? Or delightfully candid as she was at the end of what must have been a very long, very emotional day?

Not that he'd get the chance to find out. For he'd drop her at her hotel, drive back to his apartment in the city, attend the event he'd come home to attend, then get on a plane and end up someplace far, far away from here.

CHAPTER THREE

EMERSON SLUNK INTO work early Monday morning.

She'd made it home from the peninsula around lunchtime the day before, only to be met with a load of washing still in the machine, a note under her door from a grumpy neighbour about her mum's lemon tree dropping lemons over the fence, and a "gift" from Pumpkin on the kitchen floor.

Her planned recovery day on the couch listening to true crime podcasts had not eventuated. And it showed.

Strong takeaway coffee in hand, Pumpkin plodding sweetly beside her, the entire place quiet and empty that early in the morning, she—

"Happy Monday, Emerson!"

Emerson flinched and came to a halt, as Freya, her enthusiastic and highly dedicated assistant, appeared out of nowhere looking perky and fresh and wide awake. Pumpkin plonked his backside on the floor with a huff.

Freya crouched to give Pumpkin a little treat from the bag she kept on her person for the days he came into the office, then popped back up like a Jack in the box. Her eyes widened as she said, "Did you know you're still wearing your sunglasses?"

Emerson hitched her handbag on her elbow, the move making her brain hurt, and slowly lifted her hand to her face to find, yes, her Jackie O sunglasses were still perched on the end of her nose.

The thing she'd loved most about the top-floor warehouse conversion for which Pitch Perfect had been paying eye-watering rent for the past couple of years, was the light. The double-storey outer walls were mostly window—lots of tiny panels, ancient and all but impossible to clean—and the soaring ceilings boasted big, new, storm-resistant skylights.

She braced herself before sliding her sunglasses free.

"Whoa," Freya intoned. "You look wrecked. Big weekend?"

Emerson coughed out a laugh, a gentle one that didn't shake her skull too much. Yes, Freya was a natural wonder when it came to keeping Emerson's intricate schedule balanced, but she was also as blunt as a well-used pencil.

"Camille's wedding," Emerson reminded Freya.

"Of course! Saw pics on Insta. Looked amazing."

Freya, talking through the day's schedule, took Pumpkin's lead and gave it a gentle tug, then led the way past the currently uninhabited open-plan desks of the rest of the staff, towards Emerson's office at the very rear of the space.

Leaving Emerson an extra hand to check her email on her phone, only to find her photo gallery open. More precisely, a selfie of her and Holden. Her likeness was frowning, eye make-up smudged, expression bolshie. While she'd caught Holden at the apex of an utterly heart-ache-inducing smile.

She'd never ended up sending it to Camille, hardly the kind of thing she needed to worry about on her wedding night, but she'd kept it all the same.

"Who's *he*?" said Freya.

Emerson slapped her phone to her chest and gave her assistant a look.

Freya backed up an inch. "Sorry."

"No, you're not."

Freya shot Emerson a grin. "You're right. I'm not. Come on, spill. Who's the guy?"

"He's nobody." Emerson gave her screen a deliberate swipe, before tossing her phone into her bag. "Can you eke me out a little time this morning?"

"Of course," said Freya, hooking the lead over her elbow, lifting her tablet, and hovering her finger over the keyboard. Assistant Extraordinaire Mode: Activated.

"No calls till…ten. I have some work—" aka mainlining coffee and napping with her eyes open "—to catch up on."

"Done." Freya tapped the note into her calendar, before passing the lead to Emerson and angling her way to her own floating desk outside the smoky glass wall of Emerson's office.

Emerson took the opportunity to close her glass door with a soft snick. The moment she was one with her office she breathed easier. With its delicately canted rear wall, aesthetic of cream furnishings, pale wood and caramel leather accents, its aseptic beauty was like a splash of cold water to the face. In the best way.

She picked Pumpkin up, so that he didn't have to navigate the gargantuan rug covering the pale wood floor, and popped him into his bed under her desk. Then sat in the chair behind her desk, kicked off her heels, and let her face sink into her hands.

With half an ear she heard her teams starting to arrive. The Temp Team chatting about their weekends, while readying to shore up employment contracts for the regulars who kept the business ticking over. While the Head

Hunters made Monday morning plans to land a whale—
the kind of client who could pay someone's yearly salary
with one perfect placement.

After filling a spate of high-end corporate positions in
the past few months, Pitch Perfect was generating some
real buzz. Another one or two and Emerson could relax
for a stretch. Or maybe even put in place the expansion
dreams she harboured.

That was usually where her mind went, and stayed,
when she daydreamed. But that morning her mind kept
turning to the wedding.

Phillip attempting to do the dolphin and doing himself
a damage instead, the kind that would not have helped
his wedding night. Bernadette showing the bouquet to
many a wide-eyed male guest. Camille, panda eyes filled
with tears, blowing Emerson a kiss before their Mustang
rumbled off into the night.

And then there was the veritable slideshow of memorable moments featuring Holden Roarke. His hands on her
ankle as he'd helped her with her shoe. His body heat as
they'd stood side by side, looking at the stars. The rather
large *oomph* sound he'd made as he'd swept her into his
arms outside the door to her hotel room, then carried her
inside, like *The Bodyguard* poster—

Emerson's eyes popped open. Oh, no. That had happened. And not in some romantic, over-the-threshold
movie moment. Not even slightly.

She'd woken in his car. Edit. Holden had had to *wake*
her after she'd fallen asleep in his car, the muffled sound
in the back of her head the echo of her snoring.

She next remembered leaning. In the lift? Yes, there.
And again, in the hall. There had been a cool brush of
wallpaper against her shoulder as she slumped against
the wall in order to kick off a shoe. Around which time

he'd taken her by the hand, slipped an arm beneath her knees, then hoisted her into his arms.

The next bit was a little fuzzy—due to bubbly, or a self-protective brain snap—but she felt sure she'd said something, maybe even something risqué, as his eyes had gone dark, even as he'd laughed—a rough, raw, deep sound that had scraped perilously against her insides.

Then he'd let her slide to the floor, her hand running down his hard chest. His throat bobbing when she'd stayed there, bodily against him. Her nails scraping against expensive cotton as she'd curled her fingers into his shirt.

Yep, that had happened too. And he'd been nothing but a gentleman, extricating himself from her clutches and backing slowly out of the door. Then, finally, his deep voice on the other side of the door, telling her he wasn't leaving till he heard the click of the lock.

"Emerson?"

Emerson opened her eyes to find the room had changed colour, losing the sharp cool of the early hours and filling with the buttery warmth of mid-morning. She felt lost in the loose, soft warmth that came from a dream that wasn't entirely a dream.

Emerson cleared her throat. "Come on in."

Freya hustled into the room, bearing a tall, steaming glass of black coffee and a pretty plate bearing a mix of pastel macaroons.

Emerson felt Pumpkin's tail thump slowly under her desk at the scent of sugar on the air.

Freya said, "I managed to hold back the flood but it's half past ten. Perfect time for Pumpkin to have his outside time while you take your first call. Charming, but insistent this one."

"Right. Thanks. Give me thirty seconds then send it through."

Freya nodded, gathered a soft and sleepy Pumpkin, then hustled off to sprinkle whatever dark magic she practised to keep Pitch Perfect running like clockwork.

After running her fingers through her hair, Emerson reached out for the sparkly pink paperweight that sat incongruously on her spartan desk.

Before her mum passed a couple of years back—the cancer quick and ferocious, the heartache worse than the rest of them combined—she had collected paperweights, the clear kind with swirls of resin, or glitter, or flowers suspended within. When cleaning out the childhood home her mum had left to her, Emerson had kept just the one, only for it to become a touchstone. A means of infusing her with her mother's chin-up attitude, her determination to rise after every fall.

Giving the subtle dint in the paperweight one last swipe with her thumb, she put it back in place, then pressed the answer button on her speakerphone. "Emerson Adler."

"Emerson," a deep voice intoned. "It's Holden."

Emerson bumped her coffee, sending a splash over her desk. She quickly mopped up the spill with a bunch of tissues.

Then the voice returned, saying, "Holden *Roarke*," as if that might jog her memory.

And it did. She pictured the smile in his eyes as he noted her habit of calling him by both names. Then, for a second, she pictured him querying her about the List. But that couldn't possibly have happened. Meaning, maybe, other memories of the night were false too.

Awash with relief, she said, "Holden." Then, "How on earth did you get my number?"

"You gave it to me."

Her relief dissipated in a flash. "I did?"

"Work, mobile, home, email, social media. You were extremely thorough."

"That does not sound like me at all."

"Bolshie brunette? Sparkly dress? Maid of Dishonour? Before I left you to your beauty sleep, you clicked your fingers in my face till I passed my phone over. Humming a Neil Diamond medley under your breath, rather out of tune, I'm afraid to say. Then you added all your contact details, using the picture of the two of us you'd taken to send to Camille, and—"

"Yep. Okay." The clicking did sound like her. And the picture was real. Emerson slapped her hand across her eyes. "Well, this is mortifying."

His laughter rumbled down the line. "Not at all. It was, all in all, an unexpectedly fun night. Illuminating." Then, "Whoa! All good!"

"Pardon?"

"Sorry. That wasn't for you. Almost had a collision with a Great Dane. I'm in Albert Park. Running."

"Oh," she said, leaning in towards the phone, as if she might hear the slap of his feet on the path, or any kind of stress in his breath.

Then, from nowhere, she remembered him running track in high school. Remembered taking her lunch on the hillside overlooking the oval, slowly eating her warm Vegemite sandwich as she watched his long, loping stride, and the sweat patches growing down the sides of his T-shirt with each lap—

Tossing her coffee-soaked tissue in the bin, Emerson righted herself and said, "Look, I'm glad you called, actually."

"I'm glad you're glad."

"Calm down. I'm *mildly* glad, at most."

"I'll take it," he said, his voice a rough burr that made her insides go all squidgy.

"I need to thank you. For your…consideration. After the wedding."

Carrying me over the threshold, not taking it the wrong way when I clutched at your shirt, or when I gave you goo-goo eyes. The way you stayed until I locked the door.

"I'm sure any of Phillip's friends would have done the same."

"Yes. That's true. He is a collector of good people." Emerson also knew that she'd never felt light-headed talking to any of Phillip's friends. She cleared her throat. "That said, I was feeling a little tender, which, again, is unlike me. I'm not at all sentimental—"

Her eyes slid to the paperweight and away again.

"By the end of the night I wasn't handling the…" Emerson waved her hand, trying to find a word that did not stray too close to anything "heart" or "ache" related. "Anyway, I was not exactly at my best, so, thank you for seeing me through it."

"You're welcome."

Emerson squeezed the bridge of her nose, her neck feeling warm as she worked herself up to say, "Now, as to the phone number thing. Despite what that might imply, I'm actually not in the market for a…phone number."

After a spell, Holden said, "As it turns out, I'm not in the market for…a phone number, either."

"Great," she said, slumping down in her chair, her eyes rolling towards the ceiling. "That's just…"

"Great?" he offered up.

"Yes. Now, can we please wipe Saturday night from our minds? Pretend none of it ever happened?"

"Mmm. Not sure I can. Your rejection of the bouquet toss might be one of the greatest wedding moments of all time. And then there's the fact you told me I had big, manly shoulders and...what was it? Fetching eye crinkles—"

"Holden," Emerson declared, her fingers now rubbing her temples.

"Yes, Emmy."

She thought about correcting him, but the truth was, the implied intimacy of Holden calling her Emmy was the least of her worries. "Wipe it," she said. "Wipe it from your mind."

Holden laughed, all rough and raw. For a man who wasn't in the market for her *phone number*, he sure did phone call well.

Emerson rocked her chair side to side. "Now, what can I do for you, Holden?" See, she could say his name. Singularly. Not special at all.

"Right. Yes. I have a favour to ask."

"Another favour."

"Mmm?"

"Do me a favour. Protect me from the sweet young woman wielding the evil bouquet," said Emerson, her voice as deep and rough as she could manage.

Holden laughed. Something in the sound making her picture him slowing to a walk, a drip of sweat making a slow trail down the sculpted edge of his jaw.

Then suddenly she remembered what she'd said to Holden when he'd carried her into the hotel room. *Do me a favour. Don't leave, this time, without saying goodbye.*

So very glad this was a phone call not a video call, Emerson let her head fall to her desk. And there she stayed as Holden's voice said, "I'd rather think tucking you up in bed, and wishing you sweet dreams, would put me one favour up."

"You did *not* tuck me into bed." Of that she was nearly absolutely sure.

"Consider that artistic licence. Look. I truly do need a favour, Emmy. I have no problem taking no for an answer. But if you do this one thing for me, then…then we would not be even. Not even close. I would owe you, big time."

Emerson lifted her head and stared at her speaker-phone.

Yes, bumping into him had been nowhere near as horrible as she'd imagined it might be. Yes, the ache she'd once felt any time she even thought his name was long gone. But pushing it any further was tempting fate.

Unless…

Unless this was actually an opportunity. A chance to be absolutely sure that the Heartache List had done its job. That, due to the foundation built upon its lessons, no matter what life threw at her she would be okay.

"No promises," she said, "but give me the gist."

"Can do. I need you to be my date on Friday night."

Emerson may have snorted. And coughed. At the same time. Leading to a rather unladylike choking noise.

"Actually, strike that," Holden said. "*Not* a date, a plus one. Not to a wedding, for that would wipe out all the points I'd earned at the last one. The wedding I have now forgotten completely."

He stopped talking. Took a breath. Said, "What I am truly in need of is someone to accompany me to an up-coming dinner. And I was hoping you might be the one."

"A date," Emerson responded, the words flat, as if she didn't like the taste.

"But *not* a date," Holden reiterated, smiling briefly

at another runner as he moved off the path and into the speckled shade of a gum tree, pacing so that the lactic acid wouldn't start to itch. "A seat at a table, on which there will be food and drink for you to enjoy. At a place. With great people who love a chance to dress up. And have a laugh. And eat together."

Holden pressed his earbud deeper into his ear and was reminded how it had been the other night, standing danger close, their voices low and intimate, the star-spangled sky hovering silently above. He wiped his hand down the side of his shorts, actually sweating as he waited for her response.

Which was, "So long as that's clear."

They'd spent a grand total of an hour together, at most, during and after the wedding, and yet he could picture, with clarity, Emmy's expression as she deadpanned him. Gaze direct, a slight lift of her right eyebrow, her mouth twisted to the left, a healthy amount of reticence apparent on her lovely face.

"Thought you'd appreciate the delineation," he said. "Considering your aversion to phone numbers."

She laughed at that. Or maybe it was a sigh. Either way, he pictured a squint to those striking, moss-green eyes. Impossibly long lashes creating shadows over elegant cheekbones. A brief flash of teeth, the front two slightly too long, slightly too big, adding whimsy to the list of things about her that he'd found stunning.

Dappled shade fluttering over his face, Holden pressed the bud deeper into his ear again, and looked to the jut of the Melbourne city skyline, a smear of grey on the horizon.

Yes, she was stunning. Empirically. Objectively. And yes, there had been a spark, one which he'd bet quite a bit went both ways. But he was in town for a blink. A fraught blink, at that. So that wasn't what this was about.

He was asking her to accompany him because he knew she'd be able to handle herself with the dinner crowd. And when he was with her, for whatever reason, she drew his focus and kept it. Add her stated lack of interest in his "phone number" and she was perfect. The perfect non-date date.

"Look," he said, "the entire reason I am here, in Melbourne, is to catch up with some people I haven't seen in some time. There is history between us. Complicated history. And I feel that it all might go more smoothly if I bring…" *a distraction, a foil, someone shiny and lovely and bright* "…a friend."

A definite sigh that time. "And you want me for this."

"I do want you. For this," he added belatedly enough he feared he might have shot himself in the foot.

Not quite, as she said, "Surely you could get an easy yes from anyone else."

Pacing no longer cutting it, he waited for a gap, then jogged back out onto the track. "As a single man, of good fortune, 'tis true, I am hugely popular."

"Good grief," she muttered.

"Thing is, Emmy, I trust that you are savvy enough to see this for what it is, a favour done, giving you a favour in hand, should you ever need it. Nothing more."

"Let me get this straight," she said. "You're asking me to join you for some complicated mystery dinner, because you believe I won't mistake a favour date for a *date-date* and what? Accidentally fall in love with you?"

Holden grinned, as he eased around a little old lady out walking her tiny dog. "Not accidentally falling in love with me is absolutely imperative. So, if that's going to be a problem…"

"The man's ego knows no bounds."

"So?"

"Just…give me a minute."

Emmy breathed out hard, and when Holden next swallowed he had the sense memory of lime on the back of his tongue.

He picked up his pace and looked out across the acres of parkland. Parents speed-walked, prams bumped over every tiny crack in the path, shuffle runners shuffled, and bike riders wove.

To think this was the same city in which he'd grown up.

His childhood had not been so green, or nearly so free. Controlled, it had been, by a man who'd taken every chance to assure him that being a smart arse would get him nowhere.

The very best thing about finding himself in a position to retire at such a young age had been the autonomy. He could go anywhere, stay as long as he liked, leave on a whim. He could work hard, or do nothing at all. There was no overriding force holding him to any one place, holding him back.

Which meant waiting on someone to decide his fate was now rare.

"What are you worried about?" he asked when he could no longer hold his tongue.

"I'm not worried."

"Great, because I've seen you in action. You're a force to be reckoned with when…sensical."

"Sensical?"

"The opposite of—"

"Nonsensical," she finished for him, the word dripping with irony.

"Don't get me wrong, when nonsensical you're an absolute delight. But I'd be far too worried that you'd hand over your phone number, and passwords, and your address, and your mother's maiden name and—"

"Yes, thank you. I get it."

"Great. So?"

"I think I'm going to regret this. But fine, I will be your platonic, non-date, favour mandated plus one."

Holden punched the air, scaring a golden retriever. He held out a placating hand in apology to the owner, a young woman in head-to-toe pink, who smiled and tugged on her ponytail.

"I honestly can't believe I've agreed to this." Emmy's voice came through his earbuds, husky and rich, yet grounding somehow. A tether, to some point in the past. Or perhaps it was the affinity he'd felt tug between them, as she'd stood on the outside of the crowd looking in.

"You hungry?" he asked.

"Often."

"I mean now. I'm ravenous all of a sudden. Let's have lunch."

"I can't have lunch with you, Holden."

"Sure, you can." A beat, then, "Not a lunch *date*."

"Holden," she said, her voice the very height of *sensical*.

"Yes, Emmy."

"I'll go to this dinner of yours. As a *favour*. Which you will then owe me. And I will call you on that favour any time I wish, for any reason that I see fit. Unless it's illegal, or impossible, you cannot refuse me. Those are the parameters of the deal."

Parameters, discreet edges, a neat and tidy package of an agreement. Actually, that sounded entirely sensical. Especially considering what had been the perilous lack of parameters the last time he'd spent time with the family.

"Deal," he said, picturing an imaginary shaking of

hands. She with her short dark nails. The same ones that
had gripped his shirt in her hotel room as she'd looked up
at him, her eyes swimming with champagne and invitation.

"Friday," said Emmy, all business.

"Friday," he said, mirroring her tone. "I'll pick you
up. Office or home?"

"Home." She gave him an address in Kew, not far from
their old school. "I'll need to change."

"Nah," he said. "Don't change a thing."

"Smooth."

"I try."

"Stop trying. With me there is no need. For we are…
friendly…and do favours…and have clear parameters.
Till Friday." With that she rang off.

Holden punched the air again, a subtle, hip-high jab,
before yanking the bud from his ear and shoving it in
his pocket.

His return to Melbourne, for the first time in years,
had been far easier than he'd imagined. Old friends were
calling. Even the infamously changeable weather had
been spectacular. As if wounds really might heal over,
after enough time.

But he knew it wasn't that simple. Some wounds were
so deep, they never fully healed. The scar tissue became
formative, a reminder to stay frosty, and alert.

The dinner party would be his reckoning. Payment
for his soft landing.

Whether it was right or wrong to rope in Emmy Adler
would be something he'd face once it was all said and
done.

CHAPTER FOUR

FRIDAY AFTERNOON, EMERSON slid into the back seat of her ride share, mentally spent after a Women in Business lunch at which she'd hobnobbed and networked like there was no tomorrow.

Freya hopped in after her, brimming with energy and enthusiasm, talking a mile a minute about the contacts they'd made.

When Emerson's phone buzzed and she held up a "just a second" finger, Freya turned to the driver to regale him with her stories. While Emerson's heart bucked when she saw Holden's message.

All good for tonight?

Her thumb hovered over the screen. If she wanted to beg off, bone-deep weariness after a long week was a fair excuse. In the end, she typed:

All good.

Brilliant. Quick question: I'm prepping the contract, for our exchange of favours. Would you prefer it typed out in triplicate? Or should we trust we are as good as our word?

Emerson twisted in her seat, tilting her phone so that Freya—who really couldn't help herself—didn't read over her shoulder as she typed:

I have no clue how trustworthy you are. We met outside the guidance counsellor's office, after all.

Holden's reply:

Pot, meet kettle.

Excuse me. My reasons for being there were innocent and good, bordering on angelic. You?

Fair call. So, written in blood. Got it.

Emerson realised she was smiling. She told her face to calm down. Then looked out of the window, watching the cityscape flicker by, before her gaze went back to her phone. She typed:

Look, as far as I could tell, you didn't steal any money from my purse when you saw me to my room, so let's go with our word.

I thought we were never to speak of that night again.

You are not to speak of it. I am under no such gag order.

Freya glanced at Emerson, and the phone she was cradling close to her chest, curiosity written all over her face. Emerson offered up a beatific smile, and Freya lost interest, leaning forward to ask the driver to take a particular route.

Emerson glanced back at her phone. Holden had written:

If I agree to never speak of the drool you left on my car seat, can we take that as the favour returned? Partially at least.

Negative.

Then I make no promises. See you tonight.

Emerson barked out a laugh, the sound echoing in the confined space.

"You're not going to tell me what that was all about, are you?" Freya asked, curiosity leaching so patently from her skin she vibrated.

"Nope," said Emerson, sliding her phone into her bag.

"I know your phone password."

"Ha! I have no doubt. And yet I know you'd never look at my phone without asking because you are the most wonderful, dedicated, loyal assistant in the whole wide world."

"Also true."

With that, Emerson settled into the car, closed her eyes, and gave in to the rocking sensation as they trundled back to work.

Emmy sat slumped in the red plastic chair in the hallway outside Miss Kemp's office, holding her unicorn backpack to her chest, bouncing the heels of her school shoes against the linoleum floor. A loud squeak had her peeking her head around her bag to find she'd left a mark.

After a quick glance to the front desk to make sure ancient Mrs Carmichael hadn't noticed, she licked her thumb, bent at the waist, and rubbed frantically at the stain.

The door banged—the way it always did before opening—and she sat up so fast her head swam.

The sound of laughter, and a deep, warm voice, wafted out into the hall—neither of which meshed with her experiences with the earnest guidance counsellor her mum insisted she see after she told her mum, at dinner one night, that she hated her dad and always would.

Then, through the doorway, came a boy. A boy she'd never seen before. She'd have remembered those smoky blue eyes. Those shoulders—like a man's shoulders. The way he stood, as if he wasn't hyper-aware of himself every moment of the day.

That might be, she thought, *the most beautiful boy to have ever walked planet earth.*

The guidance counsellor leaned in the doorway, her face etched with concern, the way it had been on Emerson's first visit. Her voice low, private, and possibly muffled by the fluffy white clouds that had wafted into Emmy's head.

Then the boy started moving Emmy's way.

In slow motion, no less, his shoulder turning first, then hips, then feet. His head moved last, his hair swishing slightly, flicking across his face before landing in the most perfect spot for his face. Then he started to walk, slow, easy, chest out, all constrained power and vitality as he swung his near empty black backpack onto his shoulder.

Then, right when she was staring at him the very most, his eyes met hers.

Her heart stopped. Literally. *Ba-dum, ba-dum, ba-dum*…then nothing.

A smile kicked at the corner of his mouth. "Hey," he said, lifting his chin.

Emmy gulped. Eyes burning from not having blinked since the moment he'd appeared.

Then his smile grew, widening, showing actual teeth, as if he knew exactly why she sat there, unmoving. Dumbstruck. Completely and utterly crushing on him.

"I've warmed her up for you," he said, to her, in a voice that spread through her body like liquid heat.

The tip of his finger touched his brow in salute, and then he was gone.

And the guidance counsellor was calling her name as if she'd been calling it for some time.

"Emmy? *Emerson?*"

"Emerson. We're here."

Emerson blinked to find herself in the back of the ride share.

Freya slid out of the car, and Emerson went to follow before staying put.

"Are you free to take me to Kew?" she asked the driver.

He poked something into his machine and said, "You bet."

"Super. Freya, I'm clocking out. I have an...event to prepare for."

"Tonight?" Freya frowned at her trusty tablet. "It's not on the calendar."

"A private event."

"Ooh," said Freya, eyebrows waggling. "Exciting."

"No. Not like that."

"Oh," said Freya, her enthusiasm turning to disappointment on a dime.

"Can I leave it to you to make sure everyone leaves on time so they can enjoy their weekend? Can you remind the temp crew we have a meeting ten a.m. Monday? And—"

"I've got it." Freya tapped at her tablet. "I'm up to the task."

"Yes, you are."

Emerson closed the door, gave the driver her address.

With the memory of the first time she'd laid eyes on Holden Roarke still swimming in her subconscious, she made her way home to get ready for a non-date date with the guy.

Figuring a little extra time to put on a little extra armour couldn't hurt.

Emerson paced the entrance hall of her small, but lovingly refurbished childhood home, stepping from floorboard to floorboard in a repetitive pattern as the seconds slipped away till Holden was due to arrive at her door.

Pumpkin, no doubt picking up on her heightened energy, had found enough latent energy of his own in his dear old legs to leave his big, soft bed, his rheumy eyes following her as she paced.

"I'm not nervous," she said, bending to give her beautiful boy a gentle scruff behind his soft ears.

Pumpkin sniffed out a breath that appeared to be a doggy version of an eye roll.

"I'm not! I can hold up my end in *any* conversation. I spend my days going head-to-head with captains of industry. With entrenched politicians. I'm a boss, don't you know? No room in my life for nerves."

Yet as a shadow appeared at the frosted window in her front door just before a knock sounded, her heart *ba-da-boomed* in her chest.

She turned Pumpkin, gave his tail end a light nudge to send him walking back towards his bed for the evening. Then she grabbed her clutch bag, straightened her shoulders, ran a quick hand over her freshly washed and styled hair, another down the hip of her dress, and opened the door.

Only to have her mouth dry up at the sight of Holden Roarke standing on her porch, hands in pockets, smile hooking the corners of his mouth as his eyes roved over her porch swing, the bougainvillea spilling from her hanging pots, and the vintage brass lamps lit up warmly either side of her door.

It had been a little under a week since the wedding, at which time she'd seen him all dolled up. He'd even swept her off her feet that night, literally. But somehow in the days in between her subconscious had worked overtime to mitigate his impact.

Feeling an echo of that first time she'd seen him leaving the guidance counsellor's office, she swallowed at the sight of those shoulders. Those eyes. That mouth—full and relaxed, with the hint of a crescent in one cheek, as if prepared to smile at any time.

"This is not at all what I expected," said Holden, sounding utterly relaxed. While she vibrated like a freshly plucked guitar.

"Meaning?"

"I imagined something cool, modern, sleek. Scandinavian aesthetic. Slightly intimidating. But this might well be the cutest house I have ever seen."

A mite agitated by the fact he'd described her workplace to a T and feeling more than a mite exposed by having this man at her home, she murmured, "I inherited it. From my mum. I grew up here."

"And you live here still? Aw… I'm adjusting my opinion of you accordingly."

"Super."

With that, Holden's eyes finally moved to her, and the open-mouthed delight dropped from his face. A single blink and he'd taken her measure—the gunmetal-grey silk of her dress, tucked and wrapped about her like a sexy toga, the thigh split, the sweep of her hair, left down. Something dark, rich, and devouring overcame his face as he took her in. *Drank her in*, more like. In a great, heady gulp that left her swaying on her heels.

Beyond the hum of cicadas and distant traffic, she could feel the energy trapped behind his loose, cool façade. Electricity barely contained. The man was permanently lying in wait.

"Emerson Adler," he all but growled. "When you do a guy a favour, you do a guy a favour."

Fine. So she'd wanted to look good. No, she'd wanted to look *smoking*. A little bit of a *screw you* to the guy not asking her to accompany him anywhere, not even on a non-date, back when she was a sweet, gawky, smart, interesting, totally worth-it fourteen-year-old.

"You said your friends dress up for dinner," she murmured.

"And I will, from this day forth, be grateful that I did. Now, your turn."

"To?"

"Compliment me on the effort I put into looking nice for you."

"Oh, this," she said, waving a hand down her side, "is not for you."

"Is that so?"

"The more effort I put into this favour, the more effort I'll expect when I call yours in."

"Right. Well, just so we're clear, this," he said, rocking side to side, flapping his jacket open, looking utterly scrumptious while doing so, "was all for you."

Emerson rolled her eyes. "You're not giving up, are you? Fine, you look very nice."

"I try."

"Stop trying!" She shooed him backwards so that she could lock her door.

Only he ignored her and unexpectedly dropped to a crouch.

"And who is this?" Holden asked, reaching out a hand.

Emerson looked down at her feet to find Pumpkin at the door.

Oh, honey, she thought, her heart squeezing at the sight of her old boy, his whole body slowly shaking side to side as he attempted to wag his tail.

"This," said Emerson, her voice softening, "is Pumpkin. Pumpkin, meet Holden Roarke."

Holden ran a gentle hand over Pumpkin's crown, as if he knew he was fragile. "He's a gorgeous thing. Aren't you, mate?"

That he was, Emerson thought, her breath tightening, just a little. Only when seeing him through the eyes of someone new did she notice that his lustrous caramel fur was a little patchy these days, his gait a little wonky. But he was sweet and loving, and—her vet assured her—doing miraculously well for his age. And as precious to her today as when she'd first held him in her arms.

"Into bed," she said.

Holden's dark and stormy eyes lifted to hers.

"The dog," she deadpanned.

She waggled her fingers between them, motioning for Holden to move, then placed her hand under Pumpkin's chin and said, "Bed time."

With a snuffle the old dog gave her his best sad eyes, before he turned and padded back up the hall.

Emerson stood, only to find herself all but flush

against her guest, her hand lifted to steady herself, flashing her back to the hotel room, when she'd gripped his shirt.

When her eyes lifted to his, she was certain he knew exactly where her mind had gone.

"Scoot," she said. "I can't shut the door with you standing in the way."

"You're in an all-fire rush," he said, before turning and ambling onto the porch, the view from behind as good as the view from the front.

She locked up. "The sooner we get there, the sooner it will be over."

"Not sure that's how dinner parties work, but hey, happy to be proven wrong."

"Why?" she said, noting a shift in tone beneath his easy words. "Do you not *want* to go?"

Holden shot her a look, as if he hadn't meant for her to take it that way. Or hadn't expected her to pick up on it. Then he jogged down her front steps and backed down her path, a hand pressed against the stark white of his button-down shirt. "Can it not be that I am simply looking forward to being in your incandescent company for as long as I can?"

He was prevaricating. But by that stage he'd reached a sleek black sedan, different from the one he'd taken to the wedding, she was sure.

He held open the car door, smiling into her eyes as he said, "If you feel the need to fall asleep, again, I'm good with that."

"So kind of you," she gritted out, his deep, warm waves of laughter rolling through her as she closed the door.

By the time Holden pulled up by a guarded gate between a wall of long box hedges, Emerson felt faint from holding her breath so as not to drown in his delicious scent. Some magical mix of chopped wood, sea air, and clean skin.

When he slid down his window, she breathed so deeply of the fresh air she nearly choked on it.

A woman in a security uniform popped her head out of the box. "Mr Roarke! It's been—"

"It has been some while." Holden smiled.

"Saw your name on the guest list. Thought it must have been an error."

"No error," said Holden easily. "Should be down for two. This is my friend Emerson Adler. Emerson, this is Sandra."

The guard leaned down. Saw Emerson. Blinked once. "Well. Ain't it the night for surprises?"

With that, the guard moved back inside her booth, and pressed a button that set big wrought-iron gates to opening.

"Good to see you again, Sandra," said Holden.

To which the guard said, "Good luck."

Curiosity spiking in a dozen different directions, Emerson was still deciding which question to ask first when the house came into view. It was like something out of *The Great Gatsby*, three storeys, with wings, and gables and what looked like a forest sprawled out behind it.

"Holy moly," she whispered, leaning so far forward her hands gripped the dashboard.

"Careful," Holden murmured as he curved onto the huge circular drive, "you're starting to drool. Again."

Emerson shot him a look. The humour lighting the storm-cloud blue of his eyes made the backs of her knees tingle, as if he had a direct line to certain nerve clusters in her body and all he had to do was tug.

"Whose house *is* this?" she asked.

She felt rather than heard the slightest hesitation before he said, "Bettina and Chuck Sanderson."

"As in the *Sanderson Group* Sandersons?"

"The very ones."

While her work put her in the path of influential people with impressive staffing needs, the Sanderson real estate family was a whole other level.

This was not merely a favour any more, or the chance to exorcise her Heartache List demons for good. It was a huge opportunity. Perhaps even the opportunity of a lifetime.

Holden pulled the car to a stop in front of the house, its engine softening to a throaty rumble. "You need a moment?"

"Nope. I'm fine."

"Just so you know, I can practically hear the wheels cranking behind those big green eyes of yours."

Emerson looked to her lap, before shooting him a smile. "Perhaps that's the engine whimpering. You ride the clutch, you know."

A liveried gentleman opened her door right at the perfect moment, so that she could decamp the car, rather than face Holden's burst of laughter.

Only to find she had to twist and contort herself, to navigate the split in her madly dressy dress. If only she'd asked more questions she might have dressed like an enterprising HR guru rather than an awards-show presenter.

"Shall we?" Holden asked, ambling around the front of the car, hand palm-up.

Emerson gripped tighter to her clutch bag.

He noticed, the edge of his mouth kicking up. As if he was playing with her. Testing her parameters. But he didn't press her.

With a tilt of his head, he motioned for her to join him on the walk up the wide front steps.

As they neared the front door—as wide as it was tall, and taller than her by double—Emerson felt Holden hesitate. Felt the energy coiled inside him expand, felt him lock it down hard, as if in preparation for something big.

And all her wild thoughts of using this night to sell herself to the Sandersons blew away like so much dust.

Holden had asked her to accompany him for a reason. This hulking, self-sufficient, charming genius felt as if he needed someone on his side. Maybe it was time to stop thinking about her own part in this, and give the guy a break.

"Hold up for a second," she said, moving in closer and sliding her hand into the crook of his arm. Ignoring, as best she could, the warmth of his skin seeping through the fabric, the hard strength against her palm. "What's our game plan?"

"Game plan?" he asked, the clouds sweeping from his eyes as he looked down into hers.

"What have you told them about me? Do we have a backstory? Are they aware this is not a date-date? Please tell me you don't expect me to act as if I'm madly in love with you. You're right, I'm good on my feet, but that might be beyond me."

"Might?" he asked, and that smile—the one that spread across his face in a slow, easy, sensuous sweep of warmth and deliciousness—came out to play. "No pretending required. You're you. I'm me. We came together. That simple."

"Okay, then," said Emerson, even while she was becoming more and more sure that it was far more complicated than he'd let on.

She realised then that, for all that he had occupied such

an important place in *her* backstory, she knew very little about him. Apparently, he made apps and lived overseas. He definitely smelled great, and was devastatingly good-looking, and knew how to wear a suit. The rest was a puzzle that had been tipped out of the box at her feet.

"Ready?" she asked.

"As I'll ever be." With a deep breath, Holden opened the door without knocking, then waited for Emerson to precede him inside.

She barely had time to take in the soaring ceilings, the sweeping staircase, the vases of hydrangeas covering every surface, the art on the walls, when a handsome silver-haired gentleman in a wheelchair descended upon them, pulling to a stop and opening his arms wide.

"Holden, my boy!"

"Chuck," said Holden, his arm hardening beneath Emerson's hand, before he let her hand fall, and opened his arms just as wide.

Emerson held back, clutching her bag, as Holden Roarke and one of the richest men in Australia indulged in a long hug.

"So, when are you coming out of this ridiculous 'retirement' of yours to come back and work for me?" Chuck asked as Holden pulled away.

Holden laughed as he moved back to Emerson's side, putting her hand back into the crook of his arm. She tucked his arm close, aware that his laughter didn't have the same sense of release as when he laughed at her.

"I like retirement," Holden said. "It's only slightly ridiculous. Gives me the means to be a man of the modern zeitgeist, following my bliss."

Chuck's eyes narrowed, as if he didn't believe the spin. "Don't tell my wife you said that. She's constantly telling me it's time to wind back. Take up painting. Meditate. Can't imagine anything worse."

"I heard that," said an attractive ice blonde who'd ambled up behind him. Bettina Sanderson leaned to place a kiss on her husband's cheek before standing and eyeballing Holden. "Why, hello there, stranger."

"Bettina," Holden returned, his voice lit with a level of affection Emerson wasn't expecting, considering how edgy he'd seemed outside.

"One day," said Bettina, "all that rolling stone rubbish will become tiresome and someone will make you an offer you can't refuse. Mark my words."

Chuck's gaze seemed to take in Emerson for the first time, as if he'd been blinded by the man at her side, surprise flickering behind his eyes before he blinked, his face a mask of amiability.

"Well, well, well," said Chuck. "Bettina mentioned you were bringing a friend."

Holden looked to Emerson, bathing her in a smile that sent goosebumps up and down her arms. "Chuck, Bettina, this is my friend Emerson Adler. Emerson, I give you Chuck and Bettina Sanderson."

Bettina moved out from behind her husband's wheelchair, took Emerson by the hands and looked her over as if trying to commit her to memory. "We are so pleased to meet you, Emerson."

"Likewise, I assure you."

"My turn," said Chuck, rolling his chair towards her.

Emerson readied to shake, only to find herself pulled down into her own warm, solid hug.

"Oh," she said, one hand fluttering against the man's beefy shoulder, the other still gripping her clutch bag. She truly hoped she didn't look as awkward as she felt.

Until she glanced to the side to find Holden being

summarily hugged by Bettina, and he hugging her back.
Something about the shape of them, the hunched shoulders, the closed eyes, the tight mouths, made her heart
thud against her ribs. Made her look away, as if she'd accidentally witnessed something private.

"So, what do you do, Emerson? What's your *bliss*?"
said Chuck, gathering her attention, a hand still holding hers.

"My bliss? Much like you, I fear, my bliss is my work.
I run my own HR firm, Pitch Perfect. We wield a small,
exclusive pool of highly experienced temps, but at our
core we consult, source, scout, and place quality applicants into significant positions in corporate, charitable
and political environments. And...that sounded like it
came straight from our website. I'm so sorry. I was at
the Women in Business lunch today and must have said
those exact words a hundred times."

Chuck's eyes sharpened, the infamous businessman
showing beneath the mask of gracious host. "You're a
head hunter."

"I am. And a damned fine one at that."

Chuck chuckled as his wife came back to his side.
"We're going to have to watch out for this one."

"Then we shall." Bettina's smile was kind and warm.
"You're the last here—let's head in."

Emerson nodded, so starstruck she didn't realise how
quiet Holden had been since that moment with Bettina
until it was just the two of them, trailing behind their
hosts as they made their way through the house.

Emerson slowed with him, lifting an eyebrow in question.

Everything okay?

His response, a flicker below one eye, and a shake
of the head.

All good.

But he wasn't. Which was why she slowed further, till they walked side by side.

"Are you really retired? Like, actually?"

"Since I was in my mid-twenties. Though I'm dragged out of it on occasion, usually when finding myself frustrated by the lack of an app that I can't believe is yet to exist, and so have to build it myself."

She shook her head. Unable to imagine what it might feel like not to chase, not to grind, not to keep a sharp, narrow focus on one's life plan. Not to need that kind of control.

"What *have* you dragged me into, Roarke?" she asked, looking up as they passed under yet another chandelier. "Is it Stepford or Virginia Woolf?"

Holden's face broke into a quick, delighted grin, before it faded to a humourless smile. His spare hand ran the back of his neck, pinching hard. "Long story."

"Too long to tell me before dinner?"

"Much."

"I see."

He paused, forcing her to stop. "Emmy, if this is too much, if you'd prefer to leave, I will take you home. No judgement. No questions asked. Favour still owed to you in full."

She looked at him then, really looked at him. This real-life, flesh-and-blood man who needed her.

Before she could second guess herself, she held out her hand. A question flickered behind his eyes, before his long fingers closed around hers. Then they walked shoulder to shoulder, hip to hip, the fabric of his suit creating soft, rhythmic, enthralling friction all down her side.

When he leaned towards her, his mouth near her ear, and murmured, "Why do I get the feeling you've just amped up the kind of favour you plan to ask in return?" it took everything in her power not to shiver.

"Favour is such a small word for what I have in mind for you, Holden."

"Lucky me."

CHAPTER FIVE

HOLDEN'S JACKET HUNG over the back of the gilt dining chair, his shirtsleeves now rolled to his elbows. His right leg shook up and down beneath the table, dissipating the lashings of excess energy he could not hope to contain.

For the laughter, the heads tilted together in deep conversation, the random hands passing food across the table... It was years since he'd been a regular at such gatherings in this house, and yet it was so familiar to him it stung.

When he realised that he was rubbing the heel of his palm over his chest Holden dropped his hand to the table. Stretching out tight fingers. Rolling a tense shoulder till it cracked. He glanced down the table to find Emmy watching him over the top of her glass of wine.

She sat near enough that he could see the curiosity in her eyes. Too far away for his liking.

For, he was discovering, he liked having her close.

When he'd called, asking for her to join him, he hadn't exactly thought it through. It had been instinct, more than anything. An idea that, knowing she'd be there, he'd actually show up.

But the bigger truth was, he liked Emerson Adler. He found her lovely, and surprising, and hugely entertaining. Then there was the way she walked, as if a big band with a heavy bass drum played her into every room. And the way she smelled, like lime and spring time—

Holden blinked and looked deliberately about the table, to the walls, the ostentatious fresco on the ceiling, before finding Emmy's eyes again, unsurprised to find her watching him still.

So he offered up a slow smile. Intimate. Playful. Chancy, considering the company. But everything about the night was precarious; what was one more layer of exposure?

Nice digs, huh? he said with his eyes.

Emmy's glass twirled in response, the stem twisting between her fingers, catching the light which glinted and shifted across her lovely face. Then she lifted a shoulder in a shrug, the shoulder covered in the silken dark hair swept to one side like some forties siren.

Sure. Whatever.

He laughed out loud.

"Holden?"

He flinched. Then turned to Bettina, who sat to his left, at the end of the table. "Sorry. I was a million miles away."

Her chin tilted towards the other end of the table. "Not so very far as that."

His leg started jiggling once again.

"I only hope, now you're back, that you'll stay. For a while at least. All that rushing about isn't good for a person's health." Her gaze went to her husband.

Her comment, for all its sincerity, made his gut curl in on itself, like self-perpetuating quicksand. For there was enough water under that bridge to drown a man in minutes.

They were all there, ostensibly, to celebrate Chuck's seventieth birthday. But this month was ripe with unspoken anniversaries for this family. Five years since the accident that had put Chuck in that wheelchair, since Marnie had run off, Holden too.

And seven years since…since the horror that had tied them inexorably together in the first place.

Bettina looked at him and smiled. As if it had all been forgiven in five minutes. Then she asked, "Have you spoken to my daughter?"

"On occasion," Holden admitted, reaching for his iced water.

Marnie. Bettina and Chuck's daughter, who'd run off to America with the gardener. While still engaged to Holden. She now lived happily ever after in Maine with their two young kids.

"I thought she might be here."

Bettina's smile was soft. "She's always gone her own way, as you well know. But I am glad you two have kept in touch. You were always friends above all else." A sip of wine, then, "I knew she'd bounce back, she's a tough cookie. But I worried that what we did to you… I worried that whole thing might have given you all the ammunition you needed to go into your cave and stay there."

"What you did to me?" Holden reiterated, honestly stunned to hear her put it that way. "Taking me on, taking me in? Monsters, the lot of you."

She cocked her head. And waited.

"I'm fine," he assured her.

Bettina took his words at face value. Then leaned back in her chair. "I like her."

"Your daughter? I hope so."

Bettina slapped him lightly on the hand. And nodded once again towards Emmy. "I wasn't expecting to. In fact, I was ready to pretend like crazy. But she's wonderful."

"She's all right, I guess, if you can get past the toenail collection and raging kleptomania."

"Don't do that. She's *wonderful*, Holden. Stunning, which is no surprise. But that's only the half of it. She's substantial, and shrewd, with just a touch of wild. The two of you, together? Watch out, world."

Holden's chest grew tight, the muscles contracting as if weary of trying to hold all the parts of him together. "She's just a friend, Bettina. Newly minted. We knew one another for a short time a long time ago, met again at a wedding a week or so ago, and I invited her here in a fit of panic."

Bettina huffed out a small laugh. "You are the only young man I know who would do such a thing, and still end up with the gem of the ball. I've missed that. Missed you. Not just for Marnie's sake. Or Chuck's. Or Saul's."

Bettina blinked, a shimmer in her eyes that disappeared almost instantly, before she tipped her chin towards the other end of the table. "But since she is merely a friend, as you attest, then you won't mind if young Kris over there makes a play."

Though he knew he was being baited, Holden glanced down the table to find "young Kris" leaning into Emmy, resting his arm across the back of her chair.

A spike of possessiveness, for which he was not prepared or particularly proud, shot down his spine. Until Emmy turned to "young Kris", glanced pointedly at his arm, and watched as it was removed.

Feeling much better about things, Holden turned his back on the scene. "How is Chuck?"

"Retiring."

"You're kidding."

Bettina waved a placating hand. "It's time. I want him

with me. By my side. As much as I can have him. I have him ninety-nine per cent convinced."

It was a night for surprises.

"On that note…" Bettina surged to her feet, tapping a spoon against her wine glass, and the conversation fizzled to a halt. "I want to thank you all for coming tonight to help us celebrate our beloved Chuck, on his birthday. Five years ago this very week we imagined this day might not come. And two years before that…" She stopped. Swallowed. "We couldn't imagine much in the way of happiness at all. Yet here we are. With our favourite people, celebrating the good that rises. If you would all be so kind, if you have any booze left in your glasses, I'd ask you all to raise them."

Shuffle of chairs and quick pours, the clink of glass against silverware and a couple of dozen glasses lifted into the air.

"To Chuck," she said.

"And my next seventy years," Chuck added from the other end of the table.

Much laughter followed, amid *hear hears*.

Until Bettina kept her own glass raised. "And to those who could not be with us today. Our beloved Marnie, and her beautiful family, all the way over in Maine. And to our most precious boy, Saul." The shimmer no longer held as it slid over her cheeks in a silvery waterfall. "We love him. We miss him. Oh, that he was here with us still."

"To Saul," said Chuck and the rest of the table followed suit.

After dinner, nobody seemed in any way inclined to leave, moving into the library, the pool room, the halls, despite the hotbed of emotion underpinning the evening, the very air overflowing with the taste of it, the temperature, the weight.

Only half understanding the stories whispered around her, Emerson's smiles and pep had begun to wane. So she made her way around the ground floor in search of her ride home.

Bettina was talking to Kris, the super-chatty guy who'd been hitting on her all through dinner. When she caught Emerson's eye, the older woman waved a hand towards the terrace.

A quick smile of thanks then Emerson made her way outside, but not before noting Bettina grabbing Kris by the elbow and hauling him back.

Emerson made her way down the back stairs, past heavily scented gardenia bushes growing lushly by the garden walls leading down to the lawn, small fountains, tall stone statues. Music and chatter spilled from inside, creating a kind of Renaissance Eden.

The stars were out again that night but the deeper she went into the garden, the less ground the house lights touched, creating patches of velvety darkness. Then she rounded a copse of conifers to find Holden, sitting on a bench, alone, elbows on knees, back hunched, eyes closed.

He seemed to stir at her approach, as if he'd felt a shift in the air, before he opened his eyes and turned to find her. And his eyes… They were savage. Pained. Punished.

And any discomfort she felt at not being in the know fluttered off into the night like ash on the wind.

"Sorry," he said, making to stand. "I only meant to come out for a minute. What time is it?"

"Stay," she said, with a staying hand to match. For he looked far more exhausted than she felt.

Her heels sinking gently into the turf, she sat on the bench beside him, her hands curling around the cool stone.

"So," she said.

"So," he returned.

"I have questions."

He coughed out a rough laugh. "I bet you do. Do you want the long story or the short?"

"The short version is fine."

When she shivered, the cool of the night sending goosebumps down her arms, Holden lifted his jacket from the bench and moved closer to place it over her shoulders. She thanked him with a half-smile. Breathed deep, drinking in the scent of him. She could chastise herself for it later.

Holden went back to leaning forearms on his thighs, one hand rubbing over his chin, his body taut beside hers. "I must have been seventeen the first time I ate at that table, invited over by a new friend I'd made at my last high school. The one I went to after leaving East Kew, in fact. He was this towering, life-is-there-for-the-taking smile of a guy named Saul Sanderson."

We love him. We miss him. Oh, that he was here with us still.

"Chuck and Bettina's son?"

He nodded. "I went to so many dinners here after that. Spent entire school holidays. I'd been shuffling between couches of distant cousins at the time, none of whom particularly wanted me there; in comparison, this place was like a dream."

"You were a teenager. Why were you living with cousins?"

Holden glanced up, as if he'd almost forgotten she was there. Which was half the reason she'd spoken—she wanted him to remember who he was talking to.

He sat up, his hand gripping the concrete beside hers. "I grew up with my dad, though 'dad' might be too warm and fuzzy a term to describe the guy."

"How so?" she asked.

"The girl with all the questions," he said, his voice sounding far away. Then, "My father drank, he fought, he got into trouble, he pretended to look for work, he had a reputation, he owed money, and he took out all of life's frustrations on me."

Emmy thought of Chuck's open arms. Those big hugs that had stirred up all kinds of parental issues for her too. What a lure that must have been.

Emerson looked out into the night. Confronting the uncomfortable fact that when she'd been crushing on Holden Roarke, imagining him a happy, popular, easy-going hunk, she'd never once considered why a guy like that might need to see a guidance counsellor.

"Tell me about Saul," she said.

A muscle worked in his cheek. "We were like broth-ers. Even when we went to different universities we kept in touch, caught up every holiday. And then I wrote my app. The interest in the thing was insane, from right at the start. The early offers staggering for a twenty-year-old kid. Infamy ensued. Partying, travel, free hotels, more money than I knew what to do with. I lost touch with pretty much everyone who'd been a part of life in the 'before'. Including Saul."

A shadow passed over his face.

"A couple of years later I was in Amsterdam, prepping to speak at some future symposium, when there was a phone call, deep into the night. Saul was gone. Could I come home?"

"How did it happen?" she asked, her voice soft, yet it carried in the dark of the night.

"Car accident. Wet roads. Late night. Speed. Thankfully no one else was hurt."

That wasn't true. Every person inside that house at dinner had been hurt by what had happened to Saul Sanderson, and despite the festivities, and the birthday cheer, many were clearly hurting still.

"Come home, they said?" she nudged.

"So, I came home," Holden went on. "I was pall bearer. I spoke at the funeral. It was so damned sad. Yet, I seemed to make them feel as if there was still a small connection to their boy. They asked me to stick around afterwards. What could I say?"

"So you stayed."

"I stayed. And, feeling utterly useless in the face of what those good people were all going through, I wrote an app. For Chuck. As if that might somehow make up for my prior absence. And Saul's. It was twisty stuff."

"What was the app?"

"It was called Real Time. Tracked movement in the real estate market, finding patterns in house sales with regards to suburbs, streets, pockets. I'd quietly imagined it a parting gift, before running away to Bermuda. Instead, Chuck convinced me to stay on, ostensibly to teach his staff how to wield it. And then he promoted me, again and again. Even after my father showed up in Chuck's office one day, asking for money, as he was wont to do now that I'd turned out not to be so useless after all. Then there was Marnie."

She'd heard the name bandied about through the night, with both censure and delight, as if she was a polarising character in the Sandersons' story, and yet she hadn't felt the dull pain in her belly as she did when Holden said the name.

"Marnie is Saul's older sister and she did not think it

was healthy for Chuck to keep me around. Her bluntness
was a relief. Both hurting, and angry, we soon became
a thing. Got engaged, really quickly. Chuck and Bettina
wholeheartedly approved. But Marnie didn't love me. She
was working through her own pain, and I had become
the family conduit."

"Holden," Emerson whispered. Or maybe it was an
internal thing—the echo of the ache she felt for him, now
flowing freely through her.

"She snapped out of it. Started seeing the gardener. Did
fall in love. Fell pregnant. And fled. Chuck was devas-
tated. Accused her of spoiling Saul's memory by hurting
me. Watching them fall apart was the final straw. I took
the blame. Insisted she'd only left after realising I wasn't
in love with her. Excruciating. But, at least, it was true."

Holden ran both hands over his face, kept his head
tipped down, his hair falling over his forehead. "Then
I quit. Announced, in a press release no less, that I was
retiring. Moving to a beach somewhere. I knew it would
send interest in Chuck's new app through the roof, which
it did, as if that might mitigate the mess I'd let unfold.
Then I got on a plane and left.

"And while I was in the air, Chuck had a heart attack,
fell down some stairs and—"

"The wheelchair," Emmy whispered.

"The wheelchair."

"Good grief, Holden. That's…a lot." A lot for him to
walk back through that door tonight. A lot for them to
invite him to do the same. All those good people trying
their best under truly trying circumstances. No wonder
he'd needed her.

"It sounds like something out of a soap opera."

He looked to her then, a glint in his dark eyes, his
laughter sudden and rough.

Emerson slapped a hand over her mouth. "That sounded so callous. I am so sorry."

"You're spot on. Imagine how it felt being caught up in the middle of it. It felt big and important and hyper-real. I never should have stayed. I never should have let it get that far. It took me far too long to remember that I was still the outsider, looking in."

Outliers in arms. She'd thought he was being flirty when he'd said those words at the wedding; now she understood what that had meant. That it was meaningful to him.

Emerson placed her hand gently over Holden's. "They were so happy to see you tonight. You might not be their son, but they do adore you. You were not an outsider then, and neither are you now. Not to them."

A muscle worked in Holden's cheek. He turned his hand beneath hers, till he cradled hers in his own. Then he slowly, *slowly* lifted it and placed a soft, sweet kiss upon her palm.

When his face turned to hers his eyes were deep and dark, unreadable, his jaw hard. Her hand remained tucked in his. "Thank you."

"For what?" she asked, her voice a husky whisper, her body now trembling despite the warmth of his jacket, of his body heat beside her.

His eyes roved between hers. "For saying yes when I asked."

Moonlight shone on half his face, leaving the other half in shadow. All angles and character and depth and dark male beauty. His thumb began tracing the inside of her palm, spreading warmth from the place he'd kissed up her arm and into her chest.

With some effort on her part, she took back her hand, ostensibly to adjust the jacket on her shoulders, mostly so that he didn't see how his touch affected her. "It was a hell of an evening. One I won't soon forget."

"I'll bet."

Emerson felt herself whipped back to the night of the wedding, when she'd said she wasn't sure if stars were happy or sad. What had Holden said? *The most beautiful things are often both.*

A few long, quiet moments later, Emerson said, "What happened to Chuck—it's not your fault."

Holden stilled. "I know that."

Did he? Emerson wasn't sure. The "ran away to Bermuda" slip made her think otherwise. Perhaps his lifestyle had less to do with having the means, and more to do with a need to keep moving. Not just around a park, and not just in the middle of a school term without stopping to say goodbye.

The revelation pressed against an ancient bruise that lived deep inside her. He was a runner, like her dad. No wonder that particular heartache had hit so hard.

Yet she kept her gaze direct, unflinching. While Holden did the same, his body wound tight, as if breathing too deep might unravel some long-held knot behind his ribs. But the longer he looked into her eyes, the more he seemed to loosen, his face easing, his eyes softening.

And that bruised place deep inside her began to pulse.

Emerson pressed herself to standing, Holden's jacket falling off her shoulder. He caught it, stood, and placed it back on her shoulders. Adjusting it, turning her gently to tug at the lapels, and not letting go as he looked into her eyes.

"Wanna get out of here?" she said, feigning a cool she did not feel.

He smiled. "And I thought I was hiding it so well."

She turned away from him then, releasing herself from the gravity in his eyes, hooking her hand through his arm, and said, "Last to arrive, first to leave. This might just be the perfect non-date date after all."

Holden kept hold of Emmy's hand as they said their good-byes, finding her touch a comfort. An anchor. The shape of something he couldn't define but couldn't deny.

Chuck placed his hand over theirs, as if in some kind of benediction, while Bettina drew each into a long hug. And it all felt a zillion times lighter, easier, better than it had when they'd first arrived.

Then they were back in his car, heading through town, and pulling up outside her place far too soon.

As the engine cut, their breaths were loud in the sudden quiet. Moonlight fell on Emerson's quicksilver dress, her hands in her lap, her face remaining in darkness.

While Holden gripped the steering wheel, like a nervy teenager dropping off a pretty girl after the football game. If she lingered in the car, did it mean something? Would it be an invitation to tuck a hand into the heavy sweep of her hair and kiss her?

Or was it just that he *wanted* to kiss her? And had done since he'd seen her lift that glass of champagne in salute, not following anyone's rules but her own?

He'd imagined kissing her gently at first, getting a sense of her temperature, her texture, her taste. Taking his sweet time till his heart felt sluggish and thunderous all at once.

True, he'd also imagined hauling her into his lap and kissing her till he was wearing her lipstick and she was wearing none.

Either way, he might not be any good at spinning a line, but his moves were just fine.

The decision was taken out of his hands when she all but leapt from the car.

"Don't get out," she insisted, leaning back into the

window. "It's been a big night, and I'm sure you want to get home."

Home? By that she must have meant the apartment he was staying in, a modern penthouse he'd bought off plan years back and had decorated by a friend of a friend when he'd heard his dad was sick. Made plans to come home, because that was what good sons did, if you could be a good son when you hadn't seen your father in years. Only to find out his father had died earlier that month and the funeral had gone ahead without him.

The walls were blinding white, the kitchen tiles and cupboards bright red, the dining chairs a mismatched array of rainbow colours—perfect for a hyperactive kindergarten teacher. And it made him think of his father. He was seriously considering selling it when he left.

He looked over Emerson's shoulder to her white picket fence, flowers spilling abundantly over the top, her quaint cottage, the porch light glowing warmly. Invitingly.

That was a home.

"What if there's a robber?" he said.

She reached down and took off a shoe with a mighty long heel. "I'll smack them with this."

She probably would too.

"And yet," he said, pausing till he'd hopped out of the car and shut the door, "I'm seeing you to your door. You would be just as gallant if you were dropping me home."

Her hand gripped her shoe as she watched him round the car. "I can't see that happening. Me dropping you home any time. Since this was a favour, and not a date."

"True," said Holden, even while it hadn't felt that way to him. In fact, he could have kicked himself for ever suggesting it.

Then it hit him—she was right. It was unlikely they'd even see one another again, now that his reason for being in Melbourne was done. Which felt…unacceptable.

They got on. They were attracted to one another. He remembered the way her hand had trembled when he'd brought it to his lips, remembered the sweet taste of her skin, and the shards of heat that had spread throughout his body.

Date or not, asking her to dinner had felt like one of the top five decisions of his life. And he wasn't ready for it to end.

"Then consider this," he said, following her as she limped her way up her front path, shoe weapon still in hand, "me walking you to your door, at the ready to take down prowlers and peeping toms, that can be my favour returned."

"Ha," she said, shooting him a grin over her shoulder—a flash of white teeth, mischief in her eyes—as she hobbled up her front steps. "Not on your life. I am keeping that up my sleeve for when I need something huge."

"Aah. I get it." Holden stopped at the bottom of the stairs and rocked back on his heels. "You're not ready to be rid of me yet."

Something else glinted in her eyes then. A sense that she had been found out. Further proof he was *not* alone in this…curiosity.

As if she knew exactly what she'd just given away, she rolled her eyes and said, "Oh, shut up."

Holden laughed with the unexpectedness of her admission. And with that knowledge came another incremental shift in the ground beneath them both.

They weren't done here. Meaning he wasn't going anywhere. Not yet.

She shook her head side to side, as if she wasn't sure what she was going to do with him. If she'd asked, he'd have told her she could do *anything she liked*.

But she did not ask. She slid her other shoe from her foot, lowering her leg slowly to the ground, and said, "Don't go thinking I'd cry myself to sleep at the thought of never seeing you again, Holden Roarke."

Though far too late for it to have the impact it might if he didn't know she'd be thinking of him all the same.

"I survived you leaving once, I can do it again. I'm holding on to my favour. For as long as it takes to find the perfect response."

With that she turned away from him, opened her front door and took a step inside.

"Thank you for walking me to my door," she said, innate politeness coming to the fore.

"Thank you for accompanying me to dinner," he said, gripping his hands behind him and bowing at the waist.

He thought about asking if he might, in fact, make a plan to see her again. That if she said yes he could stay in town another day or two.

Then he remembered, he owed her.

She'd be in touch. When she was ready. Meaning he might have to stick around just a little longer. At least until the ledger was square.

"Goodnight, Emmy."

"Goodnight, Holden," she said, surprise and maybe even disappointment flashing across her face, before she stepped inside and closed her door.

So much for his moves.

After a few moments the front lights turned off, and a light inside turned on. He heard a soft woof, a welcome home from her lovely old dog, and he felt a sharp twist of pain deep behind his solar plexus.

Once again he found himself back where he always seemed to end up—on the outside, looking in.

CHAPTER SIX

A HANDFUL OF days later Emerson, Camille and Phillip met up for the first time since the wedding at their favourite hang-out: a rustic little hole-in-the-wall café with moth-eaten velvet couches, and mismatched wooden chairs that was funky enough to boast "atmosphere" but not so busy they couldn't hear one another talk.

"It wasn't a load-bearing wall. I'm almost certain," said Phillip at the end of a long and rambling story about their first couple of weeks of home renovations.

Avoiding the spring that poked out at the back of her couch, Emerson took a hearty gulp of her super-strong double espresso. "Did you think to, you know, maybe, check? Before going at it with a mallet?"

"Turns out we're going with a more holistic, gut-based approach." Phillip glanced towards Camille, who was, if her dramatic hand movements were anything to go by, quite possibly telling the same story to the barista behind the counter.

"Enough about us," said Phillip. "Fill me in on the goings on in the life of Emmy Adler since the wedding. From what I heard, you and a certain gentleman rather hit it off that night." He waggled his eyebrows. "By that I mean Holden Roarke."

"Did you, now?"

"Ran into him yesterday, which was nice, because I was sure he'd planned to be long gone by now. Well, not so much *ran into*, as he called to thank me for the invitation, and then we met for a drink. And he had a lot of nice things to say about—"

"Phew! I'm famished!" Camille lolloped onto the couch beside her husband.

Leaving Emmy to wonder, *A lot of nice things to say about what? Or who?* Not that it mattered. Not a jot. For it was unlikely she'd ever see him again. Yes, he owed her a favour, but she'd never had any real sense it would happen. The man didn't even live in the same country she did, so she'd quietly planned to be magnanimous and let it go.

Only, now that he was unexpectedly still in town... Maybe she *could* call it in. Should she use his IT knowledge? Too easy. Could he build her a shed? A shed would be handy for storing gardening gear, in case she one day took up gardening. And the thought of him in her back yard, using a hammer, sweat dripping down his brow—

"Did he tell you about the water damage?" said Camille around the paper straw in her huge glass of Diet Coke.

"Not yet," said Phillip. "We were talking about the wedding night."

"Hey," said Camille, slapping him on the arm with the back of her hand. "She's my best friend. That's my story to tell!"

"Not *the* wedding night," Phillip muttered. "We were talking about Holden Roarke."

Camille's gaze snapped to Emerson's. "Yeah, so my husband and your Holden had drinks yesterday, did he tell you? Mere days into our homey-moon and he's already fleeing at the first chance to meet up with another man."

"I wasn't fleeing you," said Phillip, leaving Emerson to shift on her seat at Camille's casual use of "your Holden". "I needed a little space from the *house*, in order to see things from a different perspective. And he's such an interesting guy. Well-travelled. And the success he's had. At his age. Puts our efforts to shame."

"Speak for yourself," Emmy and Camille said at the same time, before leaning in for a high five.

"Anyway," said Phillip, "it seems our Emmy has a fan."

"Oh, really?" said Camille. "Who?"

Phillip blinked at her. "Holden."

Camille's gaze snapped to Emmy's again before her face broke into a grin. "Really?"

Emmy rolled her eyes. "Calm down. We chatted at the wedding, which you know. And a little more, again, after you left. And—"

"And he dropped her at her hotel that night," Phillip added, most helpfully, cutting off Emmy before she could try to explain about dinner with the Sandersons, and the favours.

Camille smacked Phillip on the arm. "First you invite *Heartache Number Four* to our wedding without checking with me, then you find out some truly excellent gossip, which my best friend was no doubt waiting to tell me in person, and you ruin it for her! Married five minutes and you've already forgotten the rules."

"It's a lot to remember," Phillip said. "I never did apologise, though, Em. About Holden and all."

"No," Emmy insisted. "I know you didn't know. And it was fine. He was fine. He was perfectly…" What was the word he'd used? "Gallant."

Even though, several times, she'd had an inkling, a feminine rush of knowledge, that he might have been *thinking* less than gallant thoughts. About her. Good chance she was projecting, for she'd definitely been guilty of thinking less than gallant thoughts about him.

"Doth the lady protest too much?" Camille asked, wide eyes now sparkling with patent interest.

"She does not," said Emmy. "Every encounter we've had has been totally PG."

"She rated it," Camille murmured, looking at Emmy as if she was seeing a whole new side of her.

"I heard," Phillip murmured back.

Emmy breathed deep, gathering her strength.

During which time Camille said to her husband, "Before you and Holden join a bowling league, don't forget Emmy was once utterly besotted with the guy. In fact, the List came about only after *he* broke her fertile, fecund fourteen-year-old heart."

Phillip winced. Then braced himself before saying, "I am glad he came, though. It's been nice getting to know him again. He'd never talk it up, but I know he didn't charge the uni for speaking the night I bumped into him. And he's helped out a few friends, on the quiet, over the years, when they've got themselves into trouble. He acts like he's this loose, jet-setting, I-am-an-island type, but at heart he's really a good guy."

"Maybe now," Camille interjected, glancing at Emmy, her best-friend-for-ever skills right up there with the best. "But back then..."

"He was a good guy back then too," Emmy assured them. Having found a couple of the corner pieces of the Holden Roarke puzzle, she knew a little more of who he was, and what he'd been going through.

His leaving in the middle of the night back then had felt...specific. And, yes, heartbreaking. But it hadn't been his fault. And if he hadn't been a good guy back then, Emmy wouldn't have liked him so much.

He just…hadn't liked her back.

Emmy came back around to find Camille playing with one of Phillip's shirt buttons and smiling into his eyes. And felt an overwhelming sense that she had her nose pressed up against the window, as she witnessed something private.

How had Holden described it? Like an outsider, looking in.

Emmy slowly rose from her chair. "Guys, it's been fab, but I really have to scoot."

"Aw," said Camille. "Housewarming, next week. Yes?"

"Of course. Let me know if you need any help leading up."

"Will do."

Hugs all round, then Emerson left.

Standing outside the café, she looked left, then right, not, in fact, having anywhere in particular to scoot to.

But with the messy mix of thoughts nipping at her heels—the realisation she hadn't told her best friend that she'd been to dinner with Holden, and that she was pretty sure she wanted to kiss the man, along with that bitter-sweet feeling of disconnection that had hit her so hard at the wedding—she went there fast.

Keys in the door of the apartment, Holden looked to his phone as it buzzed in his hand, hoping it might be a certain green-eyed brunette.

Instead, it was a blue-eyed blonde he'd been avoiding for days.

"Joel," Holden answered, holding the phone a smidge further from his ear in preparation for his business manager's voice to come booming down the line.

"Mate!" Joel replied, his attempt at an Australian accent less than convincing.

Holden threw his keys on the frog-green kidney-shaped hall table. When he perched on a canary-yellow kitchen stool, he was forced to move as the sun slanted right in his eyes. Not that sitting anywhere else in the crazy place felt much better.

"I was expecting you to land on my doorstep a week ago," said Joel. "Jenny even had the linen washed and ready, just in case."

Yes, he could stay anywhere in the world, but he still found himself sleeping on people's couches on occasion. An old habit, a safety net from his childhood, that he just couldn't break.

Holden looked around the apartment. While he knew he couldn't spend another night in this place, he was not yet ready to get on a plane. Not while Emmy, and her favour, were out there.

"Decided to stay on for a bit," Holden said.

"Clearly. Word is out. I'm fielding offers."

"What kind of offers?"

"Teaching engagements, speaking, consultancy, investments, product spokesmanship..." Joel paused, as if he'd run out of breath. As if he'd been waiting for Holden to cut him off far sooner. "Will you be home long enough to take something on?"

Home. There was that word again. Holden flopped back on the hard yellow leather couch and threw his arm over his eyes so that the colour didn't permanently burn his retinas.

"My youngest wants to start horse-riding lessons," Joel beseeched. "Do you know how expensive they are?"

Holden laughed despite himself. "I pay you a packet whether I take on any events or not."

"Yes, you do. For which my children are eternally grateful." A pause, then, "While the kids are hankering for some Uncle Holden time, I'm glad you've stuck it out a little longer. Make new memories. And while you're at it, make some local schools, or struggling business-people, or young entrepreneurs super-happy and talk to them. For money. It'll do you the world of good."

"Fine."

"Really? Brilliant! I'll swing the list over right away." With that, Joel rang off, sounding as if he couldn't believe his luck.

While Holden called up the app he'd built, the very one he'd gifted Chuck several iterations ago, and scrolled through a list of short-term rentals, focusing on places not too dissimilar from Emmy's cosy, comfortable, suburban spot.

Freya's cheeks were bright pink, her tablet in a death grip, as she swept into Emerson's office. "Phone call. Line one."

Freya could look like the sky was falling if someone was a minute late to work, so Emmy finished reading the contract page she was on before pressing the button to bring up the speakerphone, and said, "Emerson Adler."

"Emerson. Ah, that name of yours. It's like a song. Chuck Sanderson here."

Emerson flinched so hard the top few sheets of paper swept off her desk and landed on the floor.

Freya, as if expecting it, rushed in, her eyes preternaturally wide as she neatly plucked the pages off the floor and popped them back into order on the desk, before backing out of the room in a crouch and closing the door with a soft *snick*.

"Chuck! It was such an honour to meet you the other night."

Chuck laughed, entirely aware of his own power.

"Well, you impressed me at dinner too. Even more importantly, you impressed my wife."

"That's so lovely," she said, sensing that Chuck Sanderson, CEO of the real estate and construction goliath the Sanderson Group, didn't make it a habit to call up house guests and personally thank them for attending a party. She picked up the sparkly paperweight on her desk, rubbed her thumb over the soft indent beneath, and said, "Is there something I can help you with today?"

"Well, Emerson, I find myself in need of some…key staff."

Emerson punched the air. Then reached for a notebook and pen so she didn't forget a word. "I thought I heard, at dinner the other night, that you were on the verge of retiring."

"Rumours. I'm as invigorated today as I've ever been. Now, human resources are your area of expertise, yes?"

"Very much. What are you after?"

"Temps. A few new bodies in middle management as we look towards expanding our development sector."

She jotted down a bullet list. "Temps. Middle management. Can do."

"I also have a very important position that needs filling. In the spirit of transparency, I have another couple of mobs on the case already, but they've yet to produce the goods, so I'd like you to have a go as well."

Normal business practice, at his level. "What position is that?"

"COO."

Chief Operating Officer for the Sanderson Group. A multimillion-dollar package, no doubt. With the kind of finder's fee that would pay her staff, her rent, and then some for some time. "My team and I are absolutely up to the task."

"So, you have someone in mind, then?"

She paused, mind ticking over several women and men she'd made relationships with over the years who would be ready and raring. "I just might."

"I can't tell you how glad I am to hear it. He's a stubborn fellow, but if anyone can swing him around to taking on the gig, you can."

And just like that Emerson's happy bubble popped.

Chuck Sanderson hadn't called because he'd been impressed with her. Not solely. He'd called because he thought she might be able to bring Holden on as COO of the Sanderson Group.

Emerson nibbled on the end of her pencil and thought it through.

Her own history with the guy aside, his relationship with the Sanderson family was staggeringly complicated. And he was very clearly *not* in need of a job, or looking for work, much less a high-pressure, high-investment, settle-in-one-place gig.

He was also, as far as she knew, still intending to fly off into the sunset whenever the urge took him. Because that was the kind of person he was. A man who walked into a room as easily as he left it.

And yet…

He *was* still in town, which went against his original plan. She knew because he'd begun texting her every day or so, asking if she wanted lunch. Asking after Pumpkin. Asking if she wanted help choosing her favour.

And he *had* worked for the company. He was beloved by the boss. They were all most definitely in a better place with one another than they had been before, thanks to that dinner.

If she was able to land Holden—even as a *candidate*—she had zero doubt the commission would be hers.

And Holden *did* owe her that huge favour.

No. *No.* She couldn't. She wouldn't. She didn't know the man that well, but, having heard his story, in his own words, in the silvery darkness in the Sandersons' own garden, she knew enough to know she would never ask it of him. Ever.

Holden may have given her the in, but he was not the answer.

"Chuck," she said, putting on her best I-am-the-expert-here-so-it-would-behove-you-to-listen voice, "in line with our spirit of transparency, I do not believe Holden is the right person for the job. He's brilliant, yes. He knows the business, yes. He adores you. He's in town. But as he said the other night, he's not keen on being tied down. And…"

Always better to be honest. Allowing someone to get their hopes up, knowing they'd be dashed, was, to Emerson, the cruellest thing in the world.

"I honestly believe your history together would make a partnership problematic." She paused. Let that sit. Then said, "There *is* someone else out there who is suited to the job. Someone just as brilliant, just as talented, just as charismatic—but keen. Eager. Excited by the prospect. And I am going to be the one to find them."

She would. She had to. For it would cement her position in the world of corporate HR like nothing else could.

She waited for Chuck to say something, hoping she hadn't just shot herself in the foot, but also knowing there was no way forward if he wanted her to be some kind of pawn in his get Holden game.

The man cleared his throat, and said, "I'll have my people contact your people to put the staffing contract in place. And I look forward to seeing these fantastic candidates you assure me are out there. Good day, Emerson."

"Good day—" she said, but he'd already hung up.

She stared into the middle distance, her mind whirring. The Sanderson Group. *The Sanderson Group.*

As it truly sank in, she leaned back in her chair and let out a great, "Whoop!"

Emerson turned out the lights in her office late that same evening. Moonlight spilled through the huge windows, and the only sound was the hum of the exit signs.

Still buzzing with energy as she headed down in the lift, after hours spent with her teams working through the Sanderson Group portfolio, she pulled out her phone, thumb hovering over her contacts.

It was a Tuesday, so Camille would be at bingo with her dad. Phillip—if not painting something or ripping something up—would happily chat, and he'd make all the right noises, but it wasn't quite the same.

Strangely, though, neither was the "someone" she wanted to tell.

When the lift doors opened, she pressed call before she could change her mind.

"Emerson." Holden's voice came through the phone right as she pressed the door to let her out of the building. The night air was an icy rush against her body; in contrast, with the phone to her ear, his voice was warm and welcoming.

"Holden. Um, hi."

"Um, hi, right on back. What's up? What do you need from me? Shall I rush out the door this instant, ready and raring to do your bidding?"

"There is nothing I need from you," she said, heels tapping on the footpath as she ducked around a group of young women heading out for a night on the town.

"I'm sure I could think of something."

She bet he could. "I called as I have news."

"And you thought of me. That's nice." No humour in his voice that time. Just easy acceptance. She imagined him saying so while lying back on a couch, head resting on his bent arm, bare feet on the opposite arm rest. He might have been wearing a shirt, he might not.

"The *only* reason I thought of you is because I have you to thank for said news. In a small, teeny-tiny, miniscule way."

"Now I'm really intrigued."

She reached the door leading to the car park and pulled out her key card. But held off, knowing the reception was patchy when she went underground.

There was no way she could hide her smile as she said, "I received a call from Chuck Sanderson this afternoon. Pitch Perfect is to be the Sanderson Group's new temp staffing *and* management recruitment firm."

In the beat that followed, the silence felt so loaded, she wondered if calling him had been the right thing to do at all. If she might be pressing on that ancient bruise of his after all. She opened her mouth to apologise, or take it back, or change the subject, when his voice tumbled into her ear.

"Why, Emerson Francesca Adler, that's damn fantastic news."

Emerson looked up at the dark sky and beamed, fizzy joy settling over her. "I know, right?"

Holden chuckled, enjoying her enjoyment. Which was nice. For all that the news was amazing, sharing it, with someone who understood, made it feel more real. While the sound of his laughter—deep and intimate—skittered down her arms, the sides of her torso, along her ticklish spots just above her hip bones.

"Hold up. How do you know my middle name?"

A beat. "Has it come up?"

"It has not."

"I can see it written down. Emerson Francesca Adler." His voice sounded a little faraway, as if he was tracing her name in the air. "I remember thinking it sounded like a character from an old movie. But when? It'll come to me." A moment, then, "Do you remember those mornings we both found ourselves stuck in the hall outside the guidance counsellor's office?"

Did she remember? Ha. Ha-ha-ha-ha-ha.

"Ancient Mrs Carmichael, on the front desk, had us check our medical histories constantly. One time she accidentally gave me yours."

Emerson remembered. She could feel the heat rushing into her cheeks as he'd leaned towards her, holding out the page, holding eye contact, with that gorgeous smile on his gorgeous face, as if it was happening in real time.

"I handed it straight over…after reading the first few lines," said Holden, when Emerson remained unable to say words. "The big question is, did you do the same? Or did you take the chance to read about all my many stupid feats that led to many broken bones?"

"Of course not."

"Ah. So you were a good girl," he extrapolated.

Nope. She'd simply realised all too late what she'd held in her hand.

"I was always more curious than I was careful," Holden said. "Got me into trouble. But served me when it needed to. On that note, I'm taking you to dinner. News such as yours requires celebration."

Emerson's mouth popped open but no sounds came out. She'd avoided his lunch requests, blowing them off as a bit of a running joke. But dinner? Dinner leaned precariously close to a date-type encounter.

Maybe she could look at it as a business meeting.

Maybe she could drill him for info. He had worked for the Sanderson family before, after all... No. She couldn't. *Wouldn't* ask it of him. Not even that little.

"You okay over there?" he asked, a smile in his voice. "I can hear the wheels cranking again. If you're concerned this is my way of chipping away at my favour owed, it's not. Heck, you can even pay if you'd like, just so you can be sure."

She couldn't help but laugh. "Magnanimous of you."

"Mmm. The celebration is a handy excuse, for the truth is, I would like to take you to dinner. I'd really like to see you again."

"Oh," she said on a sigh, then bit her lip to stop any more telling sounds from slipping out.

Holden Roarke wanted to see her again. And she wanted to see him too. Texting had given her a fix, but it wasn't enough. She'd started to miss that face. Miss how he looked at her, as if he liked what he saw. So much the thought of seeing him again made her feel light-headed.

Pumpkin had spent the day at home as the neighbour's university-aged daughter, Kerri, was using Emmy's sunny back sitting room to study. Kerri—who had grown up next door to Pumpkin, and house-sat if Emerson was away—had sent her usual babysitting proof-of-life picture, so Emerson didn't need to rush home.

But this couldn't be about convenience. What if she was wrong about Holden? Again? What if he was a flirty, enthusiastic, bored guy who enjoyed hanging out with her, but that was it? What if she was reliving the exact same arc as before?

Frantically swiping her card over the sensor and pulling the door open when she heard the latch unlock, she thought, *This is different*. But the only thing she could be sure of was that when he left this time, he'd say good-bye first.

"Emmy?"

"Thank you for the offer. But my mind is still spinning with ideas, and I want to get them all down before they fly off into the ether."

His outshot of breath made her wonder if his disappointment matched her own. "You've got this, Emmy. Remember, you're not the only one who's just made an excellent alliance. Chuck has too."

Emmy closed her eyes as she leaned her forehead on the cold metal door. "I'm at my parking garage and am about to lose reception, so… I'd better go."

She stepped through the door and into the dark. And just before the sensor lights flickered on, and she lost reception, Holden's voice washed over her, "Goodnight, Emmy."

She walked up the ramp to her car, their conversation playing over and over in her head. Until something he'd said snagged on something.

More careful than curious. That was how he'd described her, after a fashion.

When it came to clients, she was gung-ho, asking questions until she knew more about them—their motivations, their goals, their fears—than they did about themselves.

But when it came to her personal life she did hold back, having built big, strong firewalls around herself, and only giving a select few the password.

She pressed the remote to unlock her car as a flutter of melancholy overcame her. Somewhere along the way the young woman who had been hungry enough to start her own company had become so personally risk adverse she couldn't even allow herself to have dinner with a man she liked, just in case.

In case what? In case he didn't like her? In case he did? In case he stayed, and stuck by her, and she grew truly used to having him in her life, and *then* something bad happened? Because, according to the Heartache List, something bad always happened.

But if Holden didn't deserve his place on that list, after all, then his name wasn't a threat to that terrifying *Heartache Number Nine* slot that she so adamantly refused to fill.

The only person holding her back these days, was her.

CHAPTER SEVEN

THE NEXT MORNING, the second Emmy's eyes popped open she felt wide awake. Cleansed. Refreshed. As if she'd broken through some mental barrier.

This whole time she'd been telling herself that spending *any* time with Holden proved how much she'd grown beyond the Heartache List. For hadn't she survived a dinner, and a few cheeky texts, without a) accidentally falling in love with him, and b) having her heart broken?

So what? What did that prove? Only that *she was being too careful.*

She'd been half-hearted. If she really wanted to see where she stood, she needed to use her whole heart. So to speak.

Once at work, she waited till her teams were busy with the Sanderson brief, then, feeling tremendously determined while also slightly sick to the stomach, she punched Holden's number into her work phone and put it on speaker.

He answered, short of breath, "Hey."

"You're running," she said.

"That I am."

He's a runner, remember? Abort! Abort!

"Should I call back?" she asked.

"You can call me anytime you want. But I'm okay

to talk now, so long as you don't mind me huffing and puffing in your ear."

Emerson lifted a finger to her mouth and nibbled on the end of her fingernail as she dealt with the image that put in her head. "Something you said last night has been playing on my mind."

"Which part?"

I really want to see you again. No, *not* that. Though it had been playing on her mind. On a loop. So much so she might have even considered going for a run herself so as to shake it off, till she remembered she didn't own running shoes.

"First things first, do you know how much longer you'll be in town?"

"I do not." A beat, then, "But I have no imminent plans to leave just yet."

"Great."

"I'm glad you think so."

Warmth fluttered in her belly, reminding her that she was dealing with a guy who didn't go for lines, or games. *No pretending required.* "What does your calendar look like at the moment?"

"Is that your way of asking *me* to dinner?"

"It's my way of finding out your movements before seeing if we might implement the next phase of our... deal."

"There's a next phase?"

"There could be."

"Intriguing. Sending it to you now."

Her phone pinged, with an invitation to add Holden Roarke's calendar to her own. A shimmer shot through her at the intimacy that suggested. The trust.

Rather than battening down the hatches, she followed her newly unleashed curiosity, opened his calendar, and found herself surprised to see that it was rather impressive. Especially for a guy who considered himself "retired". "Is this for real?"

He laughed. "Turns out I'm not just a pretty face. I have skills and people are keen to hear about those skills. And, since I am a generous soul, I am willing to share those skills, for the right price."

"So, you're a mercenary," she asked as she continued scrolling through his calendar, some in bold—booked—many more in italics—possibilities. Her heart stuttered when she saw their old school listed as a possibility. And she remembered Phillip's assertion that he picked and chose who he charged.

"East Kew High School is willing to pay you the big bucks to give a talk on… Youth Entrepreneurship?" she said.

"So many bucks."

Emmy sat back in her chair, distracted from her original plan. Something Holden was extremely adept at making happen. "I don't believe you."

"That's your prerogative."

"Does it bother you that people write you off as some sort of rich, easy-going, playboy type?"

"What people? Have you been reading up on me, Ms Adler?"

"I took a photo of you in case I went missing. I've introduced you to my dog. Yes, I've read up on you. It was the only safe thing to do."

He hummed into her ear, the sound doing things to her the huffing and puffing had not. "Good for you. As to your query, people hear 'retired in his twenties' and think I spend most of my days living on a beach somewhere being served pina coladas by nubile young women in bikinis."

She looked again at the list of groups he was speaking with, mostly small groups rather than corporate gigs. As if he really was an honestly generous soul. "Why don't you? No judgement, it sounds pretty fabulous."

"You are brimming with judgement, Emerson Adler." Emerson rolled her neck. "A little bit."

"I imagine," Holden went on, "that when you go on a beach holiday, you book tours and naps and food stops down to the minute."

"That's what you imagine when you picture me on a beach holiday?" A slight pause, to let that sink in. Then, "I'm disappointed in you, Holden. I'd have thought you more imaginative."

She felt a wind of change, as if it swept over them both.

"I'm disappointed in myself," he said, his voice low, confidential. "You said something I said has been playing on your mind?"

She had? "I did. Here's my thinking. Since you are sticking around a little longer than expected, and the chances of me coming up with a favour as huge, as mighty, as worthy as the one I did for you are slim, how do you feel about chipping away at it instead? A series of…mini favours, if you like?"

"Such as?"

"Nothing comes to mind, just yet. But it will."

"And if I have a small favour I need to add to the tally?"

It might take longer to redress the imbalance. "Bring it. Only fair."

"I'm liking the sound of this. And when the tally is finally even? What then? Phase Three?" Holden suggested.

"Sure. Let's go with that."

"Okay then. I await your next call with bated breath."

"Super. Enjoy your run, Holden."

Emerson reached out and pressed the button to end the call, her hands moving to cover her mouth. Then she started to laugh.

This was going to be fun. Or terrible. It was going to be something, which, after years of living within a very tight bandwidth, felt as if the lid had just opened on a box she hadn't known she'd been living in, letting in fresh air and sunshine.

And possibility.

"I need to get to work but I'm parked in," Emerson blurted, while standing by her car one morning to find a moving truck had parked halfway across her skinny driveway.

"Give me ten," Holden said, arriving in eight in a black convertible. With track pants and running top doing a terrible job of hiding a killer body beneath.

"What's with the new car?" she asked, trying not to stare at his arms. And the veins roping towards his wrists.

"I might take a run down the coast later. Better this than a sedan. Get in."

She did. Twisting like a pretzel in order to deal with the confined space.

Biting her tongue when Holden rested his hand on the gearstick, his little finger mere millimetres from the bare thigh showing beneath her pencil skirt.

Holding her breath when she glanced sideways right when he did the same, catching his eye, sharing smiles that seemed filled with some illicit promise. As if this was the beginning of something.

"Free for lunch?" he asked when he dropped her off, the engine still running while she slid from the car.

"I thought you were going for a drive down the coast."

He levelled her with a look. "Changed my mind. Lunch?"

"Sure," she said, feeling a sweeping sense of inevita-
bility rock through her. "The place across the road. One
o'clock. You're paying."

"You're on." He grinned and she felt it, like little spot
fires all over her body.

Freya asked if she was feeling okay when she hopped
out of the lift, ten minutes late, her cheeks still warm, the
scent of him lingering on her clothes. "You look flushed.
Feverish. Should I call a doctor?"

"I'm fine," Emerson said, laughing. Before hotfoot-
ing it to her office, where she slumped in her chair and
fanned herself with a stapler.

"I need a tie," Holden said.

When Emerson showed up at his new digs—a town
house not all that far from her place—it was to find him
getting dressed for a keynote speech he was giving that
night. Dark grey suit pants, beautifully cut, hugged his
legs, his feet were bare and he was yet to put on a shirt.

"Really?" she said, trying to look anywhere bar the
sculpted wonder that was his chest.

"What?"

She lifted the bag in her hand to cover the view.

Holden looked down and his abs flexed. "Please. You'd
see more of me at the beach."

The thought of seeing more of him had her swallowing. Hard.

He noticed. His grin widened.

Emerson chose to pretend it hadn't happened, and said,
"I think we've established I'm not a beach person. More
a laze-on-a-chair-by-the-pool person, while slathered in
sunscreen, and wearing a big hat, under a huge umbrella."

"I'll remember that. If we ever find ourselves, at a
beach, together." He said it as if it was a throwaway com-

ment. But somehow it also felt like a promise. Like a plan. As if this wasn't some temporary deal they were seeing through before he went back to his real life.

"Hurry up," she said, shooing him away. "Put your shirt on, or you'll be late."

Trying not to stare at his gorgeous back, all muscle and warm skin and, *Oh, Mama*, she followed him down the hall. Then found herself in his bedroom. Where he kept his bed.

Expensive-looking sheets—no shock there—in shades of caramel and cream, lay tousled on the huge mattress. No blanket or comforter, for the man ran hot. A pair of pillows lay at one end, smushed and askew. As if he slept on one and hugged the other.

"What do you think?" he asked.

Emerson dragged her eyes from the bed, and the endearing yet aphrodisiacal story it told, to find him standing in front of a mirror holding up different shirts. Both snow-white.

She found the three ties she'd picked up at the boutique near work on her way over. Red, blue to match his eyes, and silver.

He chose the silver.

She rolled her eyes as she sat. "No ability to spin a line, and no sense of colour. Sigh."

He met her eyes in the mirror as he slowly did up the buttons on his shirt. Smiling eyes. Eyes that liked the fact that she was perched on the end of his bed. She popped up like a Jack in the box.

"Wanna come see me talk tonight?" he asked.

"I can see you talk anytime. Look at us now. Talking."

"'Tis true. But this is different. This will be me being erudite. And lauded. There may even be clapping afterwards. You never clap after I speak. It's quite the thing."

"Then, sure. That I have to see."

So she went to watch him speak to a room filled with IT types, after he made sure to snag her a seat at a table with friendly people. And he was brilliant and articulate, but also charming and warm, exactly the same man that he was when it was just the two of them.

No surprise, then, that, while a fair bit went over Emerson's head, the crowd lapped it up. She joined them in the standing ovation. And somehow, in the dark of the crowd, his eyes found hers. And he smiled. Smiled as he breathed out, a long, slow breath.

Oh, no, a voice inside her intoned, as the sense of sweeping that had been buffeting her for days swept over her so hard, so fast, it was a miracle she managed to keep her feet.

But by then, it was too late.

The next time Emmy had plans to see Camille, Holden finally took that drive down the coast road.

It was something he liked to do on occasion, just get in the car and go. Top of the car down, the wind in his hair, the engine rumbling beneath him. It satisfied the primal need to escape he'd never quite outgrown.

He'd been driving this very road when he'd had the idea for the app that had started it all. A virtual study app. Uni friends, Phillip included, had been his beta testers, before universities the world over had got wind of it and bought the app, making him a fortune. Ironic that its success had seen him never finish his degree, and not see those guys again for years.

He remembered the moment he'd realised that app might be something special. A magic trick that could yank him out of the state of impoverishment in which he'd grown up. He'd pictured himself finally having access to everything he'd wished he'd had as a kid—shelter, money, ease. And he'd been right.

What he'd not expected was the number of people who came begging, acquaintances, distant relatives, complete strangers—all after a hand-out, a leg-up, a crumb. The shine had worn off pretty quick, as soon he'd grown wary. His life was now littered with the detritus of those who'd pretended to be on his side, only to expect something in return.

Malaise set in. Loneliness. So he kept on moving, finding more out-of-the-way places, ends of the earth, depths of nowhere, as if standing still would be spitting in the face of his good fortune.

Until he built the next app. New levels of mania ensued. Bidding wars for his next app, unseen, undreamt. So was his new pattern. Build it up, then leave it behind. All the while chasing that feeling he'd felt while driving this road—dreaming what it might be like to get everything he'd ever wished for.

Till the day he'd woken up in Amsterdam, to a middle-of-the-night phone call, and realised he'd been chasing something that wasn't real. Something that would never satisfy him, even if it was.

An app functioned, or it didn't. It served a purpose, or it didn't. Success, on that score, was clear-cut. After the Sanderson debacle, he pared back, stopped wanting what it was clear he'd never have. And soon found balance that suited him.

Noisy Work—launching the occasional new app to applause and accolades and loud congratulations—which drowned out any interest in his Quiet Work—behind the scenes, sometimes anonymous, helping create frameworks for medical research, education reform, universal health care.

In order to protect that balance, his friendship groups, the people he trusted, had become restricted, or short-lived.

While unrecognisable from the life he'd dreamt of, the one people ironically thought he enjoyed, and the gruelling life he'd once known, he'd found it perfectly fulfilling.

Until Emerson Adler had come along and any feelings of fulfilment had gone out the window.

The woman confused the heck out of him.

She'd made it all too clear she wanted nothing from him, which was unbelievably refreshing. Except those times she was outright demanding something of him. Where he'd found most people obscure to a fault, she was black and white. That he had to respect.

Then there was the attraction, a living, breathing thing that was becoming harder to contain. He could have kissed her a thousand times. And he knew, if he had, it wouldn't be the end of it. He'd still want to kiss her a thousand times more.

If Joel, his business manager, who knew enough about where he'd come from, had a single clue that he was here because of a woman, he'd have laughed till he split his spleen. His wife, Jenny, would likely burst into happy tears.

Infamously impervious Holden Roarke taken down by a bolshie brunette with a penchant for asking hard questions and sweet old dogs. And he had been taken down. Brought to his knees. .

He wasn't sleeping. He had little room for ideas in his head that didn't involve ways to invent a favour he might ask or perform. And he had left behind a perfectly liveable penthouse so that he could rent a place, short-term, in the suburbs.

All so that he might be near to her.

Treading lightly all the while. His instincts assured him that was necessary. For all her big talk, there was something wildly delicate about Emerson Adler. Uncertain. Skittish.

Which was the only way he was able to stop himself from telling her how much he wanted to touch her, to hold her, to kiss her, to make love to her, to wake up beside her and do it all over again. This was the one time in his life where he had to be more careful than he was curious.

And so, rather than enjoying a delicious, torrid affair with a woman he found utterly captivating, before heading back to Stockholm or the Seychelles, or wherever the first plane he found might take him, he'd found himself in the midst of an old-fashioned courting.

And he couldn't get enough of it.

Yep. The woman confused the heck out of him.

Holden hung a left, leaving the beach huts behind and spinning up into the hills.

This he could measure. This he could enjoy without censure or self-recrimination. To be out here, midweek, while others plugged away at their office jobs, he knew himself to be a very lucky man.

He would relish these spoils of his success, before the rubber band wrapped around his heart no doubt sent him thwacking all the way back to her.

At the same time, back in Melbourne, Emerson found Camille in the succulent section of Wild Willow Plant Nursery.

"Sorry I'm late!" said Emmy. "Heck of a morning. The family next door used their new barbecue and set off my smoke alarms. And you know how Pumpkin gets with smoke alarms. Then, would you believe I had a flat tyre?"

Camille looked at Emerson's white-on-white ensemble. "Not even slightly. You should have called me. Turns out I'm now amazing with a wrench!"

"Good to know," she said. "Anyway, I called Holden, but he's off on some joy ride, so I got onto the auto club, and here I am!"

Camille's eyes widened comically. "Back up. You called *Holden*? As in Holden Roarke? As in *Heartache Number Four*?"

Emerson blinked. "Um—"

"No," said Camille, turning away, holding up a dramatic shushing hand. "I get it. I've been replaced."

"What? No!" Emerson insisted, even while she felt prickly heat swoosh into her cheeks. "Holden is… Well, we've been doing these favours for one another, you see."

When Camille clearly didn't see, Emerson gave her a quick, awkward rundown of the past few weeks. Then added, "Serendipitous timing, really, as I can't keep relying on you because you're busy, you're on your honeymoon, Phillip is your person now—"

Camille reached out and took Emerson's hands. "Stop. Breathe. I get it. It's been weird, right? This new normal?"

Emerson nodded, and smiled, relieved to be talking this out rather than shoving it down deep inside. "But getting less weird. Don't you think?"

Camille nodded, eyes a little bright. Then pointed towards the outdoor plant section before ambling that way. "So, these favours of yours. You do realise this is basically how being a couple works. You drive him somewhere, he picks up your laundry. It's a relationship without the sex. Unless… Unless this is some long-term, stretch-things-out-until-you-feel-you-might-die mode of foreplay."

Emerson, who was sniffing the leaves of a velvety plant, stilled. A lightbulb, then a thousand more, like wild, out-of-control fairy lights, were springing to life inside her head. "Oh, my."

"I knew it!" Camille spun on the spot.

"Unless—"

"Here we go."

"Unless I'm right back where I was all those years ago, feeling all these feelings and he just thinks I'm his cute little hallway friend."

"You're not cute."

"That's what you took from that?"

"Honeybun, you're *va-va-voom*. So maybe he thinks of you as his *va-va-voom* little hallway friend."

Emerson shot Camille a look. "Not helping."

"Then *ask* him! Or better yet, jump him. Either way it's gotta be better than being wound so tight."

"I'm not wound tight."

"You know what? You actually don't look it, either. What's with that?"

"I have endeavoured to make sure I don't implode with all the pent-up, built-up, you know… Let's just say Holden Roarke is mighty good fantasy material."

Camille held up a hand for a high five, which Emerson duly gave up.

"Wow. This is some huge progress you've made. Like day-one-in-therapy-then-fast-forward-to-graduation-level progress."

Emerson agreed. This was *exactly* what she'd been hoping for when she'd allowed herself to enjoy being with Holden, rather than constantly waiting for the other shoe to drop. "I do feel like a stronger, more evolved version of myself. More…open to possibility."

"By possibility do you mean giving your vibrator a

night off, dragging Holden Roarke into your bed for some good old-fashioned rumpy-pumpy?"

Emerson smiled at the grey-haired couple who gawped at them as they meandered by. "Maybe. Though without the old-fashioned bit."

Camille stopped in the middle of the aisle, sunlight dappling her face through the leaves of a row of potted palms. "Just so long as you don't forget, this is Holden Roarke."

"Meaning?"

"From what Phillip has told me—and he's told me a lot, because he is semi in love with the guy—Holden is not a stay-at-home-and-watch-true-crime-documentaries kind of man. He's a big deal. So, for all that you're having fun now, there's a really good chance he'll be heading back to his real life soon. And you… Well, you do know that people leaving you is your kryptonite. It's kind of a running theme in the… You Know List."

"I know," said Emerson.

And she did. She really did.

She still had his calendar linked to hers. Saw the eye-popping lists of people his business manager, an excitable-sounding guy named Joel, added to his "maybe" calendar—the majority of them overseas, in places like Geneva and Washington and Dubai. All of which had been crossed through, because Holden was here.

Still, hearing Camille say it sent little impacts all over her body. Like buckshot—not enough to take her down, but enough for it to sting.

Then Camille clicked her fingers. "Unless… Unless you're doing this because you *know* he'll leave. You're fooling around with him *because* there's an end point. That's genius!"

Emerson moved on, towards the fern section, Camille's theory running through her head. Maybe there was something to that too. A safety net to her experiment. Was that such a bad thing? "You make me sound so mercenary."

Camille shrugged. "You do you, boo. And, hey, when he does vamoose, after unlocking the wanton, voracious, cavalier side we all know is lurking beneath your pristine façade, I still have that list of Phillip's friends, who would ask you out in a heartbeat if only they weren't terrified of you."

"I'll keep that in mind," Emerson deadpanned. "So… plants!"

"Plants!"

While Camille talked up her idea of a wall of hanging plants in her tiny lounge, as inspired by some random Instagrammer with a much bigger house, Emmy nodded along, and tried not to think about Holden leaving, in actuality, and what that might feel like. Not having him at the end of the phone. Not being able to see him whenever the fancy took her.

And those thoughts set some small, dangerous thing alight deep inside her.

Not an ache. Nothing quite so blunt. More the sharp, painful constancy of an accidental burn.

That was the thing about burns, the small ones that travelled slowly through dry scrub. If not doused soon, a wind might whip up and soon the whole forest would burn to the ground.

"That's an A380." One eye open, Holden held his finger to the sky, tracing the underbelly of the plane as it lifted into the darkening dusk over their heads, heading to destinations unknown.

"How can you tell?" Emerson asked, while busy poking and prodding at the pile of soft blankets and cushions Holden had thrown in the back of the ute after trading it for his rental convertible.

"I know my planes," he said.

Giving up on perfection, she leaned back on her elbows, and squinted up at the plane as it lifted higher into the sky. "A man of hidden skills."

"Not so hidden, I hope. In fact, perhaps I ought to write them all down on a list, carry them on my person, so that any time people are in need of one of my many skills I can whip it out."

"Lists can be helpful." Her mouth twitched before her head turned his way. The dying rays of sunlight spilled over the dark waves of her hair, the delicate edge of her face, her shoulder. "Whip it out, you say?"

"At any time," he offered. "For the benefit of the community."

"For an ideas man, some of your ideas are whacka-doo."

"The download numbers of my apps tell a different story."

"Over-confidence is not an attractive trait."

Holden's grin hit his face before he even felt it coming. "Not in my experience."

Emerson scoffed, but didn't argue the fact. Instead, she once more became preoccupied with getting comfortable.

For all that watching her wriggle about in a bed of blankets and cushions may not have been the smartest idea for a man who was struggling not to spook her by hauling her into his arms and kissing her senseless, he felt rather good about his decision to bring her.

Their arrival at their current location—an aircraft viewing spot in Greenvale—had come about due to his latest favour request.

Andy, another friend from uni, worked for Australian air traffic control. Nearing the end of a major software update, they were keen to get his input on how to make the interface less spartan, and more user-friendly.

Emerson had called the night before, asking for a favour. One of her staff, an older, rather sophisticated gent, was having a birthday and could Holden recommend a unique gift? He'd agreed to pick something up—a signed Graham Greene book he'd spotted in a vintage store near hers—if she'd come along to a meeting as a second pair of eyes.

Partly because he had learned that spending time with her was better than not, and partly because the thought of spending any time in the bowels of the airport where his father had worked on and off his whole childhood did not entice.

Now—wriggling as if she had ants in the pants of the classy, black, all-in-one get-up that she had going on— she got her high heels caught in a blanket and it took her a good ten seconds to get free. Then she flapped a wild hand at some bug—real or imagined—that had wafted too close to her face. And huffed. Loudly.

"We can go," said Holden, not minding what they did, so long as he got to watch her do it. "If this isn't your thing."

"No! This is lovely. Really. It's…"

She looked at him a moment, her gaze a little hot, colour sweeping into her cheeks, and he felt the word *romantic* whisper on the breeze.

In the end, she went with, "Fine. If I wasn't here, I'd probably have taken Pumpkin into the office, as there is so much work to do on the Sanderson job, which is brilliant, but also a lot. My assistant, Freya—you'd have spoken to her on the phone a couple of times in the early days—sends me memes daily about ways to relax. If I tell her I lie out under the stars, on a pile of blankets, in the middle of nowhere, she'll be beside herself."

"Well, so long as you're excited to be here…"

Her grin was quick and intoxicating. The urge to stroke his thumb over that full bottom lip, to watch her eyes flash with surprise, then turn dark with longing, was a strong one. The certainty that it would change everything between them hovered on the air. Ripe and sweet.

The way her chest lifted and fell, he was sure she could feel it too. But then she lay back, and placed her hands over her chest like some kind of beatific painting. It was so damned endearing his chest hurt.

He was a goner. Truly.

With no planes in the sky, the great dome above having quickly turned dark, they watched in companionable silence as wispy clouds wafted by, blocking out the crescent moon, before wafting on again.

Emerson sighed, the sound warmed by a kind of contentment that Holden felt in his bones. "I've lived in Melbourne all my life and I never knew this was a thing."

"It's a favourite haunt of mine."

"You came here as a kid?"

"Mmm," he said. It hadn't been a thing to do, it had been a safe space, a lifesaver. "I grew up out this way."

"Really?" She lifted back to her elbows, and glanced around, taking in the great tracts of farmland. "It's lovely."

"This is. Where we were was near enough to the airport for the plane noise to be a daily grind, not near enough to live on more than a postage stamp of land in dilapidated council housing."

"You and your dad?"

"Mmm. See that farm over there," he said, pointing

over her shoulder to an undulating patch of shadowy forest green across the way. "It's a retirement home for ex-racehorses, including a few Melbourne Cup winners."

He knew she hadn't been fooled by his clumsy distraction. He only liked her more when she went with it. "Oh! That's wonderful. They get to live out their days frolicking through acres of lush pastures. Far better than the alternative."

"When they 'go to the farm', they actually go to the farm."

"Groan."

When he laughed, she lay back and smiled up into the sky. Now he wanted to trace the line of her nose, her chin, her collarbone. What was happening to him? It was like he was sixteen again, seeing a girl, liking a girl, not knowing what to do with a girl.

"So, if you grew up out this way, how did you end up in high school in Kew? And for such a brief stint?"

"You noticed that, did you?"

Her mouth twisted. "We had matching guidance counsellor sessions every single week. When you didn't show up one week, or ever again, I noticed."

Holden squinted up into the sky. "Why don't you tell me more about the memes this assistant of yours sends—are they the types you find on inspirational calendars, all bordered in flowers? Or more along the black and white dirge line?"

She turned fully on her side, her hands tucked under her head. And said nothing. He knew it cost her—the girl with all the questions—but she held her tongue.

Holden breathed out hard. "I'd call you pushy, in the hopes of sending you spiralling off in another direction, but I get the feeling you'd take it as a compliment."

He tipped his head, and found himself looking into

Emerson's curious eyes. Her lovely face, her warm body all curled up beside his. Happy to listen if he wanted to talk, or to simply be with him if he didn't. As if she wanted nothing from him bar what he was willing to give.

It cost her nothing to be that way, yet it didn't feel like nothing. In fact, it felt closer to a continental shift. If he hadn't been lying down, he might have had to reach out for something to grip.

"Change of subject," she said. "Your airport friend's proposal. It's a huge project. My advice? Don't say yes unless you see yourself surrendering to it for the next eighteen months to two years. Can you? Can you see yourself sticking to one thing for that long?"

The question was simple. And yet… That was the second time she'd asked him how long he was sticking around. Which was not an accident. Did it indicate she had a vested interest in his answer?

The continental shift cracked open a fraction wider.

When he didn't answer she huffed out a breath. Of frustration? Then she reached out blindly, grabbed a fluffy cushion and brought it to her chest. "Where on earth did you find all this stuff?"

Finally, a question he could answer. "I may have called Camille last night to ask where I might find such frippery at short notice. After two of the longest minutes of my life, in which I was asked a barrage of questions far more brazen than even you dare ask, she sent me to some frou-frou boutique. Apparently 'the plan' is that she's happy to take it all off my hands for the new house when we're done here tonight."

"She is industrious," Emmy said, with a quick smile. Then he could feel her mulling over her next words. "So, you called Camille before I called you. Meaning you were already planning this before I agreed to come. I can either assume you always liked being surrounded by pretty cushions when watching planes, or—" She breathed in, breathed out, and said, "Or you did all this for me. Knowing, somehow, how very much I needed a break."

"Sprung," he said. He smiled, she smiled back, and he felt it like an arrow in his chest fired at close range. "When I was working on my first app, I turned into a madman, locked away in my dark tower, hunched over my work, squinting if I ever accidentally stumbled into the light."

"Like Quasimodo?"

"Ah, I think you mean Batman."

"He has a cave, not a tower."

"Can't you let a man dream?"

She lifted her fingers in submission. "Dream away."

Then she turned to face the sky as a plane began its descent up high over their heads, her eyes tracking the slow movement of the big, metallic beast.

While Holden's fingertips pressed into his chest.

Dream away, she'd said. When his wish was to reach out, and cup her cheek. Or sweep that rogue lock of hair behind her ear. Or tell her that if he didn't kiss her, soon, he might literally expire, and his disappearance would be on her hands.

Unfortunately, his talk of not being able to spin a line had not been a line. Meaning all he could do was tell her the truth.

"First time I came here I was fifteen," he said. "Too young for a licence, I stole my father's car. He'd just finished telling me how worthless I was, and passed out drunk. I drove and drove, with no destination in mind, only slowing when I saw a dozen-odd cars lined up in the field here, right as a plane flew low overhead. I pulled onto the hard shoulder, the noise of the thing filling my head. My panic slowly abated, as plane after plane headed off into the wild blue yonder. My dream, as it was, from that day on, was to one day be up there, heading far, far away from here."

He squinted at the first stars hovering above the horizon.

"A few weeks later, next time my dad passed out drunk, I packed up my stuff and left. My great-aunt lived in Kew—she let me stay with her so long as I kept going to school. Counselling meant I could attend without guardian approval. Then one day my dad turned up at his aunt's place with a cricket bat and a slur. I've been on the move pretty much ever since."

She was quiet for a few long beats, before she said, "Why do you think he was like that?"

"According to him, everything that went wrong in his life began the moment I was born. My mother died in childbirth, so there was some truth to it. Made it hard to disassociate that from his drinking, his anger, his self-pity."

"How does a man like that end up with a son like you?"

His chest squeezed, the hollowness that had lived behind his ribs for so long pressed so tight it nearly popped. "So, you're saying I'm *not* worthless," he said, turning his head and adding a smile to soften the joke.

She lay back on her side, watching him, her brow furrowed. As if, if the man was still alive today she'd take a swing.

He adored her for it. This beautiful, challenging, skittish, intense creature who made him work for every smile, every laugh, every drop of trust. Made him dig deep. And speak truth.

He *adored* her.

It was the only thing that made any sense. For the way he felt, had been feeling these past weeks, was nothing he'd ever felt before. It was as wholesome as it was raw. As comforting and gentle as it was a roar in the back of his head, thunder behind his ribs, a pressing and constant need that lived and roiled at his centre, all of which was held back by the barest thread of civility.

This woman he'd never even kissed.

It was past time he did something about that.

"Emmy," he said. "Emerson." Then he reached out for her. Slowly. So she knew what was coming. As if she couldn't hear it in the raw scrape of his voice. The clawing need.

Giving her time to make it clear if this wasn't what she wanted. But, gods, he hoped it was. Hoped more than he remembered hoping for anything since he'd last been here, hoping something up there might be the answer to making his life better down here.

His fingers slid through her hair, the strands falling over his hands like heavy silk. He exhaled with relief, as it felt as if he'd been waiting for this exact moment all his life.

He cradled her gently, his thumb tracing her cheekbone, as he moved in. Caught by the heat in her eyes. By the soft catch in her breath.

When he was close enough for their lips to almost touch, he paused. Took a moment to sink into the anticipation, grateful it was finally at an end. Or was this the beginning?

And then he kissed her.

When their lips met, she sighed, as if she'd been imagining this moment as long as he had. As if she too had been holding on for dear life and could finally let go.

When he tilted her face, so he could deepen the kiss,

she opened to him, swept her tongue against his, and he was lost.

Lost to heat and need. And regret. Regret that they'd waited. And joy. Joy that they'd waited. That this moment had finally come, with the starlight raining down upon her face, as she scooted closer and wrapped herself around him, and met his kisses with her own, in this bed of blankets he'd built for her.

"Holden," she said, coming up for air. Looking into his eyes, searching.

Whatever she saw there, things soon turned frantic, desperate. As if they were trying to find a way into one another's skin.

She rolled on top of him, kissing him madly, even as her hands reached for his shirt, tugging it free of his jeans. When her hands found skin they slowed, tracing his sides with deliberation and pace, sending the painful prick of a million goosebumps racing all over his body. And it was a miracle it wasn't all over for him, then and there.

When his hands mirrored her pace, sliding slowly up her thighs, her whole body seemed to sing.

She rocked against him, setting off explosions behind his eyes, as she plied him with drugging kisses—

A car door slammed. And Holden remembered where they were.

"Emmy," he said, the word playing against her mouth.

She hummed, and rolled against him again.

With supernatural strength Holden rolled her over, till he was on top, his thigh between hers. He pressed down. Her eyes rolled back in her head, her front teeth bearing down on her bottom lip.

He gritted out, "We have company."

Her eyes flew open, her hands gripping his messed-up shirt as she lifted her head to look over his shoulder.

Glancing back, he saw a dad and three young kids pile out of a station wagon, holding apples and juice boxes, before piling into the boot when the dad opened the rear door, clearly about to set up for an evening of plane-watching at the popular spot.

Holden quickly sat up, fixed his shirt, tossed a blanket over his junk. The dad gave him a quick nod, and a wave, as if he remembered how it felt to be young and so caught up in another you forgot who you were.

Not *who* you were, where you were.

Holden was very aware of who he was—a guy whose dad would never have taken him on an "outing" such as this. Never packed him a juice box. Or told him to eat an apple. He'd offered cigarettes, drink, a kick in the backside as he shoved him out the door of a morning, telling him not to come back unless he had money in his pocket.

"Oh, my God," said Emerson, her hand flopping over her eyes. "Can you imagine if they'd been a few minutes later?"

"Whatever do you mean?" he asked, moving gently, so as not to damage himself, even as his mind spun. "Explain it to me. In lurid detail."

She laughed, the sound bright and light. And gorgeous. A sound he could listen to for ever and never tire of it.

His earlier musings lurked, like a virus—who was he to think of forever? His first real attempt at such a life with the Sandersons had been disastrous. All these years later he still hadn't learned how to settle into a life that required a fixed address. He had no clue what *home* even meant.

"Why did it take us so damn long to do that?" Emerson asked.

"You tell me."

She tipped her head to face him, so utterly gorgeous it hurt. "Should I be asking you to forget that too? It was miles outside the boundaries of our agreement after all."

Holden's jaw twitched hard enough to crack a tooth. He said, "You can ask. But then, you'd also have to ask me to forget about how much you wanted to kiss me when I dropped you to your hotel room after the wedding."

Her mouth fell open.

"Or how much I wanted to kiss you on the garden bench after dinner at the Sandersons'. Then again when I dropped you home that night. And when you brought me those ties. I can go on."

"Mmm," she said, stretching like a cat who'd got the cream.

That was neither a yes nor a no, which, as far as Holden could see, was progress. Progressing towards what, he had no idea. All he knew was that it was going in a direction that felt right.

Then she shivered. For the night had turned cold.

"Come on," he said, climbing off the back of the tray, and holding out a hand. "Let's get you home."

Home he took her. And at home he left her. After a chaste kiss at her door. A press of his lips on hers that lasted a breath or two. A kiss that left her looking dreamy and soft as she floated inside her house, her voice already calling for her dog, as if she had a story to tell.

While Holden took the throws and cushions back to the town house he was renting.

He'd buy Camille a voucher to get her own.

CHAPTER EIGHT

EMERSON HOPPED OUT of her ride share, juggling a large gift bag, a bottle of wine, and her phone. And looked, in marvel, at the changes her friends had made to their new home.

The garden bed was new, lined with little stones and boasting a string of tiny plants poking out of mounds of bark, much of which must have been done earlier that day by the team of friends and colleagues who'd turned up early for the Working Bee, Beer, and Barbecue extravaganza.

Emmy had been invited, of course, but Camille had followed up with:

do not show up before the after-party begins the rest of the day will be backbreaking love you!

With the new fence and Camille's beloved fairy lights strung along the front porch, it all looked so pretty. So very much theirs. Those bittersweet pickled feelings threatened to rise up inside Emmy again, only this time she was able to still them. For it was all okay. She was okay. They'd all be okay.

"Emmy!" cried Bernadette, Camille's lovely young cousin, when she opened the door. Dust in her hair, a scratch on her cheek, she wiped a hand down her old overalls before pulling Emmy in for a hug.

"Emmy's here!" she cried.

The crowd turned as one and called out, "Emmy!" before going back to their conversations, while Bernie took the gift bag from Emmy and popped it with the pile in the corner of the lounge.

"Did you hear?" Bernie asked, before flashing her left hand and showing off a tiny diamond on a band of gold.

"Oh. Wow! When?" *Who?*

"Barry," said Bernie, with a sigh. "We were high school sweethearts, you know. Fell apart, as you do at that age. Then reconnected at Camille and Phillip's wedding. It seems the bouquet worked after all."

Emmy's delighted laughter was genuine. "It seems so."

She wondered if Bernadette remembered trying to slip her room key into Holden's pocket. Then figured, by the lovestruck look in Bernie's eyes as she waved to Barry across the room, that she did not. Emmy decided then and there that it had never happened.

"Camille?" Emmy asked.

As if hearing her name, Camille appeared out of nowhere, looking glorious in a long green dress, her curls piled up on top of her head, making it clear she'd also managed to avoid the Working Bee part of the party.

Camille placed a glass of bubbly in Emmy's hand then gave her a quick tour. The place was still a mess, most rooms unfinished. But the pantry was huge, the light in the bedrooms gorgeous. It was on its way to being perfect.

"Do you love it?" Camille asked, as they ended up in the lounge.

"More than life itself."

"Good. Turns out we need a kettle. And a toaster. Remember we didn't put them on the wedding gift list?"

"Too bourgeois, I believe you said."

"Bit us on the backside, that did."

Emmy pointed to her gift bag. "Cream wrapping, rose-gold ribbon."

"I knew I loved you."

"These are great," said Emmy, running her fingers over the spring greens and dusty pinks of the cushions and throws draped over the couches in the lounge. Not at all like the greys and creams of the furnishings Holden had used in the ute the other night. She could still feel them under her head when he'd kissed her. Under her knees when she'd straddled him.

"New?" she asked, before clearing her throat.

"Yep! Holden gave us a very generous tab at a local boutique as a house-warming gift, so I went a little crazy."

"You came!"

Camille and Emmy both looked up at Phillip's enthusiastic outburst, only to find him looking to the front door. To Holden, standing there, holding a huge potted cactus.

Emmy's heart smacked against her ribs with such force she actually tripped forward.

They hadn't seen one another in person since the plane-watching night. They'd texted. They'd talked, sometimes late into the night. He'd called to ask for advice on a good house-warming present. Not a favour, *advice*. She'd gone with, "Something Camille can't kill." The promise of *next time* building between them like a dormant volcano.

Holden's smile when his eyes found hers was scorching. Emerson hid her own goofy smile behind her drink.

Then her view was blocked as a bunch of Phillip's

friends saw who'd arrived and descended upon Holden with questions, app ideas, requests, before the guy had even made it over the threshold.

"Sit," said Camille, pressing Emmy into her old couch, when all she wanted to do was go to him, hold out a hand and tell everyone to back the hell away.

Knowing how crazy that was, Emmy sat with a whoosh of expelled air.

"Holden!" said Camille. "Lovely to see you. Drink?"

Emmy's heart thundered in her throat as she looked up to find he'd pushed his way through the crowd just fine. He'd done so to see her. "Iced water, please. With lime if you have it."

"Do I have lime? he asks. I'll be back." Camille left.

And Holden continued smiling down at Emmy, the heat in his eyes making her wonder which part of their recent kiss *he* was reliving. She was up to the part when his tongue had traced the edges of her top teeth, sending sparks rocketing through her entire body, as if she'd been hit by lightning.

She motioned for him to sit.

And he did. Close beside her. So close that, when he pressed his hand into the seat to make himself comfortable, his little finger stroked against hers.

Phillip plonked down on the tub chair near the couch, his cheeks pink from happiness. And beer.

Holden shifted so that his arm rubbed against hers.

Emmy may have shivered from top to toe, and Holden may have noticed.

Camille reappeared, handing Holden his drink before sitting on her husband's lap, bubbly sloshing over the edge of her glass, and looking as contented as Emmy had ever seen her. She waited for a flicker of the bittersweets, only this time it didn't come. No twinge, not even an echo, too swamped with happiness was she at seeing her friends so content.

"Look at us," said Phillip, beaming. "Camille and I, all grown up in our amazing new house. Then there's Holden with his apps and his world renown."

Holden laughed, rubbing a hand up the back of his head. And was that a little flush creeping up his neck? Emmy shifted so that her knee bumped his. The look he shot her was quick, but sizzling, and she tucked her knees together so as to hold herself in one piece.

"And then there's our Emmy," said Phillip, "the Heartache List now so far in her rear-view mirror she'd have to squint to see it."

"What's the Heartache List?" Holden asked.

Camille smacked Phillip on the arm.

"What?" Phillip asked. Then, "God, Emmy. I'm so sorry. It just slipped out. I figured he knew, considering..." Phillip waved a hand at them, motioning to how close they were sitting.

"Why do I get the sense Phillip just put his foot in it?" Holden asked, leaning into Emmy's side.

"It's nothing. Don't worry about it."

His hand moved to her knee, his eyes searching hers. "I'm not worried about it. What with all the stage-whispering and arm-hitting and the panic in your eyes, I am a little intrigued. And now that I think about it, you mentioned something about the List the night of the wedding."

"Do you forget nothing?"

"Big brain," he said, tapping the side of his head.

Emmy sucked her lips between her teeth, and glanced around the room, looking for an escape. Till Camille caught her eye and mouthed, *Tell him.*

Careful Emmy would never have considered giving up that part of herself to Holden Roarke. The evolved

Emmy, the bold, brave, curious Emmy, pulled herself to standing. And motioned for Holden to follow.

Follow he did, through the lounge, the dining room, the den. But everywhere they went there were people. Eventually they ended up in the kitchen.

The pantry! Grabbing Holden by the hand, Emmy dragged him into the huge walk-in cupboard. A light flickered on as the door opened, then off again after the door closed.

In the semi-darkness, lit only by a sliver of light coming under the door, she could feel Holden's warmth. Hear the shift of his clothes, the huff of his breath.

"It looked bigger from the outside," she muttered.

"Emerson."

"Hmm?"

"Was there a reason you brought me in here?"

Darkness was nice, but as her other senses heightened, forcing her to focus on his gorgeous scent, she started to feel a little woozy. She found her phone, switched on the light, and placed it on a shelf beside a bag of pasta.

The shaft of overbright light shone on one side of Holden's face, creating shadows and valleys in the most beautiful shapes.

The slide of his hands into the pockets of his jeans were the only sign he was holding his patience in check.

"Okay," she said. "I'm going to tell you something, but you have to promise not to freak out."

"Do I seem like someone prone to freaking out?"

"Fair enough. For a number of years, I kept a notebook in which I detailed the times I'd had my heart broken."

"The Heartache List."

"The very one. I only documented the big hurts. The ones I felt sure I would never get over. My third-grade teacher leaving mid-term, the rock star whose posters covered my walls marrying some other woman."

"Those were your big hurts?"

"They were big. To me."

"Of course," he said, his expression chagrined. "Go on."

"Yes, I had other knocks, disappointments, frustrations, and sorrows that did not end up on the list. Such as when a school friend 'washed' my favourite Barbie doll's hair in the toilet. When I missed making the Dean's List at university while the kid who never showed up to lectures who also had the same name as one of the college libraries made it." She paused. "Though, to be fair, I looked up that old Barbie when it came up in one of those 'you are this old if you remember this toy' things on social media. In pristine condition they're now worth a packet."

"Emmy, I am loving this insight into what makes you *you*, but I'm not sure you needed to drag me into a cupboard to tell me about it."

"Okay. Yes. Here goes. And I can't believe I'm about to say this out loud, but maybe it's all part of the great Heartache List therapy session I'm in the midst of—I had a crush on you. Back then. At school."

In the quiet that followed, the white noise of the party permeated, but it was a blur beneath the thumping rush of blood behind Emmy's ears.

"Yeah," Holden eventually said. "I kind of figured."

Emerson stared at him. Gobsmacked. "You kind of *figured*?"

"Well, you're not exactly the most subtle person on the planet," he said, reaching out to her as if he might cup her cheek before curling his fingers into his palm. "Back then, you'd look at me with those big eyes of yours and kind of…"

"Kind of what?"

"Sigh."

Kill her now.

"Hang on a second," he said, as he came full circle. "Are you suggesting I was on your Heartbreak List?"

"Heartache."

"Oh, good. I'd hate to think I'd broken you as opposed to making you ache."

His words, while flippant, hit deep. Aching, feeling broken, these were feelings she'd worked hard to keep out of her life. Something she still hoped to do, no matter how this "therapy" worked out.

"It wasn't your fault," she said. "You did nothing wrong." She knew that now.

"Then why—?"

"It all started with my dad." Emerson leaned back, needing space, only to rattle up against a shelf that was yet to be bolted to the wall.

Holden reached out, steadied her, and said, "Your dad."

"He left when I was ten. We... I...never saw it coming. And I... I don't think I've ever really got over it. My mum tried to help me understand, that marriage can be hard work, and some people aren't built for it, but the fact he could leave *me*, and never even get in touch... It broke my heart."

Yes, broke. Every other slight after that had been like pressing into a deep wound.

"During our sojourns in the hall outside Miss Kemp's office, you were so sweet to me. During a time when life felt sour. And when you left, and I didn't see it coming, again, it brought up things I'd been trying to pretend hadn't affected me as much as they had."

"Fathers, eh?" Holden said, moving in a little closer, his thumbs moving up and down her arms.

"Camille's dad is a gem. Phillip's too. And, from what you told me, Chuck was a pretty amazing stand-in."

"So, genetically we lucked out?" he asked, a dash of irony lighting his voice, even while it remained warm and kind and understanding.

"Ha. I guess we did."

Emerson looked up into Holden's eyes, and felt that flicker of familiarity he'd said he felt when he'd spotted her on the dance floor. Outsiders looking in. Only, here in this tight space, his hands on her, she didn't feel like an outsider. She felt as if she was inside something bigger than herself. Something magical.

Refusing to think, or overthink, or mentally play out any scenarios to their possible end games, she lifted onto her toes and kissed him.

His lips were cool and smooth, the taste of lime and ice sending a beautiful chill right through her. Already holding her, keeping her steady, Holden pulled her a little higher and kissed her back.

And while their first kiss—*their first kiss!*—in the back of the ute had been scorching hot—decades of pent-up frustration hot—a dam bursting—this...

This kiss was sweet. Slow. Lingering.

Tasting, testing, learning one another's shape and feel.

The whole thing felt as if it was happening in slow motion.

Pressed as high as she could go, Emerson slid her hands up Holden's chest, and around his neck, her fingers tingling at the touch of his hair. His hands slid slowly down her arms to circle her waist, pulling her close.

This beautiful man. This good, generous, gorgeous

hulk of a man who knew what it was to hurt. To move beyond it. And to thrive.

Her limbs began to tremble as the kiss deepened. Incrementally. Unceasingly. Settling in her limbs like warm honey. Hands now roving. Touching, caressing. Finding tender spots. Finding skin.

Small sounds of pleasure backed up in her throat, keeping her breathless. Heat pooled in her centre, till her head spun. Until she was a molten puddle of gooey pleasure.

Aeons later, Emmy pulled back, needing breath. Needing to feel the ground beneath her feet.

She dropped slowly back to her heels. Rested her head against Holden's chest, her eyes filling when he wrapped his arms even tighter about her and dropped a kiss on the top of her head.

As her pulse thudded sluggishly through her body, she mused that until that moment it was entirely possible she hadn't known what heartache was.

For, like a foot that had fallen asleep, it seemed that her heart had been slumbering. And now, as it filled with blood, and warmth, and life, like pins and needles in her chest the pain was real.

This was no crush. A crush was tender, and warm. Distant.

The feelings rushing through her, the knowledge of how much she felt for this man, was wild, and raw, and out of control.

She felt as if she'd been sliced open, exposed.

His hands began sweeping over her back, calming her heart rate. Calming them both.

There was no chance he couldn't feel the thump of her heart, the tremble in her chest. No chance he didn't have some inkling that these feelings were overwhelming her. That this was not a test. That there was no going back.

"So, this Heartache List—"

"Forget about it. I have. Or, to be fair, I'm working on it."

"With the…great Heartache List therapy session that you're in the midst of."

"Mm-hmm."

"Am I a part of that?"

Emerson twisted to lay her cheek over his heart and said nothing. Not sure how he'd handle knowing he was all of that.

He lifted a hand to cradle her face, to turn it to him. "So long as you know that there is no point in asking me to forget about that kiss. It happened. And it's going to happen again."

He leaned down and kissed her once more. Pulled back to say, "And again."

Another kiss, this one rich with longing, turning her knees to jelly and her brain to mush.

He pulled back again just enough to hold eye contact as he said, "I'm done pretending this isn't happening, Emerson. I'm more than okay with you and me, if you are too."

She sucked in a slow breath, enough to gather her thoughts. "I'm more than okay with that, too." Adding, "For as long as you're in town."

His gaze intense, solid, true, he said, "I'm not going anywhere."

Then, before she could brace herself against the fresh onslaught of feelings *that* brought on, he took her by the hand and twirled her under his arm till she was tucked up against his side. With his spare hand he passed her her phone, and waited for her to turn off the light.

"Shall we?" he asked, his voice a rumble in the darkness.

She held his hand in place. And nodded.

With his arm around her he led her out into the fray.

A few wide-eyed looks from Phillip's friends, a few side-eyes from people who'd never have put "Emerson" and "public display of affection" in the same sentence. When Camille spied them her mouth dropped open, before she clapped her hands effusively, forcing everyone to look her way. "Everyone out back. Time for Strip Charades!"

Laughter and murmurs of dissent abounded before she said, "Fine. Normal charades."

Thus having provided the perfect distraction, Camille gave Emmy a quick wink and shuffled everyone outside. She gave Holden the two-fingered *I'm watching you* move. Then the party went on as if nothing had changed.

When, to Emerson's mind, it would never be the same again.

"I need a favour," Emerson blurted the moment the phone was answered. Then, "Aargh, I forgot to check your calendar. If you're busy—"

"Shoot," Holden said, no hesitation.

Emerson breathed out in relief. "It's Pumpkin."

"Is he okay?" Holden asked, his voice tight, as if he wasn't merely asking. As if he truly cared about her patchy old pup.

Emerson had no hope of muffling the warm fuzzies that crept up her insides as she said, "Yes. Yes, he's fine. I left him home today as he was super-cute and sleepy this morning. It's just, I remembered he's run out of his special food. I usually pre-order it from the vet but they were changing brands last time we visited. I ran out this morning, the vet closes really early today, in about twenty

minutes, and I have a pre-interview with an amazing
Sanderson Group COO candidate in ten minutes, and
Chuck is being very stubborn and I'm finding it harder
and harder to even find anyone to talk to about the posi-
tion much less suggest, so I won't make it in time, and
I usually use Kerri, next door, who I pay to look after
Pumpkin when I can't, but she's at uni this arvo, and—"

"Text me the details."

"Are you sure?"

"Emmy, I'm the one you call."

"Thank you."

"My pleasure," he said, in that voice of his that made
her believe it really was. His pleasure. "Where's his
bowl?"

"Don't worry about that. Kerri can feed him when
she gets home."

"Emmy, just tell me where his bowl is?"

"If you're sure…" *Two favours to tick off the tally*,
she thought. Then thought again. *Did any of that matter
any more, now that things had shifted so considerably
between them? And honestly, looking back, had it ever?*
"Pumpkin's bowl is just inside the doggy door round the
back, so if you reach a hand in you'll find it."

"Do I need a key?"

"For?"

"The side gate."

"No lock, so no key. It has been a while since you've
lived here, hasn't it? His hearing isn't great but his sense
of smell is top notch, so he'll come once you pour the
food. And…thank you."

"You said that already."

"Well, I mean it."

"I appreciate the fact that you mean it."

To think, this man, this experiment to prove to herself she'd put the Heartache List to bed once and for all, had become top of her contacts list. He was the person she called.

When Emerson realised that she was leaning her elbow on her desk, head resting in her palm, thumb rubbing the paperweight, gaze looking dreamily into the middle distance while imagining what Holden might be doing, or wearing, or not wearing, she sat bolt upright, knocking over a pen caddy.

"I owe you one," she said.

He laughed, as if he too had been mulling over the fact that they'd moved way beyond favours into…something rather wonderful. "Don't mention it."

"I'm hanging up now. So I can call the vet."

"After you," he said. And waited for her to end the call, as if he believed she might not want to.

And he was right.

Emerson came home to find Holden's rental car—now a big, black, hulking all-wheel drive—outside her house.

Using the side gate, she followed the stepping stones around to the back of the house, past her mum's beloved lemon tree, to find the man himself sitting on her back porch. Fast asleep.

Emerson slowly made her way up the wide wooden back steps, to find Holden had taken a couple of cushions from her outdoor setting, sat on one and propped another behind his back. His left knee was cocked, his hand was resting on Pumpkin's sleeping back as the dog's head lay across the man's right leg.

Emerson crouched down, reaching out a hand to touch Holden's shoulder, to gently wake him. Only her hand stopped at the last second, and she took her chance to soak him in.

The sweep of tangled lashes against his cheek, the five o'clock shadow covering his sharp jaw, the smudges under his eyes as he'd spent the week working long hours with his friend Andy, at the airport, after all. The way his hair was mussed, as if he'd run a hand through it one too many times. The strength of his collarbone, the column of his throat, the veins that roped down his beautiful forearms…

Despite his "I'm not going anywhere" line at the house-warming, convincing herself she'd be fine when he went back to his real life had become a daily mantra. And yet, seeing him in her space felt really good. It felt so right. It felt like a level of want she wasn't sure she was equipped to handle.

Pumpkin whimpered, having sensed her and woken.

Holden's eyes opened next, training instantly on hers.

Emerson stilled, like a hunter sighted by a deer, too slow, too helpless to shut down the thoughts that must be written all over her face.

"Hi," he said, his voice rough.

"Hi," she said, her voice barely a breath.

His smile was slow, and warm, and all too knowing.

But then he winced as some part of him that had been stuck in place too long pushed back.

Freed from the gravity of his gaze, Emerson quickly pressed herself to standing.

Then she clicked her fingers in front of Pumpkin's face, till the old dog groaned and eased himself away from Holden's lap to totter over to her hand for a pat. "Hey, boy, you like your new food?"

"Gobbled it down," said Holden, stretching out his long legs.

"You didn't have to stay," she said.

"Every time I tried to leave, he looked at me."

"Looked at you?"

"With sad eyes."

"Holden, he's a spaniel. Sad eyes are their superpower."

"Right." He ran a hand up the back of his neck. Boy, she loved it when he did that. "Either way, I figured it was best to settle him before I headed off."

"He looked plenty settled when I arrived."

Holden hauled his tall frame to standing. "I bet he did."

He wore old jeans, worn in all the best places, and an olive Henley T-shirt that had ridden up a fraction, revealing a flat stomach, more than one ab, and an arrow of dark hair pointing south. Not sure if she was allowed to look her fill now that they weren't "forgetting" about the attraction they both felt, she couldn't have looked away for all the world.

"Are you free now?" she asked.

He caught her eye. "As a bird."

"Do you want to come in?"

"Yes," he said, without equivocation. "I do."

"Great." She used the key to open the back door, hustled Pumpkin inside the kitchen, and watched till he found his way to his bed in the hall.

Then turned to find Holden right behind her. A wall of warmth. Of spice and cotton and fresh air. And a little bit like warm dog, which, when she imagined him sitting on her patio, his hand on Pumpkin's back, made for a very dangerous scent.

"You hungry?" she asked, then regretted it when his gaze dropped to her mouth.

"I'd love to wash up first. I feel like I'm sporting a layer of drool."

Emerson very deliberately did not offer to smell him

to make sure, knowing that kind of thing seemed to send her down mental rabbit holes she was finding it harder and harder to find her way out of.

She pointed the way to the guest bathroom, and watched him walk away. Allowing herself a quiet whistle of appreciation before she shook it off and quickly fixed herself.

Jacket off, bag away. Quick swipe of toothpaste from the spare tube in the kitchen. No particular reason—it had been a long day and it seemed rude to smell like the coffee she'd tossed back an hour before.

"So," she said, when Holden ambled back into the kitchen, stopping to lean in the doorway. All lanky legs and crossed arms, as if he was holding up the entire house by the sheer force of his presence. "Dinner."

She opened the freezer to find it fairly bare. Her fridge looked little better.

"Takeaway?" she asked, looking over her shoulder to find him watching her with a small smile on his face, heat flickering behind his eyes.

Holden pushed away from the doorframe, his pace unhurried, his gaze focused, stopping only when he was inside her personal space. Then he slowly swept her hair behind one ear, then the other, till his palms rested on her cheeks, his gaze coming to settle on hers.

"Is that a yes to takeaway?" she said.

"Thank you for inviting me in, Emmy."

His words seemed straightforward, but she couldn't help imagining he meant something deeper. Something big and wonderful and terrifying. It was the only excuse for her next words. "You sound like a vampire."

"Not a vampire. Vampires sparkle in sunlight, if I remember rightly."

Emerson snorted. "Not real vampires. They burn."

As she said the word, his fingers delved deeper into her hair, the band she'd used to loosely tie it off her face falling free.

Her nerves were so taut, her skin so sensitive, she shivered as her hair fell over her shoulders, skittering over her bare arms. While the heat from his body, so close to hers, seemed to infuse her, till she was the one in danger of burning.

"Either way," he said, his voice deepening, the colour disappearing from his eyes, "my blood is warm. My heart beats. And I'm not immortal. At least I don't think so. Only time will tell."

When he used his thumbs to tilt her chin, when she felt the sweep of his breath over her cheeks, her neck, her mouth, he could have been speaking Martian for all she knew as her head filled with clouds, her body nothing but sensation.

Her hands had curled into the front of his shirt. Was she pulling him in or holding him at bay? When her body seemed to roll into him with her next breath, she got her answer.

Her brain, the last bastion of defence, flickered one final time. "I'm not…" she managed to eke out.

"Not what?" he asked.

She licked her lips, and wild storm clouds overwhelmed the last of the deep blue in his eyes. "I know how much you've put your life on hold these past weeks. And I think… I think some of that is because of this, because of me. But I have no expectations."

"Isn't that meant to be my line?" he asked, his mouth lifting at one corner, his gaze sure and true.

"You don't do lines."

"You got me there." He breathed out through his nose.

"I'm not asking for the world, Emmy. I'd just really like to kiss you again. And I think you'd really like to kiss me."

She opened her mouth to make some Smart Alec response when his thumb moved to the corner of her mouth, before bringing it into her eyeline. "Toothpaste? Was that for me?"

Sprung.

Hands already gripping his shirt, she gave him a tug, tipped up onto her toes, and said, "Of course it was for you. So what are you waiting for?"

That, apparently. A wolfish grin lit up his face before his eyes grew so dark there was no telling what he was thinking. Or feeling. Only what he wanted.

And while, by this point, Emmy was a quivering bundle of nerves, Holden's cool held strong. And he took his sweet time.

Starting at the corner of her mouth, where toothpaste, of all things, had given her away—a kiss, then a lick.

A nudge of his lips, as close to hers as they could be without actually touching.

Then he moved to her ear, a waft of warm breath, a tug of teeth. Before he buried his nose in her neck, breathing deep as he pulled her liquefied body up against his.

"Holden," she breathed.

"Mmm," he murmured against her mouth, the tightness in his voice, the rough burr, the want spilling into his touch. Roving hands. Hardening body. Need, barely contained.

While she was melting, melting, *melting.* "Do me a favour and kiss me already."

She didn't need to ask a third time. And once his hot mouth met hers, everything changed. Her warmth became heat, her pliancy need. Her arms reaching around his neck, she lifted so high on her toes they creaked, and then, pressing herself to him, she got as close as she could, so that she might kiss him right on back.

Only this wasn't a kiss. This was an undoing. An unravelling. A revelation.

She found herself reaching for the hem of his shirt, hands frantic, desperate to find skin. When she did, it was so worth it. Warm skin, rough hair, hard muscle beneath.

His muscles twitched at the sweep of her hands. His words no more than a growl.

Relishing the fact she could cause such a reaction in such a man, she kissed him hard, deep, her hips rolling against his, her fingernails trailing down his belly. Tracing the edge of his jeans. Tugging at the button, snapping the thing free.

His moan, the hitch of his breath, the jerk of his body was like a drug. And she must have been high, as soon she was yanking his shirt up his body, her lips releasing his for a half second so she could whip the thing over his head.

Their eyes caught in that moment, their breathing rough and wild.

Her dress—black, frilly, with a deep V—was pulled off one shoulder, then the other, then tugged down her arms by strong, rough, sure hands, before it clung to her waist.

He stopped, breaths heaving in his big chest as his eyes roved over her. Her flushed skin. Her lace bra, her nipples pressing hard and painful against the fabric.

Eyes dropping, hungry eyes, he cupped her breast, his thumb sweeping over the peak.

Her head dropped back, her breath leaving her in a great long sigh.

"That's the sound," he said, his voice gruff. "That's how you used to sigh every time you saw me. I thought it was sweet. We were both too damn young to know what it meant."

Then he kissed her, his hands delving deep into her hair, before his arm tucked under her knees and she found herself lifted off the ground, literally swept off her feet. As he'd been doing to her since the beginning.

Not when they were kids. Not some foggy, long-ago era—aeons, ages, millennia before now—when she'd had no idea who she was, or what she wanted. When every turn, every decision, every comment slung her way had felt deeply personal. Deeply cutting.

Their true beginning was the moment he'd walked up to her, at that secluded bar, in that star-spangled marquee at her best friend's wedding, fairy lights dancing in his eyes, the most beautiful man she had ever seen, who had no clue how to spin a line.

She reached for him, holding his face between her hands, relishing the feel of his stubble against her sensitive palms, before she kissed him. Gently, deliciously, achingly.

"Where to?" he asked, when she pulled back to rest her forehead against his, unwilling to break the connection.

She cocked her head towards her bedroom.

His nostrils flared, his eyes a winter storm, before he all but sprinted for the bedroom, forcing Emerson to hold on for dear life, her laughter scattering behind her like sparks from a firecracker.

In her bedroom, her most private space, Emerson slid down Holden's big, strong body, took him by the hand and led him to her bed.

Where they took their time undressing one another with care. And curiosity. In equal measure.

Before tumbling onto the bed with abandon. And there

they found their rhythms, their touchstones, gentle affirmations and slippery heat.

He kissed his way down her body, taking his time, making it last, making it magic, while whirls and swirls of smoke rose inside her. She could taste the heat on her tongue, as he teased and tasted and tortured her till every thought, every fear, every last fragment of self-protection coalesced into a tiny sun bursting inside her.

And then she was lost. Dissolving, into a trillion tiny specks of light. When she came back into her body, slowly, she was all molten bones and trembling limbs.

And so it went on, savouring one another's bodies, one another's gasps, one another's sighs as the evening turned into night. And beyond.

As Emmy finally fell into a deep, boneless sleep, her head tucked into Holden's shoulder, her hand resting over his heart, her mind cresting and settling, adrift on the rise and fall of his chest, she could barely remember why she'd been so adamant as to deny herself this pleasure. This sweetness. This moment.

Her last thought was that perhaps *this* had been the way to put the Heartache List behind her for good, after all.

Emerson woke in the pre-dawn, the birds not yet chirping, Pumpkin not yet up and about, banging into walls as he tried to find his way to the doggy door. And a man's arm was slung heavily across her chest.

It was Holden Roarke's arm. For Holden Roarke was in her bed.

He'd stayed with her patchy old dog because he'd been given the sad eyes.

He'd stayed when all she'd been able to offer him for dinner was Vegemite on toast.

He'd stayed.

"Hello, gorgeous."

She blinked to find his eyes on hers. No storm within, just a clear summer blue.

She lifted a hand to the bird's nest atop her head. "That might be your worst attempt at a line yet. I'm a wreck. And it's all your fault. You wrecked me."

He ran his thumb down her cheek. "You're a gorgeous wreck."

Eyes locked onto hers, Holden shifted to cover her with his body. While she shifted to accommodate him, her breath catching in her throat as she felt exactly what she'd be accommodating.

Settled, for now, he twirled a lock of her hair around his finger, then leaned down to press a soft, sweet, place-marking kiss upon her mouth. She waited for some flutter of resistance, of instinct, reminding her that this—while lovely, and unexpected, and therapeutic—was temporary.

No expectations.

But her instincts remained quiet. Less than quiet. It was as if he'd wrecked them too.

She tipped her head so that her mouth brushed the underside of his thumb. Then, having distracted him, she rolled till she straddled his thighs.

The flimsy tank top she'd slipped into during the night twisted around her body. His big hands spanned her waist, before gently tugging the top back into place, his thumbs sweeping over the exposed sides of her breasts.

While she told herself she was in the power position, the look in Holden's eyes made her feel as if her whole world might go dark without him holding her there in place.

As if to prove it, he sat up, his arms going around her, holding her close as he buried his nose in her neck, one hand gliding into her hair, the other lining up along her spine.

Her hand went to the back of his head, the other wrapped around his shoulder till they were pressed together close. Entwined. Just breathing one another in.

Holden's lips moved to her neck, pressing, suckling, biting. Tracing her collarbone. His fingertips slipped the strap of her top over her shoulder and followed the move with his mouth till her breast was free, his mouth taking over.

By the time she was ready for him, her skin on fire, her soul stripped bare, he made quick work with a condom, waited for her to line up, then eased her down, his hard heat sliding into her.

Deeper. Deepest. Friction building, heat burning, sensation, feelings, sweeping through her, too much.

"Do me a favour," he murmured into her ear, creating sparks amongst the light.

"What?" she breathed.

"Come."

And she did. Boy, oh, boy, oh, boy, she did.

CHAPTER NINE

STRIDING DOWN THE busy city footpath on the way back to the office, after a fabulous first meeting with an excellent candidate for the Sanderson Group COO, Emerson let her mind wander to thoughts of Holden as it was wont to do. His smile when she caught him unawares. The deep notes of his voice when he'd pick up the book on her bedside table and read it to her. The sweep of his broad hand down her back as she fell asleep in his arms.

She slowed in front of a café-slash-bookshop boasting a bountiful display of classics in their beautiful front window. Her gaze picking out *Persuasion*, she imagined lying with her cheek against Holden's warm, bare chest as he read aloud Wentworth's final letter to Anne. Then she had to stop imagining it lest she expire on the street.

She looked over the artfully teetering piles till she found—there! *The Catcher in the Rye*. Way back when, she'd bought that book for Holden as a gift, as the hero had his name. She could still feel the press of it into her fingers as she'd clutched it to her chest while sitting outside Miss Kemp's office.

Before their previous session, they'd been stuck in the hallway a good half an hour, before Holden had turned to her, asking what her favourite movie was. He'd had

to write a report in English and it had been so long since
he'd seen a movie, he couldn't think of one.

"Field of Dreams," she'd blurted. "A movie about a
guy who misses his dad, starring Kevin Costner? Come
on!"

They'd moved onto favourite TV show, favourite
breakfast, favourite song.

It had felt like fate, for favourites were *her* favourite.
She kept copious lists of her favourite things, and always
had—favourite actors, favourite cakes, favourite holidays. Hanging on tight to the things that brought her joy.
And she and Holden had covered every topic, bar favourite books. Hence her gift.

That next week, Miss Kemp's door had bumped.
Emmy had held the book tighter, her breath catching,
her heart thundering in her ears.

But then some sullen grade twelve girl with long,
greasy hair had left the counsellor's room before loping morosely by.

"Where's Holden?" Emmy had asked the counsellor
as she'd approached the room, a sense of dread coming
over her.

"He's gone, honey. To another school. Come on in and
tell me about your week."

Emmy remembered nothing from that session, bar
Miss Kemp telling her that Holden, the week before, had
mentioned her love of lists. She'd told Emmy that writing things down could help some people and encouraged
her to grab a notebook, start a journal, to see if it helped
her let things go.

That afternoon, while Emmy had been laid out on her
bed, awash with tears, Camille had arrived with notebook in hand. Sparkly cactus on the cover.

Only Emmy had never used her writings to let things

go, only to hold on tight. How could letting things go be her intention when it was her actual nightmare? What Miss Kemp didn't know wouldn't hurt her.

Emmy blinked to find herself still in front of the bookshop.

In the window's reflection the sky looked ominous, meaning she should get back to the office. And yet she ducked inside, moving straight to the stationery section. No sparkles and cartoony motifs here, only high-end, leather-bound recycled paper. When she picked up a gorgeous cream notebook, with pages soft to the touch and thin black ribbon bookmarks attached, she felt a frisson of warmth run up her arm.

New notebook, and pen to match, in hand, Emmy ordered a double espresso and pointed to a table out the front. Once settled, she opened the notebook, the spine cracking just the way her Heartache List notebook had all those years ago. It too had started out clean and full of possibility, before it had become covered in her passionate scrawl, as a means to understanding why people disappointed her, why they left her behind.

The final entry?

Heartache Number Eight: twenty-five years old.

Losing Mum. That was all. No details. No questions. It had been enough. And too much.

She'd tossed that old notebook in the skip, along with so many memories from her childhood, before gutting the house and refurbishing it till it was unrecognisable. As if that put a great big underline beneath that part of her life.

All she'd kept was her mum's glass paperweight, the lovely old dog who'd marked time with her, and the façade of the house that quietly, secretly, she'd never changed in case her dad wanted to find his way home.

And, quite amazingly, since the day she'd thrown the Heartache List away, her life had been fine. Narrow, yes. Tightly controlled, sure. But *fine*.

Until Holden had strolled back in with his sexy smile, his quiet courtship, his constancy. And his favours.

Emmy popped the lid on her new pen, and the wind seemed to lift and bustle the leaves around her feet.

She let the pen hover over the page. Then, her penmanship not a lot better than it had been at fourteen, she wrote in bold capital letters atop the first page: THE FAVOURS LIST. Turning the page, she ruled a line down the centre. Put an "E" at the top of one column, an "H" at the top of the other.

Then, as if she'd been taken over by some external force, she set to noting down every single favour she and Holden had done for one another since Camille and Phillip's wedding. Starting with him helping her with her shoe, and her helping him let Bernadette down gently, and ending with his command, *Do me a favour. Come.* Before she'd fallen apart in his arms.

Her hand shook a little as she wrote those last words. The power of them. The command. Her effortless acquiescence. As if her world was no longer so very narrow, as if she no longer had control of it at all.

A frown now tightening her brow, she went back to the beginning. Some favours were bigger than others. Meaning they ought to be given ratings. Which also meant she couldn't leave out the teeny, tiny favours they'd done, those that had occurred without asking, or any expectation of return.

When done, the list was pages long. Unwieldy. And

with its scrawls and doodles and notes, and arrows, it resembled the Heartache List far more than she'd intended.

A drop of water hit the page, blurring the ink. Then another.

It had started to rain.

"Emerson?"

"What's up?"

So drenched had she been by the time she made it back to work, she'd changed into jeans and a blousy top she kept in her office in case of long late-night sessions where comfort won out over *va-va-voom*, but she hadn't thought to keep a hairdryer on hand. She added a note to her to-do list notebook on her desk and popped it under her mum's paperweight, along with her new Favour List notebook and an invitation to Bernadette's surprise wedding.

When Freya didn't answer, Emerson looked up to find her assistant in the doorway of her office, motioning over her shoulder with a pencil, to where Bettina Sanderson stood on the other side of Emerson's smoked windows, elegance personified in a drapey cream suit, hands gently clasped behind her back, gaze roving over the bright white office space beyond.

Emmy ran fingers through her damp hair, then under her eyes, hoping she didn't look like a crazed panda, as Bettina turned and caught her eye. She motioned for Bettina to come on in, moved around her desk, preparing for a handshake, but soon found herself enveloped in Bettina's warm hug.

"Thank you for seeing me at such short notice, Emerson."

"Of course. Sorry for the damp hug. I was outdoors when the rain bucketed down. In fact, I'd just had a wonderful meeting with a brilliant candidate for the COO job, which I hope balances out the fact I must look like a drowned rat."

Bettina smiled. "Not at all. Can we sit? Talk?"

Emerson motioned to the soft couches by the large triangular window at the end of her office, and quickly twirled her hair into a knot at her nape while Bettina made a happy sound as she took in all the details of the space, before choosing a chair warmed by a patch of muted sunshine.

Emerson was halfway to sitting when Bettina said, "How is Holden?"

A vision of the last time she'd seen him popped into her head, his clothes a little rumpled, shoes in hand as he'd grabbed her and kissed her as if his life depended on it, before jogging down her front steps. "He's fine. I think."

"Mmm. I'd thought we might see him again, after the dinner, but alas. Though he did send a lovely note, and a beautiful bouquet of wild flowers, to thank us for having the both of you along. A truly decent man, that one."

He really was, thought Emerson. Decent and wonderful. Solid and adventurous. Interested and interesting. A heartbreaker, yes, but only to those whose hearts were already damaged long before they'd given theirs to him.

"Now, enough about that," said Bettina. "I've come to ask a favour."

A bubble of laughter caught in Emerson's throat. Ah, the irony. She grabbed a pencil and notebook—she really did have a thing for notebooks—from the coffee table and settled them on her lap. "Tell me what you need."

"I need for you to convince Holden to consider the position of COO at the Sanderson Group."

The bubble burst, and with it came a wave of dread. "I'm sorry, Bettina. There must have been a misunderstanding. Firstly, I'm not sure anyone could convince Holden to do anything he does not wish to do. And secondly, as I told Chuck, I don't believe that would be in his best interests, or Holden's, considering their history—"

"I worked for the company—did you know that?"

Emerson blinked at Bettina's change of direction.

Bettina went on. "My name might not be on the letterhead, but the Sanderson Group is as much mine as it is Chuck's. I pulled back, a few years ago, when…family matters necessitated the move. Now that those family matters are no longer so pressing, I want my husband by my side for as long as I can have him. I'd all but convinced him, believing he might announce his retirement at his birthday dinner. Alas, seeing Holden sparked something inside him. And he's hanging on tight."

Something flashed behind Bettina's eyes—a mix of sorrow, and distress. As if, despite her elegant façade, it took an effort to be there. As if she knew what she was asking of Emmy was ill-advised, but she saw no other choice.

"I understand," said Emmy, leaning forward, her hand gripping the pencil as she madly tried to figure out a way around the request Bettina was about to reiterate. "Holden told me what you meant to one another. How you were so kind to him. How you took him in. About his wonderful friendship with Saul."

Bettina breathed out hard, her throat bobbing delicately, before she collected herself, pressing her shoulders back, lifting her chin. "Then you understand that my family has been through a lot. That I must do what I can to protect those I have left. My husband needs a reason to retire. Holden is it."

Emerson pressed her toes into her shoes, as she felt the ground tipping beneath her feet. "You are welcome to talk to Holden, Bettina, but I am certain he'll—in my opinion rightly—say no."

Bettina's smile was gentle, and painful, all at once. "I saw the way Holden deferred to you. I'd say you could convince that man of pretty much anything."

Emerson's world tipped just a little more, leaving her off kilter when Bettina steeled herself, and years of running a multimillion-dollar business came to the fore. "So here is what's going to happen. You will convince Holden to take the position, and the commission will be yours. In fact, I will double it. Personally."

Bettina's *favour* hung in the air between them. That kind of money, of prestige, was all that Emmy had dreamt of since the moment she'd opened Pitch Perfect's doors.

And yet Emerson desperately tried to come up with an alternative. Mind flitting over her best candidates, it landed on one she'd not yet considered. "Chuck clearly needs a little more time to transition into retirement. You want to spend more time with him. Maybe…maybe it's time your name did end up on the letterhead. Then, together, we can find the right team to take over when the time is right for both of you."

Bettina held up a hand and shook her head, her gaze pained, but also stubborn, as she gracefully unfolded herself from the chair. "My mind is made up."

Emerson somehow managed to get to her feet, even while her legs felt shaky, her feet numb.

"And if I can't?" Emerson asked, when what she meant was, *If I won't.*

Bettina's quick, sorry smile showed she knew it too. "You are a capable young woman with a bright future. I have every faith that together we can make this happen."

Bettina held out a hand, not to shake, but to enclose Emerson's in hers. As if she knew what she was asking was impossible, but that, as far as she saw things, she had no other choice.

And then she was gone. Leaving Emerson in the very rottenest possible position after all.

Emerson made it back to her desk and plonked herself in her chair. She slung an arm over her face, as if an answer might come to her in the darkness.

What was she to do?

Write a pro/con list? Yeah, no. A list would not help her this time.

Emerson dragged herself upright and slumped over her desk, her eye catching on the new notebook under her mum's paperweight.

She'd made it clear to Bettina, *and* to Chuck, that what they were asking was impossible. But the truth was, Bettina was right about one thing: all Emerson had to do was ask.

For, despite the many favours they had done for one another over the past weeks, officially Holden still owed her the Big One.

Could she actually do it? Would Holden understand? Was she making too big a deal of this? Holden and Chuck really did need to get in a room together and talk, so in instigating that she'd be doing him a favour!

And, a quiet yet hopeful voice piped up in the back of her head, *if, by some miracle, he accepted the job, even in the short term, he would have a reason to stay.*

He had told her, his voice earnest and deeply sexy, *I'm not going anywhere*, but he'd also swapped houses as if it was nothing and changed rental cars as though they were dirty socks.

Staying hadn't killed him so far. Staying so that they could continue their favour game. Staying as things had heated up between them. Staying, gifting her all the time she'd needed to get to know him, to trust him, to want him, to lean on him, to need him…

And to fall in love with him.

She had. She'd fallen in love with Holden Roarke. Utterly, hopelessly. Not with the shuttered gaze of a confused fourteen-year-old but the wide-open eyes of a woman who still never saw it coming.

And loving him meant she had her answer.

Asking him to go to that interview would be asking the man she loved to do something that would hurt *his* heart.

An end was coming either way. And endings, in her world, meant heartache.

Emmy picked up her phone with no plan in mind, only to find a missed call from Kerri from next door.

She called her back. "Hey, Kerri, everything okay?"

"It's Pumpkin." Kerri sniffed, as if she'd been crying.

And all the worries in Emerson's head fled, every thought coagulating into one singular fear. Ice-cold. And infinite. Her beautiful boy, her one constant through it all.

"What about Pumpkin, honey?"

"He's not moving. I fed him earlier today, but his bowl is still full. I came by to see if he wanted to go for a walk, and I can see him through the doggy door, that he's in his bed, but he won't come when I call."

"You have a key, honey. You can go in any time, you know that."

"I know. I just… I'm not sure I can."

"I'm sure he's fine," said Emmy, as she madly grabbed her keys, her jacket, and for some reason the damp notebook, and shoved them in her bag. "He's nearly deaf, remember, so maybe he just can't hear you. Is your mum home?"

"At work."

"Right. Well, I'll give her a quick buzz and let her know you're worried, then I'll be right there. You head on home and leave Pumpkin to me. Okay?"

"Okay."

Emerson rang off, then shot out the door. "I'm off for the day," she called to Freya as she ran past.

Freya, wonder that she was, sent Emmy a salute.

Running on instinct, as the lift doors opened, Emmy made one more call.

"It's Pumpkin," she said, the moment Holden answered.

Whatever he heard in her voice, all he said was, "I'm on my way."

Emerson somehow kept to the speed limit, even while adrenalin had her slightly out of sync with the world.

Pumpkin.

Her beautiful boy. Half deaf, mostly blind, fully sweet. He'd beaten kidney infections, a snake bite, a broken leg, near record old age. He'd run away. That would have been *Heartache Number Four*, except he'd come back, covered in detritus and matted fur that had taken two baths, a short clip, and a lot of gentle tugging to remove, but panting happily after his adventure.

He'd put her through the wringer, but she'd still loved him with her whole heart, all the same. Pumpkin, with his soft, sweet doggy fur, absorbing her tears when she knew for sure her dad was not coming back. Her last link to her big, funny, huggy, sad, shadowy dad, who'd left her with the words, "Life ebbs and flows, kiddo. When it feels hard, remember it'll be okay. It always gets better."

As if that might help.

As if she wouldn't use his desertion as an excuse to keep people at bay. As if she could ever again feel as if the foundations beneath her feet were truly stable. Leaving her preparing for the worst, and being happily surprised when things worked out, then believing that was a good thing.

Emmy shook her head, and blinked the tears from her eyes. Angry tears. Worried tears. Tears for Holden too. For what she might yet have to ask of him. And how he might look at her from that moment on.

There were too many feelings. She really wasn't *sensical* when faced with too many feelings.

She pulled into her driveway, the bump of the car over the old gutter rocking her from side to side.

Her hands shook as she opened the front door, her heart lodged in her throat.

She banged her feet on the floor, the reverberations in the floorboards often enough to rouse him. But no skitters of doggy claws met her ears.

"Pumpkin?" she called, as loud as her tight voice would allow.

Still he didn't appear.

Kicking off her shoes, she dumped her things on the floor and padded up the hall, her chest squeezing when she saw his sweet foot poking out over the edge of his soft bed, along with the white tip of his caramel tail.

Dropping to her hands and knees, she made her way to him slowly. "Pumpkin? Buddy?" she called, knowing he couldn't hear her.

She placed her hand on his back, her breath hitching when she felt him move, his chest rising and falling, gently, slowly. Then his eye opened, and he tried to sit up.

"Hey, boy," she said, keeping her hand on him as she leaned down to press her cheek against his. As tears slid down her cheeks, she kept whispering that she was there, that he was a good boy, the best boy. She told him how deeply and incessantly she loved him, how grateful she was to have known him, to have known that he loved her back.

Then, several minutes later, a long, slow breath left his body. And his chest did not rise again.

Tears flowing freely now, Emmy lifted the old boy gently out of his bed, his frail body lighter than it had been in years, as if he'd been slowly leaving her for a while now, but she'd been holding on so tight she'd refused to notice.

She held him in her lap, where he'd used to sleep when he was half the size, and stroked him. Breathed in his doggy scent. Committed the exact feel of his fur to memory.

A knock at the door had her heart leaping into her throat.

The door nudged open—she'd forgotten to close it.

Holden's big, broad body created a shadow in the doorway as he let himself in, his form taking shape, and colour, strength, warmth, and vigour as he padded down the hall. Such gentleness in his big body, as if he knew that was all she could take.

She felt his approach, a waft of warmth and fresh laundry, a flutter of sensation up the back of her neck, before his hand landed on her shoulder and he reached around for her chin, tipping it back, so he could plant an upside-down kiss upon her forehead. Setting off feelings inside her that at fourteen she'd never have been able to imagine, much less handle. Heck, she could barely handle them now, her heart squeezing and kicking, bucking against the constraints under which it had been imprisoned for so long.

His hair was mussed, his cheeks a little pink from the wind that had followed the rain, the rush to get to her.

This big, beautiful man who'd carved such inroads into her life. The man who had set so many things in motion. The man whose simple existence might yet tear it all apart.

The person she called when she needed to make a call.

Her person.

Her person.

He dropped to his knees, then slid in behind her, wrapped his arms around her, and hauled her close.

Careful not to disrupt the bundle in her arms, he held her as she cried and cried and cried.

Emerson blinked up at the mottled grey sky above her house as she hopped out of the car. After what had felt like a lifetime at the vet's, her brain struggled to connect with the fact that it was still daylight.

She held Pumpkin's collar in her hand as she glanced up at the façade of her childhood home, the paintwork dull despite the wash of recent rain. The home her father had left, the home her mother had gifted her, the home Pumpkin had shared with her on and off her whole life.

To think she was about to walk in there, on her own, truly alone, for the first time in her life. Legs rocky, she leaned back against her car, the warm metal a surprise against her sensitive nerves.

Holden came around the front of the car, keys in hand, and stood by her. He looked as wretched as she felt, his care for her etched into the lines and hollows of his beautiful face.

Every single atom in her being ached to reach for him. To have him envelop her in his strong arms. To lean on him. To breathe him in. So that he might absorb some of her pain. Which he would do, without question, without being asked. Not out of any favour nonsense, but just because it was who he was.

Yet when he reached out, she flinched. So thinly stretched did she feel. She'd not be surprised to look down and find herself translucent.

"Give me your house keys," he said, his voice gentle. "Let me take you inside."

It made sense. She could barely feel her feet.

But as she looked up at the house again, at the façade she'd never allowed her mum to change, even during the years she'd not lived at home, a kind of preternatural calm came over her. And she finally began to see things clearly.

"I've decided…" She swallowed against the dryness of her throat. "Decided what my favour will be."

"Favour?" Holden said, as if he'd forgotten that was ever a part of their story.

"The Big One. The one that you agreed that I could ask for any time I wished. So long as it wasn't illegal, or impossible, you could not refuse me. Remember?"

He cocked his head, the slightest smile easing across his lovely face. "You want to do this now?"

Did she? Not even slightly.

"Let's get you inside." Holden moved ever so slightly into the bubble of air surrounding her, his warmth like a balm. "I'll brew you a hot chocolate. Run you a bath. Make you dinner. And tuck you into bed, for real this time, then you can ask me any favour you want. As many as you want. As big as you want. For as long as you want."

He smiled, but his eyes were sad. Sad about Pumpkin. Sad for her. But also filled with tenderness, and steadiness, and truth. A decent man, he believed what he was promising. Even the "for as long as you want" bit. Only he had no idea that she wanted forever.

It was enough to give her a second wind, one last push of strength.

"Bettina came to see me yesterday." Or was it today?

"Did she, now?" he asked, his nostrils flaring, as if only now he sensed the fight in her and was grounding himself, ready to push back.

Emmy lifted her chin. "Chuck wants you for the COO position. He has done since the beginning. In fact, I'd go so far as to say that's why he took me on. Bettina came to my office to ask me to convince you of the same."

Time seemed to stretch and fold between them, before Holden said, "*That* is your favour? You are asking me to work for the man whose son I tried to replace, whose daughter left me, all of which put the same man into a wheelchair." He lifted his hand to the back of his neck and squeezed. "Why? For the commission? Chuck's respect? Hell, Emmy."

"No," Emerson said, her voice cracking. "That's not… I want you to refuse."

Holden's stormy blue eyes locked onto hers. "I'm not sure I understand."

"While I do think that it would do both you and Chuck the world of good to stop circling one another and actually talk, I want your authorisation to tell them no."

"My authorisation."

"Assuming that's your wish, of course. Say the word, and it's done. The Sandersons can move on and find the right person for the job. And you and I will owe one another no more favours. Decks cleared in one fell swoop."

Her declaration, such as it was, fell flat.

Especially when she saw the realisation wash across his face. For he knew her too well. He *saw* her. No wonder she'd accidentally fallen in love with him, after all.

He closed his eyes. Shook his head. "Sorry. It's been

a rough afternoon, I know. Not the time to be jumping to conclusions. Just…talk to me. Tell me what's going on in your head right now."

She glanced at her feet, unable to deal with the dislocation in his gaze, the dawning understanding. "It's been a lot, these last few weeks. The wedding, the insane workload, Pumpkin." *Falling in love with the last man I'd ever have expected could sweep me off my feet.* "I feel as if I hopped on one of your planes, thinking I was heading to a particular destination, then, mid-air, I jumped. And I've been free-falling ever since…weightless, and floaty, and still yet to land."

She glanced up to find him running a hand over his mouth, as if carefully considering his words.

"I hear that," he said. "I feel the same way."

If only…

Emmy breathed out hard. "The thing is, you're used to living like that. You feed off the adventure, the variety, the change of scenery." It was how he dealt with *his* past the same way she used lists to understand hers. "Me? I need to know I'm on solid ground. And with you… I don't. I never have."

His face, oh, his lovely face as he looked at her. As if he was the one who ached. "Emmy, I really thought—"

"You thought right," she said, not sure she'd be able to go through with this if he told her that he cared. And she knew he cared. Just as she knew that, eventually, it would no longer be enough to make him stay. "And it's been lovely. But I've seen your calendar. I know what you've given up to be here. This feels like the right time to… For us to…" She waved a hand between them.

"Say, it, Emmy. I need to hear you say the words."

Words. Like the words Miss Kemp had told her to

write, so that she might let things go. When instead she'd used them to hold on tight.

The way she'd held on to dear old Pumpkin, not even allowing herself to imagine what choices she might have to make if his health had begun to fail him.

The way she'd held tight to her best friends, suffering a physical shock to the system when it had finally hit her that they were married.

The way she'd held on to the exterior of her childhood house, just in case her dad needed to find his way home…eighteen years after he left.

The very best thing she could do for Holden, and for herself, was to let him go.

"Holden, it's time for you to go home."

His expression didn't change, as if he'd been braced, expecting it. But his voice—rough, low, and grave—gave him away. "That's what you really want?"

Emmy nodded. Just the once.

Then Holden asked, "What about what I want?"

By that point Emmy felt as if she was being held upright by a single fraught nerve. Empathy spent, softness depleted, she said, "You are retired, then not retired. You move more often than I change my sheets. You flit from car to car depending on your whims. You don't want to be here, yet you don't leave. I don't think you know what you want."

Holden took a step back. A literal step back. Then he turned and leaned his hands against the bonnet of her car, his entire body taut.

He ran a hand over his face, the skin dragging at the last. As if he too was barely holding on. "If you weren't standing there, looking like a gust of wind might blow you over, I think I'd actually throw you over my shoulder, take you inside and demand you not to say another word till you'd eaten, drunk and slept."

In his eyes, the storm was real, confusion warring with the heat that simmered between them at all times. She squeezed the skin between her thumb and forefinger so as not to find herself swept up in him.

"This isn't about Pumpkin."

"Like hell it's not," he shot back. Energy no longer contained as it seemed to flicker about him, wild and wondrous. "I keep telling you I'm not going anywhere, even when I can see you don't believe me. Do you know how it feels, to be so easily dismissed? Hell, it's my father all over again."

The rush of emotion in his voice gave her strength. "Are you comparing me to your *father*?"

He threw his hands out to the side and paced away from the car. "I have absolutely no idea what I am doing. Clearly. In fact, I've been rudderless since I looked up and saw you standing on the edge of the dance floor. You were like this silent siren, grabbing me right through the middle and refusing to let go. I've been stuck here, stuck in this place that gave me such grief for such a long time, because you... Because you..."

He reached out, fingers stretched as if he wanted to shake her. Or grab her and kiss her. Or hold her and rock her until whatever had taken over her had passed.

She licked her suddenly dry lips. "Lucky for you, then, you don't have to feel stuck any more. I'm letting you go, Holden. No more favours. Go, find work that engages you, rather than that which falls into your lap. Go, before that impressive restlessness of yours makes you regret staying. Before I—"

"Before you what?" he asked.

She bit her lip. Let it go when his eyes dropped to her mouth and stayed.

He looked up again, deep into her eyes. Soul deep.

"You think I needed *interesting work* in order to have a reason to stay?"

You, his gaze said, *you were all the reason I needed.*

He moved to her then, slowly, reaching out to hold her gently by the upper arms. Then he leaned in, slowly, till his forehead touched hers.

Emerson's eyes drifted closed. Now it was only the thousand butterflies beating against the inside of her skin that held her upright.

"This is what you really want?" he asked. "What you really need?"

"Yes," she said, "it is."

He dropped a hand over his heart, his fingers curling over his collarbone. Then he lifted his head and stepped away. Then he placed her keys on top of her car and headed towards the street.

Only to stop, turn, look at the house, then look back at her. "I heard you, Emmy. I did. But if you need company, if you don't want to go in there alone, I'll stay. Just say the word."

"I'll be fine." And she would. Eventually. She always was.

Holden nodded, every angle of his body tight and hard as he strode towards his rental car, folded his long body inside, gunned the engine, and was gone.

Emerson somehow made it up the front steps and inside her house, where she folded up like a puppet whose strings had been cut.

Sitting against the wall, she waited for panic to set in. For she'd killed the biggest deal of her life and pushed away the only man she'd ever loved.

But, like a cat with nine lives, nine heartaches were all she had. And she'd just given that ninth to the sweetest pup who'd ever lived.

She had nothing left to give.

CHAPTER TEN

A FEW DAYS LATER, Holden sat in the reception area on the twelfth floor of the Sanderson Group building, pressing at his cuticles with his thumbnails, and frowning so hard his forehead hurt.

Despite the low grey clouds blanketing the city, a shaft of sunlight slanted into his eyes. But he didn't change seats. It kept him sharp. The only possible reason why he'd ended up in such a mess was that this damnable city had blunted him. Softening his edges. Turning him to putty.

No more.

When he'd told Emmy he'd heard her, given her "authorisation" to refuse a role he'd never asked for, on his behalf, he'd never promised he'd not have words with Bettina and Chuck himself.

He wasn't exactly sure what those words would be, only that they had to be said. There had to be some sort of closure, on all of this, once and for all. Or else the hot, heavy feeling that had taken up residence behind his ribs the moment he'd seen Emmy sitting on the floor, her lovely old dog on her lap, the knowledge that her happiness meant more to him than anything ever had, would haunt him for ever.

"Holden?"

Looking up to find Bettina Sanderson heading his way, Holden stood, wiped dry hands down the sides of his jacket, before leaning in to kiss her cheek.

"So lovely to see you, dear boy. I wish you'd called; I'd have put aside time for a coffee."

"I'm not here for coffee. I'm here to interview for the COO position."

He might have relished the shock on her face if he was actually there for some damn interview. But he was not. He was there to give Chuck—Bettina too, since fate seemed to have placed her there, right on time—a piece of his mind.

Lying in bed in the plush hotel room he'd moved to a couple of days back, right after leaving Emmy's for the last time, staring at a small crack in the ceiling, he'd come to the conclusion that there was no way around the fact Emmy's happiness had come to mean more to him than his own.

That alone meant he had to heed her wishes. What else could he do?

Yet, for all that Emmy had done his head in, and his heart, and most of his major organs if the ache inside him was anything to go by, and while he knew she could absolutely take care of herself, nobody messed with her on his watch.

He would walk away. Eventually. But not until he made sure she'd be okay.

"The COO position," said Bettina, her hands wringing, her expression riddled with guilt. Good. It meant she had some semblance of an idea of the mess she had wrought. "Might I ask why?"

Holden slowly dipped his hands into the pockets of his suit pants, his throat tight, his voice a little above a growl. "If you're asking if Emerson sent me here, after your…conversation the other day, she did not. In fact, she made it clear, it was her preference that I refuse to even consider the notion."

"Oh?" Bettina blinked. Then, strangely, her shoulders dropped, and she broke out in a smile. "Well, good for her. Bright, capable, *and* formidable. I knew I liked that one."

Holden opened his mouth but found he did not have the words. What the heck was he missing?

Bettina must have seen it on his face, as she reached out and squeezed his arm. "I know. I do believe Chuck and I have not handled this whole thing as best we might. Seeing you again, while wonderful, stirred up dust we thought had been brushed away. And, while I can't speak for my stubborn husband, I do love him. Which is why I had to do whatever it took to make sure he is taken care of. I hope the both of you can understand our hearts were in the right place, even if our efforts were inelegant. I hope you can forgive us."

"Always," Holden said, as, for all that his insides were a tangled mess in no small part due to Bettina's influence, he believed her. Considering her words very much mirrored his own recent reflections, he found that he understood her too.

"Oh," said Bettina, "and the COO position has been filled."

"By whom?"

"By me." Bettina held out both arms with a flourish. "Chuck is not ready to retire. I wish to spend more time with him in our twilight years. Then it seems about time I finally have my own name on the letterhead. It was your Emerson who gave me the idea."

"She's not—" Not his Emerson. He couldn't say the

words. For, despite recent events, it still felt as if she was. His Emmy.

"Did she truly insist you not apply for the position?"

Holden nodded.

"Even while fully aware that would put her relationship with the Sanderson Group at risk. Bright, capable, formidable…and staggeringly selfless. Where you are concerned, at least."

Selfless. Holden grabbed onto that thought. He wasn't here for him. He was here for Emerson. "Back up a moment," he said, pinning Bettina with a glance. "If Emerson was the one who suggested you for the role, the commission is hers. Correct?"

Bettina's eyes widened for the briefest flash, the only sign that she'd been stymied. "Correct. And serendipitous, to have you on her side."

"Serendipity has nothing to do with it."

"No," said Bettina, "I can see that it does not. Now, dear boy, I have work to do. Was there anything else?"

Yes, there was. A good deal, in fact. "Dinner one night this week? You, me and the big guy. How about we put that dust to rest?"

Bettina's eyes misted over. "We'd like that very much."

Holden gave Bettina a quick hug, congratulated her, wished *her* luck, then headed outside where the clouds lurked low overhead, threatening to spill at any moment.

He'd done what he'd gone there to do—make sure Emerson would be okay. Which should have put a line under his time in Melbourne.

And yet…

Now he had dinner plans. And Bettina's words echoing in the back of his mind: *Your Emerson… Staggeringly selfless… Serendipitous, to have you on her side.*

He still wasn't going anywhere. Not yet.

Only now, his reasons why were shifting. Or maybe, just maybe, they were the same as they had been all along.

Thoughts now spiralling in a thousand different directions, Holden chose a number from his contacts list, and after it answered was aware of the irony as he said, "Mate. Can I ask a favour?"

Camille opened her door, eyes widening at the sight of her friend.

"Oh, honey," Camille said. "A little wet out?"

Emmy pushed her dripping hair out of her eyes. "A little."

More like a lot. It had been raining, on and off, ever since Emmy had let Holden go. Pushed him away. Told him to leave. *Semantics.*

"Wait there." Camille ran inside and came back with towels, one for Emmy to wrap around her hair, another on which to wipe her feet. Smiling apologetically, she said, "New floors."

After setting Emmy up on another huge towel on the new couch, Camille quickly made coffees before pulling her friend in for a long hug. "I'm so sorry about Pumpkin, hon."

"Thank you."

Camille pulled back, eyes fierce. "I know some would never understand, but if you need a proper funeral for the old boy, you know we'll be there."

Emmy hiccupped. It was not a laugh. It was far too soon for all that. "No funeral. I will scatter his ashes, though, beneath Mum's lemon tree."

"Well, that's far better." A pat on the knee, then, "So, did you hear Bernie's getting married?"

"Got my invitation."

"Super. We can car pool. Bernie mentioned something

about my being Matron of Honour, but intimated it's all very casual. Show up, carry flowers, sit at the big table. Though I'm considering asking for a name change. Babe of Honour, perhaps? I'm working on it. So, how are things otherwise?"

Emmy tipped forward to grab her drink, only for the towel on her head to slip over her face. Nerves a little tetchy, she quickly balled it up and hugged it to her chest.

"Super-well from the looks of things," Camille answered for her.

Emmy did laugh that time. Then reached inside her bag, pulled out the Favour List, and handed it over.

Camille—understanding the power of a good notebook—balanced it on her upturned palms. "May I?"

Emmy nodded.

Camille's eyes shifted from side to side as she read the title. "Ah. I didn't know you were still keeping track. I thought, perhaps, the two of you might have moved beyond that."

"I had. Until I hadn't."

"I see." Camille flicked through the pages. "The detail is impressive."

"Do you mean detective-impressive or the-psychopath-the-detective-is-investigating-impressive?"

"Oh, the latter, for sure." Then, "You really did all this for one another, in the past few weeks? This is more than Phillip and I would do for one another in a year. And we'd be all passive aggressive about it. Lots of huffing and puffing and muttering about being taken for granted. Does Holden mutter?"

"No muttering."

"Then the man is a saint. And clearly smitten." Camille's gaze hit a certain point in the notebook and her eyes grew wide. "Holy smokes. Did he really say that?"

"Which one?"

Camile turned the notebook and pointed, mouthing the word, *Come.*

Emmy nodded.

"That's…seriously. Wow. I mean… I'm feeling a little hot under the collar. And in need of my husband. But he's hiding in the bedroom." Camille shook herself so as to regain focus on the issue at hand. "Where is Mr Heartache, and why are you here rather than…" Camille's voice dropped an octave *"…doing one another favours?"*

Emmy held the balled-up towel closer to her chest. "He's gone."

"Gone where?"

"Gone, gone. Away. Elsewhere. Home."

Camille madly flicked to the last page, where Emmy had ruled a big angry line under the final favour. Adding squiggles. And crossing out all the space at the bottom of the page. Then, "Did he read the notebook?"

"No, he didn't read the notebook!"

"The bastard. I'll sic Phillip onto him. There's not much of him, but he's scrappy."

"No. It's fine. I'm fine."

It wasn't fine. *She* wasn't fine.

She couldn't sleep. She felt low, constantly. As if she had the flu. Yes, she'd lost her pup, and had screwed up her biggest contract to date, but she knew, *knew,* if she'd had Holden holding her through it all she'd be okay.

And yet…beneath the yuck was a sense of rightness in making sure Holden was no longer marking time. That he was out there flourishing.

"That's not what I get from this crazy manifesto of yours."

"Ignore the crazy manifesto. We had simply…run our course. Our favours finally balanced out, and that…" She stopped to take a breath, though it did sound more like a sigh even to her ears.

Camille narrowed her eyes and tapped at the Favour List. "You know that man did not stick around to pick up your laundry because he felt morally indentured to some list. That's *your* kink. The man stuck around for you."

Emmy let the towel drop into her lap. "Maybe. Yes. Of course, I know that. But it doesn't matter. Because he's gone. For ever."

For someone so okay with *nothing* lasting for ever, saying it out loud felt raw. And unbearable.

Camille watched her face, before lifting her shoulders in a shrug and handing the notebook back. "He is gone. He is dead to me. Now, we can check out Bernie's gift list later, so we can pick something wonderful and whacky, but first give me your feet. Everything feels better when you have sparkly toenails."

Emmy slid down deeper into the chair, the notebook in her hand, and propped the towel behind her head as she leaned back against the couch. Eyes closed, she toyed with the notebook ribbon.

She'd decided not to tell Camille about the texts Holden had sent since she'd sent him packing, the ones checking that she was okay. No point Camille staying attached to the guy.

Attachment only led to ache. Bone-deep ache. Soul-deep ache. She knew as she was living it. Despite all her best efforts for that not to happen, it had happened anyway. Meaning, if she'd waited any longer to end things, his leaving would surely have cleaved her neatly in half.

"Salut," said Phillip later that evening, raising his near empty beer.

Holden shuffled on the barstool and clinked the bottle with his iced water and lime. "Thanks for getting away."

"All good. Camille's at home. In the middle of what

might be days of girl talk with…you know who. I'm
meant to be hiding in the bedroom till they're done."

Holden laughed, despite himself.

"I'm not kidding," said Phillip, looking over his shoulder. "If she knew I was here, no sex for a week. The woman's stubbornness knows no bounds. So, did you call me because you wanted to talk about it too?"

"*It* being Emerson?"

Phillip winced. "Spill, whinge, get it all out. I'll say *There, there* and pretend to be on your side, even though that can never happen. Or we can say nothing at all. Talk about football. Or stock prices. Or life on Mars. Whatever you need."

"I need a drink."

Phillip breathed out. "Thank God. Two beers!"

"Light," Holden added, holding out his phone to pay.

"So, what did happen?" Phillip asked. "If you don't mind me asking. Last time I saw Emmy she was all sparkly-eyed, and floating off the ground. And Emmy does not float. She's the most pragmatic person I have ever met."

A muscle twitched under Holden's left eye. Emmy had mentioned the floating thing to him too, in an accusatory way. The way Phillip put it made it sound nice. The woman still confused the heck out of him, even in absentia.

The thing was, he liked it. He fed off it. She'd charged him with feeding off adventure and variety and change of scene, as if she wasn't all of them combined.

The same woman who wore her hair twisted into a complicated mess at home, while eating peanut butter out of the jar, raged if a temp on her books was offered less than exemplary working conditions, and in the next breath listened, actively, intently, as he talked about the minutiae of his day.

She'd also accused him of playing house, when he hadn't played at anything when it came to her. Not for a single second.

He'd been all in from day dot.

Holding back, waiting for her to catch up, he'd had to keep reminding himself it might take her more time. Reminding himself she was softer than she thought she was. Trusted her own feelings tremulously. Determined, if she needed more time, to give her as much time as it took.

That was then. Before she'd told him to go home.

Phillip passed a beer to Holden and Holden took a slow sip. "You want to know what happened?"

"Sure."

"She told me not to take a job I didn't want."

"Right. Heartless of her. Terrible." Phillip paused. "I'm imagining, being Emmy, it was a really good job."

"COO of the Sanderson Group."

Phillip whistled long and high. "You really don't want it?"

"I really don't."

"Excellent. So, you're both on the same page. Yet here you sit. Oozing misery, like a barfly waiting to happen."

Holden glanced at his *light* beer. Then said, "I thought we were on the same page. Then she skipped right to the end when I was still very much enjoying the start. She told me, outright, to go home."

"Home?"

Exactly. When the only place he'd ever thought of as *home* was any place she was. What he said was, "By which she meant away. Back to where I came from."

"Ouch. Harsh. Makes sense though. Considering."

"Considering?" Holden repeated, letting his drink drop to the bar, and slanting a hard look Phillip's way.

Phillip leaned back in his chair, hands up, conciliatory. "I mean, you know…the Heartache List."

"She said that was all in the past."

"Well, yeah. But that doesn't mean it can't ever affect the here and now. What's her big bad wolf?"

"Her—?"

"The thing that scares her the most."

Holden didn't have to think about it. *Fathers, right?* "Her dad leaving."

"Her dad. Her favourite teacher. Her childhood best friend. As you said, all in the past. Then you came along. A guy who's infamous for never staying in one place long." Phillip took a swig of his beer.

While Holden blinked. And blinked again. "She didn't much talk about her mum passing, but when she did… it nearly killed me. And then poor Pumpkin." Hell. "I'm her big bad wolf."

"Not you, *per se*, but you—someone who has loomed large in her life—leaving her? For sure."

Holden's fingers slipped off the glass to run through his hair.

How had he not seen it? She'd pushed him away before he could leave, because in her mind that was what happened to those she loved. She'd pushed him away because she believed she was holding him back.

Meaning…

"She loves me."

"Yup," said Phillip. "Hell of a thing."

He'd been so busy giving her space, giving her time, he'd not seen it when it was right in front of his eyes.

She'd refused to put his name up for the COO gig, knowing it would put her relationship with the Sanderson Group at risk. Knowing it would give him one less reason to stay. She'd protected him, and she'd faced her greatest fear, while torpedoing her own efforts in one fell swoop.

Because she loved him.

He'd felt so smacked by the "off you go" portion of her speech, as it had pressed into his own ancient wounds, he'd lost sight of the rest.

Phillip said, "If you don't want that job you mentioned, I'd take it. Do you think the renovation work we've done qualifies me for a gig in real estate?"

"Sorry, mate," said Holden, distractedly, his mind reeling. "It's already gone to someone else."

"Ah. Probably for the best. Camille wouldn't be keen on me working those kinds of hours."

Holden laughed despite himself. "Are you really as under the thumb as you make out?"

"Nah. And yeah, a bit. But I love her. She loves me. We have one another's backs no matter what. The rest we work out as we go along."

That, Holden was beginning to realise, might be the key to the whole thing.

There was no right way to be with a person, no balance sheet, or list you could tick off. No single set of qualities or interests or locations. A couple lived or died by how deeply they committed to whatever worked for them.

They both simply had to want it enough.

Later that same night, when Camille padded into the kitchen to swap coffee for wine, Emmy checked her phone to find a message from Freya.

Check the bank account!!!

The several smiley faces added to the end of the message took the edge off any concern as Emerson pulled up her bank details to see a staggering bump in the balance. Emmy typed:

What the heck?

It has to be the commission, for the COO position. Maybe one of your early suggestions impressed after all!

Maybe, thought Emmy. But surely the applicant would have let her know. The only other person it could possibly be…

"No," Emmy growled as she uncurled herself from the couch, her backside numbed from not having moved for hours. He couldn't have. He'd promised!

"Everything okay?" Camille called from the kitchen.

"Yep! Fine!" Emmy called, as she hobbled towards the bathroom. Door shut, she sat on the edge of the bath and stared at her phone. Knowing there was only one way to find out.

Yes, Holden had texted her. Several times. She'd answered him every time. But she'd yet to make the first move. She'd been the one to break things off, after all. Getting in contact, so that *she* might feel better for hearing from him, seemed cruel.

But this was different. This was insurrection! This made a mockery of the Favour List! And to Emmy such a list was sacred.

She swore, rather vociferously, as she jabbed at her phone.

Tell me you didn't!

Holden's message came back so fast it was almost as if he was waiting for it.

Didn't do what?

Take that stupid job you promised me you wouldn't take.
If you did, tear up the stupid contract right now!

A few long, painful beats slunk by.

Not necessary.

She could almost hear his voice as he typed. Picture a
small smile tugging at the corner of his beautiful, kiss-
able mouth. It was agony.

So much agony, she pressed the call button before she
had a hope of stopping herself.

He answered, but before he had the chance to draw
breath, she stage-whispered, "Holden Roarke, you listen
up and you listen good. I will not let you take that job.
I will call the bank now and have them return the commission. And if Chuck or Bettina have a problem with
that, they can go through me."

"You done?" he asked, the sound of glasses clinking
and low-level chatter in the background of whatever fabulous faraway place he was enjoying fading as if he too
was finding a quiet spot.

"So long as you do as I say."

"Ah, but that would be asking for a favour."

Emmy's heart was suddenly beating in her throat. A
favour would mean they were no longer null and void.
No. She couldn't keep doing this. She had to get over him.

"No. No favour."

"Right. Just wanted to make sure. After *the listen up
and listen good* bit—"

At the tone of his voice, warm and intimate, a smile
curled around her heart. She told it to calm down. The

fact that she could sit here, talking to the man, missing him, aching for him, and smile—surely that was the kind of progress she'd have once believed she couldn't buy.

"For transparency's sake," he said, his voice low and lovely and just for her, "I did book in for an interview."

"Holden!"

"Only so that I could tell Chuck to back the hell off. You stood up to him, for me; I wanted to do the same for you. Not as a favour, so don't panic. It was something I had to do."

Wow. "And how did that go?"

"Bettina showed up instead. Turns out, she'd already taken the position herself. Said you'd given her the idea. Hence you get your commission."

"Oh, wow. Go, Bettina. But *boo* for putting us both through that." It was cutthroat stuff, playing with the big boys and girls.

Holden laughed, the sound of it spilling over her shoulders, and she held the phone tighter.

"We can hack it," he said, stressing the *we* in a way that had Emmy wriggling on the edge of the bath. "And she apologised, to us both. Explained that she was doing what she had to do to look after the person she loved."

"Right." Emmy closed her eyes tight and hoped her voice didn't sound as pained as it felt.

"Is Chuck okay, do you know?" she asked, showing her soft spot for the old guy. Even while what she really meant was, *Are you okay?*

"Well, we've made plans to have dinner. I took what you said on board. It's past time we cleared the air. Time I let go of all the old ghosts that kept me away, from here, from home, for far too long."

"Oh, that's…wonderful." It really was. "But hang

on—how can you have dinner if—?" She swallowed her words, her hope.

"I'm far, far away? I'm still around, Emmy. Tying up loose ends. And I don't know if you remember, but I did promise you once that I wouldn't leave without saying goodbye."

Do me a favour, she'd said as he held her in his arms at the hotel after the wedding. *Don't leave, this time, without saying goodbye.*

Emmy bit her lip and tipped forward to press her forehead against the cool of the sink. "I'm glad. About you and Chuck. You'll feel so much better for having let that go."

Like she did, having let Holden go? That was a laugh. But still, apart from the great, gaping hole that had taken up residence inside her chest, it worked out for everyone. She got her commission. Bettina and Chuck would be working side by side. Holden would be truly free to live his life however he saw fit.

"Look," she said, when her throat began to feel tight, "I'd better go."

"Right. Look, Emmy—"

When she realised her hand was clutching at her shirt, right over her heart, she said, "Good luck with your future endeavours."

She heard him say something, but her thumb was already pressing the button to cut the call.

When she came out of the bathroom, Camille was quickly hopping onto the couch.

Emmy said, "You were listening at the bathroom door, weren't you?"

"A little bit. I heard talking. Had to make sure you hadn't fallen and hit your head and started hallucinating."

"I was talking to Holden."

"Well, that's…whatever you think it is. I heard mention of favours. Figured I'd better walk away before they turned into a certain kind. Of a sexual nature—"

"Yes, I get it. Thank you." As she tucked herself back into the couch, Emmy glanced at the Favour List notebook which sat innocently closed on the coffee table. "When we started the Heartache List, what did we imagine the end game might be?"

"For you to not get your heart broken." Camille looked at her through the glass of wine. "If your next question is: did it work? From where I sit, I'd say it failed pretty spectacularly."

"A little bit," Emmy admitted, the heel of her hand now rubbing the spot where it ached most. "Thing is, this one was entirely my fault. I broke my own heart. Preemptively. Before Holden had the chance."

"Might be worth rethinking the efficacy of such a move in future."

Camille lifted her wine glass and Emmy grabbed hers to tap it in agreement.

They settled in to watch some horrid reality TV show, knowing that whatever was happening in their own lives they'd never be as screwed up as the contestants. But Emmy's mind wandered.

Once upon a time Holden had said, the *only way to find out if someone you like likes you back is to be a little brave*. Choosing to protect Holden's interests over her own had been pretty brave.

Was it possible he'd known that was why she'd done it, even before she'd known it? Was that why he was still messaging her? Why he'd stayed?

Emmy sat up, while Camille snorted before falling back to sleep.

Holden hadn't left. A man known for his inability to

stay in one place for long, a man she'd accused of needing variety, adventure, and change of scene, more than he'd ever need her, Had Not Gone Anywhere.

He'd stood up for her against Chuck and Bettina, he'd looked out for her interests, he'd answered the phone the moment she'd called. As if nothing had changed at his end.

Was he trying to tell her something too?

Holden had stayed. Meaning, if she was very, very lucky, and the bravest she'd ever been, she might have one last chance to find out.

"Rain's meant to be good luck, right?" said Phillip, peering through the windscreen.

Raindrops slithered moodily down the car windows while Taylor Swift crooned softly through the speakers as they wound their way through the streets of east Melbourne.

It was the morning of Bernadette's wedding, and the perfect match for Emmy's mood, for, while she knew, in every bit of her banged-up heart, that aching for Holden while with him was far better than aching for him when not, she had no idea how to tell him. Or find him, for that matter.

She'd called Bettina, to thank her for the commission. Emmy had managed to leverage it into an even better deal for Pitch Perfect, but had not been able to trick the woman into giving away Holden's whereabouts.

She'd then bought a new notebook in which to write her "Find Holden and Tell Him How I Feel" ideas, but her list-building skills had deserted her right when she needed them most. She'd considered jotting down Phillip's idea—flashmob!—just to get things started.

Camille pulled down the sun visor to check her makeup and caught Emmy's eye. Emmy motioned for her to angle the mirror. Swiping a hand over the peacock-blue clip in her hair, then a finger along the edge of a red lip, she tried a smile on for size, only to be met with the faraway gaze of a woman who felt time slipping through her fingers.

"We're here!" Camille called as they pulled up a little way from Bernadette's parents' lovely house in Camberwell. "Look at that. Rain's stopped!"

When Emmy hopped out of the car, stepping up onto the verdant edge of the footpath, Phillip walked on tip toes to avoid the wet. While Emmy's heels sank into the wet grass. So deeply she couldn't move. Camille bit her lip before bursting into laughter.

Once Phillip and Camille had yanked Emmy out of the mire, they each took an elbow, and, arm in arm, just as they had been for so many years before this one, they made their way up the path, following the sound of laughter, and music and voices, until—

"Oh, my," Emmy gasped.

A big, round, red-and-white-striped marquee, with a wilting roof and small red flags hanging limply from the gutters every few metres, sat plonked in the centre of the huge lawn.

"It's like a giant mushroom," Phillip said, awe tinging his voice.

"A giant circus mushroom," Camille added, clapping madly. "I love it so much I can barely blink."

"It's wonderful. It could not be more perfectly Bernadette," Emmy said, a true smile lighting her up for the first time in days.

"Now I have to go find the most easy-going bride that ever lived." Camille headed off towards the house, while Phillip led Emmy towards the opening at the back of the

tent, where bunches of guests congregated, chatting happily, drinks already in hand.

Inside the circus theme continued, with flickering vintage circus videos playing across the walls of the tent like
some magical dream. And up front, where the bride and
groom would do their thing, a massive elephant statue
looked over them all.

Emmy went to grab Phillip's sleeve to point out the
monkey doll climbing a ladder to the trapeze set, when
she turned to stone.

For there, just off stage, chatting to the groom…

Holden. Holden was here!

Emmy hiked up her skirt, and darted through the
tightly packed crowd, her heels catching in the grass,
eyes locked onto the beautiful man in the dark suit.

She had no idea what she'd say, only that she had to
get to him. For after months of near constant contact,
this was the first time she'd seen his face in days, and
she could barely hold herself together.

She'd made it to the end of the aisle, right as Elvis
started singing *Can't Help Falling in Love*.

The crowd all turned, right as a spotlight swung to
land on Emmy, dress hitched, heels half sunken into the
ground, heat creeping up her neck.

Holden, after giving Barry a nudge up onto the stage,
was the last to turn. He stilled the moment he saw her,
his hands dropping slowly to his sides. Then a smile
stretched across his face. A slow, warm, charming, beautiful smile.

What could she do but smile back? A real smile. Not
the kind she'd practised in the mirror in the car. One that
started in her heart and spread out to her extremities, till
she felt bathed in light and warmth and hope.

"Emmy! Move it!"

Emmy turned to see Camille heading up the aisle, a grinning Bernadette, giving her a thumbs-up, coming up behind. Camille spun Emmy to face the front and gave her a shove.

Emmy found the beat, and made her way up the aisle, ducking off to the side at the last second and finding a spot against the wall, which gave her the perfect view of Holden, who mirrored her position on the other side of the wedding party.

And there she spent the longest half an hour of her life staring into Holden's stormy blue eyes as Bernie and Barry promised to love, honour, and cherish one another for the rest of time.

Everything went a little wild after that, for the bride and groom were playing fast and loose with scheduling and had disappeared. The guests happily headed for the booze till they were told differently.

All bar Emmy, who'd lost track of Holden once the bridal party was swept away for photos, and began to worry that he had been a mirage.

After tables and chairs were brought in, and a huge dance floor set up by a swift staging team in red noses and clown wigs, Emmy found her seat. She kicked off her sodden shoes, tucked them under her chair, and stretched out her toes.

Then, adrenalin fading, she leaned forward, rested her chin on her hand, closed her eyes, and sighed.

When she opened her eyes again, it was to find a pair of long, strong male legs decked out in a beautifully tailored suit and shiny black shoes walking slowly towards her. She knew those legs. She knew that walk. Knew that unhurried confidence.

Feeling a little trembly, Emmy pressed herself to

standing, and lifted her chin to face the man head-on. Only to remember her lack of shoes. And that he was well over six feet tall.

And so she sat, plonking back into her chair, her toes madly reaching for her shoes.

Holden, having played this game before, crouched down till his eyes were in line with hers. Tired eyes. Eyes that had seen some late nights and long days since she'd last seen them. But smiling eyes, all the same. Stormy blue and lovely. With those unfairly long lashes, and those endearing crinkles. Oh, how she'd missed that face.

"Emerson Adler," he said. "Fancy meeting you here."

"Holden Roarke," she shot back, trying to sound all confident and fine, but even she heard the note of yearning. "What are you doing here?"

"Always with the questions."

"Just one. I know Bernie didn't invite you. She doesn't even remember having met you."

His gaze hooked onto hers, as if he never wanted to let go. "Your calendar, it's still synced to mine."

"Ha!" She leaned in when she felt heads turn her way. Leaned in so close she could feel his warmth. "You totally crashed."

He leaned in a smidgeon himself, till their noses were mere inches from touching. "I don't look at it as 'crashing' so much as coming full circle. I feel somewhat involved in how those crazy kids came to fall madly in love."

Emmy shook her head. "How did you end up as Barry's leaning post?"

"Met him on the way in. Poor fellow looked ready to pass out. His best man didn't look much better. I offered my services until showtime. I can be pretty irresistible when I want to be."

"Oh, I know."

"You do?"

Emmy nodded. With no list to follow, she had to follow her gut. And it was telling her to be honest. To leave her heart wide open for once and trust it to do its thing. To trust this man to do his.

When she let out a great big sigh, filled with hope and relief, Holden reached out and swept his thumb across her cheek. Gently. So gently. The same way he went about everything, with honour and kindness and thoughtfulness and decency.

"Holden."

"Mm-hmm."

"I should never have asked you to leave."

"You didn't. You told me to go home." His gaze roved over her face, as if it had been far too long since he'd seen it last. "And here I am, doing just as you asked."

Emerson swallowed.

"It did take me a little longer to figure out *why* you said it. That and a little advice from some folks with smarter hearts than mine. You want to know what we came up with?"

"I do," Emmy said, certain she was going to like his answer.

His eyes stopped roving and landed on hers. "You did it because you love me."

A smile bloomed in her chest before landing on her face, the warmth of it like a bubble around them, keeping out the damp, the past, the people milling around them.

"But how could I?" she asked, her voice growing quiet, intimate, just for him. "We had a deal. *No* accidental falling in love."

"True," said Holden. "As I remember it, *you* promised

not to fall for *me* while I made no such promise. So, while you failed miserably, I'm off the hook."

"You are?" she asked, her voice barely a whisper now. Enough that he dropped a knee, his suit fabric sinking into the squelch, so that he could be nearer her still.

"Completely and utterly," he said, his voice raw. "Deeply, shockingly, nauseatingly, incandescently. Off. The. Hook. In love, with you." He smiled a slow, easy smile at whatever he saw on her face. "You okay there?"

Emmy nodded. Then grinned as tears started flowing down her cheeks. Happy tears. Nauseatingly incandescent tears.

"Tell me," he said, his voice rough, as if he too was overwhelmed by emotion. "I want to hear you say the words. Tell me you knew how I felt about you, how I *feel*, all along. Because I can't stand the thought that a day went by when you didn't know that I am crazy about you."

Did she? Of course she did. How could she not? His love had filled up all the tender, yearning places inside her that had craved him, even before she'd found him.

She tucked her knees together, her bare feet crossed beneath her chair, and leaned forward till her forehead touched his. And she said, "I know it."

"Tell me you believe it."

She could feel the vibration of his voice through his hand at the back of her neck, through the point where their foreheads met. "I believe it."

"Tell me you feel it."

She slid off the chair until she was on her knees before him, her slinky peacock-blue dress meeting wet grass as she cupped his face and kissed him. A kiss that was half smile, half laugh, and half utter joy.

"Hey, folks," Phillip's voice boomed over the sound

system, "Bernie and Barry have returned from wherever it is they've been, and, since this is their day, and they are doing things on their timetable, I've been told it's time for the bouquet toss. So all the singletons, please gather on the dance floor!"

Emmy lifted her head, but moved no further.

Holden did the same, a single eyebrow raising in question. "What do you say?"

She mirrored his cocked eyebrow. "I'm fine right here, thank you very much. Nice and invisible."

His eyes crinkled a moment before one side of his mouth lifted into a sexy half-smile. Their faces stayed close enough she could see an eyelash that had fallen to his cheek.

This time she lifted her hand, gently gathered it with her index finger and held it up to his lips. "Make a wish."

"You don't believe in the bouquet toss, but you do believe in eyelash wishes. You are an interesting woman, Emerson Adler." He took a hold of her wrist, pulling her finger to his lips, and blew, sending the eyelash spinning off into the ether.

Emerson grinned as she watched the eyelash flutter and disappear, and with the shift in focus came the realisation that many, many people were watching her. And Holden. On their knees in the grass. So much for invisible.

"Up," she whispered. "Up, up, up."

"Okay, okay, okay," he muttered. Pressing himself to standing, he reached down and lifted her to her feet and pulled her against him. As if, now he'd found her again, he was not about to let her go. "Much better."

"Mmm," she said, curling her hand into the front of his shirt and rather marvelling at the fact that she could do so with clear intent.

"Want to know what I wished for?" Holden asked, smiling down into her eyes.

"What if that means it won't come true?"

He seemed to think about it for a second, his mouth twisting, one eye narrowing, before saying, "I reckon it's worth the risk. I wished for you to enter the bouquet toss."

"You did not." Emmy glanced towards the makeshift dance floor, expecting to find the usual seething horde of glittery guests, only to find it was empty bar the bride, who was grinning at her like a loon. "What's happening right now?"

With a roll of her eyes, the bride all but skipped over to their table, stopped, sighed, and held out the bouquet.

"Ahh…" Emmy's gaze moved to Holden for back-up, only to find him watching her, smiling, that face she loved so much full of questions.

Take the bouquet, or don't take the bouquet.

As if one's life really could hinge on a single moment.

The post-Heartache List Emmy would have fought that notion, found it terrifying. While the *post*-post-Heart-ache List Emmy knew it could happen and that it could be wonderful.

Emmy accepted the bouquet.

Bernie took her in a tight hug. Then gave the same to Holden, holding on a fraction longer, as Holden whispered something in her ear, after which she nodded enthusiastically.

When the wedding crowd hollered and whistled, Emmy couldn't help but laugh. And curtsy. And offer up a little royal wave, the happiness rushing through her leaving her feeling as if she was floating an inch off the ground. In the best possible way.

At which point the bride headed to the dance floor, and her new husband, who met her there, right as the opening strains of *You Can Leave Your Hat On* burst from the speakers.

"Do me a favour."

Emmy turned back to Holden, her nose buried in the sweetest spray of wild jasmine. "Depends on the favour."

"I think it's high time we move on to Phase Three."

At the shift in Holden's voice—deep, husky, and compelling—her gaze skewed to his. "What's Phase Three?"

"We never did thrash that out. So, I guess it's whatever we want it to be." He took her by the hand, looked around, his expression highly focused. Then he looked back at her. "Why are you so short?"

"Took off my shoes."

Muttering under his breath about falling head over heels for a woman who couldn't keep her heels on her feet, Holden leaned around her, gathered her shoes from under her chair, then slipped an arm beneath her knees and lifted her off the ground. "First step of Phase Three," he said. "We're getting the heck out of here."

"We can't!" she said, holding on tight and brimming with breathless laughter.

Holden, holding all the cards as well as herself, ignored her, edging around tables. "The bride insisted. Just now. Said she hoped it made up for the key incident."

Emmy looked over her shoulder in search of the bride, only to find her dancing up a storm. "She *did* remember."

"Oh, yeah. Now let's go." Holden picked up the pace, a man on a mission.

Then Emmy caught Camille's eye. She gave her best friend a finger wave. Camille pretended to burst into tears, her hands clutched over her heart, before Phillip dragged her onto the dance floor.

Emmy sighed as Holden tucked her tighter against his chest and strode from the tent, just like Kevin Costner and Whitney Houston in *The Bodyguard*. It was the single sexiest moment of her life. But, considering the intention in his stride as he made his way up the side of the house, she had a feeling it would soon be pipped.

Emmy lifted a hand to Holden's cheek. "How many points do I get for bagging a Back-Up Best Man Slash Wedding Crasher?"

He slowed, just a mite, as his gaze moved to hers. "Considering how rare a breed we are, it's gotta be up near seven hundred and fifty points. Maybe even a thousand."

"Wow," she said. "To think, I had no intention of playing the game, when it turns out I'm so very good at it."

With that, she reached up and grabbed her prize by the tie and dragged his mouth to hers. Or maybe she simply caught him on the way down.

Either way, if that kiss was anything to go by, Phase Three was going to be the very best of all.

EPILOGUE

EMMY FINISHED SMEARING Vegemite on her toast, tucked a corner between her teeth, and turned to find Holden ambling into the kitchen—suit pants unbuttoned, chest bare.

Her heart still kicked at the sight of him. "Nearly ready?"

Holden spun on the spot, arms out, showing off. "Thought I'd just go like this today."

"The investors will be thrilled."

He finished his spin, and moved in, his arm sliding around her waist before hauling her close. Then he tugged her a little closer still, till she was flush up against him, his smile growing when he felt her breath hitch.

Then he grabbed the slice of toast from her mouth, placed a slow, soft kiss upon her lips, followed by a quick swipe of his tongue that had her eyes all but rolling back in her head, before taking a bite of her toast and putting it back where he found it.

"Need a lift?" she asked, when he let her go, patting down her hair, tugging on her skirt, and generally trying to feel less discombobulated.

"No, but I'll take it. Lunch?"

"Not today. I can take off early if you want to try that new Italian place around the corner."

"Done."

"When do you head to Paris?" she asked. "This Thursday or next?"

Her hand went to her phone, to check their joint calendar, but his hand closed over hers, before spinning her back into his arms, then rocking her side to side, till they were slow dancing in the kitchen.

Dust motes fluttered through the shards of buttery sunlight pouring through her kitchen window. Her mother's lemon tree, nourished by Pumpkin's ashes, flourished just outside.

While Holden's eyes, gazing into hers, were such a sharp, clear blue in the morning light. No storm, no clouds, not any more. "I think you mean, when do *we* head to Paris?"

"We?"

"Why not? I *may* have had a sly chat to Freya, before confirming the dates, to make sure you could fit it in. Freya did consider coming with me to Paris, if you refused, but in the end she chose to stay behind, keep Pitch Perfect rolling along."

"A week in Paris," Emmy said out loud.

For this was the deal. A side effect of living with a man who was more curious than cautious, who had connections the world over, who *was*—it turned out—just as happy lazing on her couch watching her true crime documentaries, or building her a shed, as he was jet-setting all over the world to talk about his new app that people were already saying would lift the ability of small businesses to compete in the global space for ever.

Having been his wildly successful beta tester, Pitch Perfect could attest to the fact that business had never looked brighter.

"What do you say?"

"I say...yes. A week in Paris, with you, sounds perfect. Now, will you do me a favour?"

"Anything."

"When you finally decide to put some clothes on, wear the pale blue. Nobody will be able to say no to you in that shirt."

"Nobody says no to me anyway."

Emerson snorted. She sure had. For quite some time.

"Fine, I'll wear the shirt. And will you do me a favour?"

"Depends on the favour."

"Always so cautious," he said, a smile in his eyes as they roved over her face.

"Not always," she said, reaching around to run her hand over his backside, before pulling him a little closer.

"Fair enough. My request is that you go a little lighter on the Vegemite for our morning toast."

"This toast?" she said, holding out her half-eaten slice. "This toast that I made for myself?"

"Mm-hmm," he said, leaning down to nibble at her neck.

"Changing up my Vegemite-to-butter ratio is a far bigger favour than the shirt." Her eyes fluttered closed as he rained a trail of kisses over her cheek. "What do I get in return?"

"Rub your feet every night this week."

Gracious, that sounded good. "Fine. What else?"

He moved to her earlobe, nipping the lobe, before whispering in her ear what he was prepared to do, nightly, in vivid detail. And Emerson was mighty glad he was holding on to her as her knees gave way.

And soon the kitchen bench proved itself good for something other than making Vegemite on toast.

And, right before her mind turned to starbursts, and happiness and pleasure and heat and want, Emerson smiled. A smile so wide she was absolutely certain it would never, ever come to an end.

* * * * *

COMING SOON!

We really hope you enjoyed reading this book.
If you're looking for more romance, be sure to
head to the shops when new books are
available on

Thursday 7th
July

To see which titles are coming soon, please visit

millsandboon.co.uk/nextmonth

MILLS & BOON

MILLS & BOON®

Coming next month

HIS MAJESTY'S FORBIDDEN FLING
Susan Meier

Jozef handed Rowan's two cards to her. "You're fired."

She settled into the chair. "No. Theoretically, you didn't hire me so you can't fire me. Plus, we have work to do. I'm thrilled that you decided to come out in public for this performance—"

"For my sons."

She inclined her head, causing her pretty curls to shuffle. "It's a good start, but you need to say something to the press when you leave. Just say, 'the opera was lovely,' while you're racing down the stairs before your security team escorts you into your private elevator that will take you to your limo in the parking facility on the ground floor."

"No."

Her delicate eyebrows rose. "No?"

He didn't want to make a scene by standing and pointing at the curtain and ordering her to leave. God knew how many camera lenses from cell phones were pointed at him right now.

He tried the easy way, smiling and saying, "I didn't hire you. I don't want you. I don't need you. I'm not going to do what you say."

She laughed.

Her impertinence infuriated him, but he suddenly noticed that her shiny auburn hair cascaded down her naked back. The color set off her creamy skin, so smooth and white that it probably never saw the sun. It also accented her green eyes.

He blinked, taken aback by the fact that he even noticed her looks. Worse, his heart rate had accelerated, and his pulse had scrambled.

He'd been married for over two decades before his wife passed five years ago, and he'd never felt this overwhelming desire to stare at a woman. He'd never been sucked in by a woman's beauty. And he wouldn't be now. If his sons or the castle staff thought it was funny to throw a beautiful woman at him to see if he turned into a wimp who would melt at her feet and do what she wanted, they were crazy.

He was a king.

Kings did not melt.

They did what the hell they wanted.

Continue reading
HIS MAJESTY'S FORBIDDEN FLING
Susan Meier

Available next month
www.millsandboon.co.uk

Copyright © 2022 Susan Meier

MILLS & BOON

THE HEART OF ROMANCE

A ROMANCE FOR EVERY READER

MODERN

Prepare to be swept off your feet by sophisticated, sexy and seductive heroes, in some of the world's most glamourous and romantic locations, where power and passion collide.

HISTORICAL

Escape with historical heroes from time gone by. Whether your passion is for wicked Regency Rakes, muscled Vikings or rugged Highlanders, awaken the romance of the past.

MEDICAL

Set your pulse racing with dedicated, delectable doctors in the high-pressure world of medicine, where emotions run high and passion, comfort and love are the best medicine.

True Love

Celebrate true love with tender stories of heartfelt romance, from the rush of falling in love to the joy a new baby can bring, and a focus on the emotional heart of a relationship.

Desire

Indulge in secrets and scandal, intense drama and plenty of sizzling hot action with powerful and passionate heroes who have it all: wealth, status, good looks…everything but the right woman.

HEROES

Experience all the excitement of a gripping thriller, with an intense romance at its heart. Resourceful, true-to-life women and strong, fearless men face danger and desire - a killer combination!

To see which titles are coming soon, please visit

millsandboon.co.uk/nextmonth

JOIN THE
MILLS & BOON
BOOKCLUB

* **FREE** delivery direct to your door

* **EXCLUSIVE** offers every month

* **EXCITING** rewards programme

50% OFF
YOUR FIRST
PARCEL

Join today at
millsandboon.co.uk/subscribe